BLOODGUARD

BLOODGUARD

INTERNATIONAL AWARD-WINNING AUTHOR

CECY ROBSON

HODDERSCAPE

First published in Great Britain in 2024 by Hodderscape
An imprint of Hodder & Stoughton Limited
An Hachette UK company

1

Copyright © Cecy Robson 2024

The right of Cecy Robson to be identified as the Author of the Work has been
asserted by her in accordance with the Copyright, Designs and Patents Act 1988.

Interior map illustration by Elizabeth Turner Stokes and Amy Acosta
Interior design by Britt Marczak
Edited by Liz Pelletier
Cover art and design by Bree Archer and
LJ Anderson, Mayhem Cover Creations

A CIP catalogue record for this title is available from the British Library

Hardback ISBN 978 1 399 73542 1
Trade Paperback ISBN 978 1 399 73543 8
ebook ISBN 978 1 399 73545 2

Printed and bound in Great Britain by Clays Ltd, Elcograf S.p.A.

Hodder & Stoughton policy is to use papers that are natural, renewable
and recyclable products and made from wood grown in sustainable
forests. The logging and manufacturing processes are expected to
conform to the environmental regulations of the country of origin.

Hodder & Stoughton Limited
Carmelite House
50 Victoria Embankment
London EC4Y 0DZ

The authorised representative in the EEA is Hachette Ireland, 8 Castlecourt
Centre, Castleknock Road, Castleknock, Dublin 15, D15 YF6A, Ireland

www.hodderscape.co.uk

To Mr. and Mrs. Harte, who loved me even though they didn't have to.

The gladiators' arena of Arrow is not for the faint of heart. *Bloodguard* includes elements that might not be suitable for all readers, including violence, gore, blood, death (*a lot* of death, including family, friends, enemies, animals, and monsters), injury and dismemberment, illness, burning, drowning, poisoning, drugging, whipping, indentured servitude, classism, xenophobia, grief, graphic language, and sexual activity on the page. Readers who may be sensitive to these elements, please take note, grab a weapon, and prepare to fight for the title of Bloodguard...

CREA TRELA

PENNOCK

MERETO

1

LEITH

The battered wagon wheels rumble over one pothole, then the next, rattling the bars of our cage and scraping the rough metal along the cut in my shoulder. I tighten my jaw in an effort not to wince. It won't do me good to remind any of the nine fighters locked in here with me that I'm injured.

Instead, I keep my gaze fixed on the dried blood still on my hands from my last match. The blood isn't mine. It's Yular's, I think. Or maybe Mundag's. Both trolls were thrown into the arena with me yesterday, and, like the rest of us, they chose to fight to the death to feed their families.

They just weren't as brutal as me. Nor were they as desperate.

Crossing my arms over the thin leather armor covering my bare chest, I lift my chin and stare at the scarred face of the fighter across from me. Two bottom tusks rise over the ogre's upper lip, the left one jagged and broken next to a gash that stretches from his mouth to his ear. His eyes catch on mine—then harden, letting me know he still has some fight left in him. I openly stare back, letting him know I'm *all* fight.

The sound of a horn announces our arrival, and the ogre huffs and looks away. No sense kicking things up in here when we might not even get paired today.

I can't help the slight sinking feeling in my gut as the horn's final note fades on the wind, reminding me there's a real chance I won't ever hear that sound again. The arena is unpredictable as fuck.

The wagon slows when it reaches the outer wall surrounding the coliseum complex, and heavy chains clank as the massive wooden gate swings open with a splintering groan.

Every foot the gate widens, chants of "Bloodguard!" from the arena build in volume like a brewing storm, rolling through the wagon.

Sullivan, the veteran fighter beside me, spits on the floor. "Filthy wretches," he mutters.

I toss him a raised brow—he nearly spat on my boot—but he just grins.

Like me, he's human. Unlike me, his skin is lighter and his hair is the color of faded straw. My skin is rich brown from all the time spent outside training, and my hair is black as tar—but both are just as dirty as Sullivan. His scraggly beard may be longer than mine, but it only barely covers the boils thickening his throat above his armor.

Sullivan is a tough old fighter. Slightly taller than my six feet and with more bulk, his size makes up for the twenty years between us. That doesn't make him better, though. It just makes him someone to watch.

"I want to be a swordsmith," he once told me. "Spend my life making weapons I'll never need again." His blue eyes had shifted to mine. "What about you, boy?"

"Me?" I'd asked. "I'll be the one you make weapons for."

Three years later and I'm thinking he had the right of it.

I glance at his forearm, where a sword and thorny vine have been tattooed, each for his two previous victories. For the next two victories he wins, he'll get a rose and a crown—and finally his freedom again. Lucky bastard.

I shift my weight on the hard bench as the chants get faster and faster. *"Bloodguard! BLOODGUARD!"*

A young gladiator, his muscles obviously bigger than his brains, seems enlivened by the crowd's excitement and raises a fist above his cloud of dark curls, barking out a quote from the recruitment pamphlet that lured most of us to this shit life. "'Fight for the gold, *win* for the glory!'"

"Glory never did the dead much good," I grumble.

"At least they fed us today." Sullivan coughs and then spits again. He's been sick for weeks and struggling to hide it. Weakness is the first thing that will get you killed around here. Stupidity runs a close second.

The wizard on the bench across from us clearly doesn't know that, though. He frowns at Sullivan, the sour expression the only thing marring the man's smooth, white face.

"What's wrong? Does my spit disgust you?" Sullivan asks, smiling. "Get over it. You're just as screwed as I am."

Sparks of magic light the wizard's dark eyes. "*You* disgust me."

"Why?" Sullivan challenges. "We can't all be fancy little lords like yourself."

The wizard lunges, and I ram my heel into his chest and kick him back into his seat.

"Save it for the arena," I warn.

The wizard gapes at me. He likely didn't expect my strength or speed. Most don't, which is why I've survived this long.

Sullivan nudges me. "Damn shame he needs his staff to control all that magic, ain't it, Leith?" His smile gathers more of an edge. "Too bad he shattered it during his last fight."

Cracking it over an ogre's skull, if memory serves. It's what secured him the win and a spot among the ten of us here.

My glare keeps the wizard in place, which is not a hard thing to do. All the rage and bitterness pulsing through my veins is surely reflected in my features. *His* features reflect only terror of the upcoming match now.

He doesn't stand a chance without his staff, and he knows it.

The rules allow us to use anything we can reach within the arena once the match starts. But even if a staff lies among the pile of swords, shields, and daggers we're offered, the wizard won't have the time to bind his power to it. He's starved and weak. We all are.

"I—I have a family," he stammers as I continue to glare. "A wife and children who need me."

Wizards, like elves and other beings with magic, have trouble conceiving, so he likely has no children and is playing for sympathy. He won't find any here.

Sullivan laughs, as do the other gladiators, and angry tears cut lines into the wizard's dirty face.

Figures. Those who are scared always cry.

I don't laugh or sympathize. We all have loved ones. It doesn't make him special.

My chest tightens just thinking of my little sister, her body ravaged by illness and not enough coin for a proper healer, but I quickly shake off the useless emotion. She doesn't need my sympathy right now. She needs me to focus—and fucking win.

The cheering builds as we rumble closer to the main structure. I try to let it galvanize me, but after years of this shit, it's hard to see the joy of either gold or glory in the fight to come.

The promise of housing, food, and money to send home lured me, just the same as all the other gladiators in this cage, to the wealthier kingdom of Arrow. And at first, this really was a land that surpassed my dreams.

But only a month after I arrived, an assassination attempt on the queen left her in a coma, and in a blink, gone were the games intended to "train" the finest warriors in Old Erth. Gone were the days of hearty meals and opportunities to heal and rest. And gone were the cheers for besting a competitor without a death blow.

Decrepit and filthy conditions claim most of us now. The arena claims the rest. Those left standing are rewarded with fairy elm soup that never quite satiates our hunger and a pittance per win. But…even a pittance helps our families, and cold broth is still food.

Eyes on the prize, I remind myself.

I blink up at the coliseum as it finally becomes visible from my spot in the corner of the wagon. A showy display of elven architecture, the stadium is made of glittering stone. Archways mark several spectator entrances, each one with a statue of a different Bloodguard—the name originally coined for the first eight generals in Arrow's army—standing guard at the top. The main entrance boasts the largest statue of all: a phoenix, the symbol of this empire.

"You can almost taste victory, eh?" Sullivan's words echo my thoughts, but there's a bleakness in his gaze. We're both so close—and yet it's hard to hold on to something as useless as hope in a place like this.

Still, he only has two matches left. Four for me. Four more out of what felt like an insurmountable hundred, and I'll win the title Bloodguard. I'll be a citizen of Arrow. I'll be rich. And I will have everything I'll ever need—and so will my family.

The tall, broad-chested moon horses hesitate as we reach the tunnel that stretches under the coliseum and widens into underground stables and staging areas, but a crack of the whip has them moving again. The steeds cast a faint glow like the moon, hence their name. Their front legs are extra-long and their haunches wide, giving them added strength to pull our heavy wagon.

Moments later, we're inside the tunnel. The shade is a welcome reprieve from the suffocating heat, but there's little time to enjoy it before the humid stench of horse manure and death steals my breath.

"Fuck me, that's awful," Sullivan mutters, reaching up to pinch his nose. I don't bother.

Eventually, the horses pull the wagon back up and out on the other side of the stands and onto the main coliseum floor, but they hesitate again, as though they can taste the scent of blood permeating the sand.

"It's been said that the sand cloaking the arena floor was once as white as the snow on the mountains of Aṁdar," the young fighter says with awe. New Guy must've *memorized* the damn recruiting pamphlet.

As a group, we eye the arena floor. After the last three years of brutality, only a field of sickly gray remains.

The carriage driver curses and snaps his whip at the steeds again, and they trudge forward, jerking us backward in our cage. This time, I can't hide my grimace.

"What do you think they'll throw at me this time?" Sullivan asks, absently scratching under his breastplate.

"Maybe a pair of fire elks?" a dwarf with a septum ring and a thick gray braid suggests, rubbing her hands along her thighs. "Those bastards from Canvol will burn through you if they don't eat you first."

"It could be anything," I answer truthfully, my tone bored.

Usually, we're paired to fight each other one-on-one, but sometimes they like to throw in a few beasts to keep things interesting. And although not a rule, everyone knows the closer a fighter gets to winning Bloodguard, the more shit they give you to try to take you out.

I pull in a deep breath and try not to focus on the fact that only *two* have made it to Bloodguard since I arrived and the High Lord took over Arrow.

"Whoever or whatever it is," Sullivan says, leaning back against the bars like he hasn't a care in the world, "I'll try to make it quick so the rest of yous can see how fast I kill and conquer."

I almost crack a smile at his cockiness, but then the air thickens in the wagon as we begin to circle the arena.

"Bloodguard! *Bloodguard!*"

I work my jaw from side to side, trying to relieve the tension pulling the cords along my throat. By all of Old Erth, I will never get used to the entirety of this warzone. In this colossal space, we are insignificant. Specks of dust along an illustrious painting. Mere saplings in a forest of gargantuan trees.

Like always, I try to pretend the size doesn't matter. Like always, I know it does. Plenty of space to run. Nowhere to hide.

I sit back, grunting a curse at everyone who couldn't wait to arrive. The stands are full today—with spectators garbed in clothes of every color instead of the black we'd grown accustomed to over the past month. My stomach sinks like a stone.

"Well, shit," Sullivan says.

"Guess the period of mourning is over," the dwarf mutters into the heavy silence, her voice pitching low as she stares at her boots.

No one speaks as we each contemplate what this will mean for our upcoming matches. The High Lord's been tempering his thirst for blood out of respect for the queen's death this last month from her nearly three-year coma. Bets have been down as well—no one wanted to seem disrespectful while the kingdom mourned the loss of their beloved monarch.

I take a deep breath and concentrate on slowing my racing heart. Panic will only get me killed faster. Because today—today, the High Lord will most likely try to gain back that loss in revenue by making a spectacle out of our lives. And our deaths.

No one is safe today.

No one.

CHAPTER

2

LEITH

F ocusing on the upcoming match, I tighten the bloodied bandage over my left hand with my teeth, glancing up at the people we pass.

The wealth among the crowd becomes less pervasive the higher the stands stretch above the stone arena. The Commons, the largest ring of rows at the top, is a sea of functional clothing stitched of simple cotton, whereas the center ring, the Middling, boasts robes of silk. But even that apparel seems mere scraps when compared to what the inner Noble Ring flaunts. Clothing of the finest silks and crinoline, flashing gemstones and gold, turns those seats practically into a treasure chest.

Eight sets of wide stairs are evenly spaced around the coliseum, and bet takers wearing bright-yellow tunics run up and down the rings, collecting wagers in exchange for tickets. And now that the crowd's got a look at us wheeling into the arena, the antes are stacking up. Banners for each fighter, our pictures painted on them but no names, unfurl above the highest ring, flag after flag stretching all the way around the arena.

I can't help but scan past each banner until I see Sullivan's familiar face—and the odds being adjusted against him—and my skin tightens. *Shit.* Since Sully only has two more matches before achieving Bloodguard, the pot is especially high—and the odds show him as a favorite.

Fortunes will be made today. And lost.

Sullivan follows my line of sight and growls low in his chest. "Fuckers."

Normally, we'd be happy for the favorable spread, hoping to make a few extra coins ourselves when we win. But not today. With odds like that, the House only wins if Sully falls. And I suspect High Lord Vitor has something extra special in mind for us now.

Everything in Arrow is crooked—and the High Lord and his son most of all.

At last, the moon horses whinny as they're pulled to a stop in front of the Regent of Arrow's personal box with four rows starting eight feet above the arena floor. Close enough that the royals can soak in the blood and violence but still at a safe distance. Their box, too, is decorated with the image of the phoenix, regal and red with swirling orange feathers. No one has seen the actual bird since it was killed a century ago, but the damn thing is painted on everything the aristocracy touches.

To hear the stories, they waited decades for the mythical bird to rise again after claiming victory over Arrow's enemies and dying in the final battle.

But it never did.

Seems absurd to continue to idolize the creature, but then again, I find most of the things these royals do to be frivolous.

The rusty wagon door is yanked open by a guard, and one by one we spill out and stand in two rows, the crowd gleefully tittering before us.

I roll my shoulders and stare up at the royal box seats.

Sadists. All of them. "I should set that box on fire."

Sullivan's laugh turns into a cough. "Aw, come on, boy. At least your fans are here." He points to a section in the Middling to our right, where a cluster of spectators waves bright scarves with my assigned banner colors—red and purple—but I pay them no mind and turn back to the royal box.

The next few minutes will decide if I have a chance to live—or die.

The High Lord's bet maker, a short human with round spectacles on the tip of his nose and a scarcity of white hair fluffed out over his ears, glances at each of us and then weighs our fates on his ledger.

With a flourish, he hands the parchment to High Lord Vitor, the ruling Regent of Arrow, who is sitting in the first row, as his status demands. The

High Lord glances down at the sheet, his thick, dark hair gathered in a wide braid that starts on the top of his head and snakes down his back, a sharp contrast against the pale skin of his pointed ears. He looks no more than forty years old, but elves tend to live hundreds of years, so there's no telling how old he really is. He's wearing the traditional elven garb of flowing silk pants and vest—in gold silk, of course—but something tells me it's to showcase his rather un-elvishly muscular frame than anything else.

Everything this man does screams intentional.

The High Lord turns to his son next to him, and they stare at each other for a beat. No words are spoken, but it's clear there's a battle brewing between the two men before the High Lord gives a quick nod of his head and turns back to the bet maker. He says something to the short man and shoves the ledger at him. The bet maker's white brows reach into his hairline as he takes the parchment, but then he makes a few sweeping lines with his quill and begins to scribble again.

Something in the High Lord's tight jaw has the hairs on the back of my neck lifting.

He turns left and snaps something I can't quite hear at his son. General Soro, who looks like a watered-down version of his father, is playing dress-up today in full military regalia, a slew of round, gold medals shaped like buttons decorating both sides of his structured navy tunic. Of course, the "general" has never served a day in the military, the title being self-proclaimed and as worthless as the man.

Father and son exchange sharp words—clearly no love lost there—before the High Lord's attention shifts to his bet maker again, his son clearly dismissed from his thoughts. Soro's jaw tightens, and his gaze catches mine, a cruel twist edging up one corner of his mouth as though he can't wait to cheer on my death in particular.

Sullivan nudges me, pulling my attention from the royal box, and I drop my hand. He motions with his head at the other gladiators in line with us and murmurs, "I have a good feeling about whoever they pair me with today."

Apparently, he's missed the exchange between Vitor and his son and instead spent his time sizing up the other competitors. The dwarf woman is thick-limbed, tough-skinned, and strong, but they tend to lack speed.

The others aren't as ruthless, not like Sullivan and me. He's right. We *should* make it through to the next round. Even as sick as he is, he's stubborn and lethal. He's also the only gladiator I dare call a friend.

Since we first met, we've shared an unspoken pledge not to turn on each other unless we're pitted against one another in a match. So far, that hasn't happened. Likely because of the coin lost to the House if the wrong one of us were to win. But I know the day is coming when the betting outweighs the risk. I just hope it's not today.

As I glance around at the other gladiators, I can't help but hope *any* of them die on my blade today instead of Sully.

A giant bell clangs, signaling a call for last bets and time for us to get back into the wagon, head to the stables, and await our paired matches.

"You ready, Leith?" Sullivan asks.

Ready to die? Or ready to kill? I nod regardless.

The dwarf stands tall, roaring and beating her chest, while a couple of elves from my homeland wave to the crowd, their thin, elegant arms swaying like reeds in the breeze. I need to keep my eyes on them. Elves are deceptively strong. The newer competitors, a minotaur and a wolverine shifter, join them and bulge their muscles. They're all trying to persuade the crowd to bet more, thinking they'll earn more that way.

Good luck with that.

Most rewards for fighters died right around the same time they started adding convicted criminals to the competitor lists.

Sullivan and I don't pander to the crowd. He cracks his neck from side to side. I stretch out my hands. The stab wound through my left palm burns, and so does the axe injury across my left shoulder blade.

I feel Soro's interest return, and I look up, expecting a glare for daring to watch his father dismiss him. Instead, he holds my gaze assessingly as a young human lord beside him laughs at something he said. I don't recall seeing this lord before, his green hair spiked with colorful jewels on the tips like some fluffed-up peacock, but it's clear he is thrilled to be in the royal box today and coveting Soro's attention. He gestures to the two lines of fighters below him, and the pair shares another laugh, making me consider my idea to set the box on fire again.

To Lord Peacock's left is an empty seat and then two more lords, one who's older with gray hair and dark-brown skin and one around my age with long, black braids, the sides of his head shaved close—a style favored by the military here. They're not cheering or laughing like the others. They're not even rushing to place bets. Why?

Suddenly, all four men's heads swivel to watch an elegant elf with light-brown skin and high cheekbones make her way toward them.

She's tall and generously curved, her strides as smooth as water as she walks along the first row and enters the royal box. If it wasn't for the way she carries herself, I'd mistake her for a member of the Middling. A plain black hooded cape is draped over her shoulders atop a well-made blue dress, tastelessly unadorned by royal standards.

As she sits gracefully in the empty seat beside Lord Peacock, the older elf to her left reaches out, capturing her in a warm embrace. As she settles, she removes her hood and shoves her wavy brown hair behind one pointed ear. This woman is poised, regal, and...scarred.

Small, raised burn marks start directly below her jawline, thickening and branching out as they slope down her throat. My guess is there's more damage along her chest, but the way she clutches her cloak against her body makes it too hard to tell.

Elves are long-lived and heal at a rapid pace. I've *never* seen one's skin marred so severely.

Lord Peacock shakes his head, openly chastising her as he lifts her hood back over her hair and attempts to further shield her scars. She removes her hood again, glaring at him, but says nothing.

Soro leans around Lord Peacock to say something to her, and the elf grits her jaw and crosses her arms, as if it's taking everything she has not to pummel both of them. A satisfied smirk turns up a corner of Soro's mouth, whatever barb he intended obviously hitting its mark, and he leans back in his seat.

I watch as she carefully smooths her cotton gown over her knees, her focus just above our heads as though she doesn't want to make eye contact with those beneath her station. Fuck that. I straighten to my full height, my fists clenching and eyes narrowing on hers, demanding she see *me*.

Like she can hear my thoughts, her head tilts lower, and our gazes collide.

Her eyes are fixed on mine now, and neither of us moves. We don't need to. The earth is moving beneath our feet *for* us.

She's no more than twelve feet away, only a few feet above me, so close I almost think I could touch her, and yet—she might as well be in another kingdom. As I continue to stare, a soft pink highlights her cheeks. But she doesn't look away, even when I raise one eyebrow in return. An emotion I haven't seen in so long I'm almost not sure I'm seeing it now flits across her delicate features. For a moment, barely a fairy's breath, I'm not a weapon or a face soon to be forgotten. I'm just a man.

Damn. I haven't felt this human in years...until she lifts her chin up and away, as though I've been dismissed. And I'm slammed back into my hellish reality.

I should know better than to assume or desire respect from one of these assholes. I thought she was giving me something—something I've gone too long without—and hell if she didn't take it all away with a simple gesture to remind me of my place.

Lord Peacock pivots his scowl from her to me. I ignore him, anger churning its way up my chest, and spread my arms, calling out to the woman, "What's wrong, princess? Feeling a little dirty that you like what you see?"

She jerks her attention to her left, away from Lord Peacock, and pretends she wasn't just eye-fucking me a minute ago. Her companion deepens his scowl at me.

"You think you can beat me?" I challenge him, my knuckles cracking as I widen my stance. "Step inside and let's go, asshole!"

"What the hell you doing, boy?" Sullivan asks low, but I don't bother responding. The truth is, I have no fucking clue what's gotten into me.

Lord Peacock leaps up, reaching for the hilt of his sword. She stands, too, pulling at his arm and speaking fast. The lord shakes her off and moves forward, his foot on the low stone ledge, appearing ready to take me on.

Nobles can challenge anyone who offends them, even a gladiator. But if that noble does so within the confines of the arena, they agree to fight to the death, just like us.

"Filip, Filip—don't do this," she begs louder. "*Please*. I need you!"

To buy her statelier dresses, no doubt.

The commotion draws the attention of High Lord Vitor, who looks like he's about to step in when his shit-for-brains son leans forward, a cruel smile dancing in his eyes, and says something to the young lord I can't quite make out. Lord Peacock tightens his jaw and steps fully onto the stone ledge.

"You'll pay for that disrespect, you filthy dog," he shouts back at me, his shoulders tensing.

The two lords beside the brown-haired woman hurry forward, but they aren't fast enough.

Lord Peacock leaps into the arena, his sword arm raised and his anger directed right at me. He swings, and I sidestep before catching him with a right hook. My punch isn't enough to knock him out, but it *is* enough to stun him into dropping his sword. It's in my hand, and I'm swinging just as he rights himself.

The steel is of the finest quality I've seen in years, the edge so sharp I barely feel more than a bump as I slice clean through his spine.

CHAPTER

3

LEITH

I toss the sword next to the headless body as the pretty elf watches her companion's peacock head roll to a stop along the blood-soaked sand. The crowd is on their feet, invigorated by the bonus match that just occurred, but I keep my eyes locked on the woman, curious how she'll react to the fact that I just beheaded her companion.

Her eyes widen with shock for only the briefest of seconds before she's rounding on...High Lord Vitor, the *regent*. He nods as if he's listening. She points in the direction of an entryway, but he only nods again. The woman says something more before lifting the hood of her cape and storming off.

That woman is cold. She didn't raise her voice or shed a single tear. *Well damn, aren't you full of surprises?*

Four old men appear from the gates that lead back to the tunnel. Two cart Filip's body away while the third hoists his head and the fourth rakes gray sand over the red-soaked areas, then picks up the sword and follows behind the other three. Shame. That was a damn nice sword.

My attention shifts back to the highest-ranking nobles—High Lord Vitor and General Soro. Technically, there's nothing they can do, but I've learned not to put anything past one of these assholes.

Vitor says something to his bet maker, who nods and scribbles on his notepad. I don't know what was said, but it can't be good if the smile Soro is fighting not to show is any indication. I almost rub my palms against my thighs but catch myself. No way will I give him the privilege of seeing me sweat.

Sudden drumbeats echo around the stadium, and my pulse quickens. The time has come to announce the matches.

A few of the fighters ease their postures, feigning courage that's long gone, and we all turn to head back to the wagon.

Typically, we're routed to the stables to wait for our match. As though the games aren't cruel enough, we never know who or what we've been matched to fight or the order until we are called. But today, before we can reach the wagon, the gate of the cage is swung closed.

The other gladiators murmur to one another at this change in protocol, but we don't have long to wait.

From the top tier of the arena, four messenger hawks, their bodies twice the size of my head and their wingspan twice my *height*, swoop into the center with large sacks gripped in their talons. Their dull auburn plumage flutters as they drop their sacks, and their wings flap furiously as they take to the sky again.

Two large ogre guards lumber to the fallen sacks and work together to dump out their contents. Weapons and shields clatter to the gray sand. Just as they finish, more hawks soar toward them and dump even more sacks with dull thuds in the middle of the arena.

Sullivan and I exchange glances, a knot forming in the pit of my stomach. The piles of weapons are larger than we're used to…large enough for *every* gladiator here to choose their starting weapons.

And instead of being herded back to the pens, a row of gladiators is nudged forward by the guards, toward the center of the arena. Their heavy feet stomp in the sand, puffs of dust floating away on the wind like funeral ash.

"Next row," the human guard calls, and my chest tightens.

"We're not being paired off." Sullivan ignores the command, his expression bleak. "It's all of us. Everyone for themselves."

My breath leaves in pained bursts. We're not just fighting a single opponent of their choosing—whether man or beast—we're also fighting *one another* to the death.

The sun is high in the sky and burns along the deep axe wound on my back, but I barely feel it, my insides twisting.

"Next row!" the guard bellows again.

I take a step forward. Sullivan follows me, spitting into the sand. He's very sick. I'm injured. But we won't slow down for anyone.

In the arena, there is no slowing down. There is only victory or death.

The moon horses squeal as they are hurried toward the exit, the rickety wagon clattering behind them, making the wizard jump.

Death thickens the air, more tangible than the coat of sand settling onto our skin.

In the piles of weapons, I spot a sword and a dagger I can use. There's a metal chest plate that would protect me more than the meager leather one I'm wearing now, but the seconds it takes to put the armor on could cost me my life.

Suddenly, the drums speed up, almost catching my racing heart and silencing the crowd, and then the percussion abruptly stops.

"Halt!" a guard shouts. "And turn!"

As one, we pivot to face the royal box, my mind racing with thoughts of which fighter I should kill first, who will be best to get out of the way quickly. *Anyone but Sully*, I argue. *Anyone but my friend.*

Just then, High Lord Vitor rises. "One hundred years," he bellows, the magic within the royal box amplifying and reverberating his voice across the massive structure.

The crowd shrieks with excitement. "One hundred!" they echo.

"Thousands of gladiators," he shouts.

The spectators cheer louder, enlivened by the thought of ten more.

"And today," Vitor continues, "we have a *special* match." He gestures to the bet makers rushing up and down the stands and then to the pile of weapons in the center. "There are two potential Bloodguards before us, and therefore there should be...*two times* the payouts!"

The crowd goes wild.

Holy hell. This son of a bitch is spinning it so this crowd can make a fortune—not lose one. And we're the ones expected to make or break their status. "Well, shit," Sullivan mutters. Neither of us saw *this* coming.

People are screaming with delight and still trying to catch the ear of the harried bet makers scribbling on pads and tossing out tickets as fast as they can. They're not even waiting to see the drop of the banner that will reveal our final odds.

The High Lord lifts his hand and pauses for the arena to quiet again. "In these final moments of betting, take in what awaits, my friends, and choose wisely, for those who thirst for water today, tomorrow may demand wine!"

The crowd's thrill escalates, their calls for action mounting.

Then something roars, the menacing sound extinguishing all others.

Even the vultures circling the skies flee.

We still.

The air around us shifts, growing thick with dread.

Sullivan and I exchange one final glance. We know what it is long before it lands.

Webbed wings the size of ship sails stretch out as talons the length of my arms slam against the arena floor. The brown dragon chuffs, the fire brewing in its belly hot enough to shoot steam from its nostrils. The elf rider on its back is covered with enchanted leather that protects his flesh from the heat. The dragon's body is the length of three moon horses. Not as large as they come, but large enough to easily squash us.

My mouth goes dry. This dragon is a young male—I can see the pair of claspers under the base of his tail as he thrashes. The only thing more ravenous than an old dragon is a young male. They need more energy to fuel their rapid growth spurts.

"Only one will rise," Vitor shouts over the gasps of the crowd. His smile takes on a malicious edge. "Will it be gladiator—or shall it be beast?"

The dragon roars once more, and the final betting bell is barely audible above the crowd's screams and cheers.

We all shift around to face the pile of weapons as fast as we can.

Sully breaks away from me. He crouches and shakes out his hands.

We don't exchange farewells. After three years of watching out for each other, it all comes down to this.

I lean forward and get ready to run, my focus on the pile of weapons and not on the man who was—dammit, *is*—my friend.

The moment the horn blasts, I charge.

CHAPTER

4

MAEVE

I can't believe this.

My leather slippers slap against the cool marble hallway that leads out of the arena with every furious step I take away from that horrible place and over to an alcove in the tunnel. This is the first time I've been to the coliseum in years, and I only came today for the formality of announcing the wedding banns. It was supposed to be easy—show up, allow the royal courts to see me and my betrothed together, say a few words to honor my grandmother's memory, and leave.

Preferably with our damn heads still attached.

Filip, bless his heart, couldn't even manage that.

Did I want to marry an egotistical, entitled oaf who had no qualms about telling me to "keep my neck covered"? No.

But I'm the daughter of "the Queen Killer." In the wake of my father's purported crimes, I've become a political pariah. While Filip wasn't the brightest torch in the cave, he *was* the only marriageable person from one of the five noble houses who was willing to overlook my father's imprisonment and my scars—*and*, more importantly, he wasn't afraid of Soro.

So, I'd made a bargain.

"Leave ruling the kingdom to me, and I'll leave the whoring to you," I'd said. And Filip—again, bless his heart—was fine with it.

We were *days* from marrying.

I should have focused on *that* when I was in the arena. The future. My imprisoned father. My brokenhearted second father. Instead, my mind—and eyes—had wandered to that gladiator. Menace cloaked him as though the arena had taken everything from him but his pride. And his rage.

He's young. No more than four or five years my senior—which means he likely volunteered for the arena at twenty-two, the minimum age of eligibility. It makes sense, given how embittered he seemed.

I could have kicked myself when Soro and Filip caught me gawking. Filip was already overly sensitive about our engagement—especially with Soro waiting in the wings, eager to marry me himself. So off Filip went into the arena…and off went his head across the sand.

My stomach twists as I pace and wait. I demanded to speak to High Lord Vitor, but my demands aren't always met, princess or not.

The crowd's excitement builds loud enough to echo against the stone walls.

"Where are you going, Maeve?" a singsong voice asks from behind me, then laughs.

I mask my expression as I turn.

Aisling, a heartless mage I've known since childhood, with lavender hair and eyes but no kind soul to match, must have followed me out of the arena.

Aisling huffs. "You really should take more care with your attire," she says, waving an irritated hand. She saunters closer, like a red weaver spider ready to pluck a juicy beetle from her web. "A hat and veil could be particularly fashionable, and maybe you could actually pull it off."

My grip on my cloak loosens. This is not the moment to try me.

Aisling, of course, does. "Honestly, Maeve, this is your first time in the arena in *ages*. Come—join Soro and me back in the stands, place a few bets, try talking to our peers."

I couldn't care less if that court of jesters ever speaks to me again. But to say "Soro and me"? Is she mad? Claiming Soro is like claiming a tiger. Yes, he'll allow a stroke or two, but he will ultimately feast on your insides.

"I won't support these games, Aisling. When I'm queen, by the phoenix, I'll put an end to these horrors."

"When you're queen?" Aisling laughs. "You'll never be queen without another noble for a fiancé." The way she eases forward is more like a slither. "Maybe you should have thought of that *before* lusting after that young gladiator for all to see." Her brows slash downward. "You know, the one who turned your last chance at the throne into an embarrassing memory?"

"Was *Filip* my last chance?" I ask and tap my chin, pretending to ponder marrying someone else. Aisling's arrogance dwindles as she realizes *Soro* is my last chance. But that's a chance I'm not willing to take. *Yet.* Not that Aisling needs to know. "No, I don't think he was."

Cheers echo from the arena floor, followed by a roar, and my head whips toward the sound fast enough to flutter my hair. Was that a... *dragon*?

Aisling's smile returns, pulling my gaze back to hers. This sadist is excited that the match has begun and likely giddy with the thought of what those poor fighters are about to endure. She can't wait to get back, and I can't wait to leave.

But as I turn, she reaches out to grab my hand, the elemental magic she's known for crackling against her skin. I jerk free of her hold. "*Come on*, Maeve. Let's see what that handsome fighter can do...before he *can't*, of course," she says.

My stomach sinks like a boulder as I edge farther away. "What makes you think he won't win?" Seeing how easily he took down a swordsman like Filip, there can't be many his equal.

But she knows something—and the glint in her eyes says she's dying to tell me.

"Just spill it, Aisling," I say. I want to scream and shout—at her, at the world—but it's been drilled into me from childhood: decorum, decorum, decorum. One day, I'm just going to decide to fuck decorum and say and do whatever I want. But probably not today. "Please," I add sweetly.

Aisling plays with a curl in her hair, her conceit as evident as the sparks of lavender magic coloring her eggshell skin. "Well..." She draws the word out, likely knowing each second she delays telling me is making my stomach knot tighter and tighter. Dread is a living, breathing thing pooling in my stomach now, and I'm fantasizing about reaching out and shaking her when she finally continues, "High Lord Vitor is adamant that *that* gladiator, and the one standing beside him, can't be allowed to live past today."

"Why?" I gasp, remembering that the veteran fighter beside mine—great, now I'm calling him *mine*—had two of the four final Bloodguard tattoos on his forearm.

"*Because*," Aisling says like I'm the dim torch, "only the gladiators of Vitor's choosing win Bloodguard. Obviously."

"What did I choose?" a male voice asks from behind me, and Aisling startles.

Her eyes widen with genuine fear before she dips into a demure bow before Arrow's regent. "My lord," she addresses him. She gives my hand one last squeeze. "Join us in the stands, Maeve."

Vitor narrows his eyes at her until she dashes away, and then he turns an indulgent smile on me. "Maeve, you look lovely. I'm so glad you decided to come today."

"Hello, Uncle Vitor," I say, my tone clipped as he draws even with me. I want to ask about his plans for the two gladiators, but I've known Vitor my whole life—and asking the High Lord to explain himself is the quickest way to never get answers.

"My condolences on your fiancé's sudden demise," he says.

He isn't sorry, of course. In fact, he looks delighted.

"Soro goaded Filip into that arena." I don't need to insist. We both know it's true.

"So what if he did?" Vitor asks, his visage spilling with relief. "You were *saved* today, my daughter. If your intended was that easily riled, he would have made a terrible king."

I can't argue that logic, but he continues, "If you want to marry a simpleton, marry Soro."

"*Uncle,*" I admonish out of habit.

It's no secret Vitor prefers me over his son—it's always been a difficulty between us.

He grins like he's made some great stride and we might somehow return to the way things used to be between us. But there is no going back. Not while Papa is dying in prison. And Uncle Vitor the one who put him there.

"Won't you consider releasing him?" I whisper, unable to bite back the question.

"This again? Maeve…" Vitor shakes his head. "Our kingdom thrives on laws. We can't bend them just because you've asked me to."

His admonishment makes my hands curl into fists, but I continue in an even tone. "I'm not asking to bend the laws or suggesting we break them. My father is *innocent*."

Papa would never have harmed Grandmother. He loved her. We all did.

Vitor's eyes soften. "I know this is hard, Maeve. But we didn't just cast Andres into a cell without consideration. And in the end, the prince confessed to striking down our great Queen Avianna. You know this, dear."

"No," I disagree for the hundredth time. Only the council was present during my father's supposed confession, but I will deny he ever said it at all until he admits the deed to my face. My father is a gentle and decent man, and I cannot imagine him capable of murder, much less murdering his own mother.

"I understand your doubts," Vitor says. "The truth can be painful." His expression turns pensive before he glances back at me. "I know you love your papa, but can't you extend that love to Arrow, too?"

I gasp. "Of course I love my country. I was willing to marry *Filip* for Arrow," I remind him.

But Vitor just stares down his nose at me. "Covering yourself up? Hiding your face in the stands?" He tips my chin up with his finger. "Avoiding these games as if you have something to hide? The people need to see you, to embrace you and know you are capable…"

He isn't trying to be callous or cruel. While Vitor isn't a blood relative, growing up in the castle with him made him as close as family. As acting Regent of Arrow, he rules in my stead.

He'll stay in that role until such time as I come of age and marry within my class. Should something happen to me, as heir to the throne, the crown would revert to the five noble houses to be shared equally. And that…that would be anarchy.

"Now, come back into the arena with me," he says. "And by the great phoenix, try to smile and at least *act* like you enjoy the games."

Vitor believes this is best for me—and for the kingdom. I recognize why…because these games are a tool.

He's a smart man, my uncle. He uses the arena to entertain the people—*all* the people—showering them with food and drink and a chance to change their fortunes. It's made him popular among the classes and solidified his position as Lord Regent. Everyone buys in. The nobles spending their time and money on this "sport." The common people betting in the hopes of a better life. The fighters willing to die to win the riches that Bloodguard brings and citizenship for their families, not to mention its coveted royal title.

My eyes widen as the words "royal title" ricochet in my chest, my heart racing.

Vitor's eyes sharpen. "What is it?"

"Nothing." I lower my gaze and try for a meek expression. "You're right, Uncle." I tuck my arm through his and lean into his shoulder. "If I want to be queen, I must act like it."

He nods approvingly and kisses the top of my head.

"Come home," he tells me. "Marry Soro, as your grandmother would have wanted, and I will believe she would understand if—sometime after the wedding, of course—I pardoned your father. The kingdom is flourishing under my rule. What Arrow needs is stability and strength, and I can continue to give it to them with my son and you by my side."

Part of me is willing to do it—I would do *anything* to save my father. But as much as I love him, I know he would never forgive me if I married Soro. There's something just not *right* about that man. He was cruel when we were children, and he's only grown worse over the years. As much as I want to believe Vitor would still be able to control him were Soro and I to wed, Soro would be *king*—and able to do so much worse. I can't risk it.

Besides…I have a better plan.

Uncle Vitor's grip tightens around my hand to steady me as we return to the arena, but I barely notice. I can't even hear the roar of the crowd over my heart pounding in my ears when we take our seats in the royal box.

I find the young gladiator, his boots digging into the sand, his body poised to sprint, and I refuse to look away. He *will* win today.

He owes me a fiancé.

CHAPTER

5

LEITH

A horn blows, and I take off.

Fifty yards separate me from the nearest pile.

My boots dig into the sand as I race across the uneven ground, my arms pumping so hard I grimace when the axe wound in my shoulder rips open again.

Forty yards.

The ogre behind me curses half a second before the air shifts from hot to scorching.

I cut right.

Thirty yards.

His screams precede those of two others crying out in agony.

I push faster.

Twenty yards.

The scent of cooking flesh fills my nose.

Ten yards.

Blistering heat pricks my skin.

The dragon turns. I dive over the pile, rolling across the sand and squelching the flames licking the exposed skin on my shoulders.

A wave of yellow and red erupts inches above me as I land on my chest, flattening my body as low to the ground as I can get, using the pile of weapons as a barrier to the dragon's fire. The crowd bursts into screams of horror and delight, all but drowning out the screeching of two more gladiators burning alive.

Five gone. Five left.

And the dragon.

I squeeze my eyes closed, trying to ignore the burning agony rampaging along my shoulder. The dragon fire sealed my axe wound, but it cost me.

My entire body trembles, the pain taking control. *Move*, I tell myself. *If you want to live, MOVE.*

I keep low as heavy claws pound the earth, and then I push up on my knees and move closer to the pile. I manage to pry my eyes open, but they ram shut again as the smoke stings them like a rake of needles. Blinking several times, I try and try again, fighting the instinct to protect my vision.

Sight is useless to a dead man, and I want to *live*.

I crawl forward and feel around. I'm not far from a stash of weapons. I need to keep moving.

My hand slips over the familiar feel of a sword. Tears blur my vision as I slap around to find the hilt. As soon as I've gripped it, I whirl, and something brushes against the sand.

My vision clears enough to see. The remaining dwarf gapes back at me on all fours. What's left of her braid is singed close to her neck. Her fingertips scratch over the hilt of a shorter sword. She snatches it, but it doesn't budge. It's melted into a shield and blazes knows what else.

"Truce until the dragon is dead?" she asks between labored breaths.

She cringes at the sound of flesh tearing from bone. The dragon found more food near the exit of the arena. At my nod, the dwarf stands and starts searching for usable weapons.

Sullivan stumbles to my side. Half of his face is red and blistered, and he's holding his left arm tight against his body, but he's still alive.

"Are you good with a bow?" I ask the dwarf.

She shakes her head. I motion to Sullivan. "He is." Given how Sullivan is guarding his arm, at least I hope he still is. Sullivan doesn't protest, so I keep talking. "You find a bow, you give it to him," I tell the dwarf, "and we'll give the dragon someone else to eat."

Understanding lights the dwarf's bloodshot eyes, and we scramble around the pile, searching for anything we can use. It won't be long before the dragon finishes his well-cooked cuisine.

"Spear!" Sullivan shouts. I look up, and he tosses it to me one-handed.

I catch the weapon and jab it into the soft sand, then grab two daggers from the pile and shove them into my belt. "There should be four," I say to myself as I pick up another sword, judge the weight, and toss it back into the pile.

"What?" Sullivan asks. He kicks a piece of armor melted into a mace.

"I count five dead since the start of the match," I explain, continuing to rummage as fast as I can. I toss him the next good sword I find. It's heavier and harder to wield, but there's little to choose from. Most of the weapons are damaged or useless, and running to the other piles will only capture the dragon's attention.

"Six with him." I jerk my chin to the mangled mess of bones the dragon just spat out.

Sullivan realizes what I'm saying. "You, me, and the dwarf make three."

It only takes a beat to find our missing man.

Mere feet from where the dragon feasts, the image of the wizard fades in and out. He's huddled against the exit, using whatever magic he has left to make himself invisible. Except wizards can't maintain spells for long without their staffs.

And if we can see the wizard, the dragon can, too.

The giant creature whips his head in the flickering wizard's direction. Without hesitation, the beast abandons the bones for fresh meat. He's either pissed that the wizard fooled him or tickled fucking pink that he gets to gobble down a magical being, because he snaps his jaws over the shrieking wizard and swallows him whole.

"Now!" I race forward, seizing the opportunity like a drowning man reaching for shore.

I'm not positive Sullivan and the dwarf will follow me. I can't be sure I'd follow them.

As I close the distance, the dragon angles toward me, taking a defensive stance. But it's not the dragon I'm aiming for, and I hurl the spear with every ounce of speed and strength I can muster.

My spear nails the dragon rider through the throat. Blood spurts from his jugular, drenching the dragon and inciting his rage further.

The crowd is on their feet, watching the dragon shake off the dead body of his master and devour it. Some scream while others are shocked into silence. I keep running and stab the dragon in the throat with my sword. The point is sharp enough to puncture the scales and weaken him, maybe even suppress his flames, but it's not enough to sever his head or prevent him from swallowing us. All I did was buy some time.

The dragon jerks in anger. I dive and roll away from his smacking wing, barely escaping the lethal blow. What I don't avoid is his hind leg that kicks me into the wall like I'm a fluttering insect.

Stars explode in my vision, and my shoulder dislocates with a gruesome *pop*. But I rise, gritting my teeth, then snap my shoulder back into place against the wall and stagger toward a sword lying near a pile of bones.

An arrow shoots through the sky, followed by two more. Sullivan found a bow—excellent.

I snag the sword and push my legs into a run.

The arrows land weakly, bouncing off the dragon's scales. Sullivan's injured arm is preventing them from having enough force. I watch as he falls to the ground and uses his feet to shoot two arrows with more power. One pierces the dragon's scales, and the beast roars loud enough to send ice shooting through my veins.

The dwarf has luck with a whip. She smacks the end across the dragon's snout, and the leather wraps around his maw, slamming it shut.

The dwarf digs her heels into the ground, laboring to straighten the scaled beast's neck.

"Kill it," she yells at us. "By the great phoenix, kill it!"

Another arrow flies past me, puncturing one of the dragon's eyes, which sends the massive dragon into a frenzy. The beast shakes his head, yanking on the whip and flinging the dwarf to the side. She loses her footing and skids across the sand, but before she can get to her feet again, the dragon eviscerates her with his claws.

The dwarf screams just as my sword comes down on his neck. My strike is vicious, but it's not enough to slice through the scales, and the dragon doesn't even flinch. He just snacks on the dwarf as if I did nothing.

His tail flicks back and forth as he eats, and I must run to avoid getting smacked across the arena again.

I can't gauge where Sullivan is until his hollers overpower the dwarf's screams. My sword is gone, and the pile of weapons is nowhere close, so I reach for the daggers in my waistband and sprint forward, toward his voice, compelling myself to move faster.

Nothing of strategy remains—only the will to survive.

I glimpse Sullivan, caught beneath the dragon, desperately trying to reload his bow while the thing snarls at him, teeth still bloodied from the dwarf.

I leap onto the dragon's neck, locking my legs around his head. I thrust both blades into his remaining eye and hammer the hilts, pounding the points deeper and deeper and deeper.

The dragon lashes violently, and I barely hold on.

My thigh muscles spasm, struggling to keep me on his back, but I know if I go down, I'll never get up again. I slam my fists onto the daggers again and again, the hilts and my hands covered in blood and tissue, using every bit of strength that remains in me to drive them all the way into the beast's brain.

When the dragon finally collapses, I do, too. I don't fully realize I've fallen until I hit the ground with a sickening *thud* and a sharp crack of bones. If anything essential actually broke this time, I have no idea. My whole body has become one giant pulse of pain.

I can't place where I am. I can only feel.

Waves of agony scrape my flesh like hot, pointy sabers. Fluid drenches my scalp. It's not sweat. I know better.

Screams of excitement pierce through my muffled hearing. This is one of those battles I can't easily rise from, and I sure as hell don't.

My weight teeters from side to side as I struggle to stand. My vision isn't much better as it fades and clears in violent waves.

I trip over the remains of the dwarf, falling to my knees beside a discarded sword. I use it to stand again. I need to keep moving. This isn't over.

Sullivan and I are the only ones left. The moment I've dreaded is finally here.

Sullivan…

He waits a few yards from me, kneeling. At least that's what I think he's doing, until I realize his legs are gone and his good arm is partially eaten. I stumble to a stop in front of him, breathing hard enough to choke.

Blood pools in his mouth. "What are you waiting for?" he slurs. "Do you think I'd let *you* live?"

I sway where I stand, my eyes burning.

He's trying to alleviate my guilt.

It doesn't work.

The tip of my sword finds his heart and pierces it clean through as the first of his tears spills across his battered face.

Those who are scared always cry.

The crowd is on their feet. I keep still, watching Sullivan's body bleeding out. A new bar of brutality has been raised in the arena today, and rage freezes the blood in my veins.

My gaze lifts to the audience, to the bloodthirsty crowd that cheered as I killed my friend. Some of them are horrified. Others are crying. But they make up the minority. Row after row of spectators are screaming with joy at my victory.

"*Bloodguard!*" they chant over and over.

They want me to celebrate with them. I won't.

Instead, I cut away a section of Sully's hair, clutching every strand in my fist as I stand before the crowd. I turn to the royal box, searching for the High Lord with an unspoken threat that he will one day die upon my sword as well. But my eyes latch onto the brown-haired elf's instead. Did she come back to watch me be torn apart?

Well, too damn bad, lady.

When she bows in respect, I all but stop breathing, then mentally shake myself. I refuse to believe there's an ounce of admiration in her cold heart. I walk right out of the arena.

Hope is the only thing that can kill a gladiator like me, and I'm not dying today.

CHAPTER

6

LEITH

I grit my teeth. After everything I endured in the arena, the tattoo the frail mage emblazons into my skin should be nothing. But since the moment the magical needle pierced my forearm, beginning to trace the lines of a sword, I understood the full meaning of pain all over again.

My body wants to pull away, every injury screaming at once for mercy. But I keep still. I've won my first Bloodguard match. It's technically an honor to have this coveted symbol on my forearm. If I win the next three, I'll be allowed to add a vine of thorns that wraps its way down the length of the blade, a rose, and a crown that circles the hilt.

When completed, the tattoo will grant me royal status and mark me as Bloodguard—a very rich, very powerful, and *very* dangerous noble. I swallow the bile rising in my throat at what I had to do today to earn this mark. This symbol was once a badge of honor. Now, it serves no purpose so well as to remind the world—and myself—that I'm a killer.

Once the mage is finished, I head straight to the barn and dunk my arm in the horse's trough. The stable boy gives me ample berth as I lean into it and splash the fresh wound with water. Nags have drunk from here for the better part of the day, and I doubt anyone has thought to clean it recently. But I won't complain. It eases the sting and floods me with relief.

I stare at the mark. A sword, pointing downward. It's strong and powerful and should make me feel the same. But all I can think about is Sullivan.

He wore the same symbol.

And it made no difference in the end.

I reach into my pocket to assure myself Sullivan's hair is still where I shoved it earlier as I left the arena floor. The first chance I get, I'll bury it someplace Sullivan would've liked. Not in the arena, nor in these crowded stables beneath it. And not in the dirty barracks where we sleep with our backs to the wall so no one can surprise us. That place reeks of piss and rotting flesh and all the sins we've committed.

Sullivan deserves better, even if those quarters were where our friendship began.

A fresh wave of pain hits me hard in the chest. The worst kind of pain. Grief. But I swallow the bitter taste before it shows on my face.

The familiar sound of wheels bumping across the cobblestones pulls my attention toward the stable entrance.

After my fight, a human guard told me someone wanted to speak to me and not to return to the barracks yet. It's likely a noble who wants me to wash his hunting dogs, chop his firewood, or some other shit they're too good to do. The pay for tasks like that is almost as piddling as what we get for winning, but even one coin is one more to help my little sister.

Yet, when I glance to the open gates, I see it's just another wagon full of gladiators, fresh from their presentation to the royal box. Looks like they will be going out as usual in pairs, no free-for-all this time.

I wonder if my win took the High Lord down a notch, and now they're having to slow the matches to cover the House's losses. I can only hope.

The wagon jostles as the other fighters hop off. Most are humans, dwarves, and elves, but one person I recognize is Luther, a giant.

His throat bubbles with boils like those that covered Sullivan, and he grimaces when he scratches them. Fresh blood and pus trickle down his neck, adding to the dry streaks painting his vest.

The guards ease away from the giant. They don't know what disease he has—they only know they don't want it. They also don't want to piss him off. Everyone knows Luther killed a bull with his bare hands during his first fight. It was a similar transgression to feed his family that got him imprisoned and thrown into the games in the first place.

As I watch, the group of gladiators is led in the direction of the pens. This is how the matches usually go: each gladiator is thrown into the arena only two or three at a time. Luther should make it. Although it's hard to tell sometimes, and I've been wrong before.

The stable boy returns to offer me a bucket of water, and I put it to my mouth, drinking hard. The rest, I pour over my head. It's only enough to refresh me, not fully wash Sullivan's blood from my hands.

My eyes remain on the gladiators as they pass. I make a show of stretching my muscles so the nearby guards don't cause a fuss. We're not supposed to speak to those in line to fight, but I'm damn well speaking to Luther. I start moving toward him, past the row of stalls.

Luther is small for a giant, maybe nine feet tall and half as wide. He walks from side to side on short, tree-trunk legs. Like most giants, the dense musculature of his chest and arms, along with the weight of his large head, bows his hips outward.

I'm almost to the end of the stable when Luther's small brown eyes shift to mine. I press my boot against a wooden plank, pretending to tie the torn laces.

"Where they?" Luther asks. Protruding jaws often make it hard for giants to speak human languages, so they keep their sentences short.

He means the group I arrived with. "They threw us all in together," I spit through my teeth.

"All?" he repeats.

The men closest to us crane their necks in our direction. "Oi. *Oi!*" Ned, an elf, yells ahead. "They just threw everyone in."

The commotion draws the attention of the guards, who stare at Luther and me but don't draw their weapons. The gladiators in the holding pens start to quiet at the realization that they, too, could have been in the group fight, except for some lucky reason the wagon they came in on was spared.

I glance at the tattoo on my arm. None in this lot bear one. Maybe killing them off quickly is less of a priority.

More likely, they intended everyone in my match to die. This wagon would've comprised round two and had very different odds.

The House always wins, but that doesn't stop the people of Arrow from trying to improve their station. I get it. I was gambling, too, when I signed on to become a Bloodguard.

Drool pools on Luther's bottom lip as he forms his next word. "Sullivan?" he asks.

Long words are hard for him, so the fact he gets a multisyllabic name out shows how important the question is to him.

Hearing Sullivan's name beats up what's left of my insides. I shake my head. There's nothing more to say.

Luther bows his head, his heavy and scruffy brow burying his beady eyes. He's grieving for Sullivan. It's brief, but it's there.

More guards arrive. I give Luther my back then. I may want to rage for Sullivan, but that rage can't help him now.

I look to the entrance again, wondering about my mystery visitor. I wish he'd hurry it up so I can get on with my day or, at the very least, leave this foul place.

Instead, a small voice catches my attention.

"I want to be you when it's my time."

It's the stable boy again. There are deep-set scars branching across his bald head, fresh pink injuries in addition to older ones. The poor kid has been beaten for years.

He backs away when he catches my scowl. I want to scream at him, tell him he's a fool for desiring any part of the gladiator life. But I'm the fool for signing up. And this kid's been through enough violence. He doesn't need me yelling at him, too.

"How old are you?" I ask.

He tilts his head as though surprised I acknowledged him. "Almost fourteen, sir," he says.

I thought he was maybe nine at most. He's probably malnourished, which must have stunted his height.

He points to my forearm, where the fresh tattoo still burns. "I'm going to get a sword like you some day," he says.

I attempt to soften my tone. He's the same age as my oldest sister, Rose. It's hard, though. My voice is still rough from battle. "What's your name?"

"Gunther," he replies.

I bend to meet his gaze and press a hand to his shoulder. "I wish you all the best, Gunther."

"You too, sir! Only three matches more." Hope that I didn't intend sparks to life in his soft brown eyes. He pumps his fist and chants as he leaves the stables, "Bloodguard. Bloodguard…"

"Make way!" one of the guards shouts as an elf on horseback rides into the stables. He's all alone and not in finery, but I recognize him as one of the two men who'd not been cheering in the royal box earlier.

He dismounts, whispering something to his brown-and-white horse that keeps the animal in place.

The lord doesn't make a sound as he unhooks a large sack tethered to his saddle or as he moves forward. Elves are like that—silent, deadly, keenly skilled. Regardless, he's no threat to me physically. I can see in his eyes that whatever fight this elf might've had in him is long gone. The lonely ones always give in.

"Congratulations on making it to the finals," he says to me with a nod. He's older, with dark-gray hair. "I'm Lord Jakeb." He says it as though being from here is a right, not a privilege. He offers me the sack. "It's Leith, right? Leith of Siertos?"

It's Leith of Grey, which is within Siertos, but I don't correct him. To people like him, everything beyond Arrow's borders is of no importance.

I take the sack and lower it to my side, my eyes narrowing. "What's this?"

"A set of clean clothes to celebrate your advancement," Jakeb explains. "I hope they fit. I had to guess your size."

"No, I can't afford this," I protest. No way am I adding more debt to my ledgers.

"It's a gift," Jakeb insists. "You don't owe me a thing."

I hold his gaze before asking, trepidation crawling over my skin, "Why?"

"To be kind," Jakeb replies. The cunning I expect from the aristocracy skates across his features. He's up to something. I just haven't figured out what yet. He adds, "You've been through a lot."

"You think?" I ask, then laugh bitterly.

Whatever the reason, I guess keep the free gifts coming. It's the least these bastards can do. I sling the pack of clothes over my shoulder and level another pointed stare at Jakeb.

He takes a half step back as though realizing he's too close for my comfort—or his. "I'd like to invite you to stay at my home. There's plenty of food, a warm bed, and someone to see to your needs. If you have any hope of winning your next three matches, trust me, you're going to need help."

My stomach curdles. I don't like this at all. I've had sponsorships before, but this feels…different. This elf doesn't frequent the arena. He isn't one of the heavy gamblers that sit along the rail, screaming for a win. Those patrons are easy to distinguish, and the kindness they show us is only to ensure they have an edge for their next bet. This elf… I don't know what his angle is.

But…a warm bed and food… This bag of clothes he's handed me alone could resell for a pretty price. My sister Dahlia needs anything she can get. Just because I can't trust this man doesn't mean I can't find a way to turn his agenda to my advantage.

"All right," I tell him carefully. "Make me a blood oath that there are no charges or fees to be tacked onto my ledger for any *kindness* you offer, and I accept."

"As you wish," he says. From deep within his robes, he produces a dagger and slices his palm, muttering the words elves use to form the binding oath. When he's done, he offers me his hand. I take it, keeping my attention on his eyes and not on the words traveling from his hand and into my arm, making the small hairs tingle as his oath disappears into my skin.

Once finished, he uses a cloth to wipe the dagger and his hand clean. "Let's move along, shall we? I've already sent word of your arrival."

I pause. "What if I'd said no?"

Jakeb chuckles. "Oh, my daughter isn't one to take no for an answer."

His *daughter*? I see. I knew there was more to the bargain. He might not be charging me coin for his kindness, but it appears I do have a duty to oblige. There are worse fates. The aristocracy are hedonistic and think nothing of paying for a good time. If fucking his daughter is the "payment" Jakeb expects for not sleeping in the barracks and pissing in a bucket tonight, I'll screw his daughter all night long.

Jakeb leaps onto his horse and motions with his hand.

Gunther walks forward with a spotted moon horse, overjoyed by leading such a fine steed. The mare's nose has a splash of white, as do her hindquarters. Gunther offers me the reins. I don't take them. This is a test, and one I should use care to pass.

Jakeb laughs, the sound strangely absent of the evil I expect from someone of his status. "You'll need a horse when you're Bloodguard. Her name is Star. She's a good one, smart and obedient. If you like her, she's yours when you win. If you don't like her, give her back to me." Humor leaves his features. "There will come a time when royals will offer you gold in exchange for favors. Use your earnings to buy a grander steed if you prefer." He seems to think about what he's saying. "Choose your allegiances wisely. Not all those in Arrow are as they appear."

The same could be said of him, but I just nod and take the reins. I'm not the best horseman. My only experience comes from riding nags to plow fields.

So I take a deep breath, shove my boot into the metal stirrup, and pull myself up and over the saddle, biting back a groan of pain from the sudden jostling of my ribs. The arena definitely broke a few bones today. Not to mention what was left of my soul. But I pay neither any mind as I grip the reins tighter.

Jakeb gives me his back, urging his steed forward, and I follow. One guard bows his head as we pass, but the other shakes his head. Whatever.

After we leave the complex, Jakeb urges his moon horse into a canter, and my mount follows with little effort. The mare has an even gait, but still, every bump and clop of her hooves rattles my broken body, and I struggle not to pass out from the pain. We turn onto the road that leads away from this hell, toward the forest lands just outside the city, and I gather my wits, focusing on everything as we pass.

Grass and wildflowers bend away from the wide road like a parting sea. My mother has never seen a flower. Neither had I until I arrived in Arrow. She'd only heard they were pretty. It's why she named my sisters Rose and Dahlia—she wanted to say she'd held a flower in her lifetime. Most of the kingdoms outside of Arrow are poor, the people fighting over the few scraps of food they're able to scrabble out of the dead earth. A flower would feel like a betrayal.

When I become Bloodguard, I'll buy my mother flowers every day if it makes her smile. I frown, taking note that as we travel farther out of town, the blooms have begun to wilt, their colors not as vivid. Weird.

My stomach twists, and I can't help but wonder if this is a bad omen.

CHAPTER

7

MAEVE

My heart nearly soared out of my chest as I watched the final gladiator rise from the sandy arena floor victorious. An hour later, I'm back in my bedroom and my insides are still twisted in knots, the image of the tall fighter covered head to toe in sweat and dirt and blood burned in my mind.

Our little estrellas chitter as they bounce along my bed like the little non-magical lemurs they resemble, their soft calico fur bristling as they watch the two smallest ones fight it out for the pillow.

"Bethina, Tibeta, behave," I admonish. "There's plenty of room—"

Quick steps racing up the stone stairs of the manor have me whipping around. My sister, Giselle, appears, her straight, honey-colored hair all a flutter, her matching eyes wild.

"It's all over the city. Filip's *dead*?" she gasps.

I barely catch her before she stumbles into my room and lands on the dark wood floor. Her escalated voice sends the estrellas into a frenzy, small but mighty claws scratching the floor as they chase one another. "Giselle, be careful!"

"*I* need to be careful?" she demands, allowing me to steady her. "Maeve, your birthday will be here in less than three months. What are we going to do now?"

My twenty-first birthday. When I'll be old enough to take the throne... provided I've married well.

My sister is only a few months younger than me, but at barely over five feet, she's short for an elf. I tower over her. It shouldn't matter, but because of her petite frame and her other, um, *abilities*, I've always felt protective of her.

My fingers brush across her cheek, smoothing her long hair behind an ear. "You don't look well," I say. "Did you take the elixir I made?"

"Yes, but I threw it up," she says, her wide eyes unblinking.

"Why?"

"Because it tasted like shit."

I sigh. "It's not supposed to be tasty. I developed it to suppress some of your...issues."

Oh, there's that questioning eyebrow lift Giselle is known for. "Well, that's one way to put it."

I quiet. "Did you give some to Papa, like I asked?" She nods. "Oh, good."

"No. Not good." She grimaces. "He threw it all up. Because it tastes like shit."

I want to laugh. If only this were a laughing matter. Instead, I step away from her and groan. "How is he?"

Her petite features soften with palpable sadness. "Terrible, Maeve, just *awful*. What are we going to do?"

"It's not we. It's *me*. And I've already come up with a new plan." I cross my arms, tilting my chin up. "I'm going to marry a Bloodguard."

Giselle nods thoughtfully, flopping onto my fluffy white bed now free of estrellas. When she turns her head, I know she's ready to talk, or at the very least tear my idea apart. "What size?" she asks.

My brows knit together. "What size Bloodguard?" I question.

"What size coffin, Maeve? Are you mad?" She throws her arms out for emphasis. "Bloodguards kill, like, everything and anyone in their path. And you want to marry one?"

My spine stiffens as I straighten to my full height. "If that's what it takes to free Papa, I'll do it."

"Which Bloodguard, Maeve? Ditrese the bear shifter is on wife number three, due to the 'accidental' demises of the first two." She blows out a breath. "Damn shame. You would have *loved* shaving his back twice a week."

"Giselle…"

She holds out a finger. "Oh, there's Aeet, the mage, but while she likes women, she's so traumatized from the arena, she won't leave her cottage. A million gold coins. That's how much she won. And she's used all of it to fortify her home against, well, everyone." She lifts her head. "No one who's tried to enter it has yet returned. Are you planning to be the first?"

"Giselle," I say.

"And let's not forget Situ. 'Where are my toes? Where are my toes? Has anyone seen my toes? I'll kill you for hiding my toes!' I mean, how many times can you tell a wizard he ate his own toes before he starts to believe you?"

"That's just a rumor."

"Is it, Maeve?" She shakes her head, quieting me as she repositions against the pillows. "There are only five Bloodguards in Arrow, all either dangerous to you or dangerously loyal to the regent. The other two moved as far away from the arena as they could go. And can you blame them?"

"No," I admit. My sister is right. Seven Bloodguards in my lifetime… Seven deeply traumatized individuals, the latest two faithfully serving Vitor. "All that senseless death…"

I move over to the wardrobe, grab the hem of my dress in my fists, and yank it over my head. I toss it into the basket next to my bed and wish it was as easy to get rid of the memories from today.

I pull my wardrobe open, grab breeches, and tug them on with jerky movements. My hands tremble as I fasten the hooks on a clean shirt, and I take a deep breath, trying to calm my racing pulse. "But someone new will soon become a Bloodguard. I just know it. And I will make a deal with him to be my husband as well."

"This is an absurd plan, Maeve. No." She scooches up on the bed, crossing her arms and glaring at me. "No. Absolutely *no*."

I don't bother arguing. There really is no other choice.

The door to my bedchamber creaks open. I don't have to turn to know it's Neela, the matron troll who's cared for us since we were children. She was our governess and tutor and family, which is why Neela was more than happy to come with us when Father, Giselle, and I left the castle in exchange for this manor.

Her extra-wide shoes tap against the oak floors as she walks over.

She blinks her small black eyes, her hooked nose crinkling as she tilts her head at me.

"What's wrong?" I ask.

"A lady of your position should dress to impress," she reminds me in a comment that bears remarkable similarity to Vitor's. She's short for a troll—coming only up to my shoulder—and ancient, as the gray tuft of hair on top of her head suggests. Her large ears droop, an unfair show of disappointment. "If you seek the throne and the crown that comes with it, you should appear worthy."

"I'm wearing a dress, Neela," Giselle says with a wide smile.

"That's nice, dear," she says, her gravelly voice cracking with age.

If Giselle had long ears, they would droop as well. Neela wasn't trying to hurt her, but the naturally brusque woman hit a very sore spot nonetheless.

Father and Giselle were given titles by Papa following his marriage to Father. Father was an accomplished soldier but had no connection to royal bloodlines. He was accepted into the court favorably due to his military accomplishments as the former High Guard of Arrow. His daughter, Giselle, never was. Short and supposedly lacking the magical prowess of her mage mother, she was snubbed.

A distant horn blasts, announcing the start of another match. "I'm going to see Papa," my sister says, and a pinch of jealousy tightens my chest. Papa has refused my visits thus far.

I nod, and Giselle heads back down the stairs, the gentle aroma of jasmine oil trailing behind her. I hope the tincture I concocted to ease her discomfort is working.

Neela waits until Giselle's light steps reach the lower level before saying, "She's upset." My hands disappear within her large grasp as she gives mine a gentle squeeze. "And so are you."

Of course I'm upset. I have no power. No way to free my father. No right to even visit him, to see with my own eyes that he's okay. And what happened today in that arena— "Neela, there was only one survivor in the match I watched. All ten gladiators were forced to fight at once, with only one winner in the end."

She sighs. "General Soro is cruel."

My uncle might sit on the throne and rule in my stead, but in doing so, he allowed Soro to rise to High General of Arrow. And the general has final say on all matches in the arena games.

"But I think Vitor is in on it, too," I tell her.

"What do you mean?" she asks.

"Aisling was all too happy to share that Vitor has been killing fighters about to be crowned Bloodguard. She said he doesn't much care for allowing gladiators he hasn't sponsored to win."

Neela *tsks*. "The High Lord has always been a fair man, Maeve. That doesn't sound like him at all." She smooths her hands down her apron as her gaze focuses in the direction of the arena. "Although…I have heard the odds have been favoring the Commons lately. And you know how the Middling hates to see a commoner rise in rank."

"Almost as much as the nobles hate for someone to join *their* rank, I'd imagine." I frown, realizing Aisling might have been right. "Between the dragon and the surprise melee combat, I must wonder if Soro intended *anyone* to walk out of that match today, favored or not."

Neela plucks a speck of fuzz from the ends of my hair, her opinions clear in the silence.

"Life should not be wagered for sport," I mutter.

"It wasn't always like this," Neela tries to soothe, but her words only make my stomach twist more. She means the fights weren't to the death *before Papa struck down my grandmother.*

"I'm going to the garden," I announce abruptly. "Father has gone to fetch a gladiator. He's hurt and needs my herbs to heal him."

Her eyes darken as she stares at me. "Be careful, child," she says. "Gladiators are not soft—or easy to win over."

She knows me too well.

"I mean it, Maeve," Neela says, her crackly voice stern. "They break those fighters down until they have nothing left to lose—and that makes them more dangerous than even *you* can realize."

As I head toward the back stairs, I toss over my shoulder the absolute truth. "That's *exactly* what I'm counting on."

CHAPTER

8

LEITH

Considering I was summoned to screw Jakeb's daughter, her staff has stuffed me dangerously close to exploding. I'm sitting alone in a small cottage away from the main house, waiting for the woman in question to appear. And waiting. And waiting some more.

I look out the only window to a garden filled with wildflowers and greens, their stems stretching tall and proud in spite of the wind. For reasons I can't explain, they remind me of the brown-haired elf from earlier. Defiance, maybe…something about sheer force of will. Or I just want an excuse to remember the first pretty face I've noticed in a while. A rusty laugh builds in my chest as I recall her reaction to Lord Peacock's untimely demise. Hell, maybe I'll even imagine her face tonight while I'm screwing whatever royal is beneath me.

The manor is a good distance away across the garden, which means whoever is coming for me probably likes to scream and yell all night, then continue the facade of a good, chaste royal when she leaves in the morning. Whatever. Coin is coin.

The dwelling holds no bed, only a large kitchen featuring a hand-pumped sink and a rack of strange, colorful spices, with a fireplace in one corner and a large empty bathtub in the other.

This is a strange place for sex, but I've seen stranger.

Two servants sweep up the remains of the meal they served an hour ago—a full loaf of bread, savory braised lamb, and perfectly crisp rosemary potatoes. The portions were enormous—enough to feed my whole family and then some—and it was a struggle to pace myself so I didn't get sick. It almost physically hurts to watch them carry the leftovers away.

Then they start filling the large tub with buckets of hot water they carry in from outside.

I cock my head when I see steam rise from the water. *A hot bath. Nice.*

I look outside again, wondering when Jakeb's daughter intends to show up, but all I find is some stable hand crouched in the garden just below my window. They set down a basket of berries, back to me and hood tucked over their head. The servant offers the fruit to a small group of estrellas who raced from where they were playing in the garden.

"Neela's coming soon, and I'll bet she brings dessert," they tell the small creatures.

That must be the daughter of the manor, I surmise, swooping in after the real work is done. Royal women are obsessed with those puffy motherfuckers—treat 'em nicer than they ever deigned to handle me, that's for sure.

This "Neela" is taking her sweet time, though. Or…is she waiting for me to bathe first? No, I must be given permission to use anything in a noble's home, even the damn chair I'm sitting on. It's the only reason I'm not already enjoying a hot bath.

I cross my arms and look around. The table seems sturdy. Maybe she'll want me to take her there.

Standing. Sitting. Crouched. Swinging. I'll do anything she wants me to do. That meal was superb, and that bath looks heavenly. I just want to get to the fucking part soon—so I can get to the sleeping part even faster. After today's fight, every inch of my body aches except the ones she plans on using.

The floorboards on the porch creak. Looks like it's finally time for the *lady* to grace me with her presence. Her guards will wait outside, I presume, to make certain I don't kill her.

Her guards, which there's still no sign of…

Instead, that servant from the garden steps through the door, a basketful of greens under their arm this time. They're taller than I thought. A lot taller—either an elven woman or a wiry human man. Given the outfit, it's safe to assume the latter. Good. Easier in a fight. His expression is blank. At least I think it is. It's hard to tell with that hood covering most of his face.

But then he sees me and jumps, dropping everything, including his jaw, on the floor.

"My, you're huge up close," he breathes. "I just might need help taking care of you."

"I don't need anyone to 'take care of me,'" I say. "I'm just waiting for Neela."

"For Neela?" He cocks his head. "Why?"

"So I can fuck her," I say, pointing out the obvious.

"*What?*" the servant shrieks. Yeah, *shrieks*. I could kill every soul in this place if I wanted—a comforting reminder, actually—and they sent a fucking teenager to watch over me. The dazzling stupidity of the noble class.

I sigh. "Fine, so I can 'make love' to her," I try, using air quotes this time.

"You can't sleep with Neela…" The boy gives it some thought. "I mean, maybe you could if you're her type." He shrugs. "Anyway, at least for the moment, you're stuck with me."

"Listen, I'm in no mood to fight with anyone right now." I fix him with a look that's sent multiple enemies sprinting far and fast. "Go back to your mistress and tell her I haven't got all night. I've had a real shitter of a day, so I'd like to get on with this and then get some actual rest. Now run along, kid."

"I am *not* a kid," he says, affronted and pulling back his hood. It's only then I realize he's a she, and she's…*her*.

Strands of hair as rich as mahogany escape her braid to fall against her cheek. She starts to brush them aside but realizes I'm staring at her, and instead she lets her hair partially cover her face.

Her braid slides along her lower back as she turns to place her cloak on the chair, and I follow it to a view of the graciously curved ass that was hidden beneath.

Tan suede breeches cover her long legs, her black boots hitting right below the knee. Her blouse is black, as is the leather corset holding her top in place and emphasizing her womanly physique. Yeah, she's a woman all right. Nothing gets past me.

"There's a lot I need to do to you," she says, then straightens and turns back to me. "Are you ready to start?"

"Start?" I ask.

She nods.

I point. "With you?"

Another nod.

"And not Neela?"

"No, not Neela..." She tilts her chin as if there's something wrong with me. "Ah, could you get in? This may take all night."

Yeah. I'll bet. I follow in the direction she motions and realize she means the tub.

"You want me in the tub?" I ask. Typical royal—she's expecting me to wash. Hell forbid I soil her body with mine.

There's that look again. "Where else would we do it?"

"The floor?" I offer.

"How in Old Erth are you still alive?" she asks. "You're completely irrational."

"And *you're* horny," I remind her.

She frowns. "I'm...*thorny*?"

I wave a hand. "Yeah, that too."

She starts toward me but thinks better of it. "Just *get in the bath*," she says, then turns to work at the stone table, her back to me.

Testy little thing.

I remove my clothes and step into the tub, then pause when my foot reaches the base. The water is blissfully hot. Not enough to burn but enough to fully realize the extent of my injuries.

As my muscles relax, my tendons pull like delicate, easily torn webs. I didn't notice how abused my feet were until now. As a gladiator, if you can run—blazes, if you can *hobble*—you're well enough to fight.

I slide my other foot in, gripping the edge of the tub as my body trembles. My mind insists it's better to ease in. Every throbbing inch of me begs otherwise.

After the initial bite, the hot water covering my thighs brings miraculous relief. And this basin is large enough for me to sink down to my neck and stretch out.

Grime and sweat from my legs drift off and pollute the water, but before it settles, the dirt is whisked away into nothingness. There must be a cleaning stone in here. A big one.

Cleaning stones can purify water for drinking in about an hour. I've never seen one work this fast before. It must have cost a small fortune.

I lower myself the rest of the way in and grimace, barely holding back my pained groans.

It's torture. All of it.

Except then…then there's peace.

I submerge completely, ignoring how the high temperature bombards my head injuries, but soon, serenity is all I know as the pain fades like dirt removed by the cleaning stone.

I ignore the growing burn of my oxygen-starved lungs and focus instead on the sweet silence, broken only by my pulse thumping in my ears.

When I break through the surface, I fling my hair away from my face, and the long ends smack against my shoulder blades. I take slow, deliberate breaths through the stomach, like I was taught, soothing my lungs.

Growing up, I learned from our elders how to survive in the caverns of Siertos during flood season, which plants I could safely eat and which would kill me. My mother taught me how to store water for the dry months and how to tend to the belladom, a cactus that only grows in Siertos and creates the most expensive and sought-after perfume in the world. It's all Siertos is known for, and it's how my family made what little money we had. Those who developed and marketed belladom were the only ones who became rich. We were just the poor farmhands who tended to the crops.

There's a clink of bottles behind me, reminding me that I'm here for a purpose, not peace.

"So," I say, and the woman turns to face me. "Ready to take me on, Princess?"

CHAPTER

9

LEITH

Jakeb's daughter comes to stand at the side of the tub, wiping ash from her fingers along the apron she's tied around her breeches. Ash? On a noble? She must have been doing something in the fireplace.

"All right, here I come," she says.

I shrug. "Really? I haven't even touched you."

"Is this seriously how we're starting?" she demands and just stands there.

I grumble. At her speed, foreplay is going to take all night.

She's beautiful—stunning, even—but still a royal. Sleeping with her is simply another task I must perform to keep me fed and to care for my family. At least that's what I tell myself.

She scatters dried mint and fruit peels along the surface of the water for several minutes, reaching back into her apron to grab another handful to sprinkle.

My eyelids grow heavy. Unsurprising, given how warm this water is.

My muscles relax, and I sink deeper, blinking several times to stay alert. Just because I willingly whored myself out tonight doesn't mean I'm safe here.

Jakeb's daughter returns to the kitchen table and shuffles around before returning. She tosses more flowers into the bath, dusting her hands against each other to get every petal, all the while pretending a gladiator doesn't lie naked in front of her, at her mercy.

She walks back to the table and this time hefts the basket. Glass clinks, and there are some scrunching noises. The way she crosses the room is more in tune with a servant accustomed to demanding work than a woman of her status.

She sets the basket on the floor and kneels down to rummage through it, probably tired of making the trek back and forth from table to tub. Maybe saving her energy for later...

There are a multitude of plants in the basket, some so bright they glow, others drying in jars sprinkled with large salt crystals. Others yet have dense black leaves I've never seen before intermixed with bright petals.

I make out juniper and eucalyptus, mostly by scent. Everything else, while fragrant, is unfamiliar and potentially poisonous. I sit up a bit in the water, muscles tensing. What is she up to?

Like a guard skilled with a sword, she pulls a long knife from a hidden pocket—

I whip my hand out, sloshing water over the edges of the tub as I snag her narrow wrist. And squeeze. She grunts but doesn't scream. I *knew* I couldn't trust her—or any of this.

Her blue eyes flare. "How *dare* you touch me."

My jaw clenches. How *dare* I? "I can't screw you without touching you. Even I'm not that good. And your father paid me to lay with you, not to lay still while you cut me. Drop the knife."

"I'm not here to cut you, gladiator, and I'm *definitely* not here to *lay* with you," she snaps. "And my father had nothing to do with it. This idea was mine."

She jerks her wrist, and I narrow my gaze. I reach out with my other hand and carefully grasp the knife, squeezing her wrist until she releases the weapon. Only then do I let her hand go.

"What idea?" I lean forward, but my sore muscles protest and I sit back again.

"I'm a healer." She answers without really answering, then points her finger to the jars lining the wall and waves her other hand around the room.

Confusion is an unfamiliar feeling that doesn't sit well with me.

Something's not right here. She wanted me. I sensed it in the way she looked at me in the arena...or was that what *I* wanted—someone to see me as more than a brutal killer? Maybe she could have if I hadn't murdered her escort.

She holds her palm out for her knife. "Well?"

"You're here to mend my injuries?" I raise one eyebrow. "And nothing else?"

She nods, and I grudgingly hand the knife back to her.

It'll be easy enough to disarm her again.

She moves to the sink area and sets the weapon down. Then she glides her fingers along a shelf of jars filled with colorful powders. I thought they were spices when I first saw them, but the way she inspects them suggests they're meant for something else. I should have guessed. The meal I had wasn't prepared here.

Using tremendous scrutiny, she chooses one as bright and orange as lily pollen and another that is so deep brown it could be mistaken for black. With a practiced flip of her hand, she shakes out enough to where she's satisfied and mashes her ingredients into a paste.

Few healers remain in Old Erth. It's why they charge as much as they do and why Mother can't help Dahlia without more coin. Many know the basics—how to stop a bleed or splint broken limbs—but when it comes to infections or poisons, you either beat it or you don't.

"Who taught you to heal?" I ask.

"I learned the fundamentals from Neela. You remember Neela? My dear, sweet, *grandmotherly* governess you couldn't wait to fu—"

"Hey." I wave a hand. "Everyone makes mistakes."

She grins.

I eye all the plants and petals floating in this tub. "Do you know what you're doing?"

My comment wipes the grin off her face.

I hadn't meant to offend. What I meant was, only the wealthiest, most powerful of Arrow have the privilege to hire healers—they don't *become* healers. From my experience, the nobles don't work, and they definitely don't get their hands dirty.

"My name is Leith," I tell her and want to kick myself. Why would she care what my name is?

She blinks at me, then answers quietly, "I'm Maeve."

There's some shift in the air between us. It makes me aware that I'm naked and that she's standing close to me. I lift some of the peels she placed in the tub and toss them closer to my feet. "What do you do with all this shit?"

"This 'shit' is meant to calm you, at least partially." She scrubs her hands on her apron, clearly irritated.

"The herbs were meant to sedate me?" I ask, realizing I would be more on edge right now if they weren't. They *had* lulled me close to sleep, but I didn't black out. I'm vulnerable in a tub filled with sleeping draught, which is a risk I can't afford to take. I abruptly pull my knees up, water sloshing, and brace my hands on the side of the tub to stand.

"I can't treat you if you start thrashing, and partially sedated or not, this is going to hurt," she insists, her gaze fixed on something on the other side of the room. "Now sit back and let me work."

When I don't move, her big eyes lock on mine. "Please, Leith."

Something in her earnest tone has me sinking down again. Dazzling stupidity? Yeah. Probably.

She wants something from me. They all do. But I'll play along for now.

The sooner I find out what the healer wants, the quicker I can use it against her.

CHAPTER

10

MAEVE

I mix a new batch of peels and leaves in a bowl and move toward the gladiator—the heavily muscled, *naked* gladiator. With my head held high, I sprinkle the contents onto the water's surface, beginning with the area over his groin.

"Something troubling you, Maeve?" he asks. "You seem distracted."

Good stars. Sometimes there just aren't enough orange peels in the world.

He chooses to look up at me then and smirk. Of course, even his smirk sets my pulse thrumming.

I return to my workstation. I must fix him. Not fixate on his body.

"Nice place," he says, taking in his surroundings.

"It's where I work," I reply. "Now quiet and let the herbs do their job. I need you slightly numb." If he's drugged enough, I should be able to treat him. And if I treat him well, he'll see that we'd make a good team. He scratches my back…damn, his hands are huge…and I'll do some scratching of my own.

"What are you thinking?" he rumbles.

I blush, because clearly I haven't humiliated myself enough.

"Oh, I see…" he says.

He winks at me, and I almost drop the jar I've pulled from the shelf. Gladiators don't wink. They don't flirt. They puncture chests and make their opponents eat their own lungs.

I shoot him a glare, then take a deep breath. He's not weak, and he doesn't act like he's hurting, even with so many injuries. He's simply—

Spectacular, if I'm honest.

I grip the sides of the stone table and bow my head, giving myself time to settle. When I've gathered my fortitude, I turn and say, "All right, Keith. This might hurt a little."

His eyes are closed, but he still manages to growl, "It's *Leith*, and there's nothing you can do to me that I haven't felt before."

Based on all the scars marring his body, I'm sure it's true. "You're a mess," I admit, and his eyes snap open. "In order to heal you, I must lance and drain the wounds your body failed to fully mend."

"I thought you were just treating the current ones." His face could chill even the harshest winter. "How long will it take all this shit to heal?"

"Probably a week."

He doesn't like what I said. "I don't have a week. They could call me back *tomorrow*."

Which is true. Gladiators don't have a posted schedule, and some can go weeks between bouts. Soro once told me they do that to whip the betting into a frenzy when a favorite reappears, but looking at the bleak expression Leith is currently trying to hide, I think it might be to break the fighters' spirits as much as their bodies.

I lift my chin. "You can't fight with your body this wounded," I say, matching his sharp tone.

"Wounds have never stopped me before, and they sure as sin won't stop me now."

No...they probably won't. "Well, if that's what you want, fine." I sigh.

He doesn't say anything for a long while. I don't, either. I can't treat him without his consent. It's unethical.

Finally, he mutters, "You can heal me fully?"

"I'll do my best."

He studies me closely. I don't know what he sees, but for once, he doesn't have much to say. He just stares at me for several long moments, judging his options—judging me. Then he mumbles, "Fine."

I shudder and hope that I really can help him as much as I claim. As committed as I am to healing, I'm incapable of miracles.

I couldn't save my grandmother. I couldn't heal myself fully. I can't seem to help Giselle.

"Lean forward and let me see your back." When he does, his skin stretches out like a map, a landscape riddled with war and pain and fire—burns, so many burns. My fingertips inadvertently pass along the scars on the right side of my jaw. I wish I could remember more about that day. All I remember are flames and pain. So *much* pain. Sometimes, I swear I can feel it still.

And still my scars are nothing compared to those Leith bears.

How is this man alive? When I'm queen, I'll free Papa, and we will end these games forever.

I dip my fingers into the paste I made, strengthening the mixture by adding the purple dust from aja mushrooms. It took months for me to find a fairy circle strong enough to grow them, but even then, I only found three and collected two.

Aja mushrooms are one of the only things that can heal not only a late-stage infection but the charred flesh that, under non-magical circumstances, would take months to painstakingly regrow.

An ache builds in my bones—that feeling of doubt that plagues me more than I wish. But if I am to be queen, there can never be doubt. Only action.

I shake off the fear. This mixture is potent, and it must be formulated just right. If I somehow missed a step, it will not only kill the infection. It will kill him.

The ingredients sparkle, brightening the paste. I exhale with relief. That's a good sign.

I apply the mixture to his left hand, starting with a stab wound straight through his palm—*it may be too late to preserve full mobility in that hand*—and onto the series of gashes crisscrossing his arms. He doesn't even flinch as I attend to these injuries.

But his jaw clenches when I move to his back. There's a large wound on his shoulder that the dragon fire only partially cauterized. Whatever made that gash dug deep. He's lucky to be alive.

He hisses as I glide my finger along the inflamed lesions and the deep burns. The paste is working as I intended. It sizzles across the skin, eating away at the damaged tissue and stirring new skin to form.

He grips the edge of the bathtub tighter.

Come on, heal...

The scar bursts open, and I gasp.

Leith twitches but otherwise remains still. I'd expected to find more injured tissue. I hadn't expected to find a pus-filled sac at the base.

"Uh...this might sting a little," I warn, trying not to gag.

With a sickening *pop*, yellow fluid mixed with spots of green oozes out.

My face puckers, and I struggle for balance. It's only because of the pain he's in that he doesn't notice my reaction. Good. Despite my chosen specialty and unusually strong stomach, this is all sorts of disgusting.

The cleaning stone absorbs the contaminants like a sponge, rapidly pulling them in and keeping the water clean. I've never treated someone this injured before. Not even close.

With a trembling hand, I add more paste.

Then add some more.

In fact, I keep adding paste like his life depends on it—because it does. Honestly, the color drains from his skin *and* mine. "Ah, this might add to your discomfort."

"Discomfort is stubbing a toe," he seethes. "Am I going to have a fucking shoulder by the time you're done?"

I take another good look and consider how much paste I have left.

"Um, maybe?" I offer.

"Maybe?" he barks back. Tremors rack his frame. He grips the edge of the bath even tighter, his knuckles discoloring. "Do you even know what you're doing?"

"Yes." *Usually*. I close my mouth tightly. It's better than vomiting on my patient. That has to be a rule, right? Thou shall not hurl on thy patient?

I order my body to settle. He still needs me, and I can't stop now.

His right shoulder makes an odd twitch. There's an eruption of fluid and—

Yes!

Leith jerks forward, and I crouch at the side of the tub. As hard as

I'm breathing, his respiration is deeper and dangerously fast. His eyes are wild, and I'm certain he'll collapse. But then his breathing slows, and relief floods me from head to toe.

"What the blazes just happened?" he groans between gritted teeth.

If I wasn't clutching the side of the tub for balance, I'd applaud. "Fresh blood is spilling from the wound."

"Wonderful," he mutters. "Indeed, miraculous news."

I shift to my knees and begin to gently cleanse the wounds with a sponge. "Don't worry. Nothing a good leeching won't fix."

"*Leeching?*" Water sloshes over the edges of the tub as he twists to gape at me, and I can't help it—I start to giggle.

"I'm joking," I say with a strangled laugh. "The next time you're in the city, see about buying a sense of humor."

"You seriously expect me to laugh? *Now?*"

"No," I say, managing a smile. "But some gratitude would be nice."

He grumbles something that may or may not be about my mother. I don't let him catch my grin this time. Squeezing the sponge, I stream water over the wounds to make sure all the infection is gone.

Leith rolls his shoulder, still looking groggy, and adjusts his back. His voice is gravelly following the stress on his body. "You helped me."

I wag a finger at him. "And saved your life. You're welcome, big guy."

He grumbles again. Surely, it's a compliment about my incredible skills.

My, there are so many scars layered one on top of another, it's difficult to discern where one ends and the next begins. I give him a moment before I slather paste over the patches of fragile, textured skin marring his back, the scars that most closely resemble my own, then tend the wound on the back of his head and what must be at least two cracked ribs.

By the time I finish treating him, the twilight owls have begun welcoming mother moon.

Leith rises when I do, steadier on his feet than he was before. That's a good sign. His attention wanders to the cleaning stone that went from white to a sickly green throughout the course of his care.

"That was all inside me?" he asks.

"Yes," I admit.

He's only a few feet away, giving me a clear view of butt cheeks capable of snapping a wand in half and making a wish. Beads of water glide over muscle as his bare feet slap against the wood floorboards. His wavy hair teases his spine right between his shoulder blades. The new skin that's replacing the burns remains pink and fresh and will need more time to toughen up.

I take a deep breath and swallow as heat flares up my neck and over my face. Leith is beautiful in the scariest way possible. I pass him a thick towel, trying to appear professional and failing miserably.

He drags the towel down his face and wraps it around his waist. "Why did you do all this? I'm nothing to you."

"That's not true." My voice quiets as I sweeten each word. "You're the biggest pain in the ass I've ever treated."

He chuckles in a way that sounds too good.

"Don't laugh," I say. "I don't come cheap."

He crosses his massive arms. "Jakeb made a blood oath that I wouldn't owe him a thing."

"I'm not my father," I remind him, ignoring his death glare. "And the way I look at it, you owe me for my services *and* for killing my fiancé."

"*Fiancé?*" he asks with one eyebrow raised and annoyance poignant in his tone.

"That's right."

When he doesn't say anything, I take a deep breath and blurt out the question that's been plaguing me since I first came up with this crazy idea. "Leith, will you marry me?"

CHAPTER

11

LEITH

This woman...

A veil of inky lashes rests over blue eyes as exquisite and fathomless as the most perilous ocean. They swallow me whole, drowning me in want, desperation, and need. Strands of her mahogany hair tease the delicate skin of her face, the thickest piece crossing the scar along her jaw. She's flushed from work and maybe more. She's beautiful, perfect, and in-fucking-sane.

"Hell no," I tell her.

Her jaw drops open. "You don't have to say it like that. Believe it or not, I'm considered a catch."

Without a word, I turn around, ready to walk back to the barracks.

She rushes to block my path and rams her hands on her hips. "Leith, you need me."

Is she trying to be funny? "For what?" I ask.

"To become Bloodguard," she insists. "You can't do it without me."

"Like hell I can't." I stomp toward her. I can break her in two, and she knows it, even though I'd never harm an innocent. And pain in the ass or not, she is definitely an innocent. If any royal can be, that is. I take another look at her.

Maybe an innocent.

Maeve saw me take out her man in less time than it took him to land his feet in the arena. She saw me win that match with a dragon…and kill my friend. Remembering Sullivan and what he was to me—father, brother, *family*—pisses me off even more.

She doesn't move, holding her ground.

"I don't need *you* to become Bloodguard," I growl. "I don't need you for anything. For three beastly years, I've managed fine all on my own."

She scans my body from the top of my head to my feet. "Yeah. It shows."

I ram my face in front of hers, the fury today stirred in me licking each word. "I'm alive, and I'm three matches away from being crowned. *I* did that. Me. With no help from anyone, especially a royal like you. I'm going to earn the money to save my family, and not just without your help—I'm going to earn it in *spite* of your kind."

Maeve's jaw tightens. I've offended her. Well, sugar breeches, just returning the favor.

Chunks of wet hair splatter water down my back when I whirl and reach for my discarded clothes. I barely have my pants tied when she speaks.

"Vitor won't let you become a royal," she says softly.

"Tell me something I don't know," I grunt. "Lord Dick and Baby Dick have tried to take me out for years."

They came to the barracks once and chatted up the fighters. A few of the ogres and humans and trolls kissed their asses. Most of us—myself included—refused to look at them. I pointedly turned away when they strolled past. I recall Sullivan spitting at their feet.

Maeve brushes off her hands and draws closer, her steps cautious despite the determination in her dainty features. "So far, they've failed," she finishes for me.

"You're damn right they failed," I mutter. "And they'll fail again. I'll make those evil bastards weep blood for what they did to us."

"They won't fail forever, Leith," she tells me quietly. "In the last three years, those who became Bloodguard are absurdly loyal to Vitor. And those who weren't… Well, there are none."

I freeze, ready to accuse her of lying, but I think back to the last two crowned Bloodguard—both were barely winning until they weren't. Then my mind shifts to the four who were on their way to winning their freedom—to Sullivan and the others—all dead now. An owl hoots in the distance. Farther away, another answers its call. The distraction provides just enough time for the healer's words to hit me harder than they should. She inches closer but just out of my reach.

The games are about money and power. I know that. I'm not ignoring what she said—I just can't get past those men who thought they were close to achieving their dreams and yet had no idea how far they really were.

Sullivan... He was supposed to become a Bloodguard. He was *that* close, and this is what they did to him. For daring to believe his fate was his own to claim. Pain floods my chest, and I grit my teeth.

Through the open window, the night breeze blows across my wet skin, but it's not the temperature icing my veins. "Liars. You're all liars. You take everything from us, even the right to decide our own fate in the end."

Compassion, or maybe pity, softens Maeve's expression. "I'm sorry, Leith."

She edges back, giving me more space, and I need it. When I finally do speak, hate has stripped me raw. "What can you do for me that I can't do for myself?"

Her eyes widen, but there's no hesitancy in her voice when she answers. "I can pay for information. I can get you the best weapons to give you the best opportunities—"

"How?" I ask.

She grimaces, but in a way that says I'm missing the obvious. "I have gold. I can buy favors from those who set up the games."

"The match makers?" I question.

"No," she admits. "I can't trust people that high. Uncle Vitor controls them."

I narrow my gaze to slits. "*Uncle* Vitor?" I growl. "Just who the hell are you, Maeve?"

She shakes her head. "He's not *really* my uncle, of course. I've just known him my whole life. He was my grandmother's favorite general, and more like family, so I guess the appellation stuck."

My body is so still, it feels like I'm made of granite. "And who exactly was your *grandmother*?"

"The queen," she says, like it should be obvious. She lifts her chin. "I don't understand. You called me 'Princess' earlier. I was certain you knew who I was."

"I wasn't being literal," I bite out, and her eyes widen.

"Oh."

"Yeah, oh." Neither of us says anything else for several minutes until I run a hand through my wet hair. "So let me get this straight—the princess of Arrow wants to help a commoner become a Bloodguard so he'll be of high enough station to marry her royal ass...*why* exactly?"

She stiffens, her posture rigid and as regal as a queen. Yeah, I see it now.

"I have my reasons," she says. "Reasons that will benefit you as well."

I cross my arms over my chest. "Prove it."

Quick as a snakebite, she takes the knife from her basket, pulls up her sleeve, and drags the blade across her forearm. The letters of her blood oath ignite and skim across her brown skin. "Promise to marry me, and I'll get you through. You'll win and earn your million gold coins. I swear it."

This is a blood oath. Breakable only by death.

She's willing to throw her lot in with mine, despite the terrible odds. Why? "What do you ask in return, besides a husband to keep you warm at night?"

"You don't *get* to keep me warm," she answers, voice firm but face flushed. "This is business, not pleasure."

"Then tell me what you want," I say with deadly calm.

She bites her bottom lip.

Does she want me to tear this place apart? "Just tell me."

"I want the throne, Leith. Do this, and I'll become queen." Her bright eyes challenge me.

"You want revenge? You want to bring the arena down...be *my king*."

CHAPTER

12

MAEVE

The sun is barely peeking over the horizon as I pound on the cottage door the next day. "Leith, wake up. It's Maeve."

Wow. I can hear him growling from here. The door's pretty thick, too. I'm rather impressed.

Leith knows who I am. About my fathers. Uncle Vitor imprisoning Papa. The murder of my grandmother, the true queen. The offer to free my father if I marry Soro.

I told him everything.

I was desperate. He was…disturbed.

But he needed to know who he was marrying, and smart man that he is, he recognized the unfathomable potential my offer may provide.

He hasn't accepted it yet. Who can blame him? I've already lost one fiancé in as many days.

I try the door again, pounding harder. "Look, you said you could be called back at any time. Your muscles have healed, but the deeper wounds may need more medicine."

Nothing. Well, nothing like words, anyway.

A thought occurs to me as I think back to how infected he was. Was he growling a minute ago, or was he dying? Oh, stars, did I *kill* him? "Shit.

Are you dead?" I shout and pound some more.

"Not yet," he answers from behind me.

I whip around, the small dagger I keep on my belt already in hand. How did he get out here so fast? He blinks at the point and not much else. I frown. Shouldn't he at least take a step back? "What were you thinking? I could have slit your throat!"

"Yeah. Okay." He scoffs, lifting his hand to the flat side of my knife and all too easily pushing it away. "You're too close to the door, and your stance is off."

"*Your* stance is off," I grumble. There's that smirk—and there's my heating face. Damn the effect he has on me. "I'll have you know I was trained by the best."

"Sure you were," he mutters.

Leith steps backward, blinking at the sun as it rises, bright rays lightening his wet hair. He's freshly bathed and evidently more awake than I am. He's also wearing the new clothes I had Father take him after his match.

"What do you want?" he asks, leveling me with a dark scowl.

"Didn't you hear me the first time?" I heave a dramatic sigh. "I want to see if you're fit for battle… Otherwise, back in the tub you go."

He shrugs and looks around. "I'll take my chances. You might *sedate* me again, and I'll wake up married."

"That's not true. I need you awake to say 'I do.'"

His eyes narrow, but he doesn't leave.

"Come on," I say, tucking my knife back into the scabbard in my belt. "Let's make certain I didn't miss something that could possibly cost you your next match."

He raises a brow. "I think I'll pass."

"But what if you get called in to fight and your wounds reopen?"

He crosses through the garden to a small training area with practice swords leaning against a stand. He looks good. *Really* good. And not merely in the healthy manner I'd intended. Eyes illuminated with cunning and swirling with lasciviousness take in this day's battlefield in one sweep as his muscles bulge and relax as he readies to take me on. He picks up one of the heavy swords, twirling it from his wrist as though it weighs no more than a twig. "Feel free to try to open them."

I sigh. *Gladiators.*

I reach him in just a few strides and pick up the other sword. When Vitor stopped training me, Father, a revered soldier himself, took over that task—if for no other reason than to thwart a possible kidnapping attempt. I think it's high time I show this cranky behemoth that not every royal is useless.

"Stay within the perimeter of the clearing or else you're out," I say and gesture to the edges of the field. "And don't worry. I promise to hold back."

"Oh, I wasn't worried," he replies casually.

I bounce in place to warm up. "You should be. I'm quite lethal."

He makes a face. "Yeah. It shows, Princess."

I lift my sword, move a few steps back, and take a practice swing to loosen up—only for Leith to knock my sword out of my hand with his. I glare at him.

"I wasn't ready." Just as a self-satisfied smirk reaches his lips, I drop down and sweep my leg under his. He falls as fast as any arrogant bastard should. I then use my instep to hook the hilt of my sword and kick it into the air. I catch it and grin. Seconds. That's all it took me to act. I stare down at him, trying not to full-out guffaw at the shock riddling his features. "I am now."

To his credit, he never dropped his weapon. Using speed uncommon to most humans, he kicks up, whirls, and strikes.

My hands and arms vibrate from the force when his practice blade collides with mine, and pain shoots all the way up to my shoulders. I try not to show it, using the momentum to spin in the air and come down in an arc.

Leith blocks my hit and the next, and I leap back when he launches forward. Back and forth, back and forth, and…shit, this is hard. I didn't expect to be better or even equal. But I still expected to do better than *this*.

I barely keep up, gritting my teeth.

"Are you smiling or snarling?" he asks, leaping when I try to sweep his leg again.

I'm actually grunting, but I don't admit it. "Just pondering what to do after I win."

"Sweetheart, the day you win is the day I crawl into a hole and die."

"Then get ready to crawl to your death," I say.

Leith laughs. I focus on my strikes and not, definitely not, the smooth motion of his hips or how the muscles in his arms bunch up before each swing.

Leith is brutal in the arena, but here, with me, his swordplay is almost...majestic.

He drops to a crouch when I take my next swing, the speed at which he moves billowing his long hair and permitting me to slice off the ends. He stares at the falling strands. "Don't look at me like that. You needed a haircut, and you know it." I blush because yes, it was a total accident. "It will continue to grow, just like your ego."

The strike he follows up with nearly causes me to lose my footing *and* my weapon. This is unfair—he's not even breathing hard. He lunges forward, forcing me closer to the perimeter. I leap and roll aside, just barely making it to my feet before he's on me again.

Aside from Uncle Vitor and Father, I've never sparred with someone at this level.

But then, rarely have I ever had to fight for my life.

Leith does this regularly, lasting however long he needs to win.

He easily deflects my next two offensive moves. "I"—slash—"can prepare a batch of medicines if your family could benefit from them"—block and pivot—"and a chest of coins for expenses they"—gasp—"might have incurred in your absence."

I barely get the words out.

Leith...he still isn't even winded.

I spin away, and he allows me a few seconds to drag air into my lungs. A tacit form of thanks, maybe.

"Tell me," I say when I can breathe again, "won't marrying a *princess* to become *king* help your family? Didn't you say you'd do anything for them?"

He growls as I bring up the family he mentioned when I told him about my predicament. Then he swings his sword at me with considerable force. "Do not..."

I raise my sword and block, pain vibrating down my arm.

He swings again. "Ever..."

I block again.

He grabs the hilt of his sword with two hands now and swings. "Question me…"

I block again, my teeth rattling.

He whips around and swings his sword again. "When it comes…"

I stumble backward and pivot out of range.

"To my family."

Each swing has gotten harder and harder to block, and only now that my arms are reduced to nothing more than quivering muscle do I realize how easy he was taking it on me earlier. And yet, as rage sparks in his eyes, I know he is *still* holding back. He wants to make a point—whether to me or himself, I'm not sure—but he's never fully lost control.

Which is why I'm not afraid. I'm horrified.

Guilt at what has been done to this man, by my own royal court, makes me want to scream, but I can't focus on his past right now. What I need to do, what I *will* do, is change his future.

I let my sword fall to the ground with a hollow *clank*. "Marry me," I plead, my gaze on his.

We stand there, me breathing hard, hurting, aching. Him scowling.

The seconds tick by, and I think I should say or do something, but before I can, he straightens. "If you really intend to be queen, you need to fight harder. I won't stick around to catch you when you fall." He tosses his sword beside mine. "Even if it means your life."

CHAPTER

13

MAEVE

I smooth my skirt and settle back against the cushioned seat of the carriage as it bumps along the rough cobblestones of the bridgeway to the castle.

Neela fussed over my gown for hours before finally deeming me ready. Its heavy layers of white lace are uncomfortable and ill-suited for warm weather. Neela, well, didn't agree. She insisted the tight cut of the bodice and thick, flowing skirt are appropriate for the Lord Regent's Summer Ball.

Lantern lights strung from the bridge to the gates hang along the walls in pretty loops of twinkling yellow and amber. When the sun sets, the glow will shine and dance along the stone. My grandmother always loved the way that looked. It's been a long time since I've seen the castle decorated this way. I only wish she was here to share it with me.

Lord Caelen, our friend and distinguished colonel, is dressed in his finest military regalia, silver jewelry gleaming against the evergreen and dark blue of Arrow. He sits across the carriage in close conversation with Giselle, her voice light and animated compared to the harsh and steady beat of hooves and the turn of the carriage wheels.

Father sits beside me, the hem of his light-blue robes brushing my skirt.

"You look nervous," he says, though his attention is outside the window, and I can tell something is weighing on his mind.

I stop fidgeting with my sleeves. "I haven't made public appearances like this in a long time."

He nods. "I'd thought giving you time to heal and focus on your grandmother was the right choice, but now I think I failed you."

"What? Never."

His light eyes are sad, and his mouth is turned down at the corners when he shifts his attention back to me.

"A ruler is visible. *Present*, Maeve." He nods to the window and the view of rows of guards lined up along the gates. "You care for the people of Arrow. But most don't know it. Not the ones with influence. Aisling and Soro are more familiar to the noble houses and militia."

"That's a scary thought."

"Yes," he agrees. "It *is*. And that's not counting their influence with the Middling and commonfolk. If you want to do this… If you want to reclaim your throne and become queen, you cannot do it by half measures. You must become the ruler our people need you to be. The ruler you were trained to be."

I frown. "You're saying I need to be popular? To wave at onlookers in the arena and pretend that all that's happening around us is fantastic even as I can see the threats mounting against Arrow every day? You want me to smile as people die for sport?"

My thoughts turn to Leith. His suffering. His pain.

I can't condone those games. I won't.

"No," he says. "I'm only saying that sometimes you must share wine with those you'd prefer swallow glass." The carriage comes to a stop, and a footman opens the door.

Father exits first, then holds his hand out to me.

"Father, I…"

"We can continue this discussion later, Maeve."

My stomach sinks. Have I disappointed him?

Though Father doesn't say it, I feel the burden of freeing Papa—his one true love. If I fail to claim the throne, everyone suffers. I take a deep breath. I won't fail. I take his hand and exit the carriage.

Giselle casts a look over her shoulder, her honey eyes wary, but like

Father, she hides it well. She smiles and allows Caelen to escort her into the main courtyard, her long silver dress fluttering as we head toward where lively music plays and dancing has already begun.

General Tut stands beside Vitor, who waits at the entryway, welcoming guests as they arrive. *Keeping tabs, more like.* Tut is tall, even for an ogre, his thick head and neck straining against the cut of his military robes. His puffs of red hair are too unruly to braid in the characteristic style that Vitor and Soro and even Caelen favor. What strands he has are shorn down to expose the shaved sides above his crooked ears.

As we approach them, I realize I have been made to feel like a guest in what is *my* home, my kingdom.

"Maeve! So lovely that you could attend this year." Vitor takes my hands and kisses them.

I choke on unexpected bitterness. I want to say something witty or cutting to defend my former absences, but instead, I smile.

"Thank you," I say, shoulders square and back straight like my grandmother taught me.

I start to move beyond the procession but then think better of it and step back and stand beside Vitor.

He beams like I've handed him the sun.

I'd like to think it's because he's proud that I'm embracing my role as the future queen, but in reality, it's likely because this serves him, too. My presence validates his position of power. And Vitor has settled *very* comfortably into the role of Lord Regent of Arrow.

"Jakeb," Vitor says to my father. And though it lacks enthusiasm or warmth, it is respectful enough. Father nods to him, then bows to me before joining the other guests. The gesture is pointed and petty, and I have to suppress a smile knowing how much Father must have enjoyed doing it.

About an hour into handshakes, introductions, and niceties, I'm beginning to regret my decision to take my rightful place in the receiving line. It would have been so much easier to join Father and Giselle in the courtyard, but easy isn't my role tonight. There's also a very annoying itch on the side of my left breast thanks to my tight, uncomfortable gown, and it's taking everything in me not to abandon decorum and reach in there to scratch it. Instead, I politely smile and nod at the noble in front of me while my grandmother's words play in my head. *"A queen does not give in to fear, anger, or discomfort before her subjects. She overcomes and endures. As will the kingdom."*

Caelen and Giselle are dancing, at Caelen's insistence, I'm sure. The lively tune is one that comes from his nearby birthplace of Tunder. Other guests linger near the buffet tables, where platters of food are laid out by the castle staff.

I notice that Aisling and Soro move from one group of nobles to another. Aisling makes small talk, her smile big and bright. She's quick to touch a shoulder or take a hand. She leans in close, her expressions almost exaggerated as she engages each guest with rapt attention. Really, she could teach a class on charm. Not that I've ever been on the receiving end of it.

Though well trained for courtly duties, my natural talents are biting my tongue, lest I cut out theirs, and herbology—traits not normally associated with ruling a kingdom. Grandmother, though—she wasn't above tongue slicing. Just not in public.

Apparently, that's one of the few things I've inherited.

At last, the line of arriving guests ends with a familiar face.

"Lord Kaysoon!" I smile genuinely for the first time in a while when the delegate from Libur approaches. I lift my hands, thumbs pressed together and fingers extended like wings in what is the welcome gesture of his land.

"Princess Maeve, a pleasure as always." He returns the gesture. The stout dwarf looks even more pleased to see Vitor. "I was hoping to catch you." He hesitates only an instant before launching into his petition. "Lord Regent, I'm sure you're aware of the droughts in our realm."

Straight to the point. I smile, ever appreciating the practicality and candor of Liburi culture.

Vitor inclines his head to his general. "Tut has kept me apprised of the situation."

We monitor *all* of the realms.

Kaysoon nods. "We've lost almost half of our annual grain harvest."

"That's a staggering amount," I whisper.

General Tut nods. "It matches the projections I shared in last week's meeting, Lord Vitor." He bows his head in a show of respect. "Things were different in the times of the great phoenix."

"May she grace our skies again," Kaysoon proclaims. Both men then make that hand gesture, which is meant to emulate a bird taking flight.

"Hmm," Vitor mumbles. The people of Libur worship the phoenix. But my uncle…he is not an elf prone to conjecture.

Vitor would never deign to worship anything.

"Can Arrow help us?" Kaysoon asks. His dark eyes flit briefly to me and then back to the regent.

"We have stockpiles of rice and legumes that can help offset this loss," Vitor says.

"Your donations will make the difference between a lean year and one in which our people go hungry."

"It's our pleasure," I say, then stop talking when Vitor grabs my hand abruptly.

"But many realms are affected by the drought," Vitor continues. "I can't say you are the first to ask for aid. We've already received many offers tonight to *purchase* these supplies from our stockpiles."

My eyes widen as I stare at Vitor. If such conversations occurred, they haven't happened in front of me.

"How much on the barrel?" Kaysoon asks.

Vitor is quiet for a moment as he appears to deliberate. "Twenty coin for the rice, fifteen for the beans."

I bite my tongue. We regularly trade with Libur for a fraction as much. There must be a great number of kingdoms suffering for prices to have climbed so dramatically.

"Is it a deal?" Vitor asks. "As supplies dwindle, there's no saying how costs might continue to rise."

"Yes, yes, of course," Kaysoon agrees quickly, but the set of his jaw says it's begrudging.

"For three months," Vitor clarifies. "We must be able to reevaluate as conditions change."

Kaysoon pauses a beat before he nods.

"Now that that bit of business is out of the way," Vitor says, "I insist that you join me in the royal box for the arena games tomorrow."

Kaysoon tugs his auburn-and-gray beard. "I accept your very generous offer, Lord Regent."

"Splendid."

General Tut gestures toward the tables set at the far end of the room. "Come, Lord Kaysoon. The chef has prepared goat coas-coas."

"My favorite!"

"I know." The ogren general smiles genuinely as he moves off with his countryman.

"Couldn't you have offered him better terms?" I whisper to Vitor when we are alone.

Vitor looks genuinely confused, then speaks slowly as if I might have trouble following. "The only terms that matter are the terms for Arrow. *Our* country's strength and prosperity. *Our* finances and caches. *Our* military."

His tone and expression lead me to believe he considers me naive, lacking the acumen to rule. He's wrong. I'm neither of those things, but my seclusion has left me ignorant. Clearly, I need to know more about what's happening in Arrow and the kingdoms beyond.

Still, I can't shake the feeling that we could've helped our neighbor through this difficult time with greater ease.

"You're right, of course," I say quickly, noticing interested eyes on us. "I was thinking of leveraging goodwill instead of focusing on our coffers."

"You weren't born in the time of the Great Wars, Maeve. Goodwill falls away faster than you can blink when people have nothing to eat."

When I glance at him, all condescension is gone, and my caring uncle stares back. "You and Grandmother have overcome such difficulties," I say. "Your sacrifices have brought Arrow wealth and peace."

"Indeed." He scans the glittering party. "There is no realm more respected, no culture that has thrived more successfully."

And yet the kingdoms around us starve and send their warriors to die in our arena. I can't help wondering again how badly other realms must be suffering for our stores of grain to already be competitively bid on. I make a mental note to ask to sit in on the next cabinet briefing.

An ogren server offers us wine from a carafe. With grace that would make my grandmother proud, I take a leaf from Aisling's book and raise a goblet to Vitor. "To Arrow."

He clinks his chalice to mine and drinks deeply.

"You will attend the games tomorrow, Maeve?" It's phrased as a question, but I know he isn't really asking.

"Of course." I sip my wine carefully to buy myself a moment's reprieve. Then I set my goblet down on a stone pedestal behind me, lest I spill cherry wine on this gown.

"Soro has something spectacular planned," Vitor says proudly. "These delegates will return home with tales of our engineering and ingenuity!"

Lovely. That doesn't sound ominous or anything.

Soro takes perverse pleasure in the games. In crafting feats that push these gladiators to the brink and keep attendance high.

I swallow hard. I don't want to think about tomorrow or the fight ahead of Leith. I need him to win, to become Bloodguard, but I don't wish anyone the torment of those games.

"What does he have planned?" I lean in conspiratorially, like Vitor might tell me the secret. Leith needs every advantage he can earn, and I vowed to help him win.

Vitor drinks more. "It's a surprise. One I think even you will find impressive."

Doubtful. Highly. People *die* in that arena.

I try venturing a few guesses, rattling off names of all manner of beasts, but Vitor only laughs. "You'll see tomorrow."

All right, if he won't confide in me, maybe I can get him to move away from fatalities within the games. "Uncle, I know the arena generates revenue and creates jobs, fosters solidarity, bringing together the community—"

"Is there a question in there?" he asks bemusedly.

I take a deep breath. I'm not good at ass-kissing, let alone being sly.

"Well, yes. I do have a question. Given all the benefits, why do we—a realm at the pinnacle of culture and civility—promote such...brutality?"

"Ah, but that's the point, my child. Look around you," Vitor says, indicating the many delegates and foreign dignitaries. "We have alliances, peace treaties. Strong relationships with the realms surrounding us and beyond. We have wealth—more so than any other sovereign nation. They fight amongst themselves." He scoffs as if our neighbors and allies are fools. "Let them. We remain neutral. We remain at peace. Why do you think that is, Maeve? What do you think keeps these warring realms from claiming what we have?"

"Well, you said it yourself. We have alliances—"

"Bah." He laughs dismissively. "Our brutality, as you put it...*that* is what keeps potential enemies at bay." Vitor accepts another goblet of wine from a passing servant and gestures with it toward his son. "Even Soro has purpose, Maeve."

To be evil? Infuriating? Elitist?

I straighten as I realize what he means. "You want them to fear us," I say slowly.

"Of course. They *must* fear us. Just as they must *need* us."

Hence the loans and the donations, the stockpiles that we trade as needed. The gambling, which isn't contingent on harvest or commerce, only desperation, ensuring a continuous stream of revenue regardless of the season.

These machinations do not sit well with me, but I'm not so naive to deny their effectiveness. And I'm certainly not dumb enough to argue— at least not yet. "Wouldn't the gladiators be of more use at the frontline of our armies?"

He nods. "Undoubtedly. But the arena serves its purpose. It feeds our greatest weapon."

"And what is that?" I ask cautiously.

His eyes gleam with malice as he takes another sip of wine. "Our nation's soul."

CHAPTER

14

LEITH

I dreamed of my sister Dahlia last night. How she held my hand in the darkness when she struggled to sleep. She'd squeeze tight through the worst of her hunger pangs, her small hand slipping from mine when she finally drifted off.

It was good to see my little shadow, even in a dream. But when I awoke, somehow all I could think of was Maeve.

She must have doused me with some kind of delirium potion as she treated my injuries. It's the only explanation for why I'm so recklessly drawn to a royal. Why I agreed to fucking marry one. Oh man, if Sullivan could see me now.

Even now, that feeling of wanting her close remains. She claims this is a business venture, but I saw the way she looked at me...

I grit my jaw and remind myself what's kept me alive these last three years. No matter what heat I see in her gaze, she's right. We should keep our distance.

This is just business.

Yeah, keep telling yourself that, Leith.

I shrug on my training gear as I stare out the small cottage window. She said she would return to check on me today, but it's not her lithe body I spy gliding toward the door.

I reach for a knife Maeve left on the table just as there's a knock. I swing the wooden door wide and find another woman with liquid-honey hair and matching eyes blinking up at me. I don't recognize her, though there's something familiar in her features. She can't be more than five foot and change, and a quick scan reveals no bulges in her clothing where a wand or weapon might reside. Still, I don't want the company.

"What?" I ask, my voice as unfriendly as my tightening features.

She doesn't say anything, just tugs her cape closed around her body—she looks no more than eighteen or nineteen—her gaze fixed on the kitchen knife in my hand.

I toss the blade onto the table with a clatter, then reach up to lean my tall frame against the door, blocking her entrance.

"What do you want?" I ask, my voice still gravelly.

"Um." She takes me in from head to toe before blurting, "You're big."

I sigh. "You must be related to Maeve."

She cocks her head. "How did you know?"

"She also loves stating the obvious," I deadpan. "Now, what do you want?"

She holds my gaze, a smile beginning to curl the corners of her mouth. "I thought today would be a splendid day to meet my future brother-in-law."

And on that note, I take a step back and move to close the door.

She chuckles and rushes on. "Wait, wait. I'm Maeve's stepsister, Giselle, and she asked me to give you this."

I glance down at her small, outstretched hand. An even smaller box with a note attached rests in her palm. I don't reach for either.

She shakes her head, patience apparently running thin, and tosses it to me. My traitorous reflexes kick in, snatching the parcel that I unequivocally do not want right out of the air. "I also have places to be," she says with one eyebrow cocked before turning with a wave. "See you later, Leith."

And just like that, the girl heads back down the path that cuts through the forest and to the manor. She fucking tricked me.

I stare at the gift in my palm like it might bite. Knowing Maeve, it probably will *at least* sting a little. I reach for the note first.

Dear Leith,

This tonic should ease your aches while you recover more today. I'm off to see how I can be of service.

Be safe,
Maeve, your charming and talented fiancée

I almost chuckle. The woman is nonsense. Alluring but pure nonsense.

Regardless, I toss the note on the table, open the small package, and pull out a vial with bright-green liquid inside. I don't even hesitate, just pop the cork and down half the elixir. And immediately regret it.

"For *fuck's* sake," I bark to the empty room as the liquid burns its way down my throat and sets my stomach on fire. The inferno soon engulfs my entire chest before sparking through my veins to muscle, skin, and bone, my blood and tendons aflame from head to toe. Sweat beads along my forehead within seconds, and I feel dizzy. I stagger, catching myself just as I stumble to my knees. The damn woman has poisoned me.

And I have no one to blame but myself. I should have known not to trust her.

I blink through the pain, my vision blurring as the agony singes away every thought but the fury at Arrow and everyone in this fucking kingdom.

But the thought has no more than formed before a cool iciness replaces the burning, then a sweet, blissful numbness. One, two breaths of nothingness, and then I'm back in my body—a body alive with feeling but no longer in pain.

I stagger back to my feet. My palm presses onto the stone table, where the note is flipped over. I reach for it when I realize there's writing on the back.

P.S. — Dilute the tonic with a large goblet of water. Otherwise, it will set your insides on fire.

"Thanks, Princess," I mutter, but I don't actually care. Not when every gouge and laceration on my body feels like new. I put the cork back in the bottle and shove the remaining half of the elixir inside my pocket.

I flex my left hand, examining the two-inch scar that now mars the space between my fourth and final finger. I curl my fingers in toward my palm and immediately recoil at the sudden, sharp discomfort. *Oh no, no, no, no.* I reach for Maeve's knife, already knowing what I'll find. *Fuck.*

My grip is weak. Too weak to effectively two-hand wield a heavy blade. I am a gladiator with one hand tied behind his back. It dawns on me that this injury could realistically cost me my life, and for the first time in a very long while, I am scared.

Another knock sounds at the door, and my stomach sinks as I swing the door open and find Jakeb on the other side. His visit can mean only one thing... I've been called in to fight again. *Fuck.*

As Jakeb escorts me back to the arena of hell, I try to find the silver lining in being called to fight again so soon. At least I'll be one fight closer to freedom.

Three more challenges.

Three more battles left to win.

One more that can save Dahlia. The second to push me to the last. And the very last to spoil my family for the rest of their lives. I'll have the means to bring them here, to Arrow, and away from the destitution found in Siertos.

Jakeb and I trot to the city on horseback, my chest roiling when we pass a rickety wagon filled with impoverished men of varying species from different parts of Old Erth. Headed to the barracks, no doubt.

There's a young wizard from Tanlita. I can tell by the intricate tattoo that runs bilaterally along her skull. She looks like she just turned twenty-two. I don't know who to be angrier with—the recruiters or her elders—for encouraging her to die.

It's too late. Everyone in that wagon signed their lives away. Even if they didn't, even if escape didn't mean death, they could never afford passage back to their homelands.

I shove the feelings of bitterness away. I can't save them. I can only save Dahlia. Maybe Maeve will do as she says and end the games when she takes the throne. I don't even consider what I might be able to do as her husband. We made a deal, and evil or not, I'd trade every gladiator's life for my sister's. I proved as much in the last match, didn't I?

In no time, we reach the city center. This section is bustling and noisy, filled with the Middling merchants and their shops.

Sprites scurry from one table to the next at their stands, cutting and sewing sheets of leather for shoes and boots, their gossamer wings flapping madly. A band of dwarves pushes a cart of fresh vegetables up the hill toward the food market, the traditional pointy yellow-and-brown hats they wear soiled from hard work in the fields. Two ogres walk hand in hand, peering at wares from a cart featuring bracelets of various shapes and colors.

A noble human in a long silk dress strolls with another human wearing garish purple, coral, and bright-green robes. She laughs and slides her arm through his crooked elbow as they meander around the market. They ignore all the workers among them, their extreme wealth worn like a mask over their eyes, until a small child pulls on the man's purple robes, seemingly begging for scraps.

The man rears back and slaps the child clean across the face, yelling something about soiling his finery. The revolting action has me seeing red, but when the woman laughs, that red deepens and my body demands action.

"Something troubling you, Leith?" Jakeb asks.

"I'm fine," I say, clenching my fists as the woman pushes past the child to continue her leisurely stroll. Those "with" rarely understand the world of those "without"—no sense wasting my breath, even on Jakeb.

When we reach the edge of the square, a horn blasts twice—a gladiator just won a match. I frown in the direction of the arena. According to the position of the sun, it's hours earlier than we usually start.

"We had better hurry," Jakeb says.

With a squeeze of my legs, my mare takes off, coming to a canter slightly behind Jakeb's horse. The sheer height of the coliseum makes it easy to spot from almost anywhere in the city, as does the magic being unleashed within the arena, making the sky above it blur and shimmer like a mirage.

From time to time, matches aren't merely gladiator against gladiator or beast. Sometimes, the audience is rewarded with magic-enhanced combat schemes. I once had to fight in the middle of a magic-made sandstorm, visibility down to nothing thanks to the tiny particles swirling around me. I kept my eyes squeezed tight and relied on my other senses to alert me to danger. Or, more accurately, just kept swinging until I hit everything trying to kill me.

Today, a storm brews above the center of the arena, gathering momentum as it swirls and expands. Thunder crashes, and lightning showers the sky above the match with color. On either side of the coliseum walls, though, there's only peace, and above the magic mirage flickering over the top of the storm, clear skies.

We ride past the manicured gardens along the wall surrounding the arena. They are enormous and as fragrant as Maeve's potions. Yet they aren't enough to counter the stench of death that permeates the air as we reach the gate.

It creaks open, and I almost hesitate to pass through.

I kick my heels, and we head toward the stables beneath the arena. Gunther beams as soon as he sees me and pumps his fist in the air.

"Bloodguard!" he shouts.

"Hello, Gunther." I keep my tone neutral. The last thing I want to do is encourage him.

He holds my horse by the reins. It's strange to dismount from a horse here, instead of being hauled through crammed inside a caged wagon like I'm used to. I'm well fed today, wearing expensive and clean clothes, with new leather armor and boots I've yet to fully break in. The stiff leather squeaks with every step.

A wave of shame burns my chest as I catch sight of a line of half-starved gladiators awaiting their turn to compete. I let the feeling glide through and past me like a breeze. Shame is an emotion I have no use for now.

As soon as Gunther leads my horse to a stall, a band of eight palace guards surrounds me.

I raise my hands in surrender to placate them. As thanks, I'm shoved forward, and my wrists and ankles are immediately shackled.

The chains feel heavier and more suffocating than I remember, but their weight helps me find that familiar hatred I need as much as weapons in the arena.

"Welcome back, friend," a guard sneers.

He punches me exactly where that axe wound was. Had Maeve not tended to me, that punch would have incapacitated me. Instead, I merely let out a curse.

The stench of animal waste burns my nose as we move toward the back. I shuffle forward, keeping pace. A new guard behind me pokes me with her sword. She's not rushing me, nor have I disobeyed. She's just reminding me she has the authority to do it.

She pokes me again, and I grit my teeth against the sharp bite of pain.

I don't make another sound, though, even as fresh blood seeps into my once-clean shirt.

Jakeb, who I thought would be sitting in the royal box by now, comes up beside me. His silver robe flutters in my periphery, but I can't see his face.

"The gladiator is not resisting," Jakeb tells the guard who poked me. His voice quavers. "There was no need to bloody him this close to battle."

I don't need to see him to hear the anger and disgust in his tone.

The guard chuckles, mistaking the tremble in his voice for fear. "Lord Caelen waits for you in the stands, Lord Jakeb," she says. "Perhaps you should join him instead of wasting your time on this corpse."

"A corpse who's better dressed and better fed than you," I point out.

My smile holds tight even as I'm shoved hard for my insolence.

"Watch your tongue, gladiator," a different guard calls out but then thinks better of it and laughs, adding, "or don't. I'm certain what awaits you today will enjoy biting it clean from your throat."

The other guards join in, laughing outright now.

Aw, hell, that doesn't sound promising.

The guards reposition to keep Jakeb out as we reach the pens, and my stomach clenches. The animals are gone, probably taken for slaughter to feed the spectators in the food tents on the opposite side of the arena. The slop and feces left behind ripen in the heat. It's a stench I'll never get used to.

"Need I remind you of my position?" Jakeb asks.

A smaller woman clears her throat but not her seedy grin. "No reminding needed, sir."

The rest of the guards ignore him, and Jakeb grows more insistent. "I have paid High Lord Vitor a hefty sum to sponsor this man—"

"He is in your care when you leave the arena grounds," a different guard interrupts. "When he's here, he's *ours* to tend to. Now leave," he spits, and I think my jaw actually drops. A castle guard giving orders to a nobleman? That comment alone would earn him a death sentence from Soro. Maybe I can't tell one lord from the next, but surely these guards recognize the man I now know is the prince's husband. Even if the prince *is* locked up.

"Your *distinguished* presence is not welcome here with the rest of us dogs," he continues. "You wouldn't want to soil your fine robes—"

"Do *not* order me about," Jakeb fires back, drawing his lean elven body to its full height. "When he finishes, return him immediately to me."

"*All* the pieces?" yet another guard offers. "Sure, if that's what you want."

Jakeb pauses, leveling a glare at each guard with a steely glint as he runs a hand over one of the gems on his robe, a subtle reminder of who has the real power and wealth here. "You will return all of him to my care. And if you ever disrespect me again, it's *you* who will be returned in pieces. Do I make myself clear?"

No apology is offered to Jakeb as he strides away, and while a few guards continue to grumble to each other, others go quiet. Prince Andres may be in prison, but Jakeb is still his husband and royal consort. They know that a lord of his status can still wield power. But he's clearly lost his grip on his position. It's the only explanation for why they screwed with him like they did.

My lip curls into a snarl. Of course the only royal offering me help is one who's clawing her way to the throne, not already sitting pretty on one. That tracks.

With a curse, I let it go, focusing ahead and away from the crowded pens stuffed with gladiators. I focus on the misery that awaits behind those stone walls as I am shoved toward the opening to the arena.

As a reminder of the pure fuckery the royals are capable of, a fresh collection of mournful gray clouds circles the arena. Lightning strikes, followed by a strong taste of metal. A mage or a wizard conjured this storm, and this spell-wielder has centuries of experience, given the heaviness in the skies.

Murmurs escalate to shouts from within the arena. More lightning in dizzying shades of green and purple strikes. The crowd applauds, enjoying the light show.

I'm shoved forward again, and from practice, I know to go with the momentum, sliding through the muck on the floor in order to stay upright rather than pushing back.

The attendees in the arena shout with glee and excitement. They're fascinated by the magic...not by the sounds of battle.

Blazes, what's happening? There's nothing indicating a match is underway.

The gate squeaks open, and I'm thrown into a pen off to the side. I slide across the mud and past Pega, an older gladiator who joined the same year I did. I haven't seen her in a while—figured she died in the arena. Again, I keep my footing, disappointing the damn guards.

The gladiators look at me, most in bewilderment, as a guard tethers me to them.

Sibor eyes me up and down. She's from Tanlita like the young wizard I saw earlier, but her blond hair is so long, the tattoo inked to her skull isn't visible. If memory serves—and it always does about these things—she fights dirty. "Hell, boy. What did you have to suck to earn that getup?" she asks.

I ignore her.

I glance around my pen, counting fighters until my stomach sinks. We're short at least four men and one giant.

"Where's Olatd?" I ask. "And Luther?"

Pega rolls her shoulder. She's shorter and leaner than most of her dwarven brethren, but her offense is superb, and her counter strikes are almost equal to mine. A commoner from Arrow, she tried making money anyway she could, but working as a blacksmith and a horse trainer and a tailor didn't provide enough for her and her orphaned nephew. So, she entered the arena with the same goal as the rest of us. Three years later, she loathes the kingdom as much as I do. As foolish as it is, I'm glad she's still around.

The left side of her face is drooped from an unfair match last month, slurring her speech. "Olatd is dead, along with the four new recruits who were dumped in first," she says. "Luther is alive. 'Cept he won't make it to midnight." Her hands clench and unclench. She likes Luther. A lot of us do. "The filthy mongrels are bringing him back now."

Ned, an elf with short brown hair and a beard shorn to a point, curses like it's his first language. His village borders the one Sullivan was from in Witoria, making his accent just as thick as my old friend's, but I can still make out most of the words damning the gentry to the bowels of Old Erth. As far as fighting ability goes, Ned's around the middle of the pack, which means sooner or later he'll die here.

I shuffle forward, my shiny boots already stained with mud. "How bad is it?"

"Real bad," Ned mutters. "This is the day we all finally bite it." Sooner, then.

Five dead and Luther dying. We're being massacred. Why?

"What time did they start today?" I ask.

Ned rubs his red eyes. "Hour past, I think."

The battle horn blasted when we reached the city. It was early, yet we thought we were late and had missed the first match. But it wasn't the first. It took barely an hour to lose almost six gladiators.

Shit.

In the arena, the show of spells continues, still without any signs of fighting.

I jerk my chin toward the sky. "That's a magical storm," I say, not that they need me to tell them.

"It is," Ned agrees, tugging on his beard, twirling the hairs into a finer point. "The bastards are trying to draw out the day. Too many died too fast, and with little effort." It's only now I see how gray his skin appears. Ned is never one to panic. Usually. "I overheard a herald in the town square promise today's game would be never-before-seen levels of horror."

My only answer is a grunt. Not much more to say than that.

Sibor stomps on the chain binding her, attempting to break it. She's ready to run, forgetting there's nowhere to go. "Whatever they picked this time must be worse than the dragon you and Sullivan met," she says.

Ned wipes his nose with the back of his hand, soiling his face further.

He grimaces, shaking his head as his red eyes glisten. "Luther was the only one who put up a fight against them, and he just about died doing it."

"Them?" I question.

Pega scratches her hurt ankle. It's infected and raw from the shackles. "We're here for their pleasure, and their pleasure means our hides. One way or another."

My voice comes out hollow. "What exactly happened to Luther?"

Sibor motions to the right. "Nothing good."

Several moon horses whinny and neigh, protesting the large, flat cart they're struggling to pull. Luther is stretched across it, secured by chains wrapped around his chest and arms.

But there's no need to shackle him. He couldn't escape if he tried.

He's pale as white ash, saturated with sweat, and naked except for the loincloth barely covering his groin. Bite marks as long as my arm ransack his body, face, and what remains of his legs. His left foot dangles, barely held on by a flap of muscle.

Luther's head droops to the side. He sees me, his expression anguished. *Water*, he mouths.

"Poor bastard," Ned says. He spits. "Those ruthless shits won't even give 'im a drink."

"Who's going back to the pen with him?" I turn to the gladiators when no one responds. "Is anyone going back with Luther?"

"Nah," Ned replies. "There's no one alive to go back with 'im, remember? No one else made it."

My focus returns to Luther as he continues to roll past us. It's another way to humiliate him and intimidate us.

Water, he mouths again.

I curl into myself like I'm just stretching my muscles. Instead, I dig into my shirt and pull out the vial Maeve sent me earlier, still half full. I kept it on me in case I needed to push through the agony again. But Luther needs it more.

"Pass this down," I mutter. "Make sure Luther gets it."

I'm met with frowns or others outright looking away. I shove it into Sibor's hand. "Do it," I hiss.

Sibor clenches her fists. I lower my stance, prepared to fight.

"It's for Luther," I snap, keeping my voice low. "It'll help him."

She eases her posture then and does as I tell her, passing the small vial down the line until it reaches the following pen. As soon as a troll takes it, he tries to pocket it.

My words slice at the air. "Do you know who I am?" I ask him. He shakes his head. "You will if you don't get that to the giant suffering on the cart."

An elf gladiator smacks the troll on the arm. "Do it," he orders.

Down the line it goes in whispers. A few guards move in to inspect the commotion. I can't let them see it. I kick, pelting them with mud. They turn around, their whips and swords raised.

"Who did that?" one demands.

More mud is flung at them, this time from three pens down. Ned kicks more at them as the wagon carrying Luther nears the exit. There're too many of us in these pens and not enough space to see for sure if the numbing vial reached him.

A guard opens the gate to my pen, and in my determination to see Luther, I don't realize what's coming until it's too late. I'm hauled out by another guard who caught me flinging mud.

He kicks me in the gut—twice. It's impossible to hold back my reaction this time. Hell, it's impossible just to *breathe*. I fall to my knees, coughing as my shackles are unlocked. This is what I get for trying to help someone. To hell with these guards. To hell with the royals.

To hell with *everyone* in Arrow.

"This one wants to go first." The guard shakes me. "Don't you, pretty boy?"

My toes drag along the soil as I'm carried, and the laces of one of my boots fall loose. The shoe slides off my foot as the sound of opening gates echoes in my ears, and a laughing guard rips off my other with a joke about how dead men don't need nice leather. I'm down to my socks now. Another disadvantage.

I try to regain my footing, but it's pointless. The bright arena opens before me, and I'm hurtled onto the sand.

CHAPTER

15

LEITH

The first thing I notice as I stumble into the arena alone is that the sand is wet. But it hasn't rained for a couple of days, not even from the magically produced storm clouds above us.

Why is the sand *wet*?

The cheers spreading along the arena at my arrival turn heady. As I push to my feet, bearing most of my weight on my right hand, the thunderous clouds roar in welcome. Lightning replies with equal menace, decorating the sky in sparks of green and alternating shades of purple.

My socks, already soaked through, leaden my steps. They'll limit my movements and could cause me to trip, so I shuck them off, my toes sinking into the wet sand. I concentrate on the human mage standing on a small terrace above the royal boxes where High Lord Vitor and General Soro sit.

The mage appears youthful, but her short gray hair gives away her true age. Either way, I would have pegged her at about three hundred years old based on the strength of her magic.

She's dressed in a gown of bloodred with lips painted the same revolting color.

To draw more attention to her presence, sparkles of purple appear above her, each detonating and showering her with bright light.

If I could reach her from this distance, I wouldn't hesitate to attack. I'd race forward, side to side, back and forth, avoiding her spells. I'd leap onto the wall and scale it. Before anyone could move to defend her, her skull would meet the lip of the terrace.

That would be my plan. It would work, too, if this damn arena wasn't so huge.

More lightning crashes, and more dark clouds appear to join the rest competing for attention. I keep waiting for something, *anything*, to happen aside from the magical performance. There are no weapons. None have been brought, and nothing indicates they're coming.

Maybe the lack of weapons is my punishment for winning too many times.

No. Forget that. Back-to-back slaughters aren't ideal for spectators thirsty for action. They're too quick. These sadists are setting up for a nice, long, torturous event.

I take deep, calming breaths. Three more matches. Only three.

I've already beaten the most extreme odds just to make it this far.

The rush I feel is familiar. It rides the knife's edge of fear, but I use it to narrow my focus and strengthen my resolve to fight, kill, survive.

To win.

I walk farther toward the center, ignoring yet another stupendous display of magic that the attendees can't get enough of. They applaud and cheer with every deadly roar of the mage's thunder and every strike of lightning that crackles across the clouds. She's riling them up and personifying the danger that awaits.

As always, I scan the area, searching for weak points and anything I can use within my reach.

When my gaze comes to the royal box, I spot Jakeb first as he makes his way down a row, his light silk robe fluttering in the breeze. A familiar black-haired elf with braids, the sides shaved close to his copper skin, stands to permit him through, his military robe of green and blue just as regal.

Jakeb shakes his head, the slow, purposeful motion a warning. He says something to the soldier, and both turn to see me, their faces as ominous as the sky above.

Very deliberately, he rights himself and sits between his daughters. Maeve's sister—Giselle, I think—hooks an arm in his, appearing to comfort Jakeb. Her robe is the color of light sandstone and blends in with the stands so well that I would have missed her entirely had she not stood when her father appeared. When she sees me, she pulls her hood up and forward so her hair is covered and her face is only partially exposed.

Weird. What is she hiding?

Jakeb nods as I pass. He's oddly calm. The soldier with black braids next to Giselle isn't. His gaze shifts from side to side, his fingers thrumming the hilt of his sword. He doesn't seem to notice me. It's just as well—I'm not here to impress him. When my attention latches on to Maeve, she pretends not to notice, but I definitely see her.

She is primped and pressed to perfection, white jewels sparkling in her rich auburn hair, her blue dress trimmed with shimmering sapphires that reflect the flashes of lightning. Maeve appears every bit the royal she is...all signs of the rustic healer from the cabin gone. Her gaze darts around the arena as though she only just arrived and is trying to catch up on anything she missed.

I wasn't sure she'd be here today. She made a blood oath to help me, but I'm not sure how she'll live up to it or if the information she finds will even be useful.

I roll my shoulders. For all she's trying to pretend not to notice me, her blue eyes finally land on mine, and she stills, her expression unreadable from this distance. All I can tell is she isn't smiling. I give no indication I recognize her. Our engagement is a ploy to help her achieve her own goals. Boasting about it or letting people know our intentions will only get me killed faster. Even if she wanted to make it public, I'm not the guy who blows kisses. I'm the man who casts the last blow.

I put her out of my mind as I continue moving. Knowing she's watching and expecting me to win is a distraction I can't afford.

Lightning and thunder continue their dance, their booming effects escalating as I close the distance between the mage and me. I pretend not to notice that I am a mere toy and this display is meant to unnerve me and inflict terror. I won't give them the satisfaction of watching me cower.

With a swoop of her hands and a flutter of fingertips, the mage lowers the tumultuous sky she's constructed, quieting the crowd as they watch to see what's coming next. As if they have anything to worry about, the royals huddle closer, using their robes and hoods to protect their fine hair and jewelry.

These fools are too spellbound to see past her conjurings. But I notice everything. Whatever magic she's concocted allows her full control of the storm. I'm not a fool, nor am I so arrogant that I don't respect her skill. What I am is a man determined to bring her down.

Having played this game enough, I understand the objective. These royals enjoy mayhem. The mage won't strike me down, *yet*, or do anything so silly as to transform me into a rabbit that a random lion thrown in could easily maul.

No. She was brought in for a specific purpose, and she will not disappoint.

She is facing in my direction now. I know her type. She's smiling and very much enjoying what she believes is the start of my inevitable doom.

I reach the center and stop. Bow my head slightly. Clasp my hands in front of me and set my back as rigid as a slab of quartz.

It's time to simply wait for weapons to arrive—if they arrive—and for her to cast the first stone. I don't have to wait long.

Ribbons of purple form around her body, the final loop winding over her throat. I expect a taunt as sharp as a battle cry and as magnified as the lords when they speak.

"Are you ready to die?" the mage asks, her voice magically amplified.

I raise my chin and reply as loudly as I can. "No. But I am ready to kill you."

Laughter scatters across the arena like pollen over a field of tulips. Some of it is forced and mocking, some of it genuine, but what interests me are those who *don't* laugh.

That group knows better than to count me out. Jakeb is among them, and Maeve, the soldier, and Giselle.

"*You* would kill *me*, gladiator?" the mage mocks. "You're a pig. Weak, whining, and so easily gutted."

"Now, now, you shouldn't talk about your father that way," I reply.

The laughter this time is almost as thunderous as her storm clouds.

"I'm going to destroy you." She sneers at the insult. Then she smiles in a way that promises a long, slow death.

I'm starting to think she doesn't like me.

At a snap of her fingers, a thunderous boom echoes across the sky, its magnitude vibrating the sand and creating small fissures along the stone walls. I crouch and spread my arms, expecting an attack from all sides.

But instead, it comes from above. A massive downpour. And because that's not enough, the arena floor rapidly sinks. I didn't even realize it could do that—and maybe it can't. Maybe magic is playing a part. For the moment, that's not my priority. I'm just trying to breathe.

There are storms that have flooded the caves of Siertos so quickly, if you aren't skilled at breath-holding, you can't make it out before drowning. I've never been so thankful in my life that the elders trained me to farm for belladom among the caves. I take as deep a breath as I can, expanding my lungs as I was taught, getting ready for that one last breath I might be allowed.

But this flooding is unlike anything I've ever endured. The rain she conjures doesn't start with a sprinkle or those heavy drops that promise soggy lands and overfilled barrels. The makeshift sky pours water like a spout into a bucket where an unsuspecting insect awaits. Except this time, the quickly sinking arena is that bucket, and I'm the bug—just as screwed.

The entirety of the arena almost instantaneously floods, even with the added volume as the floor sinks. I'm drenched and already standing in thigh-high water.

Luther...he wasn't soaked with sweat when I saw him. He was half drowned. He wasn't thirsty—he was trying to warn me. *Water.*

Except one word could not have prepared me for this.

The force with which the deluge pounds into the ground creates dangerous waves. I ride the first few, but as the level rises, I'm compelled to swim under them and across the arena.

I wrench my eyes open, trying to get my bearings. At first, it's dark, and the gritty sand scratches my exposed skin. The pitch-black storm clouds above rob me of light, and the heavy mix of soil and sand obliterates my sight.

As the water deepens, the sand settles enough that I can see.

It's been years since I've swum. During the wet season, water replaces Siertos's desert landscape, causing us to go from dry and blistering to wet and cold almost overnight.

But the swimming lessons taught me to hold strong. I concentrate on relaxing my strokes, making each come more naturally so I can move swiftly through this rage-filled sea.

I forget there's nowhere to go. I need to preserve my strength and attempt to relax.

It doesn't take long for the water to become more of a friend that I can move with and not an enemy I'm forced to fight.

The crowd cheers when I come up for air, grateful the mage didn't drown me and ruin their good time. I can't place where I am in the arena, though. The walls aren't visible through the rainfall, despite how its severity has lessened.

Nothing is close enough to guide me. I try to gauge my position based on distance from the screaming crowd, but even they are hard to hear through this weather.

All exits were likely sealed by the mage and her spell. Even if they weren't, there's no benefit to finding one. If I break through, it will take too long for the water to drain, and the force could suck me through and eliminate me for leaving the arena.

What does she have in store for me? I didn't drown, and as far as I can tell, I'm the only one in here.

I swim in the direction where the crowd is crammed and at its loudest. That's where Vitor and his cohorts are seated and where my opponent should appear. I want to be close, just not so close that I can't use the distance in my favor.

My strokes carry me smoothly across the water. This swim would be enjoyable if it weren't for the filth and death trapped in the sand from a century of battles.

Again, I come up for air, trying to get a feel for what I might be up against next.

The mage, while gifted enough to perform this degree of magic, isn't perfect. Spells of this caliber are rare and daunting. They're also impossible to maintain for long periods, as they drain the wielder's energy.

She can't kill me with another spell.

Not while she's preserving the sea she conjured.

She's the first act of what will be a very deadly play. So, what's the second act, and why all the waiting?

Something large is hurtled into the arena, followed by another. I wait a moment, just long enough to make sure they aren't alive and looking to eat me, then dive under and swim down...

Several sacks secured with rope rest at the bottom. I go back up for air, fill my lungs as much as possible, and dive down again. It takes several moments of yanking the rope to spill the contents.

The first sack contains a shield, a trident, and a glass globe the size of my head, along with a pipe. It's a device of sorts to help me breathe underwater, if only for a short while. I release it and let it float to the top. It will take me time to figure it out — time that could impede me. If the weapons are already distributed, I'm out of time and need to hurry.

The second sack is slightly easier to open. Several daggers lie on top. I push them out and grab the handle of a scythe the length of a short sword. The last two items are a rapier and a wooden sword with a sharp metal point.

What in the shit and stones is this mess?

I'm losing air at a faster rate than I intend, unable to get past the wooden sword. Its hilt is wrapped with strange plush leaves and twine, like something a child might play with, if it wasn't for the sharp, pointed tip. I determine the lords are trying to trick me and move it aside.

I decide on the trident and the largest dagger, shoving the latter into my belt as I kick for the surface again.

Whatever bit into Luther like a sweet treat is due to arrive soon. I take in the immediate area, treading water as I wait for whatever it is to strike. The wooden sword floats toward my face and stops.

How...

I swim toward the center. The weapon follows. I try returning to where I first started. The weapon shadows me the rest of the way. It's not easy for me to see and likely impossible for the royals to notice from this distance. So how is this happening?

It brushes against my arms, poking at me with its hilt and insisting I take it. I frown and dive, swimming away from the wooden sword, certain it's a trap.

My lungs were ready to burst by the time I retrieved my weapons, and they resist as I dive now. As the rain lessens to a breathable degree, I take the time to settle my nerves and surface again, pulling in several slow and deep breaths.

In the minutes it took me to forage through the sacks, the mage finished filling the arena. Waves slap at the edges where several royals crane their necks, pointing and cheering when they find me alive.

The rain, though lighter than before, remains heavy. I can't gauge my exact position. The only grace is that I can breathe and have a moment to shake out my nerves. Only a moment.

Screams and shrieks sound from ahead of me, followed by the trampling noises of a fleeing crowd. There's a sharp snap like a bear trap shutting, then another, then several more.

I dive and swim in the direction of the more terrified screams. I need to get close enough to see what's frightened them. To spare the energy I'll need against my opponent, I use the water's current to help carry me toward the commotion.

An intense succession of ripples bats against my side. I angle my body and head in the direction where they originate.

Above me, more screams pierce through the water, accompanied by that same awful snapping. There's a brief pause in the screaming before heavy objects drop into the water like boulders. Unlike last time, the newcomers thrash violently, stirring up sand at the bottom of the arena until I can barely make out my own feet.

I feel it then. A primal sort of fear, one I can't stamp out, but which sets my every sense on high alert. Higher. Humans are built for land, and I have none to stand on. Whatever creatures they dropped in here… I'm not just on their turf. I'm *in* it. My thoughts come twice as fast, and they all scream the same thing. *Survive.*

I am prey.

Strong ripples show me where they fell in and how fast the creatures are approaching. I dive, because I must do something, barely dragging myself out of the way of whatever is hunting me…

River sharks.

Fuck.

I stay low, flattening myself against the sand as they pass overhead.

One.
Two.
Three.
Four.
Five.
Five river sharks.
Longer than me.
Stronger than me.
And I'm running out of air.

CHAPTER
16
LEITH

Fear gets the better of me, and several air bubbles escape my mouth. Right away, two sharks reappear, the larger one slapping the smaller one with its tail to knock it out of the way.

They're hunting.

They're hungry.

And I'm the main course.

Hell, I'm the *only* course. And with that fresh stab wound from the guard, they'll be able to scent something *edible* in here with them. The deluge and churning waters are working in my favor for the moment, at least, diluting my scent. But these predators don't rely on scent. They can sense my every movement.

The parting clouds along the magic-born gray sky offer me only a sliver of light. My surroundings are bleak at best. Unless these creatures are right on top of me, I can't see them. The water is too murky.

They return, circling the area where I wait. When they don't find me, they dart in opposite directions away from me, but it's impossible to guess how far.

More bubbles swell from my mouth. I'm almost out of air. Again, the two monstrous sharks appear, and this time, they're followed by two friends.

They swim in circles, searching for the source of movement beneath. My lungs are on fire, and there's nothing to hide behind.

Their hunger works to my advantage, though, and they start to turn on one another. I force my arms and feet to glide, trying to avoid harsh movements as I skim the sand along the bottom. They're too busy fighting to notice me. Well, so far.

I find my opening and reach for the surface, only getting a few breaths in before a fin rises from the water and careens toward me at impossible speed.

I flip onto my back and kick away, keeping the trident aimed toward the shark as it dives under.

"There he is, my dearest. There," a royal human shouts. I'm almost to the wall when I see who it is: the male in the garish bright robes, and his companion who hurt the small child back in the square. He points to where I am so his "dearest" won't miss the fun.

The woman claps, delighted.

I dive down, furious, only to howl in agony when the shark's barbed tail strikes my arm. Their distraction cost me dearly. A fresh cloud of red swirls around me.

With a roar, I use the pain to propel myself to the surface.

I reach the air, choke and spit, greeted by the applause and enlivened commentary of that same damned royal and his partner.

With a curse hurtled at them, I push up on a small protrusion in the wall and leap high, my anger firing my will. I snag the male by his robe, bringing him *and* the woman with me when she tries to save him.

We fall into the water with a giant splash. From above, chaos erupts. I use the weight of the fall to submerge, pulling the elitist assholes with me until they thrash and disrupt the current.

Still laughing?

As carefully as I can, I make my escape.

With all my strength, I swim across the arena, hugging the wall so that at least one of my sides is covered. I stop just in time to see the feeding frenzy.

Their robes of silk aren't enough to protect their skin, and their bejeweled fingers can't shield their pretty faces. If they beg for mercy, I don't hear them—no one does—their cries of terror suppressed by those from the crowd.

The energy of the audience has completely shifted.

The sharks are hungry and greedy, fighting one another for every morsel, their bloodlust soaring with each section of human flesh they split apart.

My senses enliven with newfound hope. I think I'm onto something. What are the rules? Oh yes—*anything* in the arena within my reach. The mage forgot that essential piece of knowledge when she flooded the space. She was too occupied with impressing the crowd and the royal court to consider the consequences of her actions and what could befall her fellow tyrants. The higher the water level, the easier for me to reach them.

The rain abruptly stops, permitting me the sight I was long denied. Soro marches his way to the mage on the terrace. She might have forgotten the rules. But I'd bet my lunch he did not.

He slaps her across the face as he points angrily at the water. She grips the edge of the terrace, blood pouring down her split lip. She attempts to put distance between herself and Soro but stumbles toward the exit. Soro follows, pushing her down the rest of the way.

To her credit, her power over the arena holds strong despite the pummeling she receives. She keeps her spell going even while attempting to escape.

What a fool. She has the magic to destroy Soro and his subordinates. Instead, her goal was likely to be appointed into the royal court. Like other fools—there are so many here—she wants to belong to the inner circle. She expects a reward of gold, jewels, and connections. Her arrogance will likely cost her more than just her pride today.

Soro yells something at her and then calls to the guards, urging them into action.

I dart toward the arena seats and the two lowest rows of people as they push and trample one another, trying to reach the higher stands.

So much for that strategy.

Something pokes me in the shoulder. I whip around to see that wooden sword floating behind me. *Again.* Don't tell me *this* is Maeve's grand plan. No...she's smarter than that.

The weapon is following me like a stray and distracting me. Hell, if this is the best she can do for me, she'd better find another sap to marry.

The sharks are almost finished with their royal feast. I'm running out of time before I become dessert.

Several guards return to the lowest ring of seats, escorting dwarves in battered clothing with giant cauldrons strapped to their backs. Again, I'm reminded that time isn't my only hurdle.

Because the damn river sharks weren't enough.

The cauldrons are massive, large enough to cook the biggest shark.

Is that what they used to carry them in?

No...these wouldn't have held them all. And the dwarves, for all their combined strength and muscle, would never be able to cart them inside.

The wooden sword bumps my shoulder. I shrug it off, watching, perplexed, as the dwarves cut themselves free from the cauldrons and tip the heavy things forward.

Giant silver-and-black-spotted eels slither out, snatching three of the dwarves by their heads and zapping them as they pull them into the water. The dwarves bellow, their flesh and clothing burning.

That stunt bought me time for the sand kicked up by the eels to settle, so I dip down to do a quick survey of the sharks' locations on the other side of the arena, counting shadows moving quickly, before popping back up, looking for an advantage. The remaining dwarves curse and wave their angry fists at the guards. The sole woman among them eases away in wide-eyed shock, then kneels on the ledge where her companions fell. She audibly weeps and moves closer to the edge. Maeve pops out of nowhere and snags her around the waist. She speaks into her ear, holding tight to the dwarf as her grief continues to compel her closer to the edge.

It's not until the remaining dwarves gather around that Maeve releases her. The guards laugh. The other royals in their proximity join them. They stop laughing when Maeve yells, "Shut the fuck up or I'll throw you in next."

Vitor and Soro appear amused by her actions. Nothing in Maeve threatens them. To this gluttonous court stuffed with entitlement and riches, this is part of the spectacle they paid to experience. What else would they do—mourn? Offer comfort? I huff.

How quickly they turned from terror back to amusement once they knew they were safe.

Fuck them. I turn and swim for my life, keeping the trident close to my body.

When I stop and look back, I'm unsure where the eels have swum off to. It's certain some are fighting the sharks over the dwarves who fell in with them. The water grows redder by the second. But there's not enough food for all the predators to remain in one place. They're going to spread out—and soon.

The thought has barely formed when another fin punctures the surface and angles toward me. Then it disappears only a few yards away. And I know the shark has found me.

I couldn't outmaneuver it if I wanted to. It's moving too fast.

And I can't get away.

CHAPTER
17
LEITH

I dive, swimming toward the shark instead of away.

I'm no match for this thing power for power, but I'm superior when it comes to wit. There's no need for me to destroy it. I only need to damage it enough to win.

With the trident out in front of me, I'm protected to some extent. I swim straight toward the shark. Its maw is already open. At the last moment, I thrust my trident forward, using the shark's momentum to stab its own nose. It's not much, only enough to briefly daze and piss it off. Then I push myself over it and tilt the trident so it rakes the shark's skin as it passes me.

The points of the trident do their job. Blood spews into the water and swirls like red clouds from the wounds I create. The shark thrashes, and the turbulence rips my only decent weapon away. I use its moment of confusion to flee, but I know it will follow soon, its injuries magnifying its rage.

And alerting the others to new bait.

My body weakens with every stroke. My lungs beg for air. But my mind knows better than to stop.

I may be a skilled swimmer, but I've developed far different muscle groups and strategies over the years to keep alive on land, not water.

My body betrays me, falling into motions that resemble more of a crawl. I bump into something and finally look up. I've reached another wall, opposite from where I started. It's only now that I can gauge how far I swam.

With a pained groan, I surface. I flip onto my back, floating, permitting myself to rest long enough to slow my haggard breathing.

I'm fucked for losing my trident.

Then that fucking wooden sword bumps me on the side.

I don't slap it aside or question whether it's the mage taunting me. She's gone, taken away by the guards. I need a weapon, and I need it now.

The hilt maintains that strange, thick wrapping held together tightly with twine. I think I should peel it free until I realize it cushions my sore hand and makes my grip more comfortable. It's remarkably easy to hold. Pressing my back to the wall, I transfer the wooden sword to my injured hand and pull the dagger out of my belt with the other.

An eel skims over the water, its thin back cutting zigzag lines through the turbulent surface, but my focus jerks to the shark almost upon me. I turn and thrust the sword forward, praying my grip holds. In my weakened hands, the blow is only enough to nick the shark in the gums. I kick off the side of the wall and plunge my knife into its eye.

The blood spurting out of the shark lures the eel away from me. It takes a bite of the shark's nose, causing it to retaliate and clamp its rows of razor-sharp teeth down on the eel.

Currents of energy zap across the surface of the water and rake like burning needles across my spine. I bellow my torment for all to hear.

The crowd cheers—thrilled, applauding, and eager for more.

As the eel and shark go to war, more currents of lightning shoot through me, burning and stinging in simultaneous song. I roar, then scare myself when I abruptly quiet.

I've finally hit my limit, it seems, my vision taking turns dulling and sharpening beneath that gray and unforgiving sky. I don't know what happens. I can't hear, save for the buzzing that follows every twitch of my limbs.

This trial of strength feels like such a waste.

Drowning is the sweeter way to go.

It's my only thought…until I think of Dahlia, sick but surviving on the meager coin I send every month. My little shadow, who'd follow me to hell itself if I were to lead, needs my bravery more than ever. Self-pity won't save her life.

I try to lift a leg. It doesn't work. I'm stuck to the water like a fly on honey.

As I've done so many times in my miserable life, I force away the despair and gather my wits. But my wits don't matter so much when my body is unresponsive. I float away, somehow still holding on to that damned wooden sword. Still, I have to keep trying.

In my periphery, scorched pieces of shark and an eel head bob past me.

They killed each other. Good.

Not that it solves anything. I'm still screwed.

The remaining sharks and eels go after their dead. It's only a matter of time before they remember I'm still here and vulnerable. A very short period of time.

Cooked meat isn't more desirable than fresh to these things. What the eel tried to do to the shark, the dwarves, and me was strictly a protective response. They react out of fear and instinct.

Those poor dwarves. It's why the guards burdened them with carrying the cauldrons. The guards knew the risks and would sell their mothers if it meant sparing their own hides. Maeve knew it, too.

My head bumps against something. I've reached another section of wall. But it could be the same wall for all I know.

An elf and a sprite peer over at me.

"He's dead," the sprite says, her wings drooping as if I rained on their parade. "What a knob."

"About damn time," her elven partner adds.

"Say one more thing about that gladiator, and I'll feed numb nuts here your wings," Maeve fires off.

It's her voice that brings me back. Who needs a cheer squad when I have Maeve's sweet disposition and vocabulary to spring me back to life?

When I blink, they can't scamper away fast enough. They don't want to end up like the humans who went for a swim with me. Damn me, they're smarter than those fools.

I reach up, surprised I can move my arm. I try to kick. My legs are mostly working. I try out my other arm—it doesn't work as well as my dominant one, but it's more than I had moments ago.

And I know the sharks haven't had their fill yet. When they finish, they will find me. If I'm lucky, maybe they'll run into one another first. Except luck is a bitch I never was able to bed.

I strike the wall half-heartedly with my pathetic wooden sword. The point barely scratches the stone in my weakened state.

This thing wouldn't scare away a squirrel. What the blazes was Maeve thinking?

My body jerks at the sound of bear traps. It's the sharks snapping their teeth—the same monstrosities that chewed Luther to chunks. Wish he'd have given me a little bit more of a heads-up.

Although nothing would have prepared me for sharks. Nothing.

Well, except Luther mouthing "shark" instead of "water," but coming from fucking farmlands, he'd likely never even seen one of these monsters before.

And had I not included those royal humans in all the sporty fun, the lords wouldn't have tossed in the eels. The eels were my reward for a job too well done.

The lords are always generous that way.

Bastards.

Ripples shoot across the water. Given their speed and the broader current they create, they're made by another shark. The eels move smoothly, skimming through the water in S-shaped trajectories.

"Move, Leith. MOVE!"

It's Maeve I hear. She's right. *I can't let my baby sister down.*

From where I float, the ledge appears, ten, maybe twelve feet above me. I can't exactly scale it and escape. There are too many guards and too many beings with magic. If I so much as try, every battle before this one won't have mattered.

Neither will the way my friendship ended with Sullivan.

Deserters face a death worse than the arena.

But, while I can't leave the arena, there's nothing that says I *must* fight what's in here.

I only have to stay alive.

Stiffly, I try to move, and my body protests in spasms. It doesn't like me any better when I try a second time. It punishes me with searing pain and a terrible throbbing that reaches my head in mad bursts.

I manage to turn onto my stomach and dip my legs vertically. I almost dare a stroke when an eel spirals from the water in a terrifying leap, its maw open and targeting my face.

I raise the wooden sword—it's all I have. But as the eel reaches me, a wave lifts like a hand and slaps the eel away.

What is this?

The wave appeared in front of me and didn't move me with it. If anything, it kept me protected. Which is unnerving—but not as much as the eel at this moment.

My gaze shifts from side to side. The eel recovers quickly and comes after me again. Another joins it. Like before, a large wave slaps the first eel. A shorter wave forms right after, shielding me and striking the second.

The shark I felt coming after me before the eels appeared inexplicably spins in circles, disoriented by the miniature whirlpool it has created and is now trapped in.

Murmurs reverberate through the crowd. Something else is here. Something that may be on my side.

The ripples batting my legs warn that a second shark is approaching. By the heaviness in the current, it feels like the largest among them. Another eel surfaces, quickly swimming away from the shark's path, not wanting to meet its wrath.

I hold out my wooden sword, keen on jabbing it in the eyes or another vulnerable spot if given the chance.

What happens next can't be explained. Not by me, and certainly not by the crowd going silent in awe. The eel that slithers past the shark reappears beside it.

Its tail smacks the shark all over its head and body, any place it can find, in awkward, unnatural motions. The shark cants its head and snaps its jaws, sinking its teeth into the prey that dared assault it.

I don't lie in wait for those teeth to connect. Not after how incapacitated the last eel shock left me.

I push myself out of the water. There's a small crevice I grasp tightly, feet scrambling against the slick wall of the arena as jolts of energy course through me in waves.

I swing from left to right, trying to find someplace to rest my foot before I lose my grip.

My toe catches on another indentation along the wall, offering me a small reprieve and enough time to find another section that will better support my weight.

"Hang on!" Maeve hollers. "Whatever you do, don't let go."

Yeah. Easier said. I'm mere inches from the ledge, but it might as well be miles. Each jolt from those eels makes me wobble on my already unstable footing.

With a warrior's cry, I lurch upward and manage to catch the ledge.

At first, I can do little more than hang, my body elongating from the unintentional stretch. I barely stay in place, my torn hands begging me to let go.

Chaos has unleashed below.

The eels issue their painful currents in rapid succession. They sweep along the water in an assortment of spurts, engulfing the expanse with flashes of bright-green light. Two sharks are already dead, partially burned and floating belly-up. The one I stabbed is bleeding heavily but alive. Many more eels are shredded to mangled strings of meat.

It's smart to let them fight it out. My best guess is that each gladiator was scheduled to fight a series of sharks or eels, or hell, a school of rabid fucking jellyfish for all I know. If defeated or satiated, the other sets of predators would challenge any gladiator who remained.

Cute. But feeding the audience to the sharks had the lords scrambling for other ways to kill me. They didn't consider that their chosen instruments of torture would turn on one another, and it likely has enraged them further.

In the wild, river sharks, eels, and alike avoid each other unless there's a shortage of food. Here, they are exactly like us—gladiators fighting to the death, each one battling to emerge the victor.

An eel leaves the melee and leaps out of the water to attack me. I instinctively curl inward, shrinking myself out of reach, but not soon enough. It catches my calf and sinks its fangs to the bone. The puncture is so agonizing—so inconceivably excruciating—that I honestly consider letting go. At least the sharks would kill me.

The monster writhes, using its weight to try to drag me back into the water and damn close to succeeding. I stab it through the head with the point of my mighty driftwood blade.

It retaliates with a shock to my leg that rattles my teeth, locking every muscle in my body into place. My hold on the ledge tightens involuntarily. Finally a fucking break. I hang tight, wailing in torment and stabbing at it until it falls dead into a shark's maw. The water practically sizzles beneath me, steam rising up from the deadly waters below. Every droplet singes my skin. I reckon there's enough charge built up in there to stun a giant.

The shark goes belly-up, joining my own victim to bob lifelessly in the waves.

Another eel. I swat it aside with my sword before it can sink its needle-sharp fangs into me. It lands in the remaining shark's path and dies soon after. I am certain I will be next. Only the shark—the largest among them—doesn't jump for me. It thrashes and writhes and chomps, and it is only when the shark breaches the surface that I realize my good fortune. The creature's rough skin is riddled with puncture wounds, nose to tail, and its movements grow weaker by the second.

Good. I can only imagine the pain it's in.

The eels keep coming. Or at least I think they do. I keep stabbing. There's no strategy. It's me against them, and we all want to live.

I manage to stab several more times in a last-ditch effort to survive before my cramping, damaged hand releases my only weapon at last— and Maeve screams.

CHAPTER

18

LEITH

The moments that follow are like patches on an old man's coat, barely held together by a common thread and not enough to protect him.

There are jolts of that burning, numb feeling. They start and stop, scattered for a time or coming all at once. My body bounces in an erratic cadence.

I am in the water until I'm not.

I am choking and desperate for air until I am breathing and clearing my lungs.

Rancid water in my throat and stomach causes me to spew in surges. I'm cold, I think.

It's dark, late. Hours, maybe days since I first entered the arena. I should be dead. It's a miracle I'm not.

Well, mostly.

I think I won. I think I saved Dahlia.

Voices trail in and out, or maybe I fade in and out. The words don't make sense right away. Eventually, I start understanding the conversation.

It's about me.

"He won," Jakeb says.

"He killed Count Nathanial and his new bride. He doesn't deserve honor. I should feed him to my dogs!"

It's Soro's voice. He's a few feet from me. This is the closest I've ever been to him, and it's too bad I don't have the energy to kill him where he stands.

"All the rules were followed by this young gladiator," Jakeb says in a level tone. "He fought his opponents, and while he didn't slay them directly, his strategy bestowed him the win."

"Count Nathanial is dead!" someone else says.

"With all due respect, my lord," a young woman with a light voice replies. *Giselle.* "Count Nathanial was about as bright as a donkey's asshole at midnight. Is this really a loss for his court?"

"Giselle," Jakeb warns.

"Father," Giselle says.

There's murmuring. Lots of it. A crowd has formed around me.

"Give him to me, Soro." Jakeb addresses that bastard once again. "Leith remains in good standing. He is worth more alive than dead."

Someone nudges my side with their foot. I cough up more water.

"Father?" Soro says.

So, Vitor is here, too.

"High Lord Vitor, if I may remind you," Giselle says, addressing the regent, "Nathanial has no heir, and as your liege, his house's riches and that of his bride now belong to you."

"What say you, High Lord? May we depart?" Jakeb asks. His words are polite. His tone is not.

My legs are on fire, and my vision blurs, then goes dark again.

A few disgruntled lords and one sharp-voiced female continue to object, demanding my head. Hmm, no one put up such a fuss when I beheaded Lord Peacock. So, it's not really about *what* I did, just about *who* I did it to. Interesting.

"He followed the rules," High Lord Vitor says simply. He pauses. "He'll fight again."

Will I? I'm not so sure.

Soro argues and curses. Other voices are yelling.

"Enough," Vitor declares, and his sharp tone silences everyone around me. "This gladiator is strong and smart. In the arena, we honor these qualities. We honor our *laws.* I, for one, look forward to seeing what he does next."

There's a pat on my arm. "Do try to survive, Leith of Siertos," Vitor says smoothly. *It's Leith of Grey, asshole, but whatever.* "And if you can't, be sure to die in the arena next time, will you, young man?"

The joke has some of these lords laughing. Although it breaks the tension, there are still grumbles and mumbled complaints as strong arms hook under mine and lift me. "Try to prevent his feet from touching the ground, Caelen," Jakeb says.

"Yes, Lord Jakeb," the man holding my right side replies. There's a faint brush of long braids against my shoulder as he adjusts his hold. It's that soldier…the one who keeps Jakeb's company.

As I'm carried away, the arguing royals are replaced by familiar voices.

The gladiators. They're still here. Instead of fighting, they're headed back to the barracks.

"He's alive," Sibor mutters.

"Are ya sure?" Ned asks.

Giselle assures him as only she evidently can. "He's alive. He just looks like shit."

"He won't stay alive if we don't hurry," Caelen adds. "Look at his leg. It's twice as large as the other."

"Oh, that *is* nasty," Giselle says. "Look, it's purple and his skin is all stretched to hell and back. That can't be good."

"Eels aren't venomous," Caelen says, keeping his voice low. "They're only known to shock and bite."

"Unless they were fed poison," Jakeb adds. "Look at that red web of veins. It's spreading."

Giselle gags. She's all sorts of helpful.

I try to open my eyes at the approach of the squeaky wheels, but I can't see past my wet lashes. The back gate of a wagon drops open with a loud *thud*. Caelen's braids slap against my face when he and someone else lift me and carefully place me on the hard wagon floor.

The weight shifts on either side as two others join me — Giselle, I guess, and by the sudden annoyed huff, Jakeb.

But not Maeve. Where is she?

I don't know why my thoughts are drawn to her. It must be the poison.

"How is it possible to poison those creatures in that way?" Caelen asks. "Have you heard of such a thing?"

"There's another mage who holds Vitor's favor. Her specialty is poisons, I think," Giselle says, but she sounds distracted. "It's all right, Father. Caelen and I will take it from here. Return to the horses, and we'll meet you back home."

From one moment to the next, Jakeb is gone, the anger encapsulating the small space trailing behind him. There's a bump, then another bump. I tremble, growing hot until beads of sweat form across my forehead.

A bundle of sorts is placed beneath my head, and then the wagon lurches into motion, causing ripples of pain to flood my body like the water in the arena.

"You did well, Leith ol' boy," Giselle says from somewhere nearby. "So well, there's nothing left for your friends to play with in the arena. I suppose they owe you their lives or something like that. At the very least a bit of gratitude, don't you think?"

I don't know Giselle and especially not Caelen, but I recognize humor when it finds its way into Caelen's voice. "You talk too much, Giselle."

"I have heard that once or twice before," she says. She sighs. "Maeve prepared him well by providing all those daggers and that trident. But that sword—whatever she wrapped around the hilt prevented or damn well lessened the effects of those shocking currents." She pauses. "I don't think Leith could have fought off those eels without it."

No. Perhaps not.

We travel in silence except for the clomping of horses' hooves, the crunching of wagon wheels over dirt and rock, and my groans of pain. I groan with every bump in the road, and my skin grows slick and hot. My fever climbs with each mile that passes. Burns I don't remember receiving scrape my body raw. I jump. The pain surpasses my ability to control it. I jump again. I think it's related to the injuries, until I can no longer make sense of what's happening.

Giselle's voice is shrill. "Shit. He's convulsing. Hurry, Caelen."

I don't comprehend what happens next. I'm only partially aware of the cold slab of stone where I'm laid. Then there are hands all over me. Some touch me using care. Others rip off my clothes.

Every movement is torment. My skin is on fire.

No. *I* am on fire.

I can't move.

They're burning me.

They're burning me alive!

Voices, speaking all at once, surround me. I can't see. All I feel is the fire and those damn hands.

"Cut off his leg," Caelen says. "It's too late for him."

"No!" Maeve's voice is unyielding. "He won't last in the arena with one leg."

"You'll find another gladiator," Caelen insists.

"There is no other gladiator this close to Bloodguard," Maeve snaps back.

I'm in the small cottage where Maeve treated me before. I don't know how. I'm just there, spread out like a goat for the butcher to carve.

Maeve's hair skims over my brow, the scent of lavender distracting me for a moment.

"I must lance it," she says. "Hold him down—no, *harder*. Keep him from moving!"

What feels like a burning arrow punctures my leg. I howl, tears of agony overflowing from my eyes.

"Maeve, you're mutilating him," Jakeb warns.

"I don't have a choice," Maeve snaps back.

"Then give him something for the pain," Jakeb pleads. "He's only human."

"I know what I'm doing," Maeve counters. But the tremor in her voice belies her words.

"Are you sure?" Giselle asks. "You've never treated something like this. I don't think—"

"Do *not* question me, Giselle—not now. Just hold him," she commands. "And keep him still."

"Daughter, you must sedate him," Jakeb urges.

Maeve's voice is quiet, the warning behind it leaving no room for argument. "I need him awake. Do you understand? If he falls asleep, the poison will claim him, and he'll *never* wake again." She pauses, then adds, "He's survived worse. He'll survive this."

Have I? It sure as hell doesn't feel like it, but I latch on to the confidence in her voice anyway.

"I can't look," Giselle says, coughing and gagging. "This is too much."

"You don't have to look. Just hold him," Maeve counters sharply. "Everyone ready?"

There's a small grumble of affirmation. My arms are wrenched above me, strong hands clasp my legs—and a pain beyond belief suddenly tears through my leg. I can't keep still—I *must* make this stop—and I start to thrash against my restraints like a wild man.

Fucking hell, they are *torturing* me. Maeve was wrong—I have *never* experienced pain like this before.

If I could speak, I'd scream to let me sleep. Forever if need be. Anything to make this stop. I thrash again when a cool hand cups my cheek, a soft voice brushing against my ear as Maeve whispers for only me to hear, "You can do this, Leith. *Trust me,* just as I trust you."

Trust her? I wouldn't even know how.

Something wet drips on my cheek and slides down behind my ear as Maeve whispers again, "Please trust me, you big oaf."

Something in the way her voice breaks on the insult calms me, and I find my body settling into the waves of pain radiating up my leg. I imagine I'm bobbing on the water—granted, eel-infested water zapping me with what feels like lightning over and over. The pain is unbearable, but this time I welcome the agony—at least it means I'm still alive.

"Thank you," she says before going back to her torturing ways. I brace myself.

"I must cut deeper. The poison is trapped inside his muscle," Maeve says. "If he moves, I'll nick the artery and kill him. Do *not* let him move."

I holler in agony. I'm on fire. My "ally" is burning me alive.

"Hold him!" Maeve cries out.

This time, my ingrained need to fight swamps my mind and body. Instinct takes over, and I break free, flinging away those holding me.

I fall from a long table, disoriented and groping. I crawl a short distance before staggering upright and dragging my useless leg.

A river.

A well.

I need to find water.

My smoldering body remains my only weapon. I swing my arms, trying to feel my way as bodies surround me again.

I connect with a face, a chest, and something soft. Something burly gets in my way, but I shove through it. Glass breaks. A heavy object is thrown. I still can't see.

She's killing me. I *knew* I couldn't trust her.

My fists connect with flesh. Objects shatter at my feet.

Furniture cracks.

Where's that damn spring? The one where they get water?

I *must* put out these flames.

Someone else finds my fist, and another my injured foot.

An eruption like an avalanche of stone has me whirling and falling over. I don't quite hit the floor. Something strong snatches me up by the throat.

Maeve screams. "No!"

My legs kick hard and my fists swing, trying to connect with what has me. A roar, primal and animalistic, blasts against my face.

Whatever has me shakes me hard, trying to snap my neck.

Air is squeezed out of me. I start to sleep.

No.

I start to die.

Forgive me, Dahlia…

Maeve's screaming jolts me awake. "Caelen, rein in your beast!"

I'm thrown on something hard. A…*creature* crawls over me, holding me in place and making it almost impossible to keep breathing, words fading, then returning to scream over me.

A sword pulls free of its sheath. "He dies, you die with him," Maeve warns.

"You *dare* challenge *me*," an unearthly voice growls.

"Not a challenge," Maeve says. "A promise. Hurt him, and I'll kill you. I swear it."

Giselle's panicked and furious voice calls from across the room. "Enough. This ends now."

There's a moment when everything stills, between my almost breath and the flames blistering my skin.

Before life as I know it ends.

CHAPTER

19

LEITH

Light flickers over my closed eyes, nudging me awake. Slowly, I blink them open. I'm in a bedroom somewhere near Maeve's garden. The scent of herbs is heavy in the air. There's a circular window above me where the sun's rays peek through the branches of a fairy elm. Its branches are overgrown now, only the topmost limbs reaching the light, while lower branches are shaded and barely blooming. In the forest, a good fire would take this tree out, and its thick bark would weather the flames to bloom richer and healthier again.

A raven squawks somewhere in the garden. And a cluster of gnome cardinals swoops up and down, back and forth, round and round, showing off the aerial acrobatics they're known for.

But the best thing here is the sound of Maeve's voice.

"Leith?"

Her gorgeous face comes into view, skin flushed and eyes bright as she examines my face. She's in a white dress—no, a white nightgown—with a plunging neckline, exposing the last trail of scar just above the swell of her right breast. She reaches for a robe at the foot of the bed and slips it on, hiding a body I wish I didn't want to see.

The long braid I remember is gone. Her mountain of hair is tied up at the top of her head. "For someone who wants to become Bloodguard, you're trying really hard to die."

I laugh as she intends, though it hurts. "Believe it or not, I want to live."

She winks. "Well, then, it's a good thing you made a blood oath with a healer of exceptional skill." She reaches for a pitcher of water and pours some into a goblet.

I ease upward to drink, and as I shift, the soft sheet skims along my bare skin. The moment she passes the water to me, I gulp it down. Pain continues to throb and stab at me in various places, but the intense burning has abated.

With my bandaged hands, I lift the covers and have a look at what remains of me. I'm clean, and except for the dressings covering multiple parts of my body, I'm naked.

"Well now, Princess. You've been busy," I say. I let the covers drop. "Did you have *fun*…cleaning me up?"

She blushes and yanks the goblet from my grasp, considering, most likely, whether to cave my skull in with it. She fills the goblet instead, so the water skims along the rim. She doesn't offer it right away. Instead, she smirks, and I swear to the moon, I've never seen a sweeter sight.

"Who's Dahlia?" she asks as she hands me the water. "You spoke of her while you slept, and something about a rose."

I take several long gulps, giving myself time to decide what to tell her. "Someone special," I say.

Maeve's features dissolve into blankness, although I don't immediately understand why. She glances down. "I see," she says, forcing a laugh. "As a gladiator, you probably have lots of…fans?"

Is that what we're calling them?

"Yes. I have fans. Most of us do." Not all of them are sexual, as Maeve's implying. Some of the wealthier attendants genuinely want to reward us for our efforts. A dwarf named Wilestu treats the victors to a feast once a month. I think he does it more for the inside track on who to bet for or against, but it doesn't change the fact that he is generous and friendly.

"So, she is one of your fans, then…"

Wariness keeps me from explaining, even to her. Any information someone has about my family is information they could use against me.

I didn't survive these years in Arrow by pretending that ulterior motives don't exist among the aristocracy.

Maeve passes me the goblet once more, her gaze lowered after my blatant non-reply. "Don't drink too much, though," she warns. "Pasha is preparing supper now."

I adjust my position to better sit, and she hurries to help me. She props the pillows behind me, trying to make me comfortable. She's strong, and although I can manage on my own, I allow it. I feel like I owe her for, I don't know, letting her think Dahlia and maybe Rose are more than my sweet little sisters? I'm not trying to vex her—she just saved my life. Again. But I'm more interested in why she's so curious. She's a princess of Arrow. She can have anyone and anything.

"How long have I been asleep?" I ask.

"Almost three days," she replies, her voice oddly hesitant.

"Did anyone collect my winnings?" I ask.

"Father did the day following your last match." She falls perfectly still. "You want your earnings to go to Dahlia?"

My voice lowers to a murmur. "I do."

Her cheeks flush. She reaches for the pitcher again, then must remember she told me not to have more. She shoves her hands into the pockets of her nightrobe as if unsure what to do with them.

"Where or how should I get your winnings to her?" Maeve asks.

"There are messenger hawks trained to travel abroad and to specific realms. It's a service we pay for."

"I've never heard of that service," Maeve replies. "The only messenger hawks I'm familiar with are the ones that drop the weapons into the arena."

Why would she be? Arrow's royals have everything. They don't share with other realms, and they certainly don't send their own mail.

"All right," she says. "I'll make arrangements to send your earnings to Grey."

The unbending discipline I pride myself on evaporates the more I take her in.

Shadows ring her eyes from lack of sleep. In the recesses of my mind, I recall her voice—whispers of encouragement and maybe some light swearing. Her nightgown and bare feet suggest she's slept here and...

possibly never left my side.

A section of hair drifts slowly down and falls against her cheek. I hook my finger around it and gently bring it behind her ear, my hand lingering there.

"I don't think Dahlia would like us this close," she whispers.

I caress her face, her entire body stiffening as my knuckles glide over her soft cheek. "Dahlia won't mind, and neither will Rose," I say. "Trust me."

If there was ever a time she was going to punch me in the skull, this is it.

Regret darkens her face, and I sense her disappointment in both of us.

It doesn't sit right with me. Caution be damned.

"Maeve, Dahlia is my sister. She's almost eleven. And Rose, my other sister, should be fourteen by now. They and my mother are the only ones my winnings go to."

"Oh," Maeve says. She smiles at me playfully. "You're not such a prick after all."

"Now you've gone too far, Princess."

Her laugh is as refreshing as the first rains after a season of drought. My gaze fastens on hers. Maeve is different. And this…whatever this is, could become something more.

Shit. What am I *doing*?

No, what am I doing with *her*?

Maeve tucks the thick covers around me, then sits beside me, her hand next to mine, just barely touching, but I feel that connection down to my bones. We're quiet for several minutes. Maybe she's thinking she's lucky I didn't die, that she'd have to find herself another gladiator about to be Bloodguard. Outside of me and Sullivan, only Luther was close. I wonder if he made it through the night. If her medicine was enough to help him survive.

"Thank you," I say, "for healing me."

She had her motives, but I'm grateful all the same.

Her expression softens with concern and something more. I let the sensation between us simmer. An excitement thrums through my blood that's much like the anticipation of a match in the arena—I smile inwardly—just without the threat of being mauled by some vicious beast.

Speaking of… "There was an animal here," I say. "The night you treated me."

"There wasn't an animal." Maeve puckers her brow. "All right, maybe not an animal, but…" Her voice trails off as she frowns.

"A shifter," I say. "That's it, isn't it?"

"Sure." She shrugs, all too casually. "Anyway, if there's something special you'd like for supper, I can send word."

She's nervous, but I don't get why. Shifters are plentiful, and some high-ranking members of the royal court are shifters if I'm not mistaken. "Maeve, what is it?"

Sadness creeps along her features, but I can't assess why. It doesn't sit well with me. "Maeve?" I say, keeping my tone soft.

Impending tears glisten in her eyes, but not a single one falls. "It's just that as much as I want to, there are some things I'll never be able to change. Even if I become queen."

"Do you mean freeing your papa?"

"No. Papa is getting out no matter what I must do."

The determination in her tone is tinged with grief. "Then is it all the lives lost in the arena?" I ask.

Maeve presses her lips together. "Yes, and more."

Had I met Maeve sooner, perhaps she, *we*, could have spared those lives…including Sullivan's.

Sullivan.

I grimace when the muscle in my upper leg painfully spasms as I try to edge off the bed.

"Is something wrong?" she asks. "Do you need to adjust your position?"

"No," I say, shaking off the pain. I press my palms into the mattress, the cool cotton sheet begging me to return to its comfort. "Just been in bed too long." I glance at the oval window above, where the gnome cardinals continue to circle and play. "Is it nice out?" I ask.

"It's beautiful," she answers cautiously.

She backs away in the direction of the wall and presses a brick. With a squeak, the wall opens…revealing Maeve's workstation. I'm in a hidden room within the cottage.

"Do you mean to tell me that there was a real bedroom, with a real bed, and you had me sleep on some old cot?"

I don't admit that the cot was rather comfortable. It's the principle, damn it.

"It's not really a cot. It's more like an old dog bed," Maeve replies. She sighs dramatically. "Poor old Speckles. He likely rolled over in his grave, knowing you got fleas on it."

I chuckle, but damn does it hurt. "Don't make me laugh."

I reach toward the small, cushioned chair to my right, where a clean pair of breeches lies folded. It shouldn't be such a task, but it is, despite how I attempt to mask it.

"Leith, you're too weak to leave your bed."

Somehow, call it will or absolute stubbornness, I manage to pull on the breeches. I tie the drawstring—a hell of an accomplishment, considering how much the tight bandages along my hands restrict my movements.

I deal with the pain stabbing its way to my groin well enough, but it's those pesky spots dancing across my line of sight that warn me any position other than supine is a bad idea. I tell the spots to fuck off and force myself to my feet.

Thank the phoenix that Maeve's breasts are there to catch me when I fall forward.

All right. That's not entirely true. Her hands shoot out to catch me and clasp my shoulders. My face lands against her generous bosom because gravity is a real thing, and sometimes, the stars do align in my favor.

Maeve gasps, but she doesn't shove me away like I expect. No, rather than shove me off her, she holds me close. I close my eyes as the whole room spins.

We fall still, both of us taking our time to remember how to breathe. My cheek rests against the last few scars along her sternum, and my nose presses into the swell of her...yeah. *Those.*

Future kings don't lick their way up a future queen's throat to claim her mouth and probably everything else.

Despite how badly a future king may want to.

"Ah, Leith?" the future queen stammers.

"Mm?"

"D-did you...pass out?"

"Mm-hmm."

She strangles out a laugh as I ease away from her, ignoring the insistence of my face to return to Maeve's chest and to let my mouth linger there and then lower still.

I set my gaze on the wall and roll my shoulder, trying to gain a semblance of control.

"Fuck," I say, clamping my jaw shut when what feels like shards of glass pierce through my arm. That damn shark and that equally wretched barb at the end of its tail must have shredded the muscle. It's healing, and the bandage Maeve set holds tight, but it pinches like the stitches might split or the wound hasn't fully closed.

The pain...it's not so different from what's weighed on me since Sullivan died. But for my sake, and Maeve's, I must move forward in spite of how the dull pound along my skull increases in severity.

Maeve's steady hold lessens as I straighten further. My feet bear my weight well enough, but it's impossible not to favor one side.

"Leith, I don't know what you think you're doing, but you're not ready to go anywhere."

Pain pinches my features into a grimace I can feel. "If I don't start to move, I won't move enough when it matters." I breathe in and out slowly, trying to fight through that next wave.

Maeve sighs. "This isn't a good idea," she says.

"Never said it was." I lift my head. "Take me into the forest."

Her eyes travel up and down my body. "To *die*?"

"No," I rumble, wondering what I look like to make her say that. "Just...take me someplace pretty."

"Pretty?" she repeats.

"Yes," I answer quietly. *Some place that's the equivalent of you.*

"Please," I add when she keeps still. "There's something I've waited far too long to do..."

CHAPTER

20

MAEVE

Leith permits me to guide him. In truth, we look ridiculous. Me in my night garments and he in breeches and a dark-blue blanket draped over his shoulders. His right arm sways leisurely against his side, despite how his fingers fist around the lock of Sullivan's hair.

I didn't understand what Leith wanted until he bid me move aside the bottles of herbs on the top shelf. When my fingers felt the soft strands of hair that he'd hidden, I knew.

That gladiator, the one Leith killed the day I first saw him, must have been his friend. I wasn't certain why he cut that man's hair. I didn't know Leith, and in many ways, I still don't know him. Yet even then, I didn't see Leith's actions as coldhearted. Already, I saw more. And I was right.

What he must have felt ending his friend's life is unfathomable. I fight back tears at the thought. The tears, should any fall, belong to him. I won't steal a single drop. I don't deserve to.

While Leith slept, Father and Sonu added another coat of gold fire hornet venom to the rope that surrounds the cottage. They did a good job of covering this extra line of defense with forest debris, except the fresh, sharp scent pricks my nose and I can't fight my sneeze.

"Are you all right?" Leith asks. "Don't tell me the elf healer is getting a cold." His voice remains heavy from sleep and likely a great deal more pain.

"Elves don't get colds." I take in a deep breath, welcoming the crisp aroma of dark-green leaves, damp bark and stone, and lush, moist soil.

His focus skips from me to the planter spilling with blood orange lilies, perhaps thinking their silky black pollen stirred my sneeze. I breathe in the tangy petals, and not just to free my nose from the lingering stench of the venom, but because they also overpower the smell of the serpent oil soaking the stump they rest on. While pretty, blood orange lilies are also practical.

I pause and lift the planter so that Leith sees the match secured to the base. "If you're ever in trouble, strike it hard against the stump. It will catch fire and surround the perimeter of the cottage in a protective wall of flames."

He laughs without humor. "I noticed the rope when I first arrived, but the match and the stump are pure genius." He cocks an eyebrow. "I take it this is your way of thwarting my escape?"

"As if anything could keep you here."

It will help protect Leith, but the cottage wasn't warded for him.

He eyes the cottage carefully. "That's prairie mint covering every inch of those exterior walls."

"It is," I confirm.

He nods. "It holds a ton of water. It'd keep whoever's in there safe from the flames."

At the mention of flames, I shudder, and Leith's sharp gaze traces over me. "Those defenses aren't for me, though, are they?" he asks. "They're for you."

"Yes."

We resume walking.

"After the assassination attempt and fire at the castle...Father didn't think it safe for us to be underfoot," I explain.

"Why?"

I expel a deep breath. "Because my father didn't kill my grandmother, which means the real killer is still out there, Leith."

He pauses and reassesses the grounds as if seeing them for the first time. "Do you have a contingent of guards? Can they be trusted?" He eyes the path that leads to the main house. "This keep doesn't have high enough walls or anything protecting it from an attack from the forest side."

"Yes, well, it's better than living within the castle walls, where an enemy could be lurking around any corner," I mutter.

"Is that why you moved?" he asks, lifting a long branch out of the way for me.

I duck under. "Partially." I don't bother to add that the castle was just filled with too many memories of my grandmother and Papa. "Visiting again soon for the council meetings will be interesting."

When Leith doesn't comment, I continue, "Uncle Vitor suggested I start attending when I announced my previous engagement. I hope the invitation still stands even though my fiancé met an untimely demise."

Leith shrugs. "Not my fault he couldn't hold on to his sword."

I roll my eyes and start to respond, but Leith interrupts.

"What's that?" he asks.

I follow his line of sight and see the small house we built for our staff. "That's where Pasha, Musy, and Sonu live."

"Your cooks and the gardener?" Leith asks. "You gave them their own house? Not just a servants' quarters in your own?"

I tilt my chin. "They never had a home of their own." His deep frown lines begin to smooth, satisfied with my response. Yet... "Your query sounded more like an accusation. Do you think royal families so incapable of being kind?"

Something like guilt softens his sea-glass eyes. "Maybe not all of them."

There he goes again, curling my toes with his words, and that smirk twists my insides in all the best ways.

I veer us to the right, avoiding the small trail that leads deeper into the dense forest and instead following the path to where the trees thin and unveil the masterpiece of a hidden lake.

The water is never the same color, changing with the tones in the sky. Today, it's a pale blue, as close to white as I've ever seen. Sun storks in tricolors of pink, turquoise, and orange flap their wings wildly as they break through the waterfall, enjoying a refreshing shower before resuming their calls.

Leith takes in everything from the soothing color and light reflecting along the gentle waves, to the rainbow that always appears beneath the fall on sunny days, to the flight of toadstool butterflies and the whoosh of birds zipping back and forth.

When Leith finally speaks, I can hear his heart is breaking. He takes slow, steady breaths, his eyes closing briefly. "Will you…show me the best view of this lake?"

In the brief time we've known each other, we've experienced many things together, good and bad, hopeful and not. But I know that the most important thing we've shared is happening right here and now. I walk toward the left side of the lake, guiding Leith.

We step carefully over the quartz that casts its own unique sparkles along the water. In a few more steps, we're here, where a large bed of moss and flowers awaits. It is the best and most comfortable place to nap on warm days like this, and it's the only place where the waterfall spills pink foam.

"The boulders at the base of the fall are rose quartz," I say before he can ask. "No matter the time of year, the sun's rays always find them. The minerals in the water have healing properties, too. I think it's because it's so beautiful"—I smile—"even the Erth's magic wants to be here."

He opens his palm. Strands of withering dark-blond hair tied together with string shouldn't speak such volumes. But they do.

Leith rolls the only remains of his friend between his fingers. "His name was Sullivan. I've been waiting for the right place to bury him," he says.

I remain silent. Right now, Leith doesn't need my words. He just needs my heart.

His tormented gaze meets mine. "I killed him. That day I fought the dragon. I killed my friend so I could win the match."

I know. I saw.

I'll never forget.

Leith's features are perpetually stone, not so much as a stitch of vulnerability in sight. Even now…save his eyes.

My chest aches for Sullivan. For Leith. For what it cost them both. "Tell me about Sullivan," I say, feeling how much he needs to.

The melody of birds and the soothing sounds of the falling water melt away. Leith's silence is unbearable. When he does speak, it's worse.

"We met when I was twenty-two and he had just turned forty. I'm not sure how we started speaking—we just did, even though gladiators guard themselves carefully."

Each syllable that flows from Leith's mouth holds enough emotion to fill this lake.

"There were long, cold nights when frost licked the bars where we huddled in the driest corner of the barracks we could find. There were other moments when we thought the rain wouldn't end until it drowned us." His expression softens. "Those were the best nights with him. We shared stories of our youth, of home. He had a biting sense of humor. Sharp as an axe. Even in those darkest days, he'd find some way to make me laugh." He almost smiles as if remembering something. "If it wasn't for him, I'm not sure I'd have made it through. Maeve…coming to Arrow…we just wanted a little more than what we had. We needed it."

Leith's body falls perfectly still. The memory is still raw. "That last match…Sullivan lost his legs and part of an arm," he says. "He was hurt beyond healing." He bows his head, the extent of his actions too wrong to bear. "That doesn't make what I did right."

Leith takes a deep breath and another. "You know what he told me? He said, 'What are you waiting for? Do you think I'd let *you* live?'" He curses and clenches the hand holding the hair. "The thing is, I think he would have."

I cup his face with my hands. "Leith," I say. "The hardest lesson I've learned as a healer is that sometimes, all you can do is end the pain." My bottom lip quivers. "Sometimes it's the only grace left to give."

He shakes his head, remorse heavy in his voice. "On the toughest days, even when fear battered me, I was never a coward. I was that day. I shouldn't have given in to those fucking rules. I should have held my ground and challenged any guard demanding I kill Sullivan—I should have demanded an audience with Vitor and Soro!"

"What would that have done?" I ask. The thought of Leith challenging them scares the hell out of me. I know Soro. Leith would not have made it far. And Vitor… He will do anything for the good of the kingdom, and he believes that's the continuation of the games. "Sullivan would have succumbed to his injuries, and they'd have an excuse to kill you, too."

"But I would have taken them with me," he snaps. His eyes darken. "I would have sliced them from throat to groin and torn out their hearts for what they've made us do—all for fucking coin!"

It's mostly true. Vitor and Soro forced Leith to kill his friend to satisfy the people's greed. And not just for coin—for blood.

"They cheered, remember?" Leith says, jolting me back to the moment. "The entire crowd was on their feet when I cut Sullivan's hair from his corpse. To them, I was another barbarian fulfilling his duty to entertain." He looks at me. "They never imagined that *me*, a gladiator, a *murderer*, would have the heart to honor his friend."

"I knew you would," I say.

Leith is brutal in the arena, but he's no brute. He's a good man who did all this for his family, long before he did anything for himself. And killer or not, he's capable of kindness that men with riches have never thought to give.

I hope that he believes me. "You were a true friend."

He turns away, gazing across the lake. "Sullivan would have liked it here," he says quietly.

His hardened exterior returns, yet he slowly drops to his knees, the blanket over his shoulders slipping away onto the ground as he clutches the pieces of his fallen friend against his heart. He closes his eyes and recites an old poem reserved for the brave.

The warrior,
He led the way,
Through blood,
Through fear,
Through rage,
But when death became the foe he could not beat,
He faced it willingly and at last won his peace.

I kneel beside him and lower my head.

When he's done, Leith scoops a section of moss away with a flat stone. With care, he places the strands of Sullivan's hair into the soil and covers them with the moss he removed. The flat stone becomes the marker to Sullivan's grave. It's simple and perfect amidst the bountiful flora.

I gently pull a lily from the cluster beside that and rest it over the grave, using the language of my elven ancestors to bid Sullivan infinite serenity.

This twisted bloodbath cannot be allowed to continue. It is a stain on our kingdom, on our culture. By the great phoenix, even if it means Vitor's death, I *must be* queen.

CHAPTER

21

MAEVE

"What must be done to win?" I ask the next day.

I'm in the north wing of the castle, the section that houses the barracks and the war chambers for the lieutenants and generals.

It's a miracle Soro isn't here.

A guard with thick red hair looks around, her blue eyes darting left and right. The squat man next to her does, too. Though we're in a quiet antechamber, that doesn't mean that other guards or captains won't walk in.

I'm taking a huge risk—they are, too.

I pass along two heavy pouches of gold. One for each of them.

The female guard pauses. "We can't take bribes. The Gaming Commission would behead us if we're caught tampering with the games."

That punishment is tame compared to what Soro would do.

"It's not a bribe, merely a gesture of appreciation. I'm the future queen, after all. Should I not know what spectacle will be hosted in *my* arena?" I pull a third pouch of gold from beneath my cloak. "Such loyalty will be rewarded further when I rule."

That's not entirely true. If they can be bribed now, I should not expect them to be loyal to me in the future.

The two guards share another look.

I hold my ground and keep my chin high. My grandmother taught me to look and act the part of queen. And by the stars, I will.

The man finally snatches the gold and shoves it beneath his tunic. "We don't know much, only that there's something foul in there. We've never seen it, but I hear it from its cell. Its screams... They ain't right, Princess. Never heard anything like it before, and by the phoenix I hope I never hafta again."

That sounds...just awful. How does Soro sleep at night? I sigh. Probably with Aisling. "Thank you," I say.

The next game will pose a problem. If even the arena guards don't recognize this creature—and they've seen just about every monstrosity this continent has to offer—how am I to prepare Leith to fight it?

"General Soro has many battles planned," the woman adds, giving the antechamber another cursory glance. "There will be a number of low-level games this week, mainly throwing the criminals in, letting them kill each other." She pauses and smirks. "But that's not who you care about, is it?"

I did make a spectacle of myself during Leith's last match, but I don't like what this guard is implying or how she thinks it's acceptable to take such liberties by speaking this way to me.

I lift my chin higher. "I care about *all* of Arrow." I look down my nose at her. "You should, too. If you are to be of any use to me."

I level each of them with a cold stare and then stalk away.

Outwardly, I'm perfectly calm. But inside, I'm seething.

I keep my steps measured and my expression even. I'm done hiding. I'm finished with playing at niceties while innocent people like Sullivan die and gladiators like Leith suffer.

While my father rots in prison.

I *know* he didn't kill my grandmother, and though we've been down this road, now, more than ever, I must uncover the truth.

I stomp to the main hall, teeth gritted, and slam the doors open with my palms. When several heads turn upon my entrance, I pause and collect myself. The need for decorum drilled into me by my grandmother settles my features into a practiced, serene smile.

Servants dip into bows and curtsies. Others act like they neither saw nor heard me enter.

The castle is torn in its alliances. There are those who still treat me as the princess I am and others who stare through me as though I don't exist.

But as the daughter of the Queen Killer, I've come to expect this.

They think me unworthy to rule because of the accusations against my papa. Some even whisper that he acted with the express purpose of stealing Queen Avianna's throne for his beloved daughter. They are fools. They're so eager to believe in the kind of treachery that they themselves would commit, they ignore the fact that Grandmother was already raising me to take her place someday. That there was no need to steal a throne soon to be willingly given. I know the politics and policies of this land. I've been training to lead Arrow my entire life, and nobody is going to stop me.

Chin high, I stride through the grand main hall with its vaulted ceiling and murals and tapestries lining the walls. The floor is a beautiful, polished onyx, with dark veins and swirling lines in the translucent stone. Giselle and I used to skip across it as children, hopping and racing from line to branching line to see who was faster.

A group of wizards is in the library. Dignitaries from other large city-states like Arrow stop to stare at me, not bothering to bow as I pass them. Some are Canvolish, others from Caelen's birthplace of Tunder. They've known me for years. There was a time when they would've stopped and chatted with me. But they see me as powerless now, and therefore useless. No matter. They will come to regret this…change of heart.

Several enter the lounge where breakfast is being served, barely sparing me a second glance. Each of the thirteen halls in this part of the castle will be occupied by now or filling up soon with meetings ranging from festival planning to taxes to foreign treaties.

I wonder what Leith will think when he sees the undertakings of Arrow. Regardless of the efforts of me and my family, I think he believes that all royals laze about every day, eating and drinking and searching out our next form of entertainment.

I glide into hall four, one of the rooms reserved for military planning. I am not surprised to see Uncle Vitor. He smiles. By his side, General Tut stands stiffly at attention.

"Maeve," Soro says, his voice as slick as an eel. "I was expecting you sooner."

I am late because I rode into the city this morning with Giselle, Father, and a contingent of Caelen's guards. Caelen may be a colonel of Arrow's militia and first son of a high-ranking family, but his loyalty is first to me. And my sister. Their relationship is special...even if it can never be what they deserve.

"My apologies," I say to Soro, not that I owe him one. I address the others present in this room. "Forgive me, esteemed council members."

Vitor scoffs. "She *was* here sooner. *Before* she went about her tasks in the city this morning. After she visited the new development Lord Jakeb has undertaken, dispensing clothes and food to those who just moved in."

My uncle is right, and although my routine varies, I work every day— usually out in the communities of Arrow—aiding in the areas that need it. Not that it's elevated me in power or otherwise.

Had my grandmother not perished and Papa not been sentenced to an eternity in the dungeon, the responsibilities I bear for this kingdom may have been praised, or at the very least noticed.

But she did die.

Regardless, *I* am still the rightful heir to this throne. And once I become queen, the people in this room will answer to me.

"Uncle, a new caravan of immigrants arrived this morning," I say, squaring my shoulders and forcing the leaders in this room to listen.

"Why did you let them into Arrow?" Soro huffs.

Our policy has always been to maintain an open flow of trade and peoples in and out of Arrow, given the lack of abundance beyond our walls. I don't bother reminding Soro.

I continue, "The outskirts along the western border are becoming more cramped—"

"That shouldn't be our problem," he says to Vitor and not me.

"It is if they reside in Arrow," I counter.

Soro rounds on me. "It wouldn't be if we stop letting them in!"

I pretend he doesn't exist. It's not hard. "There's a large, abandoned warehouse close to the city where they used to mill corn. I'd like to oversee construction to create more apartments within. If we can avoid overpopulating those regions, we can limit the risks of disease and fire."

Vitor is in long, blue, formal robes, his dark hair braided tightly. He frowns at something Lord Ugeen, that ass-kisser who cheats on his *many* ex-wives, whispers into his ear, all while staring at me. Ugeen is an odious human with a shaved head and round belly, and his beady green eyes narrow on mine. He should know better than to insult me before Vitor. He's trying to either convince Vitor I am his enemy or goad me into believing I've lost Vitor's favor. It's all I can do not to kick him in the groin.

He's been a raging knob since I declined his proposal. Vitor is not a fan of Ugeen, either, so I don't understand why the vile man is even here.

I clear my throat. "Uncle? What do you think of my suggestion?"

Tut, the ogren general in charge of surveillance, rumbles a laugh. He goes as far as leaning over to the other ogren general, Pua, who's charged with overseeing special operations, just to whisper something in his ear.

They're not talking about me. They'd never be that foolish.

What they are doing is behaving as if I hadn't said a word. My stomach sinks, and anger makes my face heat.

Tut was always kind to me, even as a child, but now? Is he like the others who only see a young woman playing advisor until it's time for her dismissal?

It's been like this since Leith beheaded my fiancé. Everyone knows it's unlikely I find another royal fiancé to take the throne back except Soro, and he would see that I was given even less respect as his queen. One more reason I need to put on a genteel smile and focus on helping Leith for the time being.

I blink up at Vitor innocently. "Uncle?"

Vitor continues to frown, but any anger he holds, he directs at Ugeen. I wait and wait some more. Finally, Vitor speaks. "Take what you need in terms of supplies," he says. "But as of today, our borders will be closely monitored for suspicious activity, and all who seek entry will be vetted by our soldiers first."

"What type of suspicious activity?" I ask. Like me, the others taking up every square inch of space, save Soro, can't mask their surprise.

Soro offers a placating grin and all but tells me to run along. "Maeve, we've told you time and time again, everyone is jealous of Arrow." He adjusts the white-and-blue medal of honor pinned to the chest of his uniform. "Can you blame them?"

I can't help but wonder if he's talking about himself.

"Where are Lord Jakeb and the Lady Giselle?" Soro asks, changing the subject.

I swallow the argument about the activity along the perimeter rising in my throat. Vitor prides himself on order and discipline. Arguing with him, especially in front of others, will not accomplish anything. "Lord Jakeb is overseeing the new construction in town."

Father seldom spends his days in the castle anymore. I don't want to announce that he had a harder time than usual after his most recent visit with Papa. He left to spend yet another day helping with the construction of low-cost residential spaces in New Arrow. It was Papa's passion project, and Father is determined to complete on his behalf.

Vitor's mouth turns down the way it does when something concerns him. Then he gives a short jerk of his head as though affirming something for himself before coming around the table to stand beside me.

It may be a small show of solidarity, but declaring the borders functionally closed clearly favored Soro.

"What reports have we received, Lord Regent?" I ask, peering down at the large map of the regions surrounding Arrow.

He points to the middle of our southern border but speaks to Pua, who is more than happy to sneer my way. "Mudslides, all through here, here, and there."

"How bad?" I ask, since Pua doesn't. "The area has received nearly twice its annual rainfall already."

Vitor purses his lips. "At least a quarter of the riverfront flooded, and a quarter more was destroyed when the mud and debris swept down the mountain bordering the River Tre."

"That's a densely populated area," I say. "And the floods will impact their harvest."

Lord Ugeen places his hand on Vitor's shoulder. "It's true, my lord," he says, posturing as if he were the one who spoke. "They will be severely impacted."

Ugeen is not a general. He has no post or position. He is the head of House Olgden. He's wealthy and owns mills and controls the mountain shipping routes to the west, but he's never taken an interest in policy like this.

Vitor gestures to a segment of our northwestern border. "Here, fires burned through large swathes of farmland on both sides of the border, though the Liburi settlements fared far worse than our own."

The thought of a raging fire sends a wallop of anxiety through my chest. I idly run my fingers over the scars on my jaw, but instead of recalling the pain, I recall how Leith caressed my face as if no more than a freckle marred my skin.

Tut taps the map. "It's as Lord Kaysoon said. Libur lost a great portion of its crops."

I recall the dwarf lord and the hardships he conveyed at the Summer Ball. We sold him rice and legumes at a profit. If Libur is beset by fires now, too, they'll be in dire shape.

The fires are along Arrow's borders.

I clear my throat. "How did the fire start?" I ask.

Soro surprises me by answering and jolts me back to the moment. "Don't you mean *who* started it?" He huffs yet again. "All this 'help' you insisted on sending—water, food, those stupid children's schoolbooks?—didn't solidify alliances. This Liburi scum wants what we have. They're tired of the handouts and want to be the ones handing out."

"How do we *know* this is what's happening?" I ask, one eyebrow raised.

Soro seethes. "Because I just fucking told you."

My grandmother's words whisper through my mind. *Do not ever let them see weakness or anger. You will be queen one day.* "Forgive me, *General* Soro. I meant to ask what *evidence* you have," I say, the diplomatic composure trained into me fully in place. "Present it so I may confront Eliana and Pralin. I've known both ambassadors for years."

Vitor waits for an answer. The rest of us do, too.

"It's a hunch," Soro finally says. "A strong one that this was an intentional crime."

"But who committed the crime?" I ask, pointing to the map. "Who *specifically*? Say this *was* an attack from the outside—does it not seem a greater threat to Libur than to Arrow?" I cock my head to the side as if asking out of genuine curiosity, then shrug when he remains silent. "Regardless, if the fire *was* set intentionally, as you suggest, we must discover by whom and for what purpose this act of terror was undertaken so we can take measures to prevent it going forward."

I glance up. "Uncle Vitor, ought General Pua take ten of his officers in plain clothing and see what they may find in Libur? If this was an attack on Arrow, those involved will surely brag about their actions or perhaps use our comparatively minimal damage—though life-shattering for the affected citizens—as fuel for propaganda to bring more rebels to their cause. Also, kindly send response teams at General Tut's command to the areas affected by the landslides and fires and let us determine the resources they'll need so that, if your High Lord wishes, General Tut's designees may take as many supplies as you recommend." I am speaking with an authority most in this room do not believe I possess. I can only hope my uncle feels differently.

Vitor appears bored. But then he nods and smiles. "You heard the princess," he says. "Set the plan in motion." He doesn't say set *her* plan in motion. It's purposeful. I know it is. At least, given how he's treated me, I know it is now. But I don't care. Not if it means we extend our help.

Tut nods at me respectfully right before he bows regally to Vitor. I get it now. He wanted action, not assumptions. So did Vitor.

Did Soro really think we'd declare war on a neighbor because of his hunch? For three years, *he* has been the one to beat into me the importance of "evidence" in order to set my father free.

"That will be all. We adjourn until noon," Vitor says.

The room starts to clear. But the council and foreign delegates are scarcely out the door before Vitor whirls on his son. "You call a meeting to say we're under attack, ready to go avenge Arrow when you don't even know the culprit!" He slaps his hand on the war table. "You know better, Soro. When will you stop acting the fool and think through your next steps?"

Soro clenches his hands, hatred for his father reddening his face. "I would have found out," Soro hisses. "All I needed was your word to get there."

Vitor shakes his head. "And then you bring that jester Ugeen into the meeting. For *what*? Fool," he says again.

Soro glares at his father, then turns and steps into the hall, slamming the door behind him.

I'm the last person who would defend Soro, but I can't help but wonder if this is the best way to go about curbing him.

"Uncle," I begin, speaking softly. "Why do you humiliate Soro this way, in front of the people he's meant to lead?" It's true. I despise Soro. That doesn't mean I agree with how Vitor treats him. "I would think they need to respect him as their new High General of Arrow, ever since you became regent."

"Respect is earned, my darling daughter, as you earn it by helping and treating our people." He runs his hand down his tight braid. "My son attempts to earn it in the brothels." He reaches for the platter of fruit at the corner of the table and snags a handful of grapes. He chews angrily. "Bah," he says. "Enough of this. Tell me something good."

"Father's reconstruction project continues at a rapid pace. You should see—"

"I know your father's skills, Maeve. I also make it a point to tour the new buildings."

Of course he does. The Regent of Arrow must take credit for it, after all.

"Has your gladiator survived?" he asks.

My gladiator. I really wish to speak of anything but Leith. "He is still recovering. The wounds and envenomation were severe. It's far too early to tell…"

Vitor nods thoughtfully. "I hope he makes it. He's an inspiration for Arrow. Our people need something to believe in…"

I was going to say it's too early to tell "how long he'll take to heal fully," but if Vitor believes that Leith is still close to death, it might buy him more recovery time.

In the back of my mind, I'm reminded of Aisling's words about Bloodguards. How only the ones approved by Vitor make it to the finish. By Vitor's words, I hope Leith has his approval.

"I'm glad you think he can inspire our people, Uncle," I feel compelled to say.

"I look forward to meeting him," Vitor tells me. But something in his deep tone carries a warning that punctures my heart with wicked cold. Even as he smiles.

CHAPTER

22

MAEVE

I leave my uncle as other officials and delegates enter the room, their voices competing in varying pitches and accents, interrupting one another and requesting a moment with him. The skirt of my floor-length dress brushes the well-tailored breeches of several men scrambling to Vitor's side. It's startling how they beg for his favor. I'm not sure I'll ever get used to this switch in power. Stars willing, I won't have to.

I was at Grandmother's and Papa's sides my whole life, until three years ago. They included me in conversations, taught me how to act, what to say, how to deliberate on big decisions, and how to interpret information that we received.

"Everyone has their own agenda," Grandmother used to say.

But since her death, and with Vitor assuming control as regent—because I am too young and unmarried and, let's be honest, because no one is ready for the Queen Killer's daughter to take the throne—I am treated differently.

But the blame is partially my own. I've not been as strong or visible as I should have been. In avoiding the arena, the grand parties and interactions at court…I've diminished my presence.

If I want to be queen, I must act like it.

Yes, indeed.

I decide to adjourn to my uncle's private council room and wait to speak with him alone. The way Tut and Pua acted...I will not tolerate such petty behavior. And Ugeen...I don't trust that jackass of a human at all. He should not be privy to matters of country. Thankfully, Vitor and I are in agreement on that front.

I enter my uncle's private chambers and stop short at a loud and pronounced moan.

I jump, which makes Soro smile. Eyes never leaving mine, he uncoils Aisling's legs from around his waist and lifts her bare ass off my uncle's desk.

"Maeve," Aisling says. "This is a surprise." She shimmies her gown's skirts down, not looking the least bit embarrassed.

Sparks of lavender magic color her pale skin as she slides closer to Soro's side.

Soro crosses his arms. "What are you doing here, Maeve?"

"Mm, my guess is she hasn't spent enough time with our cherished lord regent," Aisling drawls. She plays with one of Soro's braids. "Is there perhaps a way we can be of service?"

A way *we* can be of service? Aisling is getting rather bold with her claim on Soro. But she can't make Soro king. It's the one thing—besides a soul—I have that she doesn't. I suppose that's why she makes such a grand spectacle of placing her head against his shoulder.

"No, there's just something minor I need to discuss with the regent."

"Do you think he'll listen to you?" Her eyelashes bat as she looks up at Soro. "Perhaps your desires are best made known through his son?"

Aisling is well aware that I have more clout than Soro with Vitor. I should warn her she's feeding an already bloated ego.

Soro preens. "Aisling does have a point, Maeve."

"Does she?" I ask.

He chuckles, barely acknowledging Aisling even as he speaks of her. "Aisling has many skills." He shrugs. "Perhaps they can be of value to us."

"Us?" I ask. Hell would sprout daisies and sunshine before I'd ever consider Aisling an ally. The sweet talk is as phony as she is cruel. As children, she and her friends would bully Giselle, targeting her because she was small and weak and couldn't fight back. I could, and I did. That is, until Aisling's magic sparked to life. The woman is rotten all the way through. "There is no *us*, Soro," I say. "Not with you, and definitely not with Aisling."

Swirls of shimmering magic ribbon up her bare arms as she glances down at the way I thrum the hilt of my sword

Aisling doesn't like me seeing right through her. Neither does Soro.

"Go," he says.

I think he means me until Aisling's pinched features jerk in Soro's direction. "You need me," she presses.

"Perhaps." He nods thoughtfully. "But for now, Maeve and I have business to attend to."

Aisling rights herself, her chin up and her hips swaying as she strolls past me as if it's her decision to leave. Soro watches her exit, turning only when she shuts the door tightly behind her. He's taken many lovers over the years, but it appears Aisling's charm might have at last claimed whatever shriveled-up sliver of a heart he has to give.

Soro moves smoothly across the room and to that gaudy chair Vitor swears he'll never part with. It was supposedly a gift from my grandmother.

The back and seat are heavily cushioned and covered in rich, brown leather, the frame and arms real gold. The arms stretch upward at an angle to form a phoenix taking off into the heavens on each side.

Soro strokes the head of one phoenix before leisurely dragging his hand down the length of a body resembling a peacock, which once soared over all of Old Erth.

"Vitor doesn't respect you," he says. Although directing his words at me, he fixes his attention on the lead windows behind Vitor's desk. Each panel of stained glass tells the story of the phoenix. It starts with her as a hatchling breaking free from that single egg, as legend has it. Her body grows in each proceeding pane until her fiery feathers lengthen enough to take to the sky. The panels that follow reflect her fall from grace and her ultimate death. She plummets farther and farther yet. The last panel shows her sprawled across the field, a bloody sword beside her broken form. What a terrible fate for a being once regarded as a god.

"And as you know, he doesn't respect me," Soro continues.

I cross my arms. Soro and I once played together. I have memories of us reaching for each other's hands as his mother held him and Papa held me. Soro's mother tucked him against her hip, tickling his belly and making him laugh as he stretched out his hand, wanting to link our fingers. We were maybe three or four years old at the time. It's one of my earliest memories.

My "mother" was a concubine from a distant royal house contracted for the sake of conceiving me. There was no tickling or shows of affection. There was simply a role to play and a handsome sum to play it. As soon as I was weaned, she returned to her homeland and has not set foot in Arrow since—though she was, before my grandmother's death, always welcomed. There was a brief point in my childhood in which this arrangement bothered me, but I see now how lucky I am to have two loving parents. After Soro's human mother succumbed to illness, my former friend had none.

"I don't like the way Vitor dismisses you," I admit, remembering the boy who laughed with pure glee.

Soro caresses the chair's sculpted phoenix arm as if it is alive. It's not perverse, but I still find it odd. The way his hand strokes along the phoenix's back. She's not real, but she's disturbingly real to him. My fingers drag along the scars on my neck as I push the strands that have escaped my braid behind my ear. "I think you should talk to Vitor alone. Explain how his snub affects you."

Soro laughs, the diamonds and gems sewn into his long chestnut braids gently tapping the plush leather cushion along his back. Amusement tugs the corners of his mouth, revealing a hint of that little boy who adored his mother and used to be my friend. But as quickly as that glimpse arrives, it fades in a way that leaves me chilled. "You don't think I've tried?" His expression twists with rage. "Long before Mother passed, I asked—no, I *begged*—for him to hear me. But Vitor always had someone smarter and more *experienced* to listen to. Does that sound about right, Maeve?"

I notice the way Soro refers to his father as Vitor these days. It's an intentional effort to sever their connection.

"Why aren't *we* working together?" he asks. "We're just whispers in the wind alone. Wouldn't you rather be a shout that echoes from atop a mountain for everyone in Old Erth to hear, *to heed*?"

"I've no interest in a dictatorship," I say. "My goal is to do right by Papa and Arrow."

He pushes away from the awful chair, stalking toward me, all but snarling as he readies to pounce.

I hold my ground. There's an inch at best between us as we meet face to face. "Work with me. Marry me. And let's show the High Lord who is really in control."

Dear sun above, he means it.

"And what will I get?" I say, forcing my voice to remain steady. I will never marry him, but I need to know what he plans.

Soro lifts his hand, watching me as he strokes the skin just below my ear that bears the marks from that fire. "What do you want?" he asks, his eyebrows arched. "Besides freeing Andres?"

"I want control of the games," I say, my voice stern and unyielding. He drops his hand, and I continue, "I want to return to the days where opponents could actually walk out of the arena alive—"

Soro paces to the chair and then back, fists balled. "No," he says. "That's the one thing I have in this bloody place that's all mine." He points to himself. "I make the games what they are. Vitor handles the betting side, but the obstacles, the genius behind each challenge—they come from *me*." Soro shakes his head. "Why do you think Vitor hasn't encouraged you to marry?"

The abrupt question stops me cold.

"Your birthday is fast approaching," he says. "You'll be of age at twenty-one. You've only to marry a royal, and the crown will pass to you…"

Where is Soro going with this?

"Why do you think there are no other noble houses offering up an eligible spouse for you to marry, Maeve?"

Because of you, I want to say, but I hold the words back.

"Do you think *I* influenced them?" He chuckles. "Well, maybe a little. But more so, Vitor held that honor. Why do you think he did that? Because he values you so much that he's focused on your happiness and truly finding the best husband for his dearest princess?" Soro snorts. "Don't kid yourself. Vitor only remains regent and retains power if you fail to marry."

I suck in a breath. *Oh, Vitor…*

"My father will never be king, Maeve. He knows it. It's why he doesn't openly praise you even when you're right, even when you exhibit the sort of critical thinking and leadership skills expected of a queen. He doesn't want to empower you because in doing so, he loses the power he steals from you."

It's a truth I've long seen and suspected, but I never expected to hear it out of Soro's mouth.

My "uncle" often supports me and exhibits fairness, but I'd be a fool to think him wholly benevolent. Vitor serves Arrow and himself above all things.

Soro levels his gaze. "My father will accept me as your king because through our marriage, he thinks he'll still be in control."

It's true. Vitor doesn't respect his son, and he treats me like I'm still thirteen. It's not a leap to assume he intends to rule through us. For *us*, so to speak.

If I'm to reclaim my rightful throne, I must stop conflating the uncle who taught me to fight and trained me in military strategy, the elf who carried me on his shoulders and read me stories, with the regent who is blocking me from my destiny.

Vitor loves me, I know, and he loved my grandmother so much that I often wondered at his relationship with the queen. He never left Grandmother's side after—

"Soro, what really happened the night of the fire?"

"The fuck, Maeve?" His eyes narrow, and his body tenses.

Is he rearing to hit me? I shift my stance, ready to block or counterattack if necessary. My right hand slides to the hilt of my sword again. "You know so much about everything. Tell me what happened."

I'm not stupid. The two people who have benefited the most in the wake of my grandmother's demise are Vitor and Soro.

They have motive. They have means.

They convicted and imprisoned my father.

And I...I have no memories of anything that night.

Soro's caught off guard. Why? He lived in the castle with us when it happened. He flicks a loose yellow gem free from his hair. "You actually don't remember?"

As the gem skids to a stop at my feet, a lump forms in my throat, threatening to choke me if I don't swallow down my fear. I asked for this.

Why am I so afraid?

"There was a candle on the bedside table. It toppled over, but it's not known how. Its fire caught on the canopy of the bed you were sleeping in with the queen."

By some blessing of the stars, I keep my face neutral. I've heard this story countless times. It's the same shit I heard from Vitor and even my own father. Except...I hadn't slept with Grandmother in years. Why would I do so as a grown woman?

"The smoke rendered you unconscious."

That much, I *do* believe. I coughed for weeks afterward. No number of elixirs or potions could clear my lungs completely. Because I was unconscious from the smoke, I have no memories of the fire or its immediate aftermath. I'm lucky to have survived, I know.

"Avianna tried to gather you in her arms," Soro says. "But she'd also inhaled a great deal of smoke and wasn't moving well or thinking clearly. From what Vitor says, Andres wrenched you from her arms but left her there to burn."

"Why?" I ask.

"Why do you think?" he asks, genuinely confused.

When I don't answer, Soro huffs a sigh and plops onto that ridiculous phoenix chair. "Maeve, Andres wanted your grandmother out of the way. He saved you from the fire. He got *you* out. As a general, as the *prince*, he should've saved the queen. But he didn't. I know you love your papa, but he didn't just abandon Avianna." He leans in. "He pushed her into the flames when she tried to rise. He killed the queen."

My stomach twists as disbelief mixes with anger.

Even after hearing these words over and over again...I just can't make myself believe them.

Despite the trial, the purported witnesses, even Papa not denying a single thing...it just doesn't make sense. Papa would never hurt Queen Avianna, his own mother.

Worse, Soro isn't gloating or baiting me. He isn't even trying to be cruel.

I've known him my whole life, and right now he's speaking with sincerity. Whatever the truth may be, Soro believes what he's telling me.

He expels a deep breath when all I do is stare. "Maeve, look. Forget

Avianna. She's gone. You want the throne, take it, but take it with me as your husband. I need you for the throne, and you'll need me to handle what you're incapable of doing on your own."

"And what is that?"

He smiles. "Painting your hands with blood."

CHAPTER

23

LEITH

The woman standing at the door to the cottage is not Maeve.

Giselle is wearing brown today—gloves, dress, boots, cape. She looks like a fucking tree trunk. A nice tree trunk, but still... "What do you want?"

She turns behind her, to where Caelen, his hair braided above the shaved sides of his head in the style of Arrow's military elite, raises his eyebrows at me. "Did you see where it went?" she asks him. The little thing lifts her skirt and checks her feet. "It's got to be around here somewhere."

"What are you doing?" I demand.

"Just looking for my will to live," she says. "Your idea of a good morning sent it running." She offers me one of her hands. "Care to try again?"

Her leather gloves give me pause. They're thick, closer to what a blacksmith would use, and very unlike the fine dress and cape she wears now.

She clears her throat.

I roll my eyes.

"Good morning, Giselle," I force myself to say, shaking her hand quickly.

I nod at her companion. "Caelen."

A nod is all he offers, and I could give a damn.

She claps her hands. "Splendid. Let's go. We need to be back before nightfall."

She snags my wrist, but I don't budge.

"Come on, the horses are ready. Why are you dawdling?"

I do not *dawdle*.

"Where do you think you're taking me?" I growl.

Giselle simply beams. Perhaps her will to live is back in place. "Your barracks. Maeve has business in the castle, and she asked us to escort you." She spreads her arms. "See, the fun has just begun."

I debate telling her and her companion to piss off. But I do want to return to the barracks. And there's a sentence I never thought I'd say, but I need to retrieve some things.

We mount, and they mercifully allow me to set the pace. We follow a bumpy, barely there trail through the forest surrounding the Iamond family manor, and I even manage to keep my seat as we do it. Credit for both achievements is owed exclusively to my mare, Star. Giselle rides just behind me with her bodyguard beside her. He doesn't say much, but I've noticed Caelen always shadows her, and not for the first time, I wonder at their relationship.

Star's heavy hooves pound against the moist ground, kicking mud and grass up behind her. The sound reminds me of those damn drumbeats in the arena, and I grimace, hating the way my body instinctively tenses in preparation for another fight.

As we reach a break in the trees at the top of the ridgeline, the terrain starts to change. A long, winding road snakes down this side of the incline. As we descend, the lush pines and dense forest give way to a rocky landscape littered with weeds and thorny plants and not much else.

Caelen draws to a stop partway down. "This is it?" he asks, pointing to the barracks in the distance where I lived with the other gladiators.

"Yes."

Rows and rows of large wooden buildings with poorly patched roofs fill a vast, walled square. In each tower along the points that make up the compound, royal guards, bored to pieces, pretend to keep watch.

A dense copse of thorned fire bushes—red-leafed plants that burn like hell if the leaves touch your skin—ring the barracks walls, keeping us in and everyone else out.

"Which is yours?" Caelen asks.

"The one at the end, on the left," I mumble, but it's sure as hell not *mine*. It's where I was brought as a fresh recruit and where I met Sullivan. He'd been there longer. We didn't talk right away. No one did. Why strike up a conversation with someone who'd likely be dead in a week? Or worse, someone who might become a friend.

As we follow the weather-beaten path down to the barracks past the bare patch of dirt where competitors are loaded like wild animals into the caged wagons that transport us to the arena, we have a good view of the open area where we practice. It's mostly dirt, sometimes mud or even ice depending on the season. Beq the ogre wields his favorite stick, howling a challenge to those practicing throwing longer sticks like spears on the range.

"Come!" he calls. "Fight."

Several others duel hand to hand in designated sparring circles beside him. Some turn, debating whether to take him up on the challenge. Most don't. He's good with that stick. He's also good at swiping your shit if you don't hide it well enough.

Caelen frowns as we close in on the compound's tall, spike-topped iron doors. I almost laugh at the way he looks at the old rusty things, his features alerting me that he's offended by this place.

"They don't have barracks on the front lines?" I ask.

He shakes his head. "Not like this. As a former soldier himself, Vitor provides the best care to Arrow's fighters."

Well, therein lies the difference. General—*Regent*—Vitor prizes his militia. They're valuable. We're nothing more than live entertainment.

"My lord?" the sprite guard calls from her perch at the tower. She flaps her gossamer wings as she lands. She's not greeting Caelen. She's just confounded by the fact that he's here. I get it.

"No one is permitted within a mile of these barracks unless first screened by Lord Vitor," she says. She and the others hold their ground as much as they dare. Caelen comes from a noble house, and he's a high-ranking military official in his own right.

Giselle, though, is the one who replies. "This gladiator has earned favor from our beloved Princess Maeve, and she currently sponsors him," she says. "We're here to collect his belongings and be on our way." She loses her polite tone. "Move," she tells them.

The guards flanking the sprite edge away, not wanting to offend Caelen, who has his hand on the hilt of his sword.

The sprite steps back, her beelike eyes blinking madly. Her lingering apprehension softens when Caelen drops several coins in her palm, and she damn near sinks her sword into the cohorts who rush in to demand their share.

We slide off our horses, tying their reins to a designated post out front, and Caelen motions for me to take the lead.

The slanted buildings inside the camp are made of mismatched wooden beams with colors ranging from the gray of an old man's beard to the brown of toadstools pushing through the dirt. Caelen straightens as a group of gladiators spills from the opening of the building to our left and rushes to the rear of the compound, a battle cry rising.

"Who are they attacking?" Caelen asks, sweeping Giselle behind him.

"No one," I say. "It's Tuesday. Their building gets to eat first."

We cross the yard in the direction they ran. The line stops in front of Heene, the human cook, who lifts one of the wooden bowls from the stack beside him and pours a ladle of fairy elm soup.

He's generous with his helpings. Everyone knows it, which is why they're all but stoning one another to be first.

Never mind. They *are* stoning one another.

"They're hitting each other with rocks!" Giselle gasps, echoing my thoughts.

"Yes." I shrug. "Except for some wooden swords you couldn't stab through parchment, weapons aren't easy to come by here."

The guards march forward to break up the fight. Not quickly, mind you—like I mentioned, they're bored to shit. Heene pours a bowl and hands it to the troll who's smart enough to move away from the escalating brawl. He dips all six fingers of his right hand into the soup and licks them clean. He must enjoy his broth with a dash of dirt and sweat.

Caelen pulls Giselle along to keep pace with me. They had stopped to watch, not understanding the gladiators in the food line were probably going extra hard in the hopes of winning Caelen's or Giselle's favor. No.

They're not in danger of being killed. Not here with me. But they will get more attention than they're ready for.

"They feed you broth here?" Caelen says. "That's your meal."

He doesn't bother calling it fairy elm soup. Probably because it's not damn soup. It's just like he said. Broth. And broth is bullshit.

"It has protein, and the cook adds minerals." I point back toward the barren, rocky expanse that we traveled over in the last leg. "This was a quarry at some point," I say, explaining.

"They add rock dust to your soup?" Giselle is incredulous.

A pang of resentment builds, and I tamp it down. It wasn't always like this here. And the circumstances I—we—found ourselves in were not of Caelen's or Giselle's making.

I cut a sharp left, stepping over a body. The barely conscious elf came from my homeland of Siertos. He arrived less than a month ago. He claimed he'd never heard of my family and walked away from me into a group of gator shifters that had impressed him more. The bite mark along his bare chest tells me they weren't as impressed by him.

Every new arrival is "tested." Some fare better than my countryman did.

The barrack where I sleep is the next one we reach. I think that, like the rest of the buildings, it once had a porch. The pillars that support the overhang remain, but the wall that should separate the outdoors from the indoors is long gone, to create more space for all the idiots like me who were recruited for a game no one really wins.

I step into the empty room, thankful we arrived during mealtime. Dragging two nobles through a barrack full of gladiators is *not* my idea of fun. Our wooden "bunks" are really just stacks of large, rectangular crates, piled five high and open on one side. The bucket of water in the corner is our sink, and the uselessly barred window at the rear is a place to relieve ourselves when the weather is too perilous to reach the shitter.

I arrived from Siertos during one of the worst summers Arrow was said to have endured. I almost chose the bunk in the center, where I could stick my head out and enjoy some semblance of a breeze. But then I noticed that older men, even giants, all chose beds against the walls. There was one left with a few people eyeing it, so I claimed that one for myself. Everyone else took a bed in the center. Though the heat made it tough to sleep that first summer, I thought about hanging a blanket from the top beam for privacy, and I eventually did. Not even for the peace I sought, but to keep out the harsh wind and cold that struck us the moment summer surrendered to fall. The actual walls in this place did little more to buffer against that cold.

When it came to attacks during the night, the middle bunks took the brunt of them. Vulnerable in all directions.

Since then, I graduated to the third level of bunks. I feel for the tear in my meager bed pad, rummaging through the lumpy, straw-filled sack until I find the letters from my family hidden inside. I tuck them into my shirt. It's the only thing I came here for. The only object in the world I care about. Just holding them grounds me so much that I almost smile, remembering the day I showed Rose how to sneak her letters into the courier's cart to send for free. In my absence, Beq the ogre may claim my spot. Let him. I'll take it back, but I'll be damned if I let him screw with the things I can truly call my own.

I've started to lead them out when Pega, Ioni, and Rye saunter in.

"Told ya it was Leith," Rye says. A gash on his forehead held together by stitches Ioni or someone sewed is bright red and infected.

My injuries aren't infected, my clothes aren't hanging by threads, and I'm not dirty. I'm healthy. I'm fed.

I don't think I've ever felt worse.

Rye wipes his dirty face with the back of his hand. It doesn't do him any good, since his arms are about as clean as his bare feet.

Pega tries to smooth out her bright hair when she sees Giselle. "Nice cape," she says, not meaning it. The dwarf looks no worse off than the last time I saw her. No better, either. "Ya nanny press it for ya?"

Giselle unfastens her cape and hands it to her. "I'm glad you like it. Consider it yours."

Pega stares at it hard. She wants it, but we all have our pride. It's a constant tension, accepting help versus surviving when we can only depend on ourselves. "I'm not your charity case, Princess."

Giselle makes a face. "And I'm not a princess." She pulls a large pouch from a pocket hidden in the folds of her skirt. "What I am is your new sponsor who is generous with gifts."

Ioni tries to take the cape. Pega bites his hand. "Ouch!" he yelps.

"My sponsor, my cape," Pega tells him. She beams proudly.

Sponsorships used to be more plentiful. But with matches to the death, gladiators aren't a great investment anymore.

A shadow thumps its way into the barracks. Holy hell. Luther!

Relief showers me like a warm summer's rain. He's better, but his leg still looks bad. "Heard…you…here." He grunts and I think even smiles. I know I do.

"No…touch!" he grunts.

I turn and realize he's talking to Caelen, who's leaning over Pega's bunk, looking into her cups. Some are filled with dirt and others with filthy water. "Yeah. Don't touch them," I warn.

"I wouldn't," Caelen says. He eyes me closely. "They're maggots."

"And leeches," Pega adds, smiling proudly with what remains of her teeth.

"They're not her pets," Caelen says, stating the obvious. He sighs, weary. "This is what you use to clean your wounds?"

I keep quiet. He already stated the truth.

"What else do we have?" she asks. She looks back to Rye. "Come on. You need a good leeching if we're gonna keep what's left of your forehead."

Rye takes a seat opposite Luther. Luther used to sleep on the floor, but a few weeks ago, a bunch of us removed two of the bunks and put them end to end so he could have a bed. It was Sullivan's idea, even though he got mad when Luther thanked him.

"Um, before you use your little buddies over there," Giselle says, appearing a little green, "take these."

Luther's small eyes widen to their fullest when Giselle pulls out several small vials from the pouch. "For…me?" he asks carefully.

Giselle nods and starts handing out Maeve's treatments. "For all of Leith's friends."

Ioni laughs. "So, we're friends now. Is that right, Leith?"

Maybe they are. Shared misery has a way of bonding people. Why not? I answer with a small nod. Ioni's eyebrows shoot up into his hairline, and then his mouth curves into a tremulous grin. Pega opens one of the vials and scrunches her wide nose. "How do we know these work?" She's smart to whisper. We might be alone for now, but the walls are thin, and you never know who will pass by.

Luther holds out his leg. It's not perfect, and neither is his health, but it's a damn sight better than what it would've been. "It work," he says.

The gladiators hurry forward. I help Luther, and Pega and Giselle alternate between Ioni and Rye. We try to keep quiet and move fast. Around here, these potions are worth more than gold. I can ask Maeve for more later, but for now, I want to help those closest to me.

Caelen ambles to my side, watching me rub the paste Maeve created onto Luther's red and oozing knee.

"There's supposed to be an infirmary," Caelen says. "Was that a lie, too?"

"Nah," Pega says. "That's still there."

"Why not go, then?" Caelen presses. His revulsion is as obvious as the damage to Luther's leg. He's not disgusted by the injuries. He's disgusted by our situation.

"Why should we?" Ioni mumbles. "So they can drug us, cut off our limbs because it's cheaper than healin 'em, and claim to have saved us? Nah, then we really wouldn't survive, would we?"

Giselle shakes her head and hands out envelopes stuffed with mixtures of healing herbs.

"Make sure Ned gets some," I add softly.

Luther nods.

"The ones with red ink treat burns," Giselle explains, taking a cue from the gladiators to lower her voice. "The blues and greens fight infection. Yellow, mix with water and drink it slowly. That one's for fever."

Maeve wrote instructions on the envelopes, but Giselle is the one who recognizes that not everyone present can read.

There's a shift in the wind and voices approaching. I don't have to tell the gladiators to hide their stashes.

"Time to leave," I say.

Giselle takes Pega's wrist and pulls her along. I guess she's going to take that sponsorship seriously.

"You remind me of my nephew," Pega says, her tone gathering a sadness I haven't seen before in her. "Always dragging me about, showing me something."

Caelen turns before we leave. "The gladiator Pega will stay with me, but I shall return with whatever you need."

Luther, Rye, and Ioni nod and smile their thanks, and for them, that's a lot.

The sun has just begun to set as we head out.

A group of guards is carting an ogre's body away as two others fight over his abandoned stick. Beq is dead.

I don't have to worry about him taking my spot.

I just have to make sure I'm not next.

CHAPTER
24

MAEVE

The guards step away from the doors leading to the dungeon. I am wearing one of my brighter dresses in Papa's favorite shade of gold. I lift the hem so I don't trip. Vitor notices, and he takes my arm to keep me steady as we make our way down the uneven stone steps.

His hand on my arm doesn't offer the warmth or comfort it once had. How can it when the seeds of doubt have grown such deep roots?

The torches barely illuminate this dank place as their weak flames flicker, casting shadows that writhe like living things across the stone walls.

I wish I could remember what happened. What *really* happened the night of the fire.

All I recall is following my grandmother through a corridor—nothing of sleeping in her bed or other such nonsense, despite what I've been told. The only thing I remember after that is Father's voice calling out to me, telling me to come back to him. I awoke the next morning in Papa's and Father's chambers with my grandmother unmoving beside me, covered in burns.

It was awful. I remember screaming and Father comforting me. Papa no longer could because he was here, in this horrible dungeon.

I jerk when the torch just above us sparks.

"It's all right, Maeve," Vitor says, stopping so I can gain my balance. "It's just going out."

I nod. Everything about fire now haunts me.

My thoughts drift to my grandmother as we continue our way down.

Vitor adored the great Avianna of House Iamond, perhaps more than duty required in the century following my grandfather's death.

During the three years she wasted away in a coma, he spent hours a day at her bedside, always hoping for a cure and commissioning healers from every corner of the world.

If he wanted the throne so badly, why would he go to such drastic measures to save her?

When Grandmother died, Vitor was gutted.

Clutching my skirt in one hand and Vitor's arm with the other as we descend lower still, I try to reconcile the conversation I had with Soro with what I've known of the elf beside me, and I struggle.

We are nearing the bottom when a low, guttural moan echoes off the walls—the only sound save for my own heavy breaths.

I drop my gaze as a hundred doubts creep in.

Up until my grandmother died, I'd clung to the hope that she would awaken and clear Papa's name. When she died last month, that hope died with her. Now, it's up to me.

If I can't clear Papa's name and discover who truly killed the queen, marrying Leith is ultimately the best choice, and not just because of how hard I'm falling for him.

"I'll wait for you here," Vitor says, erasing Leith's face from my mind. He takes a few steps back and crosses his arms.

I adjust my skirt and step into the dark corridor that leads to the cell at the end where I'm told Papa spends his time.

I take several long breaths, my eyes already moist with tears. Giselle says Papa is in terrible health. He won't get better unless I get him out, and damn it, I *will* get him out and I will heal him. I pass several empty cells. Because of the recent "attacks" along our borders, I know Soro will fill them soon. If he doesn't send everyone straight to the arena, that is. If Soro had his way in the council chambers, he'd be leading a raid along our western border already.

The cells are nothing more than small stone rooms with a plank to sleep on and a bucket in the corner. Surely Papa isn't kept in one of these. He can't be. His health has deteriorated too much for him to endure these conditions.

When we reach the end and I see him, my stomach lurches. His living quarters are better than the cells we passed, but not by much. Within a half-moon space, beyond the curve of a containment wall no higher than my waist, sits my sweet papa. No bars or locked doors needed, only a gate that swings easily open. He is too frail to even stand. At least he has a cot rather than a plank, and some bedding. On a battered wooden stool next to his cot are several books and Father's silver hairbrush. I kneel slowly in front of him, forcing a smile, though it's nearly impossible.

He's curled into himself, the blanket Neela knitted covering his skeletal frame as he stares blankly at my face. His hazed eyes widen with recognition, and he reaches out for my hand.

Vitor, who has decided to follow me after all, places his hand on my shoulder. "Be careful. He might hurt you."

I shake my head. Failing state or not, my papa couldn't hurt a stinkfly. And he definitely wouldn't hurt me. "Hi, Papa," I say in an uncertain voice. I smile, cupping his hand gently. "Hi, Papa," I say again.

I turn my hands so he can hold them in both of his.

His long gray beard tapers around his face in smooth strands, brushed to a shine—no doubt by Father, who Giselle says visits daily. Besides feeding him, it's the only way Father has left to express his love. It doesn't sound like much, but it is everything to Father, and maybe to Papa, too.

Right on time, a kitchen servant bustles down the steps and offers me a wooden bowl filled with stew. Steam from the soup rises in a cloud in the frigid air. I reach into the pocket deep in my skirt and remove a potion embedded with herbs that should help his appetite.

"Thank you," I tell the kindly troll, whom I recognize from our days in the castle.

My smile dwindles when I look up at Vitor standing beside me.

His features are hard like the stones lining this dungeon. He doesn't seem to want to speak. No, that's not it. He doesn't want me here at all.

I've stayed away because I was told Papa had asked for me not to visit, but after my conversation with Soro earlier, I decided to come anyway. Maybe he doesn't want me to see him like this, but if he changed his mind and decided he wants me here after all, he's too weak to even speak the words now. Tears blur my vision as I dip the spoon in the bowl.

Vitor's attention sways between Papa and me as I feed my father. I talk to him about what I've done since the last time I saw him. I tell him of Giselle and the estrellas and how Father and Neela have taken up chess again. I don't talk about Leith, not with Vitor standing over my shoulder. When I wipe Papa's lips with the hem of my robe, a rat scurries up his shoulder, and two more on the opposite side.

"Did you make friends, Papa?" I ask.

My father has always had a special connection with small animals. All of our estrellas followed him home. My grandmother had a similar one with birds. He must have bonded with these little creatures. Good. I don't want him to be alone.

Evidently convinced I'm in no danger, or maybe just bored by our one-sided conversation, Vitor leaves us and climbs the stairs, his footsteps growing fainter as he nears the top.

I don't realize I'm crying until Papa pats my tears with a section of his beard. But then he releases his beard to trace my scars as if he's never seen them before. "It's okay," I assure him. "They don't hurt."

I hold Papa's hand and stare into his glazed eyes. "I swear I'll get you out," I promise.

There's no response from him as I say my farewell and kiss his cheek, and my heart feels as empty as the rows of cells lining the corridor.

I rise to leave, but Papa's voice, gravelly from years of disuse, holds me in place. "Bye, Maeve. Love, Maeve."

I freeze, tears dripping over each syllable I manage. "I love you, too, Papa."

CHAPTER

25

LEITH

I shadow Maeve for several hours through Arrow's main market in Ellehna Square. Caelen or Giselle must have reported back to her about our barracks visit yesterday, because we've been winding through the crowded market for hours now, in search of herbs and plants. What seems like every variety of them.

I'm alert to anyone who might harm her. It feels unnecessary—the people of Arrow are far less a threat to their princess than her own noble class—but old habits die hard.

Maeve seems distracted, her eyebrows drawn together and her lips pressed thin. She's different today. Sad or frustrated, maybe.

I'm not sure what changed her mood, and though I'm of a mind to ask, sometimes we need to hold fast to our grief and anger. It gives us the strength to do the things we need to do.

And Maeve does a *lot* of things, I'm learning.

She gathers whole handfuls of dried herbs from a market stall and shoves them into the basket she carries before handing over several coins from her belt pouch without haggling. We move to the next stall, where an elderly ogre greets her in his native tongue, a series of clicks and words that feature chuffing and whistling sounds.

I glance at Maeve again. I think she intends to heal every fighter in the barracks. Maybe she'll be able to return things to the way they used to be in the arena.

What stands out most about her is that she doesn't do anything by half measures, and, well, I like this trait of hers a whole lot.

Her hair is loose around her shoulders today, two thin braids on the sides keeping the rest of those smooth strands off her face. A faint breeze blesses us, and the smell of her homemade mint-and-rosemary shampoo distracts me momentarily.

When she looks up, I pretend I've been watching a little girl with brown curls and brown eyes who's holding tight to her mother's skirt with one hand and a doll in the other. The mother is placing an order for purple flowers for the upcoming festival commemorating the death of the phoenix. "Hmph," I say.

"My, you're in a chatty mood today," she teases. She nudges me with her elbow. "What's on your mind this time, you wizard of words?"

You, I want to tell her, but I don't because that's the way it should be. I think. "That little girl looks like Dahlia," I say. "Except Dahlia never had a doll. The only thing she really had to call her own were these green shoes Rose passed down to her. She slept with those things, she loved them so much. And when she slept, Rose would sew any small holes shut and reinforce the stitching so she never had to take them off."

"Oh," Maeve says, suddenly lost in thought.

I cock an eyebrow, unsure whether she's pitying me, my sisters, or all of us. But I don't push. Not this time.

"Leith, look." Maeve points ahead excitedly.

My hand drops to the hilt of the sword Jakeb gave me as I narrow my gaze. I don't see any immediate threat, and our exit pathways are plentiful.

Maeve hurries forward, and I follow her to another market stall. This one has red silks draping over the top and amber flags anchored above it that hang lankly and slither in the slack breeze.

The colors are of my home country.

"Belladom," she says.

I frown as I draw even with her and the dwarf manning this booth. His bright smile is smarmy, and I wonder for a second if I should just take him down. Probably not, though. *Pity.*

"Come, Princess," the dwarf says. He lifts a vial containing belladom oil and removes the stopper. He wafts his hand over the perfume. "The rarest and most prized scent in all the realms."

I huff. "Our ancestors used it for bug repellant."

The dwarf frowns at me. He recovers his smile and continues selling Maeve on his wares. "The scent is nature's purest aphrodisiac." He waggles his eyebrows.

As if she needs any help in that department.

I reach for one of the actual seeds. It's large, about the size of my fist, and oblong. Holding it triggers a slew of memories. Roasting the outer leaves over the fire, my mother wrapping rice and legumes in them to give us extra nourishment. It was the main staple of my people's diets for centuries. Until the outsiders discovered the hard seed's unique scent and the wealthy classes of the realms began to covet it.

Maeve's brow furrows with confusion as she addresses the peddler. "It attracts…"

"Any one you wish to attract," he promises.

Bullshit.

"I always thought belladom was some sort of cactus," Maeve says, eyeing the seed I hold and glancing between it and the many perfume bottles the dwarf has arranged.

"Belladom grows in the desert," I say, "but it sprouts underwater during the flood season. Don't ask me how, but the floodwater mixes with the sand in a way that fertilizes the plants. Each flower produces a single, prickly fruit containing one of these. The needles must be scraped off with a knife before you can eat the flesh or get to the seed."

Maeve's hair sweeps over her shoulder as she turns to me. "That's very laborious."

Indeed. I spent eighteen hours a day suffering in those belladom fields, and this merchant will make more money off the sale of one vial than I made in a year. I set the seed down. A vicious urge to grab the man and drag him out of his fancy stall has my hands curling into fists.

I step away before I do something stupid.

"Don't go, my lord. Come, have a sample," the dwarf insists.

I'm not his lord, and I want no part of this. The mere aroma of that shit churns my gut and brings back harsh memories I'd sooner forget.

"Leith, wait," Maeve calls.

But I keep walking.

"Leith."

I pause farther down the line of market vendors. It's not her I'm mad at. It's the memories that surfaced upon seeing belladom again.

She grabs my hands when she catches up to me, and I look down at them, hardly recognizing them anymore.

"We'd wrap our hands the best we could," I tell her. "It was painful. And it was hard watching the children learn — "

"Children?" Maeve asks, horror puckering her brow.

I don't need a mirror to know my features harden. The kids would cry, thinking they were being punished. I push away the memory of when Rose and Dahlia were old enough to work. Dahlia sobbed as I pulled the needles from her bloody hands every night, and Rose would clamp her jaw and go deathly silent as I removed the spikes rammed into her nail beds. I curse a few times. It's what ultimately led me here. I just wanted my family to stop hurting.

Maeve's fierce eyes stare straight ahead. "That perfume will be banned."

Yeah, it should be. I agree. But…what would Siertos have to barter or sell without it? The region relies on belladom for its entire economy now. "I don't think it's as simple as that, Maeve."

She sighs. She knows it isn't.

"Come on," I say, turning away from her. "Let's finish this excursion and head back to the manor."

"I'm almost finished here," Maeve says, grabbing my hand to lead me around an ogre pushing a fruit cart.

I thread our fingers together. I don't question the rightness of it. I just enjoy the feel of her hand in mine and the reassuring squeeze of her fingers as she offers me a silent comfort for all the pains of my past.

There is no need. I am determined to live in the present.

Eye on the prize, I remind myself.

She leads us to craftsmakers section of the market, plopping me in front of a case of big, shiny knives while she speaks to a man selling baby toys at the next cart over. I look at her quizzically, and she mouths the word *estrellas* with a smile. I can't help but smile back. Of course the lemur puffs get a gift, too.

"This will be perfect for Toso," I hear her tell the man. "He's learning advanced commands already. Can you believe it?"

Keeping one eye on Maeve, I allow myself to admire the gorgeous feats of blade smithing in front of me. It only takes a moment for my eyes to catch on something wonderful.

"May I?" I ask, reaching for the lone boomerang blade on display. I can hardly believe she even has one—what citizen of Arrow is going to purchase a weapon native to the southeastern deserts of Siertos? Other than me, of course. Once I secure my Bloodguard winnings, perhaps I'll commission a few. I always meant to teach Dahlia and Rose the art of its wielding.

"Good…taste." The giantess nods eagerly. "One of…my favorite."

"Mine too," I say, testing its balance in my hands. "This is beautifully crafted. And wicked sharp, too."

The blacksmith beams, then even more so when I toss the weapon in the air, one end spinning over the other in consistent, precise rotations, and catch it with ease.

"Ah! Not many…can wield…boom…er…ang." I toss it once more, even higher this time, and once more on top of that, to make us both happy.

"Impressive!" Maeve says, returning to my side. "Where'd you learn to do that?"

"Back home." I shrug, but pride is brimming in my chest.

"Then we'll take it," she says to the bladesmith, passing over quite a few coins more than it's worth. I should probably protest, but, well, I *want* it, this little slice of home. And who am I to take coin out of such a lovely craftsmaker's hands?

"Thank you, Maeve," I breathe. "Really. I'll pay you back as soon as I can."

"My, there's no need for all that." She winks. "You'll be a great help to me with this thing. The wizard's elm grows all its most potent leaves at the very top, after all, and it's not the only one."

"Then those branches don't stand a chance." I grin and tuck the boomerang blade into my waistband. I honestly can't remember the last time I had a day this good.

Maeve takes my hand and guides us out of the market and down a desolate alleyway.

The quality of the homes diminishes quickly.

"Where are we going?" I ask, unease settling in my bones.

"I have one last stop," Maeve says. She must sense my tension, because she adds, "I'm sorry, Leith. I'm not purposely trying to frustrate you."

"I'm used to it," I grumble.

She chuckles, and I feel my mood lighten even more. Funny how a day out with Maeve will do that to a person.

There are few shops on this primarily residential street. One barely the size of Maeve's cottage, but with tables spilling out into the street before it, advertises hot, spicy cider and meat breads. The scent has my stomach growling, and luckily for me, this seems to be our destination. Unluckily, Maeve drops my hand before stepping inside. The place is nothing special by noble standards, but it's dark and defensible, and the scent of warm bread mingles with that of freshly brewed ale. It's my kind of place.

A seleno fairy, as sensual as they are frightening, fans the hot cups of cider she places on a large tray with the fingered tips of her leathery black wings. I tense. In terms of mobility, winged creatures have a natural upper hand. Thankfully, the room we're in is too small for flight. Her ebony bat ears droop when the *bang, bang, bang, crash* of steins and ceramic plates precedes a row of cursing.

A guapilla struggles to place the broken plates and cups she's dropped back onto her tray, her long green-and-blue hair as frazzled as she is and her gray skin blushing to purple. "Stasia, I'm so sorry," she says. "It won't happen again."

Stasia, the seleno fairy, blinks back at Maeve and gives her a look — one that says she curses the day she hired the girl. "It's *fine*, Gabi," she bites out through her fangs.

It's not fine. Not for Gabi. At least not on land. In water, guapillas use their flippers to swim impressively quickly and majestically. On land, be it genes or some type of curse cast onto her people, their feet face backward. She must have some reason for being here instead of her homeland, but I'm sure as shit not asking her.

Gabi walks forward — I mean, backward — or...never fucking mind.

I don't know where the hell she's going, and neither does she. The precariously stacked pieces of plate and stein *clink*, *clink* on her tray. She kicks forward—yes, definitely forward this time, seeing as her knees are backward, too.

"Your order will be up soon, Princess," Stasia tells Maeve—two meat pies, four sausage rolls, one cup of hot cider, and their tallest mug of ale. I almost swooned when she said it. Stasia takes in Maeve's scars. She reaches out to hold her chin. Maeve, understandably caught off guard, freezes. Gently, Stasia tips Maeve's face to the side to better see the injured tissue. It's only because Maeve allows it that I allow it, too. Stasia releases her. "I'm sorry this happened to you."

"Thank you, Stasia," Maeve says quietly.

"But it is good to see you again after all these years." Stasia bares her fangs, and Maeve responds with a smile.

Gabi finally makes it back to the serving station. Stasia, who looks tired and broken for reasons bigger than anyone present today, pats Maeve with her leathery wing-hand. More vampiric than their colorful and pretty fairy cousins, the seleno are fierce warriors. They fought against Arrow when Old Erth was still young. It's odd to find one here.

"A friend?" I ask.

Maeve doesn't answer me until Stasia enters the small kitchen. "I cared for her daughter," she says.

"A child?"

"No," she replies. "Stasia and her daughter, Sueneh, came to Arrow like many others looking for work. When they couldn't find a way to support themselves, Sueneh signed a contract to fight in the arena. She... didn't win her last fight, and I couldn't save her. What little she earned was enough for Stasia to start her business. It wasn't enough to mend her heart. Losing her daughter broke her."

"I can only imagine," I say bitterly. I don't have children, but may the heavens help anyone who hurts my little sisters.

Maeve glances up and rises to greet a pair she introduces to me as Uni and Neh-Neh, a cyclops couple and proud new parents. Maeve gushes when she sees the baby girl clutched in Uni's beefy arms—apparently, she not only delivered the little thing but saved her life somehow. "She's so curious," Maeve says. "Look at the way her eye darts all around, taking everything in. Smart baby!" she coos.

After a brief catch-up—and who knew there were so many questions one could ask about one newborn baby?—Maeve returns to her seat and reaches for the cider Gabi successfully dropped off along with our food, pausing to blow on it before taking a sip. "I love babies." She tastes her drink and smiles, then asks, "Do you…" Her voice trails off as a red flush creeps over her face.

Want children? Dream of family? I don't know exactly what she's about to ask me about babies. I only know that I refuse to let myself think that far ahead about my life. Not yet. Not until I'm Bloodguard. "We should eat quick. It's late," I say, shoveling in a bite.

It takes only a few minutes to finish our meals, and soon we are headed back toward the market square to retrieve our horses.

The squalor of Arrow is too vast to hide in this area. The houses, which I can imagine were once made of brightly colored stones and sweeping curved roofs, with blooms overflowing their flower boxes, have been reduced to dull, empty spaces with broken roofs, the plant life dead and hanging like the long, blackened fingers of a goblin oak.

"I never would have known this part of Arrow existed," I admit. "Even if I did and reported it back to those in Siertos, they'd never believe me." I curse under my breath. "None of the realms would. Everyone outside this kingdom thinks it's a paradise. What fools we've been."

"You're not fools," Maeve quietly insists. "It was better when my grandmother still ruled, but it wasn't perfect even then. Upon her injury, Arrow suffered—and it's not just our realm but also abroad. Vitor balances our interests with the larger economy of Old Erth. We send aid to our allies where needed, and we barter and trade to keep our defenses and coffers strong. But the entirety of Old Erth is strained. Soro believes war is inevitable." She glances at me. "Maybe it is."

"What will Arrow do then?" I ask.

Maeve's face stills, but she keeps walking. "Arrow will fight."

"What about Vitor?" He's the one in control now. He makes the decisions.

She lowers her voice. "My uncle will do whatever he must to keep Arrow strong."

Maeve's hair flutters like wings against her back as a brisk wind cuts through the alley. *Mm, rosemary and mint.* I wish she would wear it loose like this all the time. It suits her.

We proceed. Some ransacked shops and two-story homes are roofless, their wooden upper floors falling through the ceiling and pushing out through once-grand windows.

"Many of these houses look abandoned," I say.

Maeve nods. "Soro claimed he was stopping crime in these poor areas, but it appears all he succeeded in doing is ridding the poor areas of people."

She glances at the remains of a home three stories tall. "Papa loved Arrow. He would have been a good king—the best—following in my grandmother's footsteps. When Papa is free, things will be different."

"If you free your papa, will you step aside and allow him to rule until it's your time again?"

"I thought I would. For a long time, that was my plan." She's quiet for a moment. "But this *is* my time, Leith," she says, her voice reflecting her determination and her misery, too. "Papa will never be the same after... everything." She lifts her chin like the queen she will be. "I will free him *and* make Arrow as wonderful as he dreamed."

The fierceness Maeve regards me with when speaking of liberating her biological father rivals some of the worst opponents I've encountered in the arena.

I thought we had nothing in common, but here we are, both willing to take on monsters to help the ones we love.

My duty was to play bodyguard today. Between watching out for potential threats and dissecting our conversations, I haven't contributed much...but some things should be said. "Maeve, you could take on the world."

Her reddening cheeks don't stir a grin from me this time. I regard her as intensely as she regards me.

She looks away first, whispering, "With you by my side, nothing shall stop me."

CHAPTER

26

LEITH

The moment doesn't last long. I'm on edge, my instincts warning me that something is wrong as we walk through this run-down neighborhood.

The sound of soldiers marching is distant at first but quickly strengthens in volume and numbers.

"We should get out of here," I say, taking her hand and pulling her down a side street.

"Wait. What are you doing?" Maeve asks.

"Soldiers are approaching in droves. Why? It's late. Too late to do anything good."

We don't get far. Maeve digs in her heels. "I'm the princess of Arrow, Leith. I'm not running and hiding."

I don't think she understands the danger her own soldiers present with that knob of a lord and general in charge.

Wood splinters from somewhere behind us. "By the order of Lord Soro, we demand you open up!"

Maeve whirls. "It's a raid." Her shocked eyes narrow to slits. "He's looking for more immigrants to imprison."

I grab her elbow and pull her back.

"Let me go," she bites out. "I must stop this."

"No," I hiss under my breath.

"Ye can't come in my home without a royal order!" an old woman yells.

"Get out of my house, you filthy bastards!" a man with an accent similar to Ioni's hollers.

Breaking glass follows the echoes of furniture and bodies being shoved away. "The princess shall hear of it," another man adds.

"I'm counting on it," Soro shouts back.

It's this last comment that has Maeve fighting me. I pull her close, taking care not to hurt her as I drag her around the back of the building.

"They need me," she insists, voice cracking.

"Not in pieces," I counter.

When we hit the alleyway, I don't stop to argue. I run ahead, my hand around her wrist. If she digs in again, there's a good chance I'll pull her arm from its socket.

"Keep moving," I order.

We weave down a series of alleyways. I don't know where the hell we are, and after taking two consecutive lefts we run the risk of turning a square and circling right back to where we started.

"Shit."

I pause. Maeve sighs. She points to a red house. "There. That building."

I look ahead to the horizon, where the sun has begun to disappear behind the mountains. That's when it occurs to me how truly late it is. The encroaching darkness will cover any trail we leave, so there's that. We can weave through this town and lose them before circling back around to our horses at the market.

But the cover of night will also benefit Soro and his pack of guards, concealing whatever atrocities they might commit.

"Do you know this place very well?" I ask.

She still isn't thrilled with the idea of running, but she's resigned to my plan—at least for the moment.

"We're just at the outskirts of the new development project Father took over for Papa."

The red house has a heavy metal door, and even I can't get it to open.

The stomping footfalls of many guards echo along the narrow streets.

They're coming. And at a quick clip.

I can't let them get to Maeve. There's no telling what Soro would do to her in a sadistic state like this.

I spin and draw my sword.

She slaps her hand over the scabbard. "Not yet."

She points up to the second-floor balcony on the bright-orange house next door. Maeve takes a running leap, barely making a sound, flips over the rail, and lands. She turns and offers me a hand. *I'm good*, I mouth, hoping she doesn't expect me to pirouette or some shit.

I follow without any help, though not as quietly. And without any flipping. Bloody hell, it's like she's a damn acrobat. We leave the balcony door open. I can hear the guards close by — maybe even below — and any movement would only attract their attention.

I glance around the dim room.

Well, hell. This is a kitchen. It has maybe one or two rooms branching off it and stairs that lead into the rest of the house. Multiple families must live here.

We're mice in a box.

Maeve checks the closed doors. One has shelves stacked with bowls and wood platters, a bag of dried beans, and a second sack of grains. The other opens into the bedroom next to it. A dead end. So not real helpful, either.

"There," I whisper. I point to the hearth.

Maeve doesn't question me. She hurries over, glides around the cooking vat, and squats down. After a quick look up the chute, she glances back at me, grimaces, and then starts to shimmy up.

I can't fit around that giant cauldron the way Maeve did. It's suspended on a beam by iron hooks, so thankfully I can swing it out and slip behind. As I squat in the hearth, taking care to step on the edges of the hearthstone and not the ash or burned logs at the center, I see what Maeve was grimacing about. It's tight as a sewer pipe. I don't know that I'm going to fit. And sure as shit, this isn't the best idea, but something tells me confronting Soro and his guards right now would be even worse.

She swears her papa is innocent, and that means her grandmother's killer is walking around free. Vitor is in control right now, and by extension, so is Soro. Being alone in an isolated part of the city, where he's stirring up trouble to have an excuse to arrest the innocent...

No good comes of us crossing paths tonight.

If Maeve dies, there is nobody to stand in the way of one of them taking over the throne—permanently. I've heard all about the crown reverting to the other five houses, but I for one think they'd have a hard time supplanting Vitor. Like a sabre-cat, he's sunk his teeth in deep.

Cinders and ash are dislodged while Maeve shimmies upward, hands and feet against the wall in front of her, leaning back so her body is wedged against the other wall of the chimney. I follow her lead, back pressed against the opposite wall, and then pause, remembering I moved the cauldron. I drop down a few feet and extend my leg to pull the beam back in. By the time it's in place, the clomp of feet on the stairwell echoes through the walls.

Maeve braces and spreads her legs so I can climb up higher.

We're near the top, and I can see a spattering of stars overhead through gaps in the chimney's cap. I debate knocking the cap off and getting us both to the roof, but I don't think we can risk the noise with Soro's militia so close.

In this position, Maeve's arms are on either side of my face. My arms brace beneath hers. And her legs...sweet baby phoenix, her legs are on the outside of mine, so she's sitting on top of me. And that yellow dress—it's bunched around her waist.

She starts to slip, and I reflexively grab her by the hip.

Big mistake. Her thigh is toned, and she curls her leg around my waist, anchoring us together more tightly.

"I was hoping it'd be bigger," she rasps.

I don't think she means me, because, yeah... "The chimney?" I ask in a strangled voice.

"Yes. Let me try something," Maeve says, moving around on top of me for a different angle.

She's trying to help.

She is positively no help.

Her front is now getting better acquainted with my front. And the tightened tips of her breasts are now pushing into my chest.

It has a very immediate effect.

"Uh," Maeve whispers. "Leith?"

I don't mean to rub against her. She's the one moving against me. She spreads her hands against the wall, shuddering. "I'm sorry," she breathes. "I don't mean to, to…"

My chin falls to rest against her shoulder, and my lips graze her ear. "You don't mean to what?" I whisper, clinging to the last shred of my honor.

Maeve swallows hard. She groans.

It's not her fault we're in this tight space—figuratively or literally. And as for my body's reaction… Well, I guess my body could give a damn that there are a dozen guards stomping up the stairs. Danger isn't doing a thing to dampen this woman's effect on me.

Maeve squirms and makes a small sound that causes a big reaction. I grit my teeth.

"I'm not trying to p-play games," she whispers.

"I didn't take it that way," I whisper back. I'm glad it's dark in here, because I swear on my life I might actually be blushing right now. She seems nervous—possibly more about sitting on top of me in a chimney than about the guards searching the house. I'm making her anxious, and that doesn't sit well with me.

I try to lean away, but I don't get far. There's nowhere to go.

The door to this room slams open, and we both freeze. The other doors are opened and closed. The table is flipped on its side. Glass shatters, and it sounds like shelves are broken.

I lean forward until my lips brush her ear, and in the softest voice I say, "If they find us, I'll drop down and distract them. You climb up to the roof. Hit the cap as hard as you can manage and run—"

She shakes her head. Her lips brush my neck. "No." Her arms and legs tighten around me. "Together."

Well, that's not happening. Only one of us can drop out of this cramped space and hope to draw a weapon, let alone fight off enough of Soro's guards for the other to escape.

"I saw them, Lord Soro," one of the female guards says. "I swear to you, they came in through the balcony."

That we did. More doors slam as the rest of the guards are likely sweeping through the rest of this home.

"I'm not your lord," Soro says. "What I am is the future king who will cut out your tongue if I find out you have misguided me."

There's a chance we'll still be discovered, and I change the position of my hands so that if I must drop, I can pry Maeve off me.

The guards' yells echo through the chimney as they continue to ransack this place. I'm grateful that whoever lives here, if they even still do, doesn't seem to be home. I don't imagine this search would have ended well for them. Soro is known to keep dogs, although mercifully they don't appear to be with him tonight.

As it is, I hope there are no shifters among his guards. Their sense of smell is above all others.

Little by little, the room goes quiet as everyone leaves. I swear Soro lingers. It's like I can feel his presence, patiently waiting like a coiled snake. The slightest bit of movement, and he'll strike.

Seconds stretch to minutes. Maeve's breasts rise and fall against my chest with every intake of air, hardening her nipples further. I rub my face against the side of hers, intending to bring comfort. "It's all right," I whisper.

My lips graze the side of her neck, sliding over a scar until soft skin is all I feel. Not quite a kiss but close, and closer yet. She leans into me, breath hitching. My mouth is almost on hers when I realize what I'm doing. I'd slap myself upside the head if I didn't need my arms to hold us up.

We're wedged in a chimney right now, far from her home or any reinforcements. At least a dozen guards and one very vicious lord general could still be searching for us. No. This is *not* how I keep Maeve safe.

I crane my head away from hers. "Climb up," I tell her.

Her gasp this time isn't one of pleasure but one of hurt. Then she's moving, as agile as a spider, climbing over me and scaling her way to the rooftop. Soot and who knows what else fall as she goes. I wait for her to flip the cap. It gives easily, but it's still louder than I'd like. Thankfully, there aren't any other sounds from the house. No one coming. No one going.

My arms are trembling from holding us up for so long, and my leg—the one shredded by eels—is shaking so bad I'm not sure it's going to hold my weight on the other side of this.

Soro and his guards could still be in the house. If it was me in his place, I'd continue to wait.

"I don't see them," Maeve whispers down to me.

That doesn't mean they haven't laid a trap. I inch my way to the top and pull myself out. I'm too tall and too big to bend a leg, so it's awkward dragging myself up to a sit and then working each leg, one at a time, out of the chimney. The only upside is it gives me a minute to rest, so when I do land, I don't collapse.

"Go," I tell her. "Don't look back. I'm right behind you."

She doesn't hesitate. Maeve runs along the rooftops, nimbly leaping from one to the next. I'm not familiar with this part of Arrow, and I follow her, hoping she's leading us toward her home or a busier section of the city where more people will provide a distraction or at least bear witness to whatever Soro was plotting.

I grab her hand when we're at the last house closest to the market. From here, we can see the hitching post where we tied the horses.

They're gone.

Maeve curses.

I consider our options. We could circle back and find a rooftop to hunker down until morning. We could take our chances and head toward the castle, relying on Maeve to rally the troops and all those still loyal to her family. Or we could try to make it back to Jakeb's manor on foot—

A hulking cyclops comes into view, holding the reins of both our horses. It's Uni. He pauses and looks up as if to say, *What are you waiting for?* Maeve jumps right off the roof.

Damn it, woman!

She leaps toward the house beside this one, catching onto the second-story window ledge, then stretches down with her toes to balance on the top of the first-floor door casing before dropping quietly to the street in a crouch, her sooty skirt billowing around her as she lands.

I'm strong and agile, but I don't possess that kind of balance. I lower myself over the side and straddle the walls between the buildings, dropping and catching the walls with my hands and feet to slow my descent.

Maeve mounts and waits for me.

"Is the road clear?" I ask Uni.

"Go," he bids us. "May the phoenix keep you safe."

CHAPTER

27

LEITH

"I didn't get to ask Uni... Do you think Neh-Neh and the baby are safe?" she asks.

I hope so. Soro and his guards were mere blocks away when we reached the city limits. "He wouldn't have waited for us with the horses if she wasn't."

She nods, and something of a burden seems to lift off her shoulders. Her horse, Knight, trots silently next to Star and me. For such massive animals, moon horses can be shockingly stealthy.

"You seem close with them and their community," I say.

Maeve grows quiet. "When a family of wolf shifters from Tanlita arrived, an odd infection plagued them and many in the surrounding area. I've never seen such an illness—fever with these odd patches of stripped skin. With knowledge from Neela's people, I was eventually able to brew an elixir that helped them heal. But the shifters didn't make it."

"Damn," I say. "They're so hearty."

Maeve plays with the reins, fiddling with the straps when she realizes how badly they're twisted. "I know. But they were infected first, and I couldn't come up with a remedy in time. I was able to help everyone else—specifically those in Uni and Neh-Neh's part of the city." She sighs but doesn't seem to beat herself up about it. That's good. A healer with perspective. Maeve really is the finest person I know. "I just hope Soro doesn't seek them out."

"Would he have a reason to target them?" I ask. I don't know enough about Arrow's internal politics.

"No. But..." She shrugs. "It's hard to say. Soro doesn't trust any of the newcomers to Arrow. The infection I just mentioned, along with a few others that were just as unfamiliar, sparked prejudice. If he had his way, he'd cast them all out and not let anyone in."

That's a sentiment that contradicts everything Arrow stands for. It's long been a realm of peace, of opportunity, of equality...or so the stories go.

Well, I learned firsthand that most of that is bullshit, but this is the first I'm hearing of a high-ranking royal—a general, no less—actively campaigning to abolish open borders or to punish immigrants.

"Soro picks fights solely for an excuse to fine them." She quiets. "Or worse, as you know."

She means the "criminals" that they've started throwing in the arena with us.

"Vitor...as regent," she whispers. "He could stop these raids. But he doesn't, and I truly cannot conceive of why. I've asked several times. Instead, he'll throw me a bone on something less controversial. He's not the same man I once considered family."

We ride into the Iamond family stables, dismounting and passing the reins to a sleepy attendant. I scratch my steed behind the ears and promise to bring her an apple in the morning.

Before we even leave the stables, Maeve is swarmed with chittering balls of fuzz. The estrellas reach into her saddlebags with grabby fingers, and Maeve—laughing, radiant with joy—pulls out the little trinkets she bought them at the toy stand today. A particularly large one delicately plucks a stuffed dog from her palm, sniffs it, then bounces away, tail high. Maeve is still beaming as we cross the lawn to the main house.

Candlelight flickers at every window of the manor, and moonlight doves huddle along the eaves, the brightening moon adding a sheen to their dark-purple plumage as we step onto the slate terrace and make our way toward the rear entrance of the manor.

Maybe I shouldn't, but I take her hand in mine. Maeve stiffens at the contact but almost immediately clutches my hand as if afraid to let go. The way I hold her isn't the same way I clutched and half dragged her during our escape. It's gentle, intimate in a way I've never felt before.

"Leith, Vitor has his moments where he hears me so well and is so incredibly kind." Her hold on me tightens. "And then he does something like tonight, where he turns his back and allows Soro to run amuck…"

I find it hard to believe Vitor is ever really kind. It's simply a side he shows Maeve so what little power he grants her, she actually believes she wields. But they have a history, and tonight is not a night for scrutiny. She needs someone to hear her, so I do.

I look back, continuing to ensure that we weren't followed. I couldn't have defeated Soro and all his guards alone, but had they threatened Maeve, I damn well would have tried.

"You'll need to increase security," I tell her. "You know that, right?"

Whatever the status quo was with her "uncle" and his heinous son, I'd bet my sword arm that things have changed. Tonight was proof of that.

She nods.

"Thank you for helping me today," Maeve says. "Can I tell you something without you taking offense?"

I shrug. "Probably not."

She laughs, then bites her lower lip.

"What is it?" I ask.

"I paid for a messenger hawk to deliver your earnings after your last fight, like you wanted," she says.

"And…?"

"I did something without your blessing," she admits.

I square my jaw. "What else is new?"

She laughs in that way that lights her eyes despite the dimness. "It's something good. I promise," she tells me.

On an evening this dark, Maeve shouldn't appear so exquisite. But like the sun's, the moon's rays are her friend, reflecting off the shiny strands of her loose hair.

"Oh," she says. "I almost forgot. I'll just be a second." She opens the door to the manor and lifts an envelope from the kitchen table, leaving me in suspense. She returns to the terrace when she realizes that I didn't follow her inside.

The soles of her leather slippers scrape along the slate stone. She extends her hand. "Here," she says, practically bouncing in place.

I close the distance between us until she's near enough to touch. But I don't take what she offers, too engrossed in her gaze to spare a glance at her hands.

Maeve saves me the trouble of drawing closer when she inches forward to roll the ties on the front of my shirt between her fingers. "You mentioned your family doesn't have much in the way of clothes."

I tilt my head. "That's right, which is why you sent them as much as you did when we made our agreement."

"Well, I sent them more, and blankets, and a couple of children's stories, too."

"Why…" I hold out a hand. I know why she did it. She's Maeve, and this is what Maeve does. She cares for those who need caring. "How did you manage?"

"The messenger hawks you told me about. Neela—you know Neela? Our grandmother troll you want to do naughty things with?"

Oh, she'll never let this go. "Yes, I remember," I admit. I also remember how Neela pelted me in the back of the head with an apple the first day I took a walk around the grounds. In her defense, it was a damn good throw, and that apple was delicious.

Maeve shrugs playfully. "Well, Neela secured several. I didn't realize how much they can carry and decided to make it worth the trip." She smiles. "When Neela paid the remaining charge today, there was something waiting for you."

She offers me the small envelope.

"What's this?" I ask.

"A letter from home," she says.

Joy pierces my heart. My pause is brief. I attack the envelope containing the letter. Mother never learned to read or write, but Rose has learned enough to scrawl words onto a ratty piece of parchment paper.

Deer Leith,

Erth quaqes hav sterted heer. They hav us all skared. Wee receeved wut u sent. It helpt Dahlia. It helpt us.

Thang u. We mis u n r blest by ur sakrifeyce.

All ower luv,

Rose

"I helped them," I say. I look up at Maeve. "Dahlia is doing better."

Maeve jumps and claps in place. "Leith, you saved your little sister and helped your family."

I frown when something occurs to me. Maeve leans in. "What's wrong?"

"No, it's just…" I reread Rose's letter. "Something is off."

She tilts her head, questioning me but careful to avoid reading the letter. "How so?"

Again, I take in each word. "You sent my winnings from my last match."

"Well, technically Neela had them sent." She's so close her arm brushes mine. "Given your family's situation, we sent everything as soon as we could manage. What are you upset about?" she asks.

"It's probably nothing," I say. "But it usually takes longer to hear back from them. A month, sometimes two." Perhaps Rose is getting faster and they were able to send this letter back with the messenger hawks. The thought makes me happy.

She bites her bottom lip. I wish she wouldn't. *I* want to do it for her.

"I sent all the medicines and elixirs I had."

"Thank you, Maeve." And damn it if my voice doesn't quiver.

"I don't have any more aja mushrooms. But the moment they come into bloom, I'll get them. I know a spot now. I promise—"

"I know you will."

She saved my baby sister.

No. Maeve saved them all.

It doesn't matter if the terrace is dimly lit. It's clear Maeve is blushing. I cock a brow. "Is there something I should know?"

"You mentioned earlier today that Dahlia never had a doll," she says. "So, I went ahead and placed an order to get one made and sent to her." Is this why it took so bloody long to pick out estrella toys this afternoon? She was ordering a custom doll, too. "One with big brown eyes and short black curls, as you described her. Oh, and with the green leather shoes you said she always wore—"

I haul her to me and kiss her. It's not a hasty kiss. I take my time, passing my lips over her lush mouth. With this woman...I'm lost.

I cup the base of her head and encircle her waist with my free arm.

Maeve's stunned pause is brief, and then her body melts against mine.

Her fingers slide into my hair, her lips moving in concert with mine.

Then there's no time for thoughts.

There's only the feel of her skin and the sounds that she makes, those little breathy moans that I feel down to my bones.

I'm lost completely in the feel and taste of her. The way my arm fits perfectly around her waist, and her pounding heart as it beats against mine.

I nip at her throat, and she releases a gasp. I silence it by feathering my lips over hers.

One pass.

Two.

Three.

That's all the restraint I have in me before I devour her.

I press myself tighter against her, bowing her back, my tongue seeking more of her taste.

Her impassioned moans stir awake fireflies as large as my hand. They flutter up and out from deep within the garden, circling us as silver cicadas and glen-berry frogs greet the bright moon with a serenade.

I'm barely aware of them. Beneath the moon, the stars, the dark-blue sky, there's only Maeve...

CHAPTER

28

LEITH

That kiss marked the first of many.

It's not something I meant to happen the first time—or many times thereafter—but I won't regret it. With Maeve, each moment seems to take on more meaning. Or maybe it's just that time is not on our side.

Maeve's birthday draws near.

Only a couple of weeks away.

Soon, I'll be called back to the arena. If it wasn't for this Memorial of the Phoenix festival, I could've been summoned to fight *today*. I'm healing but not near my normal bearing. I can only hope I regain as much of my strength as I can during this reprieve.

"This is foolish," I tell her. "If you wanted to attend the parade, you should've gone in your carriage with your father and sister and a full regiment of guards, as your station demands."

"I wanted to go with you," she says simply.

I let those words settle over me.

Her eyes are bright and hopeful, her smile tremulous.

She tugs the hood of my cloak down, covering the top half of my face completely. "It's more dangerous for you than for me."

I debate reminding her that there is no escaping the danger ahead. I need to become Bloodguard. She needs to become queen. Instead, I say, "It's fine. It'll be dark soon."

"This way," she whispers.

Her smooth hand wraps around mine, and then she's tugging me ahead, through the steep, upward-sloping alley at the north side of the city, closer to the castle.

Maeve continues to keep her head down, and I do as well. She leads us through a small gate and into a garden, where vines of starberries the size and color of ripe plums twine along the dilapidated posts of a graying fence that's one strong gust of wind away from falling apart.

Maeve kneels in front of the fence and motions me over. I steal another glance behind me before closing the gate and falling to one knee beside her.

I peer out and down to possibly the very best view of the main street. A fairy with light-green skin zings from side to side above the crowd, her shimmering wings fluttering with the escalating frenzy of the stragglers trying to find a good view.

"Sweet bread, fresh sweet bread!" she yells. Her accent, faded from her years in Arrow, reminds me of Sullivan. Her homeland must be Witoria. I make a fist when that familiar sense of grief threatens to pull me in. He should still be here, strategizing with me to take these evil games down. But he's not. I'll need to figure out things on my own in order to prevail the next time my feet press into that filthy sand in the arena.

Maeve rests her head on my shoulder, and as naturally as I blink, my anxiety fades. I curve an arm around her, relaxing my clenching fist, and sweep a kiss along the top of her head. With her, loneliness fades and the grief lessens.

"Ale," the light voices of sprites carrying mugs call out. They zip down the street opposite and then back, their strength far surpassing their tiny bodies. "Some ale to enjoy during the parade," they say in unison.

We're high enough to easily see everything through the wide slats in the fence. But it's almost impossible for anyone to see us, even without the camouflage the berries and vines provide. Beings from all walks of life take up every inch of space along the sidewalks and rooftops below. Given the garden rests almost at the peak of this hill, we're well above the winged sprites flying below.

I have a good view of what's coming, and I'm fairly comfortable. There's just one last thing I missed. Maeve squeaks as I yank her into my lap, her back resting against my chest. I tug her earlobe with my teeth. "Shh," I say. "The show's about to begin."

Her back bounces against me when she laughs, and while I can't see her, I can picture her smile.

"How in Old Erth did you ever find this place?" I ask.

Maeve angles her neck so I can see her face, but she's no longer smiling. "The house with the white door used to be Neela's home when she was little. Her family couldn't afford it, so they lost it. She used to bring Giselle and me here as children. I think she missed living here, but I also think she wanted to show us how easy it is to gain and lose in Arrow."

I nod.

Many fortunes are made—and lost—in the arena.

Maeve motions around. "Father built this garden for her in honor of her family. It was something her mother always wanted. And he purchased her home so that she'd never lose it again." Tears find their way into Maeve's voice. But like always, she forces them away. "As queen, I'll make sure everyone can have a home." She turns to see my expression. "You think I'm foolish, don't you?"

"No." Optimistic, perhaps, but never foolish.

"There are ways to create opportunities. It isn't simple, but it *is* possible. Investing in our communities benefits all of Arrow." She waves a hand, and I sense her frustration. "I've shown Vitor the programs I want to implement. When I'm queen, I won't have to ask or plead to initiate my plans." She takes a deep breath. "I won't have to try and convince my peers to do the right thing."

I only nod. She has ideals and hope, and though I suspect she recognizes she won't always win and her plans won't always yield the results she seeks, Maeve will not give up the fight. Of that much, I'm certain.

When those dreadful drums begin, I clutch her hand harder than I intend.

"Leith?"

"Sorry," I mumble.

She pats my hand. "As queen, I'll end these games."

She felt my tension, and again she eased it.

Cheers erupt along the winding road, closest to the edge of town, and they grow as the procession commences.

The celebration of the phoenix has begun.

The purples and blues of twilight have barely begun to crawl across the horizon when the first eruption of magic paints the sky in a mix of green, gold, orange, and red. Oh, what lengths Vitor and his minions must have gone through to put on this farce of a show.

The speckles of color spread out, and the shape of that damn phoenix forms, her wings expanding before soaring ahead, evaporating as she passes us.

"That fucking bird," I mutter, watching the fragments of her wings dissolve above us. I think these nobles will look for any excuse to celebrate.

"That fucking bird was actually a monster," Maeve says in the same enthusiastic tone.

I wouldn't know. In Grey, we had only the belladom fields and our dry and rainy seasons, the caverns and cisterns. We have no mythic history like Arrow's. Or if we do, they stopped teaching it long ago.

The drumbeats draw closer.

Boom.

Boom.

Boom.

My heart beats hard and fast in my chest. The rush of my blood makes my muscles tense, and I squeeze my eyes closed, focusing on Maeve and her presence. I breathe in her sweet scent, like mint and sunflower oil, allowing me to return my attention to the road. The drummers are in the lead, a band of acrobats mere feet behind them. The entertainers walk forward, each holding a partner balancing on their shoulders, save for a giant and a cyclops who balance their partners out to their sides on their hands.

With each bang of the drum, members of the troupe are thrown in the air by the strong bases charged with catching and then flinging them to each beat.

Boom.

Boom.

Boom.

Those horrid beats increase in speed, pushing the performers to toss higher and faster, inciting the crowds to scream and clap, demanding more, even as sweat soaks the cyclops's dark-brown skin and blood reddens the faces of those attempting to stay balanced on just their toes.

Boom.

Boom.

Boom.

Maeve angles her body, swinging her legs so she rests over my lap. She nuzzles her face into my throat, and her arms wrap around me. I didn't realize how on edge I was…until I'm not. At least not as much.

Hell, she really is *everything*.

"Will you please distract me?" I ask.

She smiles softly as her face meets mine. *"Leith,"* she says as if it's the most important word she knows—no, as if I'm the most important person she knows.

But that can't be right.

That *shouldn't* be right.

Even if we marry like we're supposed to, like we planned—and I become a king—she will always be a princess, and I'll always be that poverty-ridden boy who just wanted more.

Until she says, "Don't you know that I would do anything for you?"

I lift my hand when she nibbles on her bottom lip as she does when she's nervous, and I glide my thumb across it. Her large eyes melt me in their bottomless blue depths, and I want to kiss her.

Instead, I ask, "So, what is so important about the bird?"

Her mouth briefly dips. But then her expression evens out. If she's disappointed in me, she hides it well.

I want to tell her, to admit to the longing, the sheer adoration I feel for her in my heart—to give her those three short words that will convey it all.

In the time I've known Maeve, I've come to see that she deserves them. But until I'm Bloodguard, I have no control over my life, and I need to take care of my family before I can think about my own happiness.

Still, the weight of her is nice, and the scent of her skin. I tug her closer, hoping she understands.

She pats my hand again.

"Killing 'the bird,'" she says, using the same wry tone I did, "is what elevated Arrow to greatness." She leans forward for a better view. "Ah, that's Kopper."

"What?"

"Not a 'what'—well, I suppose it is. Though more of a 'who.'" She points at the parade. They carry lanterns and blow whistles that make a sharp call. "The noble houses have begun their procession. Kopper is the first."

The first fifteen black-robed people form a triangle, and then every member behind them—all garbed in red—fans out. Their long red robes have wide, thick sleeves, and as they lift and lower their arms in waves, the fabric ripples. From our height, the full effect is clearly visible.

"It's a beak," she says.

I huff, wondering how I didn't realize as much. "The beak of the phoenix," I say. The red-robed members of the house walk in formation to create the shape of a head and neck.

Maeve makes a face when they blow their whistles again. "And *that* is its supposed call."

"They should have opted for the talons," I mumble, wincing when they let that caw rip once more. "They're quieter."

Maeve surprises me by laughing, though it lacks genuine humor. "The honor of talons belongs to Olgden, but Damella is next. Their symbol is the wings of the phoenix, purple with ribbons of red spiraling from the feathers." She sighs, mumbling as an afterthought, "This is Aisling's house."

Sure enough, here comes Damella. All women. All in purple. All pirouetting in tiny dresses of, you guessed it, *purple*. Their sole accompaniment is a male soprano on horseback, his eyes rimmed in black.

Fifty or so feet below us, on the other side of the street, I spot Neh-Neh, then Uni beside her, their little one strapped against his chest.

Damella is a house of mages, it seems. Arcs of their magic light the sky above the beak formation, and streams of red fall from the sky. The women of Damella cascade red ribbons over the crowd with their magic.

"The phoenix..." I know the answer, but I feel compelled to ask anyway. "Queen Avianna of House Iamond killed it?"

"Yes." Maeve slides her hand along mine so that when our fingers meet, they intertwine. "That's what the realms decided—that the phoenix must die. From what Uncle— I mean, from what Vitor and my grandmother shared with me, the phoenix circled the sky at every battle during the great wars, her flames raining down on all those engaged in combat."

"That's horrifying."

"That's one way to describe it," she says, shuddering against me. "Good stars, can you imagine fighting your mortal enemy, unsure if you'd ever see your home or your family again, only for some giant fiery bird to burn you alive?"

"The former, yes. The latter, no thanks."

She groans. "I'm sorry. I didn't mean to be so insensitive."

No. She didn't. Which is why I squeeze her hand in comfort and support.

We're quiet as we watch the mages continue to draw on their elemental magic. Their wind scatters red ribbons and purple flower petals through the sky like ash. The mages at the fore of those assembled— Aisling and her family members, Maeve points out—conjure a giant bird of pure fire that soars overhead.

The display is impressive, and the crowd claps and cheers.

Maeve and I stay silent.

I wonder why her house isn't represented, why she isn't down there with Jakeb and Giselle. I want to ask, but she looks sad again.

"Which house is this one?" I ask to distract her.

"This is Olgden. Ugh."

"Olgdenuh?"

"What? No. I was just grumbling." She chuckles and points to a short, heavy-set human leading the procession. "That's Ugeen."

I've heard his name mentioned around the manor.

"He proposed to me," Maeve says.

"He's old enough to be your father."

"Not technically. But he's power hungry. The man cares for nothing save amassing more wealth. He has no interest in politics and nothing but disdain for the Middling and Commons."

Sounds like most of these houses. "Do any of your nobles care much about those beneath them?"

"Some do. But Ugeen..." Her eyes narrow. "He's a liar and a cheat,

Leith. Ugeen was one of the witnesses who claimed my papa had long been plotting against my grandmother."

So Ugeen wanted Andres to fall. It's not surprising. He no doubt stood to gain.

"Vitor despises him," Maeve says.

"Because of what he did to your papa?" I didn't think Vitor believed in Andres's innocence.

"No. Because he dared to try and become king through me."

We watch his house. They don't dance or sing. They wear gold, from the cloaks that drape across their backs to the bright-gold shoes with upturned tips. Ugeen waves haughtily, his brethren pausing occasionally to toss coins to the crowd.

I thought Soro and Vitor were the worst foes Maeve would face. But she'll have a hard time with these other nobles, too.

"There go the talons," Maeve says, rolling her eyes when Ugeen's family members lift their hands and curve their fingers to resemble claws.

It's a weak display at best. We're already looking ahead as the next wave of the parade approaches.

Each house member rides on a black moon horse. They carry black flags. "House Paragrin, body of the phoenix," Maeve says quietly. "You decapitated the last eligible bachelor of their family."

"Oh, Filip. Your former fiancé... Sorry about that," I say, not meaning a word. Giselle mentioned how he frequently berated Maeve about keeping her scars covered.

Between Ugeen and Filip, I can't help but ask, "Were there no other eligible options for you?"

I've watched throngs of nobles from four houses parade by. Surely there is some other suitable partner?

I don't want Maeve to marry someone else. But the fact remains that I might not survive the arena. And Soro—hell, I know that won't end well for her.

She looks at me, and her eyes are sad. "I *did* make the rounds, Leith. Not many nobles are willing to challenge Soro. He made his claim clear the moment the queen became incapacitated. And, uh, Filip was not my first fiancé. I was engaged to a childhood friend from House Kopper. But he...died."

So they're threatening any potential suitors.

I can't say I'm surprised.

Soro was quick to goad Filip into the arena that day. I don't think he would bat an eye at murder. Does Maeve suspect foul play?

The drums beat again.

Boom.

Boom.

Boom.

Maeve stands. "This is the tail. House Revlis."

Vitor's house.

They progress in military fashion. Equal rows. A mix of genders, all garbed in silver robes. Then a few feet behind the nobles, a full regiment of Arrow's actual army marches, shields and swords, maces and clubs held at the ready.

"Crowd control or part of Soro's detail?" I ask.

Maeve huffs, and I have my answer.

I rise until I'm standing beside her.

She crosses her arms. "Vitor has hired a wizard for a magic display that will light up the night sky. There will be music and more performances."

I see some of the commoners already walking in the direction of the castle.

But then those dreaded drums start up again.

Vitor sits upon a throne that is carried by a slew of servants. He is surrounded by guards.

"Revlis. Revlis," the crowd chants.

But Vitor and his entourage aren't wearing the same colors that Soro and the other members did.

"Vitor's colors are silver and blue," Maeve says. "Same as Soro's." She sounds so far away even as she remains in my arms.

"Yet they wear Arrow's colors," I acknowledge. Blue and green trimmed with gold.

The strands of her thick braid slide along my chest as she shakes her head. "No, Leith. Those are the colors of House Iamond." She looks up at me. "The colors of *my* family."

CHAPTER
29

MAEVE

Before Leith can stop me, I leap the fence and run down the alleyway, throwing my hood back and untying my cloak as I go, letting it fall to the cobblestone street.

Vitor said he wasn't participating in the parade. And yet here he is. On my grandmother's throne. Wearing *my* colors!

Uni and Neh-Neh see me first, and there is some commotion as they shoulder their way across the street, cutting through the last of Vitor's procession until they reach me.

"What are you doing?" Leith hisses as he catches up.

His legs are far from mended. Running as he did is not good.

"I need to do this," I tell him. *"Alone."*

He flinches but doesn't argue. "I'll escort you."

I want to kiss him. To go up on my toes and show him—show everyone—that he matters to me.

But that would make him a target. And the arena will be hard enough without Soro's enmity. So while I'm so grateful that Leith would risk himself for me, I cannot let him go through with it.

"This isn't your fight, Leith. *I* need to make my presence known. Not just in the castle or the council but to all of Arrow."

Leith grimaces but ultimately nods. It isn't because of my title. Leith simply respects that I must make my own choices.

He turns to Uni. "Can you accompany her?"

Uni shares a look with his wife. Neh-Neh's mouth trembles, and then she nods encouragingly and holds her hands out for the baby. They will not abandon me, though there is risk to themselves if they stand beside me.

"Thank you," I whisper.

"Is your father at the castle?" Leith asks, his gaze darting around. "Jakeb, I mean."

"No, he's at the manor."

Many of the Middling and Commoners assembled are taking notice. Rather than follow toward the castle, they're staring at us. Pointing at us.

I hear whispers of "Bloodguard."

It won't be long before they all recognize Leith.

"Can you go to Father?" I clasp Leith's hands. "Tell him to meet me at the castle to accompany me home."

Leith nods, and with one long look at Uni, he takes off in the opposite direction, away from the crowd. The moment he clears the heavier throngs, he breaks into a run.

I know how much that must hurt him.

"What can we do, Princess?" Uni asks.

I see so many familiar faces. Stasia, the seleno fairy, and Gabi, the guapilla who works at her tavern, eye me expectantly. There are others, too, who I've known or treated.

"Tell us," Uni says.

"Sing. Please sing," I say. "The Anthem of Arrow."

I take Uni's hand and Stasia's, and we step into the now-empty path of the parade.

The rest of the friends and townsfolk, the merchants and off-duty guards, the faces known to me and those who simply sense my sincerity—they fall in line behind us.

The crowd grows.

The crowd sings.

I walk onward. Though we are last and the parade has progressed ahead, our numbers expand. The onlookers pause, and when they see me, people from all classes of Arrow fall into line and join me.

What begins as a handful of friends merges into dozens, then hundreds of bodies, large and small, young and old.

We are not the color of any one house, but many.

My heart has never been more full.

We continue up the streets, more and more citizens of Arrow joining along. As we turn onto the main road, I see the lanterns lining the bridge, the purple haze of magic in the sky as Aisling and other mages from Damella join Soro on the parapet walls. And there, at the gates to the castle, is Vitor.

He sits upon my grandmother's throne.

I have never seen the huge seat moved from its place in the palace, let alone lifted and carried along like some mobile stage for the monarchy.

Vitor arches a brow.

He instructs his guards to lower the throne, and he leaps to the ground.

I don't pause.

I lead my people along the street to the bridgeway. The crowd parts, creating a gap for me to walk through as the other assembled persons and houses turn to see what's happening.

The singing quiets.

Vitor reaches me, and his expression is indecipherable.

"I wasn't expecting to see you in the procession, Lord Regent," I say.

"Nor I you."

He told me he would remain in the castle to coordinate the night-sky display. There was no mention of him parading himself on a throne through Arrow's city streets.

Vitor takes my hand and lifts it. He escorts me forward, all the way up to the gates, until we're standing in front of Arrow's seat of power.

I turn and address the people before he can. "Tonight, we celebrate. We commemorate the day Queen Avianna defeated the great phoenix!"

The crowd cheers.

"I am Princess Maeve, granddaughter of Avianna of Iamond, ninth ruler of the Iamond Royal Line. My house is the house of the people!"

Raucous cheers go up.

"Well played, child." Vitor grins at me.

He lifts our joined hands toward the sky, and the cheers grow louder.

As if we'd choreographed this from the start, the hired wizard and supporting mages send up sparks and spectacles of color. The crowds gaze up.

I focus on Vitor.

"You spoke of purpose, Uncle," I say in a low voice so only he can hear. "This is mine."

He reflects on that for a long moment, then says angrily, "I also spoke of fear and need. And you *did not* heed my warning." I only smile back at him.

You don't scare me anymore.

CHAPTER

30

LEITH

I race the distance back to the manor on horseback.

My muscles ache and burn. Sweat drips from my brow, and nausea pitches into my throat. Pain is my companion. Pain and terror, because every second away from Maeve is one in which she is surrounded by enemies.

"Jakeb!"

I scream his name twice more to be heard over the colorful explosions that are visible even from this distance.

He rushes out of the manor toward the gates, Neela close on his heels and Giselle just behind. Her eyes are glowing with odd light.

"It's Maeve," I say between heaving breaths. "She's joined the memorial parade. She'll be at the castle by now."

Jakeb moves with unnatural speed. He's across the yard and slamming into the stables in a blink. I hear the moon horses startle and whinny.

"Is she all right, Leith?" Giselle's body is shaking. Ripples of multicolored sparks spray from her hands. Her eyes are a blend of swirling hues. I think I understand the need for the gloves now.

I instinctively take a step back.

"Giselle!" Caelen yells.

His harsh tone seems to ground her. Her eyes blink rapidly before turning into liquid honey again.

"She wasn't in any immediate danger." I relay what we saw and how Vitor made a spectacle of showing himself as some kind of ruler supreme.

Giselle lets loose a string of curses.

We mount as soon as Jakeb returns with the horses, and Star launches into a run before I can even reposition myself. I grab the reins and lean against her neck, my legs tightening to keep my seat.

"I told her not to go." Giselle overtakes me on the right. She's riding faster than the rest of us, her small frame looking even slighter atop the spotted moon horse. "But oh no, no one ever listens to me!"

It's not long before we're back in the city, rose petals and red ribbons strewn on the streets.

When I glance back over my shoulder, I see more of Jakeb's house riding to catch up. Pega, the groundskeeper, and several of the guards who are stationed at the manor gates join us.

We follow the path the parade took, which is easy to see from the stragglers and trail of flowers.

As the castle comes into sight, Jakeb yells, "Halt!" which causes our horses to stop so short, my face nearly rams into Star's neck.

Maeve stands before the castle gates, beside Vitor.

Her face is bright and joyous, smiling.

The night sky pulses with bursts of magic and color, and the crowd claps and cheers, some of them chanting Maeve's name.

My face heats. I've rallied her family and we've raced here as if her life hung in the balance, but she's not in danger. She's laughing and grinning with her "uncle."

I lower my head. "I, uh…"

Jakeb lays a hand on my shoulder. "You made the right call, Leith."

Giselle edges her horse back toward mine. "Last time we participated in the Memorial of the Phoenix, it was not so pleasant, was it, Father?"

"No," Jakeb says. "They booed and heckled us. Maeve cried for days."

I imagine the crowd treating Maeve with such open hostility and derision, and it makes me violent.

"Everyone was upset in the aftermath of the trial," Giselle explains.

"It was a good lesson for all of us," Jakeb says.

For me, it's just one more glimpse into Maeve's character.

In the arena, I'm jeered. It's common for the bettors to do that—they're looking for any advantage they can gain. But that doesn't make their words any less hurtful. I act like I'm impervious, but any gladiator will tell you, we *hate* the crowds. Whether they're for us or against us, we're just a thing to them. The crowds don't care about the harm they inflict. They just want to win. And nobody deserves to die with such cruel taunts in their ears.

"Stop growling, Leith," Giselle tells me. "You're starting to sound like him."

She jerks her head toward Caelen, who merely grunts.

"My daughter could've hidden behind those high walls." Jakeb points to the castle. "But she didn't. At great risk to herself, Maeve made it a point to regain the trust of the community." He inclines his head to where Maeve basks in the adoration of Arrow. "She took a chance."

I nod. "And it paid off."

There are tears in Jakeb's eyes when he turns back to me. "Yes, it did."

We say nothing for several minutes.

Giselle is the first to break the silence. "Caelen, I'm in the mood for a jug of ale."

He sighs. "Of course you are."

She turns to her gladiator. "Pega, dearest, I imagine you're parched, too."

Pega looks between me and Giselle. "I could use a wee bit of ale to wet my mouth. It was a rough ride here."

The three of them move off while I remain behind with Jakeb and the guards.

I keep my hood drawn and my gaze on Maeve. It takes a while, but my heart rate gradually settles. As the overwhelming sense of dread fades, I find myself wanting to smile.

Maeve has done it.

She's won over the people of Arrow with kindness and hope.

The same as she did with me.

"Hi-ho, Bloodguard," a voice calls. We pivot our horses as a dwarf approaches. He has wealth. It's evident in his clothes and bearing and in the way he holds out his hand to Jakeb as if they're equals.

"Lord Kaysoon." Jakeb clasps the dwarf's hand and then makes some symbol with his fingers before lifting his arms skyward.

I look around nervously. Last thing I need is to draw attention. My leg feels like it's been ripped off and used to clobber my arm.

Despite the time I've spent in Maeve's care, I'm not fully recovered. Between the venom and the deep wounds to my legs and my slow progress at regaining full mobility in my left hand, I may never be.

"I'd hoped to see your next two bouts," the dwarf tells me. "It's been a long time since a gladiator of your ilk made it to the last matches. Hoped that other fighter, the one from Witoria, would've won, too. I've been tracking his career for years. A fine fighter, he made."

Sullivan.

"Are you heading out?" Jakeb asks, sparing me from having to answer.

Kaysoon nods. "Things are…changing. Tensions are running high, both in Libur and among the other realms."

Jakeb nods solemnly. "May the lands be replenished and peace prevail."

Kaysoon makes that odd hand gesture again. "We, too, pray for peace." He gives me a short nod, then offers one last parting bit of advice to Jakeb. "But prayers go unanswered. Preparedness wins wars. Keep a close eye on the princess. I fear for her safety, and she *cannot* fall…"

CHAPTER
31
MAEVE

"Gladiators don't dance," Leith tells me flatly.

It's been a few days since the night of the parade, when I fell asleep beside him on the couch in my bedroom.

I think he was expecting something else when I told him to come with me this evening. He didn't protest when I led him to the manor house for my father's dinner party. Truth be told, with his mouth on mine, I'd been thinking of something else, too.

I'm *still* thinking of those things.

I close my eyes and imagine his strong hands streaking across my skin, his mouth following. I rub my legs together, a delicious ache throbbing at my core.

Leith's mouth curves into that little smirk like he can sense what I'm imagining.

But this soiree is one my father planned, and I want Leith to be here with us.

He turns from where Father's mastery of the lute sweeps a melodious tune through the open glass doors. The sun has started its descent, painting the faded dark wood of the manor's exterior in hues of peach and gold.

It bathes Leith, making his hair shine and eyes sparkle. All in black, he remains this imposing, unyielding force of wrath. Except now that we've kissed, I know he does yield, at least to me.

"You said supper, Princess. Not dancing. 'Dancing' never came out of your mouth."

I wag a finger at him. "You're in another embarrassingly cheery mood again, aren't you?"

The way his thumb grazes over the back of my hand broadens my smile. He bends to kiss my cheek.

"You're lucky I like you," he says, and my whole body flushes.

He looks ahead, his eyes focused on a distant point.

"I need to be Bloodguard," he whispers, his lips brushing the top of my head. I start to nod, but then his next words hold me in place. "I need to be your king."

"Yes, you do," I whisper.

His smile fades as we pass our large dining room and enter the ballroom, but mine stays firmly intact. Though we've wrestled with when to tell my family that our relationship has evolved, since they still perceive Leith as dangerous, I'm desperate to shout it to the world.

Musy and Pasha step to the joyful song Father plays on the lute. Sonu, our groundskeeper, claps his hands with delight. He's quite buff for a human his age. And Pega, dressed in a silky yellow shirt and breeches that match her spiky yellow hair, jumps in place in front of Sonu. I think she's trying to dance… Never mind, it appears her breeches were getting better acquainted with her womanly butt crack.

"She's not used to wearing underwear," Leith whispers.

"Thank you for sharing."

Neela accompanies Father on her violin. My sweet estrellas bounce along the furniture to the beat of the music, chittering away and enjoying the fun.

In the corner, Giselle sits on a stool, flipping through pages of music.

"It must be hard turning those pages wearing those leather gloves," Leith says.

"Mm," I say, hoping he doesn't press for more.

Caelen whispers to Giselle, and she looks up at us and grins. She abandons the pages and heads our way with Caelen shadowing.

Leith and Caelen more or less growl at each other in a way of a greeting. Giselle beams. "You boys are going to be best friends," she says. "I can feel it."

Another exchange of growls. Aren't they fun?

Giselle grabs my hand and pulls me closer to the dance floor. She grins at me. It's a forced smile. She's getting worse, and we both know it. But what plagues her is beyond my abilities.

Giselle spins us back toward Pega and Sonu, adjusting her gloves when she stops. "Pega, be a dear and ask Maeve to dance?"

"You want me to dance?" Pega points a finger at me. *"With her?"*

I sigh. "Believe me, I'm equally thrilled by the idea," I reply.

The rotten little fox I call my sister shoves me against Pega. She catches me, curses, and drags me onto the dance floor, in the same manner she would an old goat that broke free of his pen.

Pega places her hand lightly—well, lightly for someone of her strength—on my waist, eyes level with my chest, and her other hand takes my own. I place my palm on her shoulder. Like with Giselle, I tower over her, but unlike Giselle, this dwarf would break me in half if I irked her.

I mean to see how Leith is doing, but for this moment, I can't. I'm too taken by Giselle and Caelen. Her smile slowly vanishes as the distinguished soldier regards her with unmitigated affection, taking a beat to fold her gloved fingers over his and press a gentle kiss to the back of her hand, his eyes never leaving hers. I *feel* her breath hitch as much as I see it, her attention dropping briefly to her knuckles before she returns her gaze to his sparkling irises.

With his careful hold and sweeping movements, Caelen makes certain Giselle knows that *she* is the exquisite beauty he's honored to stand by. Caelen loves my sister, even if he knows he shouldn't.

"This is wrong," Pega says, looking down at our feet. "I think it's you."

She steps awkwardly back and forth, back and forth, back and forth. "What are you doing?" I ask, trying to match her movements.

She furrows her fuzzy yellow brows. "I'm making the square," she says as if it's obvious. "Musy 'splained that you're supposed to dance like you're trying to draw a square with your feet."

Giselle and Caelen spin smoothly past us, her straight hair flowing like a flag in the breeze.

Pega scowls. "Don't hate the dancers who can dance. Hate the dancer who told you to make a square," Giselle teases.

She brushes the drooping side of her face, notices the flaky crust of an hors d'oeuvre, and licks it off. "You're not doing your square correctly, and Musy wouldn't lie about somethin' like a square."

"Says the gladiator whose legs don't bend," Giselle replies. "Did you forget you have knees?"

Leith prowls toward us. "May I?"

He smirks and closes the space between us as Pega steps away, clearly pleased to do so.

"I think it's time I show you what a real gladiator can do," he murmurs in my ear.

Pega flings her arms as if in pain from simply holding me. "Good luck," she says to Leith. "She can't dance worth shit."

My body heats as I reach for Leith's hand. "You're not going to do that stupid square thing, are you?" I ask.

He shakes his head.

Then he comes alive, moving with exuberance and athleticism becoming of a Bloodguard as the music speeds up.

My gaze bounces from our feet to his face.

"Don't be too impressed, Princess. This is the only dance my mother taught me."

Leith leans into me, and without thinking, I rest my head on his shoulder. But when I realize what I've done, I try to pull away.

"Don't," Leith tells me, holding me close.

I swallow with great difficulty. "But everyone will see," I remind him.

"Let them see," he says.

And they do.

Leith leads me along, and I follow every motion, relishing the feeling of being held in his strong arms.

I need you, I want to say.

Please don't leave, I wish to beg.

His full attention is on me, and it's as if we are the only two people in the world as everything and everyone else fade away.

It takes Giselle jerking away from Caelen with a gasp to pull me back to reality.

My body tenses when she backs away from him and that irritating charge crackles against my skin.

Caelen is at her heels as she strides toward the door. "What is it?" he asks. "Did I hurt you?"

She looks at him, her eyes wide with stark fear.

"I think I'm going to explode," she whispers.

Caelen pulls her close, circling her waist with his arm and quickly leading her away.

"Sorry. Too much wine. I need to walk it off," she stammers to the rest of us as they go.

Pega hurries after them, stopping dead when the strings on Father's large lute thrum an awkward chord caused by the vibrations from Giselle's uncontrolled magic as she passes—but only for a second. She would never admit it, but anyone can see she's grown protective of the younger woman.

Father sets down his lute and follows them, too.

Giselle and Caelen's abrupt departure takes our cheer with them.

Pasha and Musy can read a room. As the tension muddles the air, they bustle back into the kitchen with Sonu to finish the final preparations for supper. Leith holds me, easing my growing anxiety.

Father returns far more quickly than I'd expect, his skin flushed and wrinkles deepening along the creases of his eyes.

"Father... Did something happen to Giselle?" I ask.

He shakes his head slowly. "It's not that. We have company. Vitor and Soro are here."

CHAPTER

32

MAEVE

I instinctively release Leith and take several steps back.

He straightens. "Can you make it to the cottage?"

"There's no time," Father says.

Leith's features ice over as we follow Father from the ballroom to the entry hall. Leith brushes his sword hilt and then, arms loose at his sides, faces the door.

"Are you ready to greet our guests?" Father asks.

I glance at Leith, who stands next to me, more marble than flesh. "Always, Father," I say, straightening my shoulders and lifting my chin.

Father kisses my head. "That's my daughter, the future queen."

I grimace when the muffled gallop of hooves striking the front lawn pricks at my ears. Ten, maybe twelve guards on horseback and the rumble of at least three carriages.

Taking a deep breath, I clasp my trembling hands in front of me.

Unlike me, Father is rock steady. He walks to Neela and carefully takes her heavy hands in his. "My most distinguished friend," he begins. "If I'm not arrested this eve for cracking a wine bottle over these fools, we will meet later for tea and reading as promised." He chuckles when Neela doesn't budge. "Please leave us. This is neither your battle to fight nor your war to win." He bows and kisses her crooked knuckles. It's only when her bushy gray eyebrows lower that I know she's conceded.

I press my lips together as she shuffles up the stairs, her movements slow and careful so she doesn't slip, even as she shoos away the herd of estrellas poking their heads over and through the railings. Pasha returns from the kitchen. She wipes her wet hands on her apron and quickly takes the position by the door.

Leith is most dangerous when he's quiet. And he's very quiet now, his gaze unwavering on the door. My ears prick again when the horses chuff and stomp as they come to a stop outside the front of the manor and several guards dismount, shouting orders. The sounds carry clearly to us through the open windows.

When Leith checks his sword again, I give him a small bow. "If you would, my future king, kindly suppress your great urge to stab Vitor and Soro on their way in."

His lips barely move when he mutters, "I'm not making any promises."

The hem of my skirt slides over the marble floor as I straighten. "Leith," I whisper, "the last thing either of us needs is to have the entirety of Vitor's and Soro's allies calling for your head."

"Maeve." Pasha's hands are shaking horribly as she peers out the window. "The high lord and his son are almost to the door."

There's a pitter-patter of little feet. Lots of little feet. I exchange glances with Father. He shrugs, unaffected. "If you would, sweet Pasha, please let them in."

Pasha, her tight gray curls askew from dancing, wipes her hands on her white apron one last time and casts a final look at Leith. Then, after only one knock, she throws open the door and steps aside, bowing.

My eyes practically shoot from my skull when the first of five...six... eight...*twelve* pageboys in pale-blue silk shirts, white breeches, and round flat caps march in, their arms full of golden and midnight roses.

Leith turns to me, his features darkening to those of the Bloodguard he's destined to be. "I'll ram every last flower down Soro's decapitated throat if he so much as reaches for you."

I've come to think of Leith as more wolf than man. The way he eliminates his competition, the way he moves—ready for a fight that may come without notice—and how protective he is of those he considers his pack.

"We can't accomplish everything we mean to if you're sentenced to death." My voice trembles when Father steps forward to greet the lords outside. "Leith, you're not in the arena, and neither are they. Any harm upon a noble outside that battle zone results in execution. They will find you, and they will kill you." I squeeze his arm. "Please, Leith. I need you." I'm not thinking of the throne now. No, I'm terrified for *him*.

"What are you doing here?" Father demands. As proper as he is, he's never forgiven Vitor for imprisoning Papa.

Vitor strolls in like the king he believes himself to be, gallantly removes his robe of gold-and-white silk, and passes it to Pasha without even looking at her. He adjusts his long, thick braid of dark hair so it lies over his left shoulder. "Now, is that any way to greet your High Lord?" Vitor laughs wholeheartedly as he motions around the entry hall and the rooms beyond, proclaiming them his to conquer. "Especially after such a grand gesture from my child to yours."

I pinch the bridge of my nose when the small *clink* of Leith's sword against his buckle announces he already has his hand over the hilt.

Several of the flower arrangements are placed along the sills of the densely leaded windows that overlook our front garden. Some are placed on tables and mantels in the library and parlor, and more are arranged along the length of the buffet tables in the ballroom.

"Bloodguard. Bloodguard," one of the pageboys chants in a whisper.

It's hard to know who's chanting. All the pageboys are running circles around Musy as she directs them where to set the vases. Yet the chant continues, loud enough for the little boy to alert Leith to his presence but not so obvious that he may immediately be discovered.

"A friend of yours?" I ask.

Leith thrums the hilt of his sword, choosing to keep his eyes on Vitor and Father's exchange instead of answering me.

"Please don't do anything, my champion," I whisper.

"I'm going to tear out his throat," my champion replies.

Vitor's ogren generals, Tut and Pua, step into the entry hall. Their oversize helmets make Tut appear bald and scrunch Pua's braids against his shoulders. They're here to witness their High Lord's triumph, yet they fixate on me, Tut mouthing something to Pua that I can't fully make out. What I do recognize is the name Ugeen.

Vitor jerks his chin and dismisses the generals. A few of the royal moon horses whinny, and more chuff and stomp their hooves into the soft grass as the two generals return to the front lawn.

What just happened?

Ugeen is here? Father would never let him inside. The man lied to the council, falsely condemning his husband.

Vitor raises his hands as he does when addressing the arena. "The Great Avianna of Iamond would have relished this day," Vitor tells Father. "Remember how she spoke of Soro and our lovely Maeve becoming one?"

Father glances at me. "Actually," Father says, his smile widening, "if my memory serves, I believe she once called Soro a 'sadistic pig of a child.'"

As if called directly, Soro storms into the foyer. He tears the collar of his burgundy cape as he whips it off and tosses it away to square off with Father. And Father still smiles as he continues, "Or perhaps I am mistaken?"

"Take caution of how you speak of your general," Soro bites out.

When I take a step forward, Leith's grip on my arm tightens. "Not your fight," Leith tells me. "That's my job."

"Not today," I whisper.

"I am no longer a mere soldier," Father says. "I am the lord of this house and spouse of the real king."

"The *disgraced* king." The cold sneer that forms beneath Soro's pointy nose makes me shudder. "You've made many mistakes, Jakeb. It won't be long before you regret each one."

"We all make mistakes, don't we?" Father says casually. "Like opening the door to uninvited guests. And you are correct. I regret it already."

Soro doesn't frighten Father, but he frightens me enough *for* Father. At least it looks like Soro is backing down this time as he wanders the entry hall, peeking into various rooms as if inspecting the ridiculous flowers the pageboys have carefully set upon every available surface.

Empty-handed now, the pageboys make a quick exit, each afraid to draw attention to themselves, except for the smallest, who continues to chant. He rushes to Leith and curls his thin arms around his waist.

"Bloodguard, Bloodguard," he whisper-chants.

Leith solidifies his imposing form, clearly surprised by the contact. He recovers quickly and places his hand on the boy's shoulder. Using care, he moves the little boy gently away. "Be wary of those who watch you. I don't want you hurt," he says in a voice so low, only the two of us can hear him. "Run along, Gunther, and I'll see you soon."

The sweet child fiddles with the collar of his shirt, which is two sizes too big for his lean body. He heard Leith, but even as he steals a quick look in Soro's direction, his fascination with Leith keeps him in place.

"Out!" Soro commands from the ballroom archway, and the little boy flinches. With a nod from Leith, Gunther runs.

Vitor approaches, all smiles, takes my hand, and raises it to his lips. "Maeve, my darling. How are you this evening?"

He squeezes my fingers tight, drawing my attention from the door where Gunther disappeared. It takes everything in me to bow in greeting. "Uncle."

Vitor releases me and turns to Leith as if just noticing him. "Good evening," he says. "I am High Lord Vitor of Revlis, Arrow's Regent and Defender. And you are?"

"You know who I am," Leith says.

Anger singes me from head to toe, and I grip the fine satin of my gown in my fists. The regent gives me a warning glare, but I look away without acknowledging him. Furious prickles of heat creep up my neck. The *nerve* of him, to pretend not to know Leith after he has bled him in that damn arena time and time again.

I'm taking a breath in preparation to tell Vitor exactly what I think when strong hands grasp my shoulders and whip me around.

"Daughter, this is not the time to confront Vitor," Father whispers, having come up behind me. His voice is soothing, and it calms me as it has since the day he and Papa made us all a family. "But your time will come. You will soon be queen. Do not lose sight of it." He braces himself, looking straight ahead. "No matter what this filth says."

With that, Father takes my arm and leads me away from our unwelcome guests and into the library, where candles in the wall sconces cast shadows that dance along dark wood bookcases and across heavy brocade chairs on one end of the room. At the other end is Papa's desk, all his personal items placed upon it exactly as they had been in the castle. The only things missing are the ancestral swords, which were placed in glass casings and set into the wall behind the desk. When Vitor took over as regent, he claimed my grandfather's and grandmother's swords. To this day, he promises they're somewhere safe and swears I will receive them when I take the throne.

Father wraps an arm around my shoulders as I take several calming breaths. I pull away and sit on a green silk settee as Soro and Vitor enter with Leith following them. Father lowers himself onto the settee to my left, but instead of sitting in the chair next to me like I wish, Leith stands behind my right shoulder with his hands clasped in front of him and his full attention on Vitor and Soro as they position themselves in high-backed chairs opposite us.

Pasha and Musy bustle into the room and can't seem to move fast enough as they serve cherry wine in shimmering goblets, careful not to spill a drop.

Vitor nudges Soro covertly, but I notice it. Soro clears his throat. "You look lovely tonight, Maeve." He shifts uncomfortably in the chair that looks too small for him. "I hope the flowers suit. They are your favorite, I believe." His rote delivery sounds like he's reading from one of the manners primers I had to study as a child.

Fine. Two can play the false-civility game—at least until Vitor and Soro reveal why they are really here. In a cordial voice, I reply, "Thank you, Soro, for your kind words. I do love roses, but the dahlia will forever hold a special place in my heart."

Behind me, Leith shifts slightly at my tribute.

The corners of Soro's mouth lift. "Then they shall adorn every last open space at our wedding."

Wedding? Shit.

It takes a great deal of composure and several visuals of Soro being tarred and feathered to not shriek and throw furniture, but I manage to calmly say, "Oh, have you and Aisling announced your affections at last? Congratulations. You are perfect together."

Soro's face remains expressionless as he balances his goblet in his fingers. "She can't make me king." He used the same tone at last year's Winter Solstice Ball when he complained the duck was too dry. "I need a queen for that."

How...sweet.

Vitor takes a sip of his wine, the crinkles at the corners of his eyes deepening as he scrutinizes me and the way Leith shields me like a lover. Stars above. Does he know what I'm up to?

"You will make a fine queen, Maeve," Vitor says. "Provided you choose your king wisely."

Leith's spine is so rigid I could build a roof on top of him. I'm no less relaxed.

Vitor raises his chalice so Pasha knows to fill it. "Your birthday is fast approaching, my dear," he says. "It's time to decide."

Father reaches over and squeezes my hand. He knows Vitor is onto me, too.

Vitor wants me to marry Soro. There's no way he'll risk sharing that power with the other noble houses. As Soro pointed out, Vitor has not been pressuring me—the longer I am ineligible to rule, the longer he retains power—but I can see how that would be a liability. Once I'm of age, the law of succession states that I can marry *anyone* of nobility.

Is that why he closed the borders? To limit my opportunities?

My full attention returns to Soro, who is studying me with a self-satisfied smirk. "Come now, Maeve," he says. "You knew this was coming."

I did—but not so soon, and I have other plans now. I'm to marry Leith. But I do understand Soro's haste. While the noble houses of Arrow might not be suitable, there are other lineages outside of Arrow. Soro knows I mean to marry to free my father. *Soro* is running out of time, not me.

"Now, gentlemen, just because I'll shortly be of age doesn't mean I'll marry the day after my birthday." I make a point to toss my hair as if flirting. It's not something I ordinarily do. Flirting and hair-tossing are Aisling's gifts and not mine. I don't do either well.

Soro finishes swallowing a gulp of wine. "Then when?" he asks.

Just a day after Leith wins Bloodguard so I may tell you no.

"Just enough time so I feel comfortable." Which, of course, will be never, and Soro knows it. He narrows his eyes on me, and I shrug. "This is a big decision." I lean back and take a sip of wine. "I will need time to consider it."

Soro snorts and rolls his eyes. "I'll give you one week, Princess."

Or else what? Is he trying to tell me that I no longer have a choice?

If Leith had the power to freeze others with his glare, Vitor would be chiseling shards of Soro from his chair from now until next spring. Someone may die tonight. *Please, don't let it be Leith.*

CHAPTER

33

LEITH

Vitor beckons Pasha and Musy closer. "We ate before our arrival. But there's always room for tea and cake..." He laughs. "And, of course, more wine."

Lord Dickless isn't asking. He's behaving as if this is yet another space he commands.

Pasha and Musy respond as if fearful of angering a nest of hornets as they back out of the way when Vitor, with his head high, stands abruptly and strolls from the library, crosses the hall, and opens the door to the parlor as if he owns it. I don't understand the look Vitor throws to Maeve's father, but Jakeb must, because he nods slightly and rises from his chair.

Soro rises as well, pausing when Jakeb offers Maeve his arm.

Pasha and Musy, their hair a mess and sweat darkening the cloth of their light-blue dresses, look to Jakeb for guidance.

"Please set up drinks on the terrace, if you will," Jakeb instructs the women. "And kindly enjoy your supper without us. We will take ours later."

Maeve leans her head against Jakeb's shoulder, and Soro follows them toward the terrace. It's only because Jakeb motions me with a jerk of his chin in the direction of the parlor that I don't shadow them. *What is he thinking?*

If Soro tries something with Maeve, I'm confident Jakeb can protect her long enough for me to kill Vitor and his bastard son. It's the only reason I stalk in the direction of the parlor.

Sonofabitch, tensions are high. Soro is a hairsbreadth away from snapping. I've seen his type before. He's too entitled. And the entitled don't do well with opposition.

I enter the parlor almost silently. Vitor stands before the marble fireplace with his hands clasped behind his back, the tip of his dark braid a breath from touching his wrists. It's a beautiful room from its brilliant floors to the domed ceiling of white birch. But it's absolutely my least favorite room in the manor.

There's no warmth to it. No sense of the family Jakeb has created. It's as if every exquisite item they brought from the castle was dumped in here. But the one thing I dislike most in this room is the painting that hangs over the fireplace—the very one Vitor is studying.

He knows I'm in here. It bugs the shit out of me that he doesn't turn to acknowledge me. My fingers grip the hilt of my sword. I'm dangerous. Didn't he, himself, make me this way? I walk closer, entertaining ways to kill him. I could stab him through the throat with my dagger or hang him from the rope tassels tied to the drapes. They're thick enough to hold him. And maybe Pasha will find it in her heart to forgive me for the amount of blood she'll have to clean. I can picture it so vividly—Vitor swinging from side to side, the blood from his opened throat spraying the leaded glass and the pristine white window coverings, turning the marble floor red.

Side to side, he'll swing. Kicking until he can't. The last twitches of his feet signaling his highly anticipated death.

One swipe of my sword could do it, too. It would be clean, quick, quiet. But that's too easy. This bastard deserves far worse.

From near the left row of windows, a moon horse whinnies, followed by another, their impatient stomps along the moist landscape expressing their demands to return to their stalls. Heavy voices curse them and order them to settle. A resounding slap of a hand strikes the haunches of a moon horse farther down the lawn. The guards should know better than to treat creatures bred for war—and capable of understanding human speech, no less—so poorly.

Another slap and more harsh reprimands. Hell, at this point that entire herd would bond with anyone who offered a gentle hand or word. But within those ranks, they'll never find that kindness that drives them to please. Not when their own high lord throws people like meat to ravenous dragons. Just as he did during my final moments with Sullivan.

I glance at the ornate stone table near the fireplace. A black onyx statue of the phoenix rests at the table's center. Hmm. Looks about heavy enough to crush Vitor's skull and cave in his chest. Yes, chest first, and just his face. That will hurt. Almost as much as it hurt me to kill Sullivan… if only it wouldn't make so much noise. Then again, who would stop me?

I come to stand beside Vitor, setting aside, for now, all the ways I could kill him.

"Have you considered how hard it will be to be king?" he asks.

I don't take the bait and barely blink. "I'm sure any son of yours could handle it," I say.

"Is that so?" he asks.

His attention is on me. Mine is on him, too.

"Do you like her?" he asks.

I almost deny it, believing he's referring to Maeve. But his obsession with the painting above the mantel stops me. Not that he wasn't intentionally trying to trick me.

The imposing portrait is of the Great Avianna of Iamond, Maeve's beloved grandmother. Her battle armor is depicted in hues of black and gray, symbolic of the night all light abandoned the sky as she slaughtered the phoenix. It's a hell of a morbid scene. Dead soldiers spread out around her, their broken bodies partially burned. Avianna could pass for Maeve's twin were it not for the brutal glint in her eyes.

Avianna stands with her feet at parade rest, a silver-hilted sword dripping blood in one hand and a gold sword with a massive ruby in the pommel held skyward in the other. I offer Vitor a one-shouldered shrug. "I didn't know her," I finally reply.

"That's true. How would you?" Vitor chuckles but then loses his humor. "Avianna was a remarkable leader. A true ruler who followed the law absolutely. Her granddaughter, though…" He shakes his head. "Maeve is soft. Too tender for what must be done for Arrow." He watches me closely. "It's why she will need a strong king to support her."

What the fuck is he getting at?

In the fireplace, a small log perched atop of a stouter chunk of wood cracks in half and tumbles to the bricks below, its crumbling remains hissing. Vitor waits for me to say something. I'm happy to disappoint.

He keeps his arms behind his back. "What happens after you win and help your family?"

Mm. It's like he wants me to kill him. "What makes you think I have family?"

Vitor chuckles. "I make it a point to know about everyone and everything that affects my court." He raises a thin eyebrow. "So, tell me, gladiator. What comes next? You help your family in Siertos—what of the others? What of the realms that may soon encroach upon the borders of Arrow, where your family, I presume, may soon reside? And what about the threats to the *other people* you care about?"

He means Maeve. But it's not a threat—it's something I wasn't expecting. Vitor appears to be feeling *me* out as Maeve's king.

Vitor motions back to the painting with a jerk of his narrow chin. "The questions I present to you... She'd already have the answers. That's what an amazing woman Avianna was."

I edge closer to the picture. Bloody hell. That coveted mark—the one with the sword and vines, the one *I'm* all but throwing myself into a lion's mouth to earn—is etched into several of those dead soldiers' arms. They're faint but definitely there. I walk closer to the painting.

I point upward. "There." Vitor follows the motion as I continue to point. At least nine have the emblem traced into their skin. Whoever Avianna solicited to create this supposed masterpiece painted the faces of the dead away from the viewer to give them anonymity and soften the horror of the murder scene it is. To Avianna, this was a moment of celebration. To me, it's not even close.

Vitor doesn't react. Which means this ball-less bastard already knew what I do now. I don't bother to sugarcoat my response. "Nine," I say. "I count nine dead Bloodguards. You see an amazing woman," I tell him flatly. "I see a killer queen, a fallen king, and too many who recklessly died for glory."

He doesn't react other than to say calmly, "We saved Old Erth that day. The phoenix was a herald of death, razing friend and foe in the thick of battles."

"How many died so that Arrow could claim victory that day and every one since?"

Vitor chuckles. He nods as if I didn't just insult his precious Avianna. "One of our most costly victories, indeed," he says and looks at me. "I should know. I was there."

CHAPTER

34

MAEVE

W e don't move from the terrace railing until Vitor and his entourage disappear into the darkness.

"Odd for the generals to accompany Vitor when his own guards followed him here," Leith says.

Father sniffs with disgust. "Keep your gators close and your vipers closer."

Leith rocks back on his heels. "You think he doesn't trust his own son."

"Vitor has certainly embarrassed Soro enough for Soro to turn against him," I offer.

Father nods. "Ugeen's presence bothers me more."

"Ugeen?" Leith asks. "He was here?"

I nod. "Soro laughed about it when you were in the parlor. He said something about him groveling to Vitor to be permitted to accompany him here. Vitor allowed it but then confined him to his carriage like a rotten child."

Father nods carefully. "Why come just to be humiliated? Ugeen knows better than to think that I'd allow him in. If Vitor thinks Ugeen or maybe even Soro will turn on him, he'll want Tut and Pua close by."

Pua carries a bardiche, an axe as long as his body, with him at all times. The immense ogre likely sleeps with it. Tut keeps a double-headed war axe strapped to him always. Add in their strength and size, and the best way to survive a fight with them is to flee.

"Ugeen is too weak to lead nightcrawlers to a fish," Leith says.

"Soro isn't much better," Father says. "He's too reckless, and I believe he fears Vitor just as much as he may love him. For now, Vitor will remain the High Lord. And for now, we must take heed of the start of a potential war. As much as I don't want to agree with Vitor, too many want the resources Arrow has."

Misery and dread clamp my chest like a vise. War may be upon my country, and many of my people will die if it comes to pass. And on top of everything, I still have Soro to contend with.

Leith offers a short bow…and then offers us a moment alone.

Father gathers me to him again, and for a moment, I'm that little girl who always sought his kindness in times of distress. "War or not, Vitor will never grant me power, will he?" I ask.

Father kisses my head. "Not unless it directly benefits him."

"I'm worried for Leith."

"Stay by his side," Father tells me quietly. "You'll need his strength and his heart in the days ahead."

He's giving me his blessing. I only wish Papa could, too.

He chuckles as I squeeze him tighter. "I love you, Father."

Sadness clouds his tired eyes, ringing the orbits with deep shadows. "And I will always love you, my dear, dear daughter."

My smile arrives with unexpected tears.

"Now go," he says. "Find your gladiator."

I run, snagging my cloak as I practically leap through the terrace doors.

But Leith is gone.

Along the perimeter of the rear lawn, there's only the chorus of twilight owls and moonlight doves who flap their wings to add to their song. I race through the dark, my heart aching when I catch sight of the bench where Papa, Father, Giselle, and I used to sit and watch the sunset, each of us taking turns telling a story. My throat pricks as I hope that one day we will all sit on that long wooden bench again so Papa and Father can share their stories with their grandbabies.

My hair flies behind me as I run faster, toward the cottage. When I catch up to him, Leith is already past the blood orange lilies, their petals squeezed tight as they sleep, awaiting dawn. I stumble to a stop, the chill of the night cooling my lungs as I take long, deep breaths.

Leith takes me in, his stance rod straight and his grip tight over the hilt of his sword.

The petals along the starfire wisteria draping the weeping willow to my right open and close beneath the stars, releasing their tangy perfume and sweet nectar in drips that splatter along the ferns.

"What's wrong, Maeve?" he asks.

"They're all lies," I say.

He cocks his head. "What?"

It's one thing to know it and quite another to speak it aloud, especially in front of someone who I'd like to see me as his equal. "The power and influence I supposedly have as the princess are lies," I say.

He brushes my windblown hair behind my shoulders.

"I'm disturbed by Soro's sudden need to have me as his queen," I admit.

"I am, too," Leith agrees. Ah, and there's that rage again, simmering at the surface.

He watches me as I take his hands. "There's more," I say. "As much as I stubbornly believed that when I am queen, Vitor must heed me, he won't. To him, I'll always be a child."

"He will heed you if he wants to keep his head firmly on his shoulders," Leith says.

"I can't kill him for the same reason I know he won't kill me." I stare at our clasped hands. "He loves me as I love him. He's Uncle Vitor, the same man who used to carry and fret over me as his own."

"Vitor *would* kill you, Maeve, even if he loved you, if he saw you as a threat to his station. You know that, don't you?" Leith shakes his head. "He talked of my family, even as he spoke of threats at the borders…"

I frown.

"He knows, Maeve. The elf is not daft. He was…feeling me out. He sees me as the threat that I am, and he'll either come after me in the arena or make sure that I never fight another match."

He does know. I hadn't fully thought about the dangers to Leith outside the arena, should Vitor realize my plan… How on Erth hadn't I realized this sooner?

My whole plan centers on Leith surviving the arena and becoming Bloodguard.

He rakes a hand through his hair, the strands falling back in place to frame his face. Stars, he's beautiful. And strong. And good.

"We come back to the same two options," he tells me.

"And they are?"

"I kill Vitor and Soro. Or you wind up marrying one of them."

I swallow hard. "Or we free Papa. He's innocent. If I can prove that, Vitor must relinquish the throne."

"And do you think Arrow would actually embrace him?"

No. I'm not sure they would. Even exonerated…he's not fit to lead.

"Probably not," I acknowledge, wishing I didn't have to. "But maybe it will buy us some time."

I wonder what he's thinking. What he's feeling.

After a few long moments, he sighs.

His sea-glass eyes are tormented as he takes me in, like the thought of me coming to harm is more than he can bear. "I thought we'd have more time, Maeve."

Vitor and Soro have seen that he's well. That he can fight. And knowing that I don't want to marry Soro… Yes. Vitor has no doubt figured out my plan.

Once Soro does, too, he'll come for Leith. With everything he has.

Leith's hands frame my face, and he tilts my chin up to his. My mouth parts, already anticipating the feel of his kiss. But he doesn't kiss me. Not yet.

His thumb rubs across my bottom lip.

I shudder in his arms and say what's in my heart. "I want all my tomorrows to be with you."

His eyes flare, the pale green glittering in the moonlight. "Whatever time we have, I shall forever cherish."

I go up on my toes and press my mouth to his before I take his hand and guide us toward my favorite place in the world. To our personal slice of paradise. "Then let's not waste it…"

CHAPTER
35

MAEVE

My trembling hands relax to the sound of the waterfall on the other side of the lake.

My racing heart… Well, that's something else. It pounds against my ribcage as it demands I give every last bit of it to Leith.

I unfasten the back of my dress. Leith would never pressure me. He wouldn't even ask. And for that reason and so many others, I want him to have it. To have *me*. Slowly, my clumsy fingers tug each button free, and I pull one sleeve down, then the other, exposing all that I am. Every curve. Every bit of pretty.

Every flaw. Every imperfection. Every piece of me that I've respected and even more I've wished away. For Leith, I bare it all.

He quiets, drinking me in. But his chest rises and falls fast, and his eyes are darker, the pupils dilated so that only a thin rim of pale green shimmers in the moonlight.

I hold my hand out to him, and he takes it. His thick, curved lashes fan over his eyes as he bows his head and kisses the back of my hand. "Are you certain?"

I've never been more sure of anything. "Yes, Leith—"

In the next heartbeat, I'm in his arms, his mouth hot on mine, tongue teasing and tasting. I gasp against his mouth at the feel of his big, rough hands gliding over my skin.

There's a clang when he drops his scabbard to the grass, a pull of cloth as he removes his cape, a slide of leather as he peels off his boots, and a slip of fabric as he loses his breeches.

Leith stops briefly to catch his breath and lift his shirt over his head, his dark hair falling to cascade against his shoulders. Mesmerized eyes skim over my face and drag down my body.

"You're so fucking beautiful," he whispers.

Then his hands are trailing along my skin, his lips following close behind. One hand strokes my waist, testing the side of my hip and curve of my ass, his fingers gripping me as if anticipating the way we will fit together. The other hand caresses my neck, touches my face, angling my head up so he can begin a leisurely exploration along my throat with his mouth and fingertips.

My back arches as Leith threads his fingers through my hair, sweeping his luscious mouth over every portion of damaged skin. He walks us backward until the trunk of the adoni wisteria tree is pressed against my back, his hard body against my front.

My breasts are sensitive, the hardened tips rasping against the muscles of his chest. He moves his torso back and forth, and I gasp. He smirks against my lips and then lifts each breast and cups them, rubbing across the tips with his thumbs.

I can't control my breaths.

Leith's shoulders are twice the breadth of mine and thick with corded muscle. Every raised scar and wound on his body—so many that I personally healed—makes me want to do as he does and reverently kiss each one. I touch him, my hands skimming over hard muscle and smooth skin.

He has known so much pain, my gladiator.

But this night, I can bring him pleasure. Of that I am profoundly certain.

His hands pluck at my nipples until I'm writhing against him. As I feel that long, hard part of him thrusting up between us, I switch my attention from his shoulders and chest to stroke my hand over the top of him. Leith tears his mouth away with a loud groan.

I'm not alone in this tempest.

He hefts one of my legs up and around his waist. When his hand trails below, I'm hot. Wet. I gasp at the way he touches me, and I use my leg hooked around him to pull him closer so the aching part of me slides over his erection, and he chokes on a muffled curse.

I grin against his mouth and then take us both under again.

His fingers tease a rhythm, dipping in, retreating, somehow making me hotter, more needy, as the incredible sensation building in my core makes my legs shake.

"Stay with me," he mutters.

As if I could be anywhere else. "Always," I whisper.

He kisses me, then rests his forehead against mine for a moment.

His thumb makes fast, tiny circles over my sensitive nub, and I tug at his neck and hair, each exquisite stroke of his hands taking me higher. And, *oh stars*, even higher. When I explode, he holds me through it, drawing each pulse of pleasure until my legs fold.

I'm swept up in the next instant, held close against his chest, wrapped in all that strength and tenderness. I marvel at how a man so formidable, so deadly in the arena, can be so soft, bringing me to such heights of happiness. I smile, and he smiles back.

He lowers me onto the bed of moss I've spent so many hours lying upon alone. I draw him in for a kiss, and I pour myself into it. Neither of us is alone anymore.

My trust. My faith. My love.

Yes, *love*.

This gladiator is kind and good and strong. He's everything I need and all I've ever wanted.

"Leith, I..."

He rests his forehead against mine once again. Then kisses me gently.

He rolls his hips, rocking against me and starting those tiny pulses all over again. On the next stroke, I grab hold of him, bringing his smooth, round head to my core.

He stills. His muscles tense.

I put my heels on the ground and arch up. There is pressure and fullness, and a quick flash of discomfort that is already abating.

Leith shudders and waits.

His body is as taut as a string of a violin, and inside me, his thick length flexes in a way that makes me moan. He withdraws a little and then pushes forward again. The friction—it's so good. I gasp, and it's all the encouragement he needs.

He pulls back nearly all the way out and then enters me again. And again.

And again. He starts gently, too gently. I need more of him, and I need it *now*.

"Leith." I practically growl his name, spurring him to go faster and deeper until I'm bowing my hips to meet him at every thrust.

I drag my hands down his back, urging him to continue.

And then there's only the slap of our bodies, our breaths harsh and intermingling, the scent of flowers and grass, summer and skin. Love and lust and pure, unadulterated pleasure.

I scream his name when I come undone again, each pulse dragging him closer, deeper. Leith groans but doesn't quit. He rides me through pleasure so intense I weep from it. He groans and praises me, his hands moving over my body like he can't stop touching me.

He slows only enough to roll so that he's on the ground and I'm seated atop him. When I straighten, he somehow sinks deeper, and I release a low-pitched rumble of shock.

He pumps his hips from below me, and I shudder. *"Fuck!"*

"Maeve. My sweet, sweet Maeve…we're just getting started."

CHAPTER

36

LEITH

Caelen and I have spent the better part of the day galloping to his birthplace of Tunder.

I'm atop Star and riding at a breakneck pace. Moon horses, being the masochists that they are, always want to go faster. We had to fight with them twice just to convince them to rest and drink from a creek.

Maeve insisted on going to the castle, despite my arguments to stay at the cottage. The blood oath she swore to help me win in the arena compelled her to learn what she could of the upcoming matches.

It's a miracle I wasn't called back to fight this morning.

My hands curl at the memory of waking before dawn, Maeve's lush body pressed against mine, her dark hair fanned out around us. Her blue eyes were so bright and wondrous as they gazed up at me. And later, as the sun rose and we waited for news of a match to be carried to the manor, for the banners to rise above the arena, declaring the odds and who would be fighting for the day…there were a few painful moments when she clung to me, her head on my chest and her arms wrapped tight around me.

It's been a long time since someone's cared about what would become of me.

"We're almost there," Caelen mumbles.

"You're certain we can secure this crew?" He claims he knows someone who can help my family escape Siertos.

Caelen's face remains stoic, and his braids shift along his back as he pivots on his saddle. "No. I'm not certain of anything. But we must try, and this is the only way."

Vitor knows about my family. He could harm them to get to me. I must get them out. Hide them someplace safe.

I adjust my hold on the reins. Like Caelen, I rise and lower, leaning forward and back on the saddle, pretending that Star isn't doing all the work.

I catch Caelen's smirk. "Something funny, elf?" I ask over the pounding melody of hooves.

He grins, an expression I've rarely seen on this soldier. "No. But it would have been if your horse hadn't kept your ass in that saddle, gladiator."

"It's too late in the game to develop a personality," I retort, forcing my features to still when Star skids along a sharp curve and all but kills us both.

Caelen shoots out his hand, careening to a halt, a cue that Star follows abruptly. The splatter of mud that accompanies our stop barely finishes hitting the dense grass before Caelen's head cranes to the far right. "Take off your cape," he says quickly. "We're nearly to the border."

My pause is brief as he removes his military robe of green and blue and throws it to me, unveiling his uniform in the same colors beneath. The colors of Arrow. No, of House Iamond, Maeve's family.

"Drape it over your clothes and pull down the hood," Caelen tells me.

I do as he says as he positions himself beside me. His horse and Star chuff and stomp their hooves, eager to resume their run. It takes Caelen stiffening for the horses to pick up on his unease and settle.

I follow his gaze to the south as small drops of rain splatter against my nose. The rain clouds move in the direction he's watching. The storm is moving quickly, though, with clear skies across the whole eastern horizon.

It's then I see a band of people break through a distant stand of trees and run across the field, headed in the direction we rode through. A giant—bigger than Luther, from what I can tell from my position—forces his short legs forward with a baby strapped to his back. The human men ahead of him are faster, as are the ogren women lifting their skirts as they sprint ahead, screaming.

A literal army chases them on horseback, four surrounding the giant and his child first before he's able to return to the trees. More soldiers appear in the direction the others are running, their bows and arrows aimed at the migrants. The migrants—for surely that's what they are—skid to a halt, many of them falling onto the damp grass before they rise with their hands up.

A scout in a muted uniform of Arrow's green and blue leads her horse toward the large group, pausing when she notices us. Caelen acknowledges her with a tilt of his chin. I follow suit, but it's only when the scout returns the motion that I think we're clear.

"They almost made it," Caelen mutters. He turns his horse away and toward the stand of trees they emerged from. "Let's go while they're occupied."

I urge Star to follow, but like me, she isn't keen on leaving just yet. The soldiers round up the migrants. To the west, a troll rides a wagon similar to the one used to escort the gladiators to the arena. Hell if I don't know where they're headed.

My scowl fixes on Caelen. "Is this what my family is in for?"

I've never known Caelen to sugarcoat a damn thing. And he doesn't start now. "Yes," he says. He shakes his head when I curse. "I never said it was easy, but if anyone can get them through, Xavier will. Come. It's just through here," he says.

Star hesitates because I do. "You can't help them," Caelen says, speaking through his teeth. "But you can help your family, and that's what we've come to do."

He's right, and I fucking hate him for it. Without another glance back, Caelen stirs his horse into a canter and then a gallop.

Star and I don't take long to catch them.

We tear away from the open field, slowing when we reach the dirt path that leads through the forest. Like most of the ground we crossed, it's muddy, but here, large and small stones cover the uneven path.

"A few years ago, Tunder decided to build a direct route into Arrow and a network of supporting roads on both sides of the border."

"I imagine that was good for commerce."

He shrugs. "Trade flourished for a time. But once migrants started to use it, Arrow reconsidered, and their portions of the roads have not been maintained since."

"Have we crossed into Tunder?"

"Not yet."

He motions upward. Hidden within a canopy of green and yellow leaves is a square stand where three more soldiers in Arrow uniforms wait. Once he points it out, it's easy for me to spot others. I catch one and then another, mostly patrolled by humans, elves, and a few trolls with wrinkled skin that blends into the bark.

Shit. According to Maeve, Soro has repeatedly asked Vitor to close the borders. Looks like the bitch has finally decided to throw his mangy mutt a bone. And man, if it isn't one hell of a bone.

But these watchtowers... They weren't erected overnight. This plot has been in place for some time, I realize. I wonder what this will mean for the future of Arrow and its surrounding realms.

Guards are stationed every dozen yards here.

"I used to think Arrow prided itself on open borders."

Caelen's wry expression isn't lost on me. "Open to those that Arrow wants to welcome." He makes a show of adjusting the medals along his uniform so his high rank is evident to any guards mounted in the trees. "The new laws are being enforced *aggressively*. Even royal envoys are being turned away."

Of course they are. There will be no more potential suitors for Maeve.

"Is this the only path?" I ask. I can't see how anyone could make it past unnoticed.

"There are gaps along the borders that aren't manned," Caelen whispers. "Only due to lack of patrols. But the penalty for breaching them is imprisonment." He looks at me. "That's not the way your family will be escorted in. They'll have to traverse the mountain passes."

"Good," I say. As he well knows, criminals find themselves in the arena nowadays. For most, that's a fate worse than death.

I'd prefer not to risk moving my family at all, but there is nothing stopping Soro or Vitor from having them killed or capturing them so they can control me. And just moving them out of Siertos isn't enough—the

Regent of Arrow's reach extends anywhere my family could go, except under my own protection.

Plus, once they're in Arrow, they'll have better access to Maeve's healing herbs. A permanent cure for Dahlia, better food and shelter for my family, and at last an education for Rose, who's always dreamed of writing stories.

Star chuffs as she splashes through a puddle, splattering mud onto her legs and mine. Maybe I should care about how badly I'm soiling Caelen's robe. Nah, there's so much more to be concerned about.

I'm due for my next match, and Soro's made no secret of wanting me dead. If I'm caught today, I must hope they'll throw me back into the arena rather than having me executed on the spot.

Though I'd put higher odds on Soro just calling for my head.

I glance at Caelen. He's taking a major risk accompanying me and disguising me as one of his own. He seems to be fiercely loyal to Maeve and her family, but I wonder if that loyalty will hold if something happens during our time in Tunder and he's put to the test.

A few minutes later, the steep forest path widens, and we begin to ascend the side of a plateau.

"*Now* we're in Tunder," he tells me.

Forget about watchtowers. There are walls high enough here to rival the height of the arena.

We guide our horses along the whitewashed stone border.

"Tell me more about Xavier," I say. "If that's even his real name."

Caelen doesn't bother defending him, turning his horse onto the dense ground to avoid another wide puddle in the road. "I'm told he leads a band of heavily armed mountaineers. Together, they make frequent runs. He's a mountain troll and swears he and his crew can survive under any conditions."

"Do his charges survive under his watch?" I ask.

"The terrain can be treacherous, but I'm told they reliably deliver."

I'm already worried about my mother and sisters traveling with strangers across dangerous territories. I suppose that's why his mention of a heavily armed crew gives me pause.

"Are outlaws a problem?"

Caelen shrugs. "They can be. People in the denser forests are poor and desperate, depending on the time of year. They'll attack anyone they can secure goods from. Xavier's crews are prepared to protect themselves as well as those they transport."

I have questions. Many of them. Like why does Arrow's military let this troll run free? If they know of him and wish to stop goods or persons from trespassing, then why haven't they set a trap for Xavier before? I'd ask, but I don't think Caelen will be forthcoming with answers.

And the fact remains that I have few options.

As the ancient trees thin, I catch my first real sight of Tunder. And that view only becomes larger and wider as we cross the plateau. The city center comes into view above the walls like a giant rising from sleep. I expected Tunder to be smaller. Much smaller. I suppose after all my time in Arrow and the constant reminder of how *awesome* Arrow is, I've developed a prejudice and can no longer imagine any realm close to Arrow's equal.

"This is your homeland?" I ask, taking in the immense white towers and concentric levels of the city that appear to ascend like a spiral.

He nods. "It is. But Arrow is more home than Tunder ever was."

"Why?" I ask.

"My father and Maeve's grandfather — the Good King Masone — were cousins. My mother was never a part of my life, and my father didn't seem to want to be, either. I attempted to excel in academics and athleticism to win his respect. And while I never earned his, I did catch the queen's attention. She invited me to Arrow the summer I turned eight. I never left, nor was I asked to return to Tunder."

"You grew up with Maeve and Giselle," I say.

He nods, and I almost catch him smiling, but then his demeanor and his stance turn rigid. "There was an agreement made between the queen and my father in exchange for me staying in Arrow. But yes, my childhood was spent with Maeve and Giselle. Mostly Giselle. Maeve had other duties. Giselle didn't have enough."

My guess is that he and Giselle found enough to do together. I rub my jaw. I almost ask him if it was love at first sight or if their friendship became more with time. But ultimately, I don't. If he wants me to know something, he'll tell me. He's already shared more than I ever expected to know. No need to pry.

We ride up to a line of people, the adults fretting with each step closer to the wall while their mercifully innocent children chase each other and play. The Commons are easy to recognize. These people could be my family, could be me, but fate had something else in mind. Shit. What wicked blows fate can wield.

All it takes is a glance at the colors we wear for the guards to allow us through. We don't wait in line. We don't open our saddlebags or answer any questions.

I pretend to be indifferent. It's a skill I developed over time, and by now it should be second nature. Today, it takes some doing to bring my apathy forth. The guards stationed here nod and salute Caelen. They may be doing their jobs, but I detest them on sight.

Ahead of us, a battalion of foot soldiers marches our way. I try not to react when the ones in the lead lurch forward in a sprint.

"You there! Halt!"

CHAPTER

37

LEITH

Hand on my sword under my cloak, I ready for attack.

"Just keep moving," Caelen murmurs.

"Halt," the elf in the lead calls again, his voice carrying over the growing discord behind us at the gate. "You!" he shouts, and I glance back to see that he's pointing at a giant with a huge pack slung over his shoulder.

I release my sword and let out a breath, resisting the urge to look back while the unmistakable sounds of clubs striking flesh break out behind me as the soldiers subdue the resisting giant.

"This way," Caelen says. He leads us through the bailey into an open courtyard flanked on either side by tall battlements. Wait…this isn't a courtyard, even if there are fountains and draping flowers and pruned trees. This is a clever funnel. It's the only way into Tunder—which leaves us like fish in a barrel.

If the many archers upon those battlements decide to shoot down on the procession of travelers crowding along with us toward the next gate, we're screwed.

"I take it Tunder is about as receptive to immigrants as Arrow?" I grumble.

Caelen nods stiffly.

Once we're through, I twist in my saddle for a better look at the trolls and giants, the humans and elves, the shifters and fairies who are screaming back at the first gate. As guards with drawn swords surround the giant who is now face down on the ground, I hear that lead elf's voice again, ordering someone to get on their knees.

"Quit fidgeting," Caelen tells me. "Focus forward."

Though it's hard, I force my gaze ahead.

One block. Two blocks. Three. That's how long it takes before I manage a breath that isn't painful to take.

All the structures along the cobblestone main street are constructed of white stone. Their rooftops resemble a field in bloom—all bright colors, although I notice some method to the hues. Blues on the bigger homes, yellows for what appear to be businesses, reds for restaurants and taverns. The colors are bright, sweeping like strokes of a very thick paintbrush.

Caelen offers a stiff nod to pedestrians on the way to market. Everyone from a troll with soot on her hem to a young elf dressed from head to toe in silk gives Caelen ample space the moment they catch sight of his green-and-blue military uniform and how his hair is shaved on the sides. They know he's a legitimate member of Arrow's army—a high-ranking member—even if they recognize that he was once one of their own.

We reach the top of one street and descend another before either of us speaks again. "The inn where we're meeting him is not much farther. Giselle should already be there."

"Giselle?" I ask.

Caelen presses his lips into a thin line. "Giselle does what she wants, when she wants, and her steed, Usic, is faster than any moon horse, save for a few in the army. With her royal crest, she would have been permitted entry automatically." He sighs. "I know she wants to see an herbalist here, and in her own way, she wants to watch over us. She'll be here. On my life, it's only a matter of time before she shows herself."

Watch over us? I glance at the fearsome soldier next to me who clearly needs no watching over but decide to keep my mouth shut.

He's done talking about Giselle, and despite wanting to, I don't ask about the affliction that no one dares speak of. Maeve's secrecy about it bothered me at first—and I still want to understand the gloves and know what threat, if any, Giselle might pose—but I respect her loyalty and Caelen's, too.

Our moon horses pick up to a trot as we reach Tunder's main square. Two streets past, and then down another four. There are lefts and rights, and though I try to commit the directions to memory, it feels like we are turning circles in this place.

Finally, Caelen pauses. "We're here," he says.

A stable girl reaches for his horse's reins.

Another young girl reaches for Star's bridle as I idle beside where Caelen strokes his white-and-tan mare. He looks up, so I do, too, releasing a string of curses when I catch the name of the pub.

Your Mother's Bloomers

Now there's a place you want to meet the man charged with your mother's and sisters' safety.

The roof of Your Mother's Bloomers is more moss than shingles, coating the tiles in red and green patches. The pointed roof arches go this way and that, more of a last-minute thought.

I glance into the elegant tea shop beside it. Through the window, I see an assortment of well-dressed patrons sipping from teacups and sating their appetites on towered plates of pastries and pies.

"Tell me we're going into that tea shop," I say through my teeth. The last thing I want to do is sip tea with my pinkie high in the air or whatever the fuck, but the pub looks like where murderers go to put hits on their grandmothers, not a place we'll find someone trustworthy to safely transport my family.

Caelen strokes his horse one last time. "We're going into the tea shop," he says.

I hop down beside him, staring at my mud-splattered boots, and scratch Star behind the ears before she's led away. "We are?" I asked, relieved.

"Nope," Caelen says. "I'm just telling you what you wanted to hear."

Caelen strides toward the pub as a dwarf and a very naked giant stumble out. An enthusiastic roar of the crowd in the tavern shouts, "Drink, drink, drink," loud enough to overtake the busy street.

The naked giant holds the door for us before joining his gentleman friend…vomiting into a sewer. Yes, indeed. This is a classy establishment.

"Drink, drink, *drink*!"

A crowd gathers around a small table where an ogre with spiky fair hair and black clothing guzzles down a pint of beer. The changeling in front of him morphs from a large cat to a pink possum and then to a stunning, brown-skinned human before slamming her metal cup down.

Caelen stops briefly, taking in the madness and the scathing looks tossed our way—can't blame them, I'm dressed like a real asshole right now—before he quietly crosses the room and into a dark corner.

He slips into a booth, and I follow, sitting beside him. My companion raps twice against the wooden table, pauses for a moment, and adds a third. As if materializing from the shadows, a mountain troll appears, pushing our table out of the way to make room for his massive body on the bench across from us. Traces of barely there black strands poke through a mostly bald head.

The troll smooths out what little hair he has like someone with bountiful locks, starting from his forehead. As he glides his palm over his scalp, I catch sight of a deep scar in the shape of an *X* carved into his forehead.

"Xavier." Caelen nods.

The troll huffs, annoyed. "I go by many names. Pick the right one, and you might get what you need."

Caelen tosses a small sack filled with coins to the middle of the table. Xavier scowls at it and then at Caelen, who asks, "Do I have the right man now?"

Xavier doesn't open the sack. Just smacks a meaty claw over it and drags it to his side. "What do you need, soldier?" he asks.

"A human woman and her two young daughters brought to Arrow."

A strike of a match lights the scars that mar his face. A stab wound along his cheek is fresh and still not fully sealed. He takes a drag from whatever fragrant herbs he's rolled and releases puffs of smoke through his large nostrils and the gash on his cheek. "To sell?" he asks.

His exhale is strangled by my sudden grip on his throat. I'm not sure I could actually strangle a mountain troll, but I'm willing to try.

"Do not insult my bride," Caelen offers casually.

Bride? Does he mean my mother? Rose?

"My companion here knows I don't like to play games," Caelen says.

Xavier coughs, smoke billowing from his nostrils and mouth. Caelen is taking responsibility for my family. He's trying to help, and I'm only impeding his efforts.

Xavier gestures with his eyes for me to look down. I may have him by the throat, but he has me by the balls.

He smirks, jabbing my crotch with the flat side of his knife. "I think you may want to keep that."

Why, yes. As a matter of fact, I do.

I release Xavier's neck and ease back slowly.

He waves a hand, leaving a swirl of smoke in the air. "I only ask because I *don't* sell or buy," he growls. He narrows his gaze at Caelen, using the rolled-up herb in his beefy fingers to point at him. "But three bodies means three passes, means three times the price, Cael. And my rates have gone up."

It's clear Xavier knows *exactly* who Caelen is.

In the next blink, Caelen has the troll lifted with one arm and slammed against the wall. Xavier is easily four times the soldier's weight.

"I said no games," Caelen growls. His eyes are glowing amber, and the skin on his arm is expanding. His voice... It isn't elven.

The troll grins.

Before I can get a word out, Caelen releases him. Without further negotiation, my companion tosses three small sacks of coin to the troll. "I've brought no more than usual, Xavier. Take it or leave it."

Xavier peeks inside each bag, weighs them crudely between his hands, and eventually tucks the pouches into his very large pocket.

"And there will be three more when they come back to me." Caelen transfers a note into the troll's hand. I recognize it as the one Maeve wrote with descriptions of my family. She made it so I wouldn't have to come here myself, but I refused to entrust my mother and sisters to a smuggler I hadn't seen with my own eyes.

I have my own dagger out now. "Or three times more torture if you fail."

Xavier jabs himself in the chest with each word. "I don't fail. Neither does my crew." He pauses. "Two weeks from this day. And they'll be with you." His eyes dart around the room before settling back on us. "Here."

I frown as the chanting crowd bellows and the newest chugging-contest participant, a mage, face-plants onto the floor, sparkles of red floating from his unmoving form. "Here?" I question.

Xavier nods. "Here and safe, Cael," he promises.

Caelen jerks his chin toward the door. I follow him outside.

The purpose was to get them into Arrow. But perhaps that isn't possible? Even through the mountains.

"Caelen—"

"Steady, soldier," he says. "The last bit was for anyone eavesdropping. Xavier knows where to find me."

Rather than head toward where the horses are being watered, Caelen marches to the establishment next door.

Where the tavern was dim and smoky, here everything is pristine and white, and I feel as out of place as a donkey in a palace.

"What are we doing here?" I ask as we're led by a very tall female elf toward a table beside the front window.

"Drinking tea."

We sit. Caelen orders. Tea is served.

I guess he isn't going to bring up what transpired in the tavern, but my suspicions are already confirmed. The night Maeve lanced the wounds on my legs, that ungodly roar, the weight and menacing voice of the shifter that constrained me...it was him.

"So, there's a warm and fuzzy side to you," I say. "What are you? Some super-sized bunny shifter?"

Caelen's offended expression makes me snicker, then laugh outright. The sound is rusty, but even his lips twitch at this brief moment of levity. And he doesn't deny it.

I realize why I feel good. Because for the first time in a very long time, I have hope. Getting my family out of Siertos means they'll have a chance at a better life. Even if I don't survive to make Bloodguard, they'll be supported.

I can imagine them in a small house near the manor, helping Jakeb and his staff and being cared for by Neela and Maeve. My sisters will swim in the lake and pick flowers in the fields.

"Something to eat, sir?" The human serving our table addresses me, but her gaze stays on Caelen as if he's someone important.

"No, thank you," I mumble. Little cakes don't call to me like the scents of the stewed meat and tangy ale the tavern had. I can't help looking at the door.

Caelen follows my gaze. "We can go back if you want, but I'd prefer to scout the place from here. We'll draw less attention this way."

"We wouldn't have drawn *any* attention if you hadn't started to shift and lifted a troll over your head."

He takes a beat, then makes a face that says *fair enough, man*. And then I'm smiling for the second time today. Maeve would be over the moon.

"I *meant*," Caelen clarifies, "we'll stand out less among the other military officials here."

He has a point. Though the colors are different—purple and white—there are uniformed members of Tunder's guard here, along with what look to be merchants and members of the Middling class.

This may not be Arrow...but there are many similarities.

We sip tea and stare out the window at the sun setting over the walls. A muscle starts to tick in Caelen's jaw. "She should have found us by now," he says, worry casting a dull glow along his copper skin. "She knows we can't afford to be here for long."

Bells toll. The loud ringing makes my blood hammer through my veins and my heart beat fast. It's the feeling I get before I step into the arena.

Caelen stands abruptly.

"What's happening?"

Outside the tea shop, guards sweep the streets. They bear the colors of Tunder—*and* Arrow.

"Damn. I'd hoped we'd gone unnoticed." Caelen drops a handful of coins on the table. "Time to go."

The bells continue ringing as we rush to reclaim our horses.

"We need to find Giselle and get out. Now."

"And if we don't?" I ask.

"We will," Caelen insists. "We must."

I mount Star and follow him. The streets are too busy to hurry the horses, a fact that both mounts resent. We stand out on their tall backs, and where the colors of Arrow gained us entrance to the city, I worry that now those colors make us a target.

And still those damn bells ring. "What do they mean?"

Caelen's expression is grim. "They're closing the gates. Early."

Shit. How are we supposed to leave this walled city?

We could find a place to scale the wall, but we can't abandon the horses. On foot, it would take days to make the trek over the mountains— also, I'll admit I've grown quite fond of my mare and don't want to leave her behind. We can't hunker down and hide, either. The penalty for missing an event in the arena is death. I *must* get back to Arrow.

"This way," Caelen instructs, guiding his moon horse along backstreets until we're approaching the main bailey at an angle.

I spot the platoon of blue-and-green-uniformed soldiers at the same time Caelen does. He growls something I can't make out.

They block the only open path out of this walled city.

I reach for my sword.

"Wait!" Caelen says.

Then I see her. The Arrow guards have surrounded Giselle. "I'm a citizen of Arrow," she proclaims. "Get your hands off me!"

"She knows we're here," Caelen whispers. "She's providing us a diversion. Don't waste it."

"You dimwitted, arse-sniffing, swine-kissing fools, you have no right to detain me!" She starts pushing and shoving the soldiers as we walk our horses through the crowded courtyard toward the main gate.

Caelen has a bag of gold in his hand, and he drops it into the palm of a Tunder guard stationed near the gate. He's a giant several feet taller than Luther. The guard strides ahead of us, blocking us from view. We clear the gate.

I know I shouldn't look back, but I can't stop myself. That's Maeve's sister. I can't leave her.

The gate is closing. "Caelen…"

"Give it a moment," he tells me.

His voice is a low, rumbling growl. His beast is at the surface. Maybe that's his plan—to shift and go back for her.

But if they seal the gate…

The air around me charges like it did in the arena before that mage-made storm. I can smell the change in the air. It reminds me of the days leading up to flood season in Siertos, when heat-lightning would streak across the sky as the clouds continued to circle and grow.

The last thing I see as the gate shuts is Giselle peeling off her gloves.

Right before a massive ball of fire erupts.

CHAPTER

38

MAEVE

Leith and Caelen have been gone for hours, but I know it will be many more before they return. The trip takes between seven and eight hours in each direction—and that's without stopping or taking the time to meet the smuggler, Xavier, if he was even there. I worry that Caelen's contacts in his homeland may not be reliable or that relations with Arrow might test their loyalties. Every minute that passes feels like days.

I look up from the ledger I'm reading through and stare out of the parlor window. Within that spread of forest lies our spot beside the lake.

My thoughts keep circling to the events of last night with Leith.

The passion he awakened in me is like some invisible ribbon tethering us together. I want to do what we shared again. I want to do *everything* with my gladiator.

I feel my mouth curving, and I get it now. I understand what makes Leith so arrogant. Be it in the arena, beneath the stars, in a bed, or against the wall, he is...unequaled.

I want to dwell in the blissful memories. I want to take us back to those intimate moments again and again. But as beautiful as the memories of last night are, there are too many other harsh realities staring me in the face.

Leith still faces two matches in the arena.

My birthday is twelve days away—and I can only imagine what will unfold with Soro and Vitor when I'm fully eligible to marry and rule.

Leith's family is vulnerable.

There is unrest along the borders following Vitor's decision to close them.

Rumors of war abroad.

And here within our own realm are the stirrings of dissent. Ugeen, Aisling, Soro, Vitor.

All this while Papa rots in prison, Dahlia's health fails, and more fighters fall in the arena at Soro's whim.

"Maeve," Neela calls as she enters the parlor. "The courier came."

I rise when she hands me two letters, her expression grim. I'm not sure I can take more bad news or much more stress.

The first letter comes from Soro's desk and is addressed to Leith.

I hesitate only for a second before ripping the seal and unfolding the parchment.

> *Leith of Siertos, you are hereby ordered by General Soro of*
> *Revlis in observance of your contract heretofore signed upon*
> *your arrival in Arrow to report to the arena tomorrow, where*
> *you may or may not be summoned to compete in battle.*

Shit. Legs unsteady, I lower myself into my chair near the window.

I knew this was coming, but seeing the proof of it makes my stomach churn with dread. They will show Leith no mercy. I already visited the castle this morning to speak to the guards I've bribed. They claimed they had no new information, and I believe them. Whatever Soro has planned, he is not discussing it with anyone.

This is bad.

I wring my hands, then catch myself and settle them on my breeches. Leith will be exhausted when he returns. I already have tonics prepared, fresh blankets on the bed, and food waiting, so he can rest and eat and sleep. But he might not have time for any of that. And I hate to think of him being disadvantaged when he steps into the arena.

He still isn't fully healed from the last match.

I force myself to remain calm. I need to think. I ready for the second letter, and when I see the scribbled marking on the cover, my heart skips a beat. I shouldn't open it, but I need to know that my medicine arrived in time. Need to prepare myself to care of Leith's family in the event that it did not. In this moment, I choose to ask forgiveness rather than permission.

It's a short, barely legible note, scribbled by Leith's sister Rose's hand. I skim it quickly and sigh in relief.

His "little shadow" is still sick with fever, but she lives. It's hot where they are instead of cold and rainy as it should be this time of year. Perhaps the instability of the weather plays a part in why sweet Dahlia continues to fall ill. Stars know it's causing problems in every other corner of this world.

I hope Leith's mission with Caelen will prove fruitful.

It won't be easy. With the borders closed, arranging passage out of Siertos may be impossible. But as Father pointed out, we have a better chance of defending them here.

But if they can't reach Arrow...

I return to the ledger I was skimming through, only to slam it shut and toss it back on Papa's desk, stirring Toso awake from where he naps on the windowsill.

Toso is our largest estrella, his size similar to a full-grown lemur. I smile when he chirps and leaps onto my shoulder, and I stroke the fur on top of his head. Estrellas are smart and can understand sentiments and even some words. Not like moon horses but more than any non-magical beast, to be sure. And while I don't think he can understand me now, I speak aloud nonetheless. "I'm worried about Leith," I say.

Toso nestles against me.

I can't just wait here. I must do something. *Think, Maeve. Think.*

Should Leith and Caelen fail to secure passage for Leith's family, if they must remain in Leith's home of Grey, then they'll need food and supplies in order to survive.

My darling fuzz ball chitters and clings to me. It wouldn't hurt to have a little company, especially from someone protective. "Neela, do we have a large sack I can fit Toso in?"

Neela eyes me. "And why, my dear?"

"I need to get to town, and I'd like a little company."

Neela crosses her arms. "Why can't your company consist of guards, as your station requires?"

I scratch Toso's furry back, making his hind leg twitch. "Guards would attract attention." I shrug. "Attention is not something I need right now. I'll only be to the aviary and back."

Neela raises her bushy eyebrows but doesn't question me further. "Fine. But don't dawdle and be back before supper."

She flaps her hands and heads in the direction of the kitchen. Toso leaps from my shoulder and races after her.

I hurry to the stables. I saddle Knight and mount quickly, then circle back to the manor, where Neela waits. She lifts Toso, who grips a leather sack with a long strap in his teeth. The moment I loop the strap over my shoulder, Toso jumps in, burrowing and squirming inside the thick leather until he's comfortable.

Then Neela hands me three pouches of gold. "The proprietor drives a hard bargain."

"Of course he does."

"The aviary is in Lady Ashara's former abode."

I nod.

"Be careful, Maeve. Don't draw attention."

She knows what I mean to do, and she's not trying to talk me out of it. I urge Knight forward, and he charges away from the manor.

"Try not to look so smug," I tell Knight when we pass the main city stables. Moon horses are intelligent and full of personality, too. He knows what I'm saying.

He huffs and swings his tail, communicating that he can't help it if he's pretty. I laugh and stroke his mane. "Yes, you're the prettiest," I agree.

The elderly human woman who sells turkey legs looks up from her stand as I enter the city, her thick brush dripping with the honey, salt, and pepper combination she uses to baste the legs. "Princess—" she begins.

I cut her off by pressing a finger to my lips. She nods and whispers to the fairy helping her. He flutters off to spread the word that I'm trying to go unnoticed.

Neela mentioned that the mailing service is in what used to be Lady Ashara's home before she was stripped of her title and banished from Arrow. I never met her, but Papa told me she was one of the few ladies of privilege to openly speak out against Vitor and my grandmother for their role in slaughtering the phoenix.

Lady Ashara was tough and loud, and it cost her. Grandmother could be generous, but she had little patience for anyone she suspected of disloyalty.

Knight's hooves *clop-clop* along the cobblestone path that leads to the older part of town. The run-down neighborhood once brimmed with affluence. As we reach the top of the hill and look down, I catch sight of the glass dome of Lady Ashara's former home.

Papa mentioned that she was a bird and butterfly aficionado and that she kept them in a massive solarium. "It makes sense that the mailing service would set up their shop there," I tell Knight and Toso. "It's the perfect place to rest and care for the messenger hawks." As I say it, one takes flight from the rooftop, its large wings stretched and several packages tied to its talons.

When I dismount from Knight in front of the shop, I tug my hood farther down my face. I readjust Toso's bag so it's more comfortable over my shoulder, then grab my saddlebag.

I reach the entrance, noting all the available merchandise lining the windows. There's quite an eclectic collection of everything. A bell rings above me as I open the door to the shop.

"Hello? Hello?" a voice calls.

I deepen my voice to mimic Leith's and do a terrible job. "Good day," I say. "I need to place an order."

The front of the shop is what was likely a grand foyer. Erected walls have cut the room in half, and they feature rows of shelves filled with trinkets, bags of rice, beans, flour, and even sweets. Soaps, perfumes, and more luxury items line the shelves behind a long counter where the shop owner waits. The counter takes up almost the entire wall save for the two closed doors at the far end. The glass cases display simple jewelry, silver pipes, and frames of gold sparkling with crushed stones—none well-made or befitting of the royals of Arrow's court. They are made for those of far less fortune.

A human man not much older than me with long blond hair motions me to the desk, scroll and plume ready in hand. A chain links the piercings on his nose and ear—oddly regal and expensive jewelry for a simple shopkeeper.

"What do you wish, and where, son?"

His voice is quick and animated. I slip the wide strap of Toso's pouch off my shoulder and set it gently on the floor, flap closed, then fumble through my saddlebag and pull out several vials of carefully wrapped elixirs and crushed herbs that help with fever. He places them on a scale.

I hold tight to my altered voice. "I'd like to send these to the village of Grey in Siertos."

He stiffens, his bright-green eyes shifting in my direction. "It's good that you came. This is the only way to get anything there," he says. "Who is this on behalf of, boy?"

My muscles tense, and I slide my hand to the hilt of my sword, camouflaged by my cloak. I'm unsure he knows who I really am, but his stiff demeanor bothers me. "It's on behalf of Leith—"

"The gladiator," he says. "Yes, yes, I know of him." He scribbles the weight on parchment, resuming his work. "Anything else you wish to add?" he asks.

"A bag of flour, a sack of rice, and a pot for boiling."

His eyes light up, no doubt because he charges by weight. "My hawks can carry a bag of dried corn as well, if that is to your liking," he adds, trying to sound subtle and failing miserably. I get the feeling he's trying to take advantage of my need to get things to Siertos. While I'm certain Vitor taxes him an outrageous amount, the jewelry he wears suggests he does remarkably well.

Something here is off.

Toso must feel it, too, because he climbs out of the leather pouch to stand defensively at my feet. Behind the counter, the shop owner is too busy tabulating the riches he'll make ripping me off to notice.

"Yes, corn," I say, voice pitched low, "and five pounds of dried bison meat."

It's all this man can do not to dance. "We only sell increments of ten pounds," he says. When I sigh and nod, he adds, "I must warn you, boy, such a heavy transport will require more coin and, well, more hawks. We can't overburden my children."

No, we can't, can we? "That's fine," I say, unable to keep the bite from my tone as I toss more coin on the counter. Is it a wonder these gladiators must save money to send money?

"Anything else?" he asks. "Perhaps something pretty from my shop?"

Before I can reply, there's a smack of wings and a deep shriek from a hawk behind the set of double doors. "A delivery," the shop owner announces. He scoops up the payment with a large smile and pockets it before slinking away. "I'll be right back with your receipt. Please, look around. I discount my items with every mailing."

"Sure you do," I say.

He grins, not caring what I say now that he has his payment, and disappears through the double doors behind the counter. I sigh and do indeed look around while I wait for his return. Perhaps I'll find some yarn Neela could use to knit Papa another blanket. The way he gathered it against his face during our last visit makes me think he misses the smell of home. As I walk down the display case, I notice a pair of sparkly hair clips. Perhaps Leith's mother and his sisters might enjoy something pretty of their very own. I step around the counter to get a better look.

They are dazzling and better quality than the other items on display. The price isn't terrible, even for this sleazy owner's standards. Mailing shouldn't be much, and perhaps I can convince him to waive the fee. I start to lift them when something in a cubby beneath the counter catches my eye.

Feet.

Doll feet.

Covered with green leather shoes just like Leith told me his little sister wears.

I wouldn't have seen the doll from the other side. I wouldn't have seen it from this side had the owner shoved the doll in just another inch.

Anger heats my skin. I pull out the doll with big brown eyes and short black curls I had made for a little girl who has never had a *fucking doll*.

As I do, several envelopes fall to the floor. When I recognize the handwriting as Rose's, I stop breathing. Toso, shadowing my every move, takes a sniff. Each envelope is marked with a number scribbled in what I recognize as the shop owner's hand. I reach for one, fury causing me to tremble.

I pull out the letter written on a tattered scroll. Unlike the other letters Leith received from home, this one has a date on top.

A date from *three years ago*.

The heat my anger stirred plummets, replaced by a frigid spike of cold down my spine. "No," I say. "Please, no."

I gather the envelopes from the floor and several others that remain in the cubby and sort through them by number, starting with the lowest first. My breathing is quick and painful. Every single letter is from three years ago.

There are several out of order—and it wasn't because of the extreme weather affecting the seasons. It's that Rose never learned her months in the right order, misleading the shop owner into numbering them incorrectly.

I must go by the seasons to properly sort them and read them. It's the only way I finally learn the truth. One by one, I read the brief letters.

Wer r u, Leith? Did u fawget us?

I cover my mouth. *No, sweet one, he never did. He* never *would*.

Dahlia is verry sic.

No.

Mama is sic. Shee gaeve Dahlia all her fude.

No.

Mama did ent make it.

Oh, stars.

Dahlia wonet waek up. Leith, help me. Whut do i do 2 waek hr up.

No!

Dahlia dyd. Imma lone. R u ded? Please dount be ded, 2.

In the last few letters, Rose's handwriting is barely legible. I know she's sick and starving even before she finally admits that she's dying, too. She pleads for Leith to help her, to save her, that she's scared and doesn't want to die alone.

The final letter is from a leader from Leith's village. It's dated fourteen months after Leith arrived in Arrow.

Two Leith of Grey,

I'm surry. We fond ur family and buried dem together. Dey wer ded a long time.

CHAPTER
39
MAEVE

I brace myself against the counter to remain upright, tears blurring the writing before me. Years. His family's been dead for *years*.

All this time, he's stayed alive, fighting to fulfill the dreams of a family long dead, a family he's trying to bring home.

The shop owner skips out from the back room, abruptly stopping when he sees the doll laying on the desk and the letters surrounding it.

His eyes widen as realization strikes.

But realization doesn't strike him nearly as hard as I intend to.

I intend to strike him dead.

I unhook my cloak. It flutters as I toss it away and unsheathe my sword. Toso hisses, leaping up and racing on all fours along the counter. Now that the shop owner sees my face, he damn well knows exactly who I am. He barely calls me by my title before he races behind the doors and locks them tight.

My anger makes me strong. I kick open the doors and sweep into a dark storage room. It's large and dusty, shelves piled and spilling over with valuable goods this devious little shit hoards for his own profit.

How much hurt has this man caused? How many lives has he ruined? How did no one realize this sooner?

I start forward, spinning away from the first shelf that the shopkeeper topples over to stop me and dodging the others that follow. The heavy and sharp contents slam and break against the old wooden floors. They create large piles covering the entry to the solarium.

The owner is pushing and throwing everything he can at me. I hop over tools, toys, clothing, and boxes of dried goods, my quick footwork mimicking an odd dance.

Toso bounds over the mess, his growls growing more menacing. I stalk toward the solarium, taking my time so my sensitive eyes adjust from the dark storage room to the bright space filled with sunlight. I freeze beneath the archway.

A dome encompasses the entire roof of the aviary. There's a large opening in the corner where the glass dome ends and the tiled roof of the remainder of the house begins. It allows the enormous birds access in and out, as well as exposing them to the elements, including those harsh enough to kill them.

Tethered across several posts are incredibly old and malnourished hawks, straining their bodies to reach the scraps of food intermixed with their waste on the floor. Their feathers are brittle from age and the disgusting conditions they're kept in. These birds are barely capable of flight. To task them with carrying supplies is heartless.

And to send them to the distant regions where migrants and gladiators arrive from? Impossible.

"How long have you been pocketing money and supplies meant for starving families?" I demand of the shopkeeper who's nearly halfway across the aviary.

He stills with his back to me. "Who said I've done that?"

"Are you this much of a monster?" I challenge. "Or are you so ignorant that you'd insult someone with a sword?"

Fingers wrapped around my sword hilt and attention still on the man, I point to the rope binding the hawk with my free hand. Toso follows my direction and skitters to the perch. "Set them free," I tell him, opening and closing my fingers in a biting motion, and off he goes. He gnaws through the rope anchoring the bird before bouncing along to the next perch.

It's only my anger that keeps my gasp from escaping. The hawk's ankle is shredded and unnaturally twisted. He is the oldest among the aerie, his glazed eyes and lowered head telling me that he gave up on life a long time ago.

"Go," I tell the hawk with a shooing motion, still keeping an eye on the man.

The poor hawk tilts his head from side to side, wary, then turns to his master for instruction, his loyalty evident despite the neglect and abuse. The man shakes his head, and the defeated hawk remains in place, wings drooping, and I'm infuriated even more.

"Toso," I say. "Fly. Go. Tell them."

Toso angles his furry head to the side, taking a moment to interpret my request before he enthusiastically repeats it in his own magical tongue. The hawk's eyes widen. He squawks once and expands his wings, soaring through the opening and not looking back.

"How dare you?" the owner asks, his voice rumbling. "They belong to me!"

"You don't need them anymore," I assure him. "As of now, you're permanently out of business."

"Says who?" he challenges.

"Says me!" I yell. "The heir to the throne!"

I tighten my grip on the sword when the bones along his spine crack and his ribs realign. A shifter. *Hmm*. But what kind?

He curses when the next hawk takes off, followed by another.

"Did you ever send anything you were supposed to?" I demand.

He laughs—yes, *laughs*. "Sure. At first. I needed proof I sent something, now, didn't I? And the wealthy always check."

He hurls a perch at me. Then a bag of grain. He's running around the room, and I weave to the other side so he can't backtrack.

My voice shakes from my hatred. "What about the gladiators?"

"Which one?" he mocks as he runs in the opposite direction.

"All of them!" I shout my words as I fling a dirty water bowl at him. He ducks, and it shatters against the wall beside his head. Coarse white fur sprouts along his back.

Two more hawks take flight at the sound. They used to drink from that filthy thing. They won't have to anymore.

The owner turns his head, and the long black nose of a badger twitches back at me. "Most die anyway!" he hisses. "How do you think I pay your royal taxes?"

My hands turn to lead. "You evil little worm."

His fingernails have grown into thick, sharp claws. Instead of running, now he stalks me.

Good.

He's challenging me, clearly to the death. "You're making a mistake," I tell him, my voice seared with rage. "And I swear it will be your last."

He leaps at me, finishing his shift midair.

I pivot and swipe, cutting off his greedy hand. A cry of agony rattles my eardrums. But chopped arm or not, he's fast and hits back, using his weight to send me crashing into a feeding station. My wrist strikes the corner, and I lose my sword. I barely catch the swinging claw he aims at my face.

Toso hurtles himself on top of the owner's head, biting and scratching. I follow Toso's lead, biting the exposed flesh of the owner's other arm. He screeches like the swine he is and violently shakes his head, flinging Toso away.

We roll along the dirty floor, wrestling and trying to kill each other. In his shifted form, he's able to put up a hell of a fight against me. The struggle is intense. He's heavy and strong, but I'm elven, mad as hell, and refuse to let him go. I turn, adjusting my body until I manage to clutch his trembling good arm between my legs. With all my strength, I twist. The limb is hard to break in his animal form. It takes some effort, but the *crunch* when I succeed is pure satisfaction, as are my blows that follow.

I punch him in the throat and kick him far enough away to give me time to scramble to my sword.

The shopkeeper leaps again, but Toso bites down on his ankle, surprising him and limiting the height of his jump.

Not a problem. It's high enough. Arcing my blade horizontally through the space between us, I sever his spine.

My first kill. I think I ought to feel worse about it.

Two halves of the shopkeeper land at my feet, but it offers me little satisfaction. He got off a lot easier than he deserved. Breathing deep, I stomp back toward the entrance and snag my cloak, draping it over myself to cover my bloodstained shirt.

When I reach the front door, Toso right behind, I kick it open, blood-slicked sword in one hand and Dahlia's doll in the other. It's only by luck that the streets are empty.

"Princess?" a familiar voice asks.

Or not.

I don't notice Uni right away. His old brown shirt and breeches blend into the siding of the house he stands before. He pulls his baby girl in a wagon and uses his free arm to carry a stack of firewood he must have just purchased, given he's so far from his neighborhood.

"Princess?" he says again.

I swallow hard. That title hurts me now. Princesses do better by their people.

As queen, my first task will be freeing Papa. The second, ending the combat in the arena. And every task that follows will involve seeing to those who need me and protecting them from the likes of that shifter lying dead on the floor of the shop.

My steps feel heavy as I walk toward him. "Uni, will you help me with something?"

He drops his pile of wood and looks from his child to me. "You saved my little girl. I'll do anything for you, Princess."

My eyes sting. Yes, he would.

"I want you to bring everyone who's in need to this store. Take whatever you want. Food, jewelry, gold—anything—oh, but first close the door to the aviary so no one sees the dead body. Will you do that for me, Uni?"

His eye sweeps down to look at his daughter. His sweet baby is wrapped in the towels I used to bathe her the day she was born. They don't have much. Today, they'll have more, as will everyone Uni brings here.

"Are you sure, Princess?"

"Yes," I tell him. "Just two stipulations. One, you didn't see me."

He nods. "What's the other?"

I take another look at that building that made its fortune in lies. "When the shop is cleared and everyone's gone, burn it to the ground."

CHAPTER

40

MAEVE

My hands continue to shake as I ride through town.

Dead. Leith's entire family is dead.

Good stars, how am I going to tell him?

The painful thud in my chest grows more pronounced as I remember that Leith is right now trying to secure a crew to bring his family home.

He risked his life traveling to Tunder. He's risked his life in the arena countless times. Everything he's done is for his family.

My stomach clenches. My heart *aches*.

"Great phoenix." I breathe in and out, blinking back tears. I bring Knight to a stop in front of a fountain and wipe my face on my cloak. This is an area of town with quaint little shops where one can buy fabric or candles, herbs or books. I dismount, and Toso peeks out from his bag. I tie the reins over a post. "Stay here with Knight, will you?" I ask him.

He nods, his large eyes fraught with sadness.

"Princess!" Ula hurries out before I make it to the front stoop of her shop. She's a stunning troll, her silver skin sparkling and her carrot-orange hair spilling past her apron. Her bookshop is a safe bet for where to find Father and Neela spending the afternoon. "It's so good to see you. Thank you for helping Obert."

Her husband is one of the miners I treated following a cave-in. "How is he?" I ask.

"Oh, the slippery devil can't keep his hands to himself." She bats the air. "In other words, good as new." She pauses when she looks at me. "Princess, have you been crying?"

I try to smile and fail miserably. "I just need to speak to my father." I glance past her shoulder. "Is he here?"

"Not anymore, dear," Ula says. "He went on to New Arrow a bit ago."

"Right."

"Are you listening, dear?" Ula asks.

"Yes. I'm sorry." I meet her eyes. "I need to speak to Father."

Ula nods and points. "Just cut through the alleyway there. One block from the end, make a right, then go straight until you reach the new inn. That's what he's working on today."

"Thank you." I pull my hood back over my puffy, crying eyes.

I don't have to walk long before the steady beat of hammers and the back-and-forth sliding of saws echo down the alleyway. My duties at the castle and in service of my community have kept me busy, and I haven't stopped in to see how New Arrow is coming along in a few weeks, but my, have they made progress.

Several elven and ogren women call from a rooftop, demanding more shingles.

"Come on with ye, Ostie!" an elf says. "We need to finish before the rain comes."

A giant with auburn curls down to his butt replies something in clicks and hisses and throws a large stack of tied shingles at them, not to them.

The elf, who has a tattoo on her face and piercings all along her eyebrows, catches it and places it between the two other women and scowls. "Ostie, there was no need to comment on my mother like that. I toldye ye can help us on the next roof that can better support ye weight."

Oh, and Ostie is not happy about it. More clicks and hisses precede a very angry fist and one irate finger.

"Come on, Ostie, ye know I didn't mean it that way!"

Just last week, they were working on the other block. At this rate, they'll be onto the next in a few days.

My feet have never failed me, and they don't fail me now. I jump out of the way, barely missing getting soaked when a troll empties a large bin of water and lye soap out from a third-floor window.

"Sorry, lad," he tells me, his beard soaked with sweat. "Didn't see you there."

I wave to those who smile as I rush by. They're not welcoming me as a princess. They're welcoming me as another of their own. Many women stroll along in simple cotton dresses in dark shades of red, green, and gray, their baskets stuffed with fresh vegetables and their faces absolutely beaming as they speak in their native languages.

A troll laughs with his wife as he turns a goat on a spit. Across from them, just a few yards from me, an elderly giantess sweeps her front stoop.

This is the Arrow I always wanted for my people. It may have been Papa's dream, but Father turned it into a reality. I never imagined the wonders a group made up of so many people from different walks of life and languages could create.

In another block, I'm at the inn. "I was told my father Jakeb is here?" I say to the human painting the exterior of the brick structure.

He smiles. "Down the hall, last room."

My hand slips over the handle more than once when I reach the door, my palms sweaty and shaking. With more effort than it should reasonably take, I push it open.

In a barren room, with a paintbrush in hand, wearing an old pair of overalls and his graying hair tied in a high bun, stands the great Lord Jakeb of Iamond, husband to Andres the once future king.

Royal by marriage.

Former High Guard of Arrow.

Philanthropist.

And a man with a broken heart.

In large, bold letters, **ANDRES** is emblazoned across the wall. Father must have written Papa's name with the blue paint he's using. As I watch, he paints over Papa's name with quick brushstrokes. "Sorry," he says. "I was just thinking of him."

There's no masking his sorrow.

My father's eyes widen. "You're upset."

He sets aside the paint and hastily wipes his hands on a rag.

I'm shaking by the time he reaches me. I think I might be in shock.

"Maeve!"

"It has to stop," I whisper.

"What?"

"All of it. The games. The lies. The deception."

My father looks fearful for me, like maybe I'm not in control of myself.

"We must get Papa out." None of this would have happened, *none of it*, if Papa had been on the throne.

Father strokes a few strands of hair away from my face. "Maeve, stop," he pleads. "You must stop."

"I can't!" I shout at no one and nothing in particular. "I can't stop. Not when Papa is innocent! Not when he—"

My voice trails off when Father holds up a hand, eyes brimming with tears. "Andres is not innocent, Maeve."

I jerk away from him, furious. But as I start to turn, Father clasps his hand over mine. "The night of the fire, he tried to save you, but he left Avianna there to die. Intentionally."

I whirl on him. "If he wanted Grandmother dead, he must have had a damn good reason."

Father shakes his head slowly. "None of that matters. He could have had the best intentions or the worst. Regardless, Andres must atone for her death."

My voice trembles with grief. "If that's true, why didn't you ever tell me? Why did you let me believe—"

"I *did* tell you, Maeve, that same day you woke. *Everyone* has told you, even Vitor. You choose not to listen."

My thoughts and memories tumble like leaves in the wind. I don't remember Father ever flat-out saying Papa was responsible for Grandmother's death. I look at the window, where a wren has decided to weave her nest. Have I been so set on defending and protecting Papa that I've ignored everything else? I shake my head. No. That can't be right. None of this can be right.

"You've been crying," Father says quietly. "Did something else happen?"

Stars. What's wrong with me?

"Maeve, what happened to you?" Father asks carefully.

254

I can't think about… I press my palms to my temples. No, this is too much. Everything is too much right now. Father kneels beside me when I slump to the floor.

"Maeve?" He grasps my shoulder gently. "Tell me what happened to you."

In the streets, the music and laughter continue to grow in contrast to the gloom surrounding this man who wants his lover back, the one who only barely speaks. The one who…who *isn't* innocent?

My mind is too bogged down to think clearly. This thing with Papa—I can't fix it now. And unless I become queen, I won't be able to make it right.

"I need to talk to you about Leith," I manage.

I tell him everything that happened in that aviary, every gut-wrenching word. When I remove my cloak and reveal my bloodstained clothing, Father's eyes grow as wide as saucers. By the time I finish, all I want to do is curl in a ball and weep.

"You mustn't let him know," Father says as if it's the only logical choice. "Nor must you tell another soul. This is a travesty for every last gladiator."

"Father, he *has* to know," I insist. "They all do."

Father leans closer to me where we remain on the floor. "No, Maeve. Not if you want Leith to win."

It's something I wish he didn't say. "I can't keep something like this from him," I bite out.

"You can if it means his life."

He might as well have thrown cold water on me with how chilled his words make me feel.

"Do you hear me, Maeve?" He looks back to the wall where he wrote Papa's name, now nothing but a smeared patch, blue paint dripping down the wall like tears. "A man, even a man as strong as Leith, does *not* come back from losing someone he loves."

CHAPTER

41

LEITH

What a fucking day.

Caelen and I huddle into our cloaks. The temperature dropped sharply as we reached the outskirts of Tunder, and we've been riding in the pouring rain for seven *fucking* hours. It wasn't until we reached the border with Arrow that the storm finally subsided. But by then, we were soaked to the bone and freezing, except, oddly enough, for Giselle, who seems to thrive in the rain.

The sun set hours ago. Night looms as we pass through the gates and onto Jakeb's lands.

"You should rest," Caelen says.

How can I? We were nearly caught. The fate of my family rests in the hands of a suspicious mountain troll. The borders are closed. And I...I likely have to return to the arena in the morning.

Caelen and Giselle wait for me to dismount. I'm not a rider by any stretch, but Star took pity on me. She butts me gently with her head, and I rub a hand down her long face. "You're all right," I tell her.

The horse whinnies at my pitiful excuse for praise. She loves apples. That could make up for it. But I can also bring her a different treat tomorrow. Maybe a carrot or something.

She nudges me once more, and I head toward the cottage.

It'll be dawn soon.

Fatigue and fear for my family weigh my steps. I could try to sleep, but I don't think I'd manage more than an hour, and that would dull my senses rather than sharpen them.

Neela waits outside the cottage beneath the awning, tucked out of the rain. She hands me a basket.

"Eat something, gladiator," the old troll says. "You're due back in the arena come morning."

My stomach plummets.

I knew as much, but hearing those words...

"Where is Maeve?" The whole ride back from Tunder, I've wanted to see her face.

"She's at the manor, but I'll alert her of your return," Neela replies.

I start to ask Neela why she was the one waiting here instead of Maeve, but she bypasses me and heads toward the manor.

I was already in a horrible mood, and knowing I'm returning to the arena makes it worse.

Still wet and shivering, I light the fireplace. Damn. That rainstorm seemed more magically charged than anything from nature, just like the fire that set the gate ablaze, creating all manner of havoc. I'm certain both were conjured by Giselle.

She's a powerful mage.

But despite my questions, she said nothing of what happened—even when I thanked her for her assistance.

I close my eyes and let out a deep sigh. I just want this day to end.

I strip out of my wet clothes and place them over the hearth. I change into dry breeches and a freshly laundered linen shirt, then wrap myself in a blanket, but even with the fire blazing, I'm absurdly cold.

Maybe tea would help. I approach the sink, and the exhaustion of the day punches me down once more. After filling the kettle, I lean forward, my head dropping against my arm as the water heats. Damn, I could curl up in bed and sleep forever. Maybe Maeve and I can lie in bed for a short while... She always knows how to keep me warm.

I lift my head and freeze. I'm not sure how I missed it when I first came in. Perhaps it was because I was damn well frozen.

Sitting on a mound of gold and black flower petals is a giant crystal bottle of belladom. What the hell? Maeve knows what my people go through just to get one tiny drop. I grit my teeth.

This fucking day.

My glare trains on the bottle and then, of course, on the stupid note.

My dearest Maeve,

Dropped by to give you an early birthday gift and to resume the conversation we had in Vitor's office. You know what I want. I know what you need. Find me.

Yours,

Soro of Revlis

Lord and General

That little shit stopped in again.

I seethe, then seethe some more. My family probably tore their hands up to harvest every drop that went into that vial. My people have suffered and died for centuries producing that shit. I can't believe this is even here.

The door is flung open, and Maeve rushes in. She's in a plain, deep-orange dress, and her cloak is soaked through. But that's not what gives me pause. Her eyes are swollen and red as if she's been crying. Maeve isn't a crier. She's shed maybe five tears since I've met her, and she practically sucked each of them back in.

"What's wrong? Did something happen to your papa?" I pull the kettle off the fire and hurry forward when she shakes her head. I wrap my arms around her and pull her to me. "Is it Soro? Did that piece of shit hurt you?"

"W-what?" she asks. She takes a good look at me. "Leith, you're shaking. Let me take care of you."

"I don't care about me," I say. I search her face. "Tell me what he did to you."

Maeve starts to speak only to abruptly quiet. She's seen the bottle of belladom. I release her as she walks toward the sink. "Where did this come from?" she asks, then reads the note and looks up. "He was *here*?"

Yeah. It does not bode well that Soro can penetrate the defenses of Jakeb's property so easily.

"Is this about your papa? Is Soro offering something to get him out?"

Her eyes well. "Soro can't release him. Papa killed the queen."

Now I'm the one confused. "Who told you that? Whoever it was is a liar."

"It was Father," she says. "Earlier this evening. In town. He said…he said everyone had told me, I just chose not to believe. Vitor likely only spared him for me."

Damn. "He could have had a reason…"

The slow shake of her head silences me instantly. I fold the blanket over the chair, certain she'll explain, but she doesn't. She doesn't mention the belladom or Soro. It's like she's at a loss for words. I decide not to press in order to give her time to, I don't know, settle or something.

"Papa killed my grandmother, Leith."

Is that why she blocks out the memories? Because she doesn't want to believe it? But then…when her eyes lift up to mine, they're haunted, like there's more.

"Maeve, did something else happen?"

She blinks, her lips parting only to abruptly press tight. My already frozen body chills further. "Maeve? What's wrong?"

Her light-brown skin blanches. Like splintering wood, she all but falls apart. I gather her to me.

"Tell me," I say. "Tell me what happened, and we'll fix it together."

"We *can't* fix this," she whispers. "I'm so sorry, Leith."

Is she sorry for crying? She doesn't ever have to apologize for that. I stroke her hair and kiss her head, trying to comfort her. She came to me. I have to find a way to give her what she needs. "What can I do to help?"

It takes her a moment to look at me, but when she does, it's as if every emotion, every kindness, every tender moment she's ever shared with me floods her gaze.

"You can't help me," she says, her voice shaking. "But by all the moon, please, let me help you."

She pushes up on her toes and pulls me in for one long, sweet kiss.

I circle her waist when our kiss deepens, every stroke of her tongue erasing all the frustration, uncertainty, and inhumanity the day brought.

My grip tightens as she deepens the kiss, my hands lowering to cup her ass.

As I squeeze, she abruptly breaks from my hold. I think I somehow scared her and try to step away and allow her a moment. But then she moves closer, watching me in that way that begs me to see and know only her. Even as she unties my breeches, her gaze never leaves mine.

"I love you with all my heart," she says. "*Please*, Leith—tonight, let me love you with my body."

My eyes widen, and my body thrums with heat at her words.

The soft fabric of my breeches falls to my ankles, and I kick them away in time for her to grab a tight hold of my stiffening dick.

Holy shit.

My eyes scrunch as my chin lifts to where the reflection of the flames dances along the ceiling. She starts working my dick from the base, gliding her hands up and down the length of me as she makes her way to the head, each pass of her thumb over the tip inciting a few drops to emerge.

She releases me long enough to pull her dress over her head and fall to her knees, opening her mouth to take me deep, her eyes never leaving me as she sucks hard. With every pull from her hand and her mouth, I grow dizzy as she removes what remains of her clothes with her free hand.

Her nails dig into my ass, encouraging me to pump in and out of the back of her throat. I don't have to tell her how damn good it feels, but I do anyway, my head spinning with how bad I want her.

I lift her in one motion and lay her across the worktable, spreading her legs so I can taste her tender flesh.

She jerks when I lick her. So I do it again, my tongue feathering over her center, working her faster when her fingers tangle into my hair and she pulls me closer.

Over and over, she calls my name, her body thrashing so hard I have to haul her back again and again to the edge of the table, my arms hooked around her legs to keep her in place.

Her back arches as she orgasms, tremors of bliss causing her body to quake. She writhes, the remains of the red-and-purple powder she was grinding on this worktable dusting her skin.

When she finishes, perspiration beads between her breasts and glides down her stomach. I flip her over, guiding her toward me until her feet touch the floor. She bends forward, her regal features flushed with lust as she tosses her hair over her left shoulder.

"Don't stop," she begs. *"Please."*

And I don't.

She watches me over her shoulder as I glide my dick in between her folds. Goose bumps splay across her back as I retreat slowly and push in harder.

Bang.

The table slams into a cabinet at my first hard thrust. But as her core slickens with each pump, the banging increases, as does her call for more.

Bang. Bang. Bang. Bang. Bang.

The rhythm is steady, building in time with the pounding of our flesh.

"You like this?" I ask. "You like me fucking you?"

"Yes," she rasps.

She grips the edge of the table as I increase my speed to match her surging desire.

"Harder," she begs, her head and messy hair falling forward. *"Harder."*

The fragrance of sweet pollen and sharp eucalyptus intertwines with the aroma of sweat and passion.

She finishes multiple times, but I keep going.

I turn her once more, throwing her legs over my shoulders, and her hands clasp my neck as our eyes meet.

I love her.

I don't know the exact moment that it happened. I only know that it did.

As I reach completion, I haul her into my arms, her legs snaking around my waist as I fill her.

I can't tell her I love her. Not yet.

That doesn't mean that I won't fucking love her forever.

CHAPTER

42

MAEVE

Leith claimed my body with aching tenderness.

He'd ridden for hours without rest or sleep, yet he made love to me as if I was the only thing that mattered in the world.

I held him and tried to show him how much I loved him, but then the pale rays of morning arrived, bringing reality with them.

Father insisted on escorting Leith to the arena, and I followed an hour later with Caelen and Giselle.

We were all exhausted, all broken and beaten down with worries and regrets. I sat in the royal box, my body strung taut as a bow, watching as each banner was raised. Soro toasted me each round, no doubt enjoying the torture.

But Leith didn't fight that day.

Or the next.

Or the next.

It's deliberate cruelty on Soro's part. Each day finds me sitting in the stands, my stomach churning as my fear for Leith makes it almost impossible to breathe.

My position as princess requires I sit and watch as fighters die, and it sickens me. I was able to avoid it for a time but not as long as I'd wished.

I cringe at the cheers and fervor of the crowd, their focus more on the coin they wager than the lives lost in the arena. Each night, when we return home, Neela has food for us and a hot tub of water waiting.

We bathe. We make love. We hold each other and sleep. Or at least try to.

It's hard to rest when we both know that the next day could sever us forever. Leith frets over his family and how to ensure their safety.

Everything he does is for them…and knowing the truth as I do… It ruins me.

There's a harsh knock followed by a pause. I know it's Caelen. Just like I can guess why he's here. "Gladiator, you're being summoned to the arena."

Again.

Leith is already dressed. I slip into my nightshirt as I watch him fasten his sword to his hip. He smiles at me—that crooked, confident smile that I know so well. I don't smile in return. The guilt of knowing his mother and sisters are dead is eating me alive. I'd decided to tell him, despite Father's warning, because I thought it was the right thing to do, but then I couldn't.

I just *couldn't*.

"Hey," Leith says, returning to me. He cups my face and brushes away a tear with his thumb. "Are you still not feeling well?"

I nod. The guilt of hiding this secret has ravaged me. And ever since Father told me Papa killed his own mother, I barely sleep or eat anymore. Bad dreams—that's my big excuse for the mess I've become.

"Gladiator," Caelen calls. "We haven't much time."

Leith kisses me, caressing my face gently. "Two more matches," he reminds me.

"Two more," I say. "Don't forget—there's supposed to be fire. Lots of it. The guard I spoke to warns that it's crucial you don't engage your opponent directly. Even he seemed scared of whatever they have planned for you."

"What of the weapons?" he asks.

"He kept the ones I intended for your previous matches and promised to sneak as many into the arena as he can."

He presses a kiss to my forehead. "Thank you."

"Leith," Caelen says. "If we're late…"

Still, Leith takes a moment to embrace me tightly.

It's only when I force a weak smile that he finally releases me.

I watch him and Caelen trot away on their moon horses. Caelen tosses his braids behind him as he looks back at me, his features troubled. I suspect he's heard of the fire at the aviary by now.

I wonder if he's figured out the full extent of it.

I should be riding with Leith, and it annoys me that I'm not, but the fewer who know about us, the better. And the less likely it is that Soro's hand will be forced.

My stomach rumbles, but the thought of food makes me nauseous. And forget how terrified I'll be seeing Leith go through whatever those monsters have designed for him.

Father and Giselle plan to see Papa after the match, unless I need help with Leith. I'd love to see Papa, too. If Leith fares well, maybe we both could visit him. And maybe, just maybe, I can somehow get Papa to tell me what happened. Or at least possibly admit his guilt. Could I maybe believe it then?

"Hello, Maeve."

I startle.

Soro is here.

In my cottage.

Dear sun above, where the hell did he come from?

I take several steps back. "What are you doing here?"

He's leaning against the counter as if he has all the time in the world. His gaze takes in the whole room, including Leith's clothes and mine tossed all over the place.

My face heats.

"Why do you think I'm here, Maeve?" His thin lips press into a line. "You're nearly twenty-one. I'm here to marry you before Vitor convinces you that someone else would make a better king."

"Come now, Soro. I'd think Vitor would welcome any delays. He remains Regent of Arrow, and you continue to lead as High General. I can't imagine that Vitor would *ever* want the status quo to change."

My reasoning seems to strike a chord. But Soro doesn't look wholly convinced. "No?" He taps his chin. "Vitor has taken a liking to your gladiator..."

He's referring to his father as Vitor again. It's not a good sign.

Soro drums his fingers along the edge of the counter, posing as if he's relaxed even as his gaze fixes on mine. "You know what he told me just last night?"

His peculiar calmness unnerves me more than any mood I've ever seen him in. "Soro, tell me what you're doing here."

He ignores me. "He told me, his son, his general, the lord at his side, the constant in his life, that I don't deserve the throne." His laugh carries enough bitterness to taste. "Vitor actually said that should something happen to him, some uneducated brute could lead Arrow better than I ever could."

"*Is* something going to happen to him?" I ask, barely getting the words out.

His darkening eyes travel from my face to the front opening of my nightgown. I clutch it and step back.

"Shall we sit?" he asks.

He's not really asking. Vitor has pushed him to the brink, and I think the rest of us are meant to pay for it.

I nod, trying to steady my nerves as I lower myself onto a wooden chair at the kitchen table. Soro sits opposite me, brushing the eucalyptus leaves I meant to mash today onto the floor. "He doesn't believe in me, Maeve. After all I've done for him…" He reaches for my hand. I give it to him, only to keep him calm. There's something very wrong with him.

"You believe in me, don't you? You know that I'm better than Filip ever was and that I'll always be better than anyone else."

"Soro, we already discussed this. I need time. We don't need to rush into this." I try to give a carefree laugh, which fails miserably. I stop myself from looking in the direction of the door. Does he know Leith just left? Of course he does.

He spreads his hands. "You're out of time, my wife. Say you'll marry me, and I'll have your papa released from jail. Hell, I'll free Andres myself." He leans forward. "Now, say it."

I hold my breath. How am I going to get out of this? I only need to hold him off until Leith wins two more matches, but by the look on his face, I doubt Soro is willing to wait.

I jump back when he whips out a dagger.

He arches an eyebrow and grins, then slices his palm. Words of the blood oath he intends for me to take flare and spiral along his arm. "No more games, Maeve." The shadows darkening his eyes leave me cold. "Swear on your life that you'll marry me."

I rise. "I'm not marrying you unless you free my father first," I tell him.

Time. I need to buy Leith and me more time.

"And not before my birthday," I add.

Soro pushes away from the table and slowly rises, lifting his sliced hand to his face. He swirls his tongue against his palm until the blood is licked clean and the words from the oath disappear into his skin. I shudder with disgust.

His demeanor is disturbingly hollow, but the way the corner of his mouth delivers a sudden twitch scares me in ways Soro has never done before. "I'm no longer asking, Maeve," he says. "Tell me yes. Last chance. Or I'll make you fucking regret it."

There goes another odd twitch in his otherwise ghostly features. It's haunting. No…it's evil.

"Soro, listen to me—"

"I am done listening. I am done waiting. You no longer have a choice, and neither do I." He walks around the table. I walk, too, keeping the slab of stone between us. "How else will you sit on that throne? How else will you free your papa…" He closes his eyes, leans back on his heels, and smiles. Sin cuts into that grin. "Never mind. You mustn't worry about him anymore."

I feel the blood drain from my face.

"One royal hand washes the other, Maeve," he says. "But if…" He shakes his finger at me. "If it doesn't, it's time to cut that hand off."

"Soro, what did you do?" I think that he's threatening me, that he hasn't acted yet, but I can't be sure.

"Consider it motivation to become my bride," he says. He watches me for a moment, quiet, calculating in a way that has me stepping back in search of a weapon. "And consider it a taste of what's coming if you deny me. Now say it. Say you'll marry me, or I swear to the great phoenix you *will* regret it."

CHAPTER

43

MAEVE

Forget fear. Anger rushes to the surface, heating my face. "Get out. Get the fuck out!"

This time when he looks at me, every plane along his sharp features hollers that he's won. "Very well. If you prefer things the hard way, that's exactly what we'll do."

He calmly strides across the room and leaves, shutting the door quietly behind him. It would have been less menacing if he'd come at me with the knife.

My body feels numb, and I swallow several times, so unnerved that I can't move right away…until the prickly feeling of being watched creeps over my skin. I rush to the window that overlooks the garden. No one is here.

But I'm not alone. I feel it in my bones.

I back away in the direction of the open bedroom.

It doesn't make a difference. It's already too late to hide. The door opens.

A royal guard with dark hair stands in the doorway, eyeing me like something he'd rather taste than respect. He leans against the frame, rubbing his jaw as he takes in my barely covered body. "Good morning, Princess."

A second guard laughs and joins him. His hair is all silver and hangs in two braids past his waist. Now a third with deep-red hair waits just outside the door.

Fear should incapacitate me. I'm a woman, and these men can't wait to hurt me in the most sadistic of ways.

But I won't be afraid.

Not in my own home.

And not when my family needs me.

"*Get out*," I hiss.

They laugh, crossing the threshold into my cottage.

"I don't think we will, Princess." The first man reaches for the collar of my nightgown, and I smack his hand away.

The dark-haired guard sidles up behind me, leaning close to whisper in my ear. "Guess what? We just broke down the doors of the manor." He drops his voice. "How shall we celebrate?"

He yanks me by my hair and slams me against my workstation. The sharp and painful blow spills blood from my nose.

"Tie her up," the red-haired one instructs. "Our future king is waiting."

Invading my home was their first mistake.

Making me bleed is their second.

Not securing me hard enough is their third.

And their last.

My heart pounds against the table, my body ready to respond with the skills Vitor himself ingrained in me.

Fight anyone who tries to hurt you, he told me. *Fight dirty. Make them bleed. Make them pay.*

I wait for the guard to reposition himself.

And then, like Vitor taught me, I make him pay.

I break free and snatch the two very long knives hidden beneath my table and whirl. The first knife slices across the neck of the dark-haired soldier who held me down. The kill should have been instant, but it's not deep enough. Blood gurgles between his fingers as he stumbles back. The second, I flip in my hand and plunge deep into the other man's groin. He collapses, screaming, the color draining from his face to match his pale silver braids.

The one with red hair jumps from my reach and circles back, punching me in the face. Throbbing pain overwhelms me as my back slams against the wall.

I choke on blood and swipe my face.

The dark-haired guard comes at me again. I step away from his swinging arm and the punch that follows. I can tell he's losing blood fast. I drop into a crouch and rebound upward with a fist. The guard's head snaps back, skin and armor stained a gruesome shade of red, and he falls unconscious to the ground.

I dive into the bedroom and reach for the sword I keep under the mattress.

Strong hands clasp my ankles, pulling me out from beneath the bed and dragging me across the floor. I throw my weight to the side, spinning and breaking the soldier's hold.

I can't confidently fight him hand to hand. The man is bulkier and better trained than I.

Except my hands are no longer empty.

The red-haired guard who ripped me out from under the bed goes pale and tips over.

It's understandable, seeing as his shins were sliced clean through when I swung my sword.

"You bitch!" the guard clutching his groin hollers from the ground. "That's my twin. You're dead. You're dead!"

"We need her alive, Tav!" his twin screams.

Slice.

His mouth stays open as his head rolls away.

I slip out the back door.

Thick black smoke billows from the manor. My stomach sinks and pulse quickens. Oh, phoenix, why did it have to be fire? I look around. The long way through the forest is the safest way, but there's no time to be safe.

Every member of my household who's not at the arena is in the manor.

I start for the trail, doubling back when seven guards on horseback thunder toward me. They crash through the natural flora and my well-kept gardens, their steeds trampling everything in their path.

There are too many. I run to the other side of the cottage. Three of them laugh and turn their horses, intent on chasing me down. The other four stay put, expecting to catch me when I round the other side of the cottage.

I run as fast as I can, my muscles straining from the effort. I round the side of the house and head back to the front. I start for the path to the manor but not before lifting the planter of lilies and slamming the hidden match into the stump soaked with serpent oil.

My body is flushed with heat from the wall of fire that immediately erupts behind me, encircling the perimeter of the cottage. There are frightened neighs and shrieks as the guard in the lead is launched into the flames when his steed abruptly stops. The rest of their horses refuse to move any closer to the flames, backing away and balking when urged to skirt around them. This buys me time to sprint to the manor unfollowed.

My bare feet press over pebbles and sharp forest debris as I cut to Pasha, Musy, and Sonu's house.

Sonu is the first I see, his face pressed into mud, the hilts of four daggers protruding from his back. Musy, dear sweet Musy lies on her side, her body spilling blood from deep gashes across her chest.

Her mouth is stuffed with a soiled rag, and her blank stare is fixed to where Pasha's body swings from a tree.

Pasha's feet dangle above the brush, her toes disrupting the leaves as she sways in the breeze. Instantly, I fall to my hands and knees, bile burning a path through my throat and nose and onto the blood-soaked ground before me. *No, please! Let this be some cruel dream. Please.*

But it's not.

They weren't fighters. They were friends. A scream claws its way up my throat, and my eyes burn with tears I don't have time to shed. I must keep going. Damn it, I must! I drag myself from the ground and take off at a sprint. I fucking hope I run into soldiers now. I will kill every. Last. One.

My ears twitch when I'm halfway to the house. Knight is neighing in panic and kicking at the stable doors. But there's more—he's in pain. I glance to the left of the house, where a separate and smaller cloud of smoke is building. It wasn't enough to set the manor on fire. The guards are burning the stables.

"Knight, we must protect our home!"

His frightened neighs morph into fury, fueling the adrenaline soaking my veins.

Splintering wood never sounded so sweet. My brave moon horse is taking action.

And I follow his lead.

A guard on horseback charges up the forest path toward me, and I run right back at him. I spent every summer in this forest. I played beneath the trees and napped on its cool floor. No one knows this place better than me.

With the war cry of my female ancestors, I leap onto the flat rock ahead and push off it.

Anger makes me strong. We collide, both of us falling away from his horse. He gets to his feet first, raising his sword. I'm right behind him, bringing my blade up to meet his when he tries to gut me.

My next few strikes are defensive. Once I gain a sense of his pattern, I become the aggressor. I spin, slicing across his stomach. He's injured, but his mail protects him from mortal damage. I try again. He blocks my strike, cutting into my right arm in the process.

The gash burns.

I suck in air through my teeth, and using both hands, I drive my sword underneath his mail and through his torso.

Knight barrels through the brush, kicking the guard's falling body furiously away. There are burned patches on his skin that I'll need to fix. But there's no time to see to my friend.

My head pounds with what I need to do.

Make them bleed. Make them pay.

I grab Knight's mane and swing my leg over his back. He takes off like a shooting star. We break from the dark forest, riding uphill and into the full sun.

Make them bleed. Make them pay.

I lift my sword and sever the head from the body of the first guard we encounter. He drops an armful of jewelry that belonged to my grandmother.

He was trying to hide it from the others.

But it's not his to hide.

Make them bleed.

Knight races to the rear of the manor. I choke out a cry when I see estrellas lying dead.

They were scared. Why didn't they run?

I think about how loyal estrellas are to those they consider family. We're their family. We're their home. They didn't want to leave us.

Ahead, a guard is stabbing Toso. I scream with heartache and hatred.

Toso hisses and snaps his sharp teeth, fighting back until his wounded body collapses.

The guard looks up, his eyes widening as he sees my blood-soaked sword. "I don't want to hurt you," he tells me. *The feeling isn't mutual.*

No. He wants me alive so Soro can do it himself.

His hesitation costs him. I punch my sword through his skull.

Toso, my dearest Toso—so dedicated to protecting us, he took on an elf four times his size.

"Maeve!" Neela calls to me from the roof, a cast iron pan clutched tight in her hands. She doesn't care about the raging fire eating through the house. She only cares about us.

"Maeve, they're after you." She looks the opposite way. "They're coming, child. *Run!*"

She's bleeding and covered in soot. Her anguish is thick in every word. I guide Knight with my knees to cut to the left, trying to make my way to the front, where I can help.

My stomach lurches as we pass the stables, the smell from a slew of tiny burning bodies curling me inward. All these babies, all these estrellas, hiding in the stables only to be burned alive.

Grief overwhelms me. I don't see the cluster of guards rushing me from behind.

Father does.

I barely have time to lift my sword.

Swish.

Swish.

Swish.

Swish.

Their helmets were of no use. Father's arrows angle through their eyes and out the bases of their skulls.

I'm almost to the terrace when I glance behind me and see our bench.

The one where my family and I watched the sunsets. Back when Papa was free, we lived in peace, and the manor was our summer home. But now…now our home burns, and I can't save it!

That moment of distraction is all the guards need.

One races across the terrace, striking me with a heavy dining chair and knocking me from my horse.

Another guard jumps from the ledge and prowls forward. A tiny estrella leaps at his face, biting and scratching the guard to try and save me. He smacks her away, and the crunch of tiny bones makes me scream.

Something knocks me in the head.

"Fool!" a deep voice barks. "You were told not to kill her."

I open my eyes, I think. It's hard to tell with the shadows framing my vision.

Something chitters. Another estrella.

She bats at my nose.

Tibeta.

"Go," I tell her. "Go, now."

My voice is slurred. I hope she understands.

I roll to my side. It's the best I can do. Around me, the house is falling apart. Glass shatters, and smoke pours out. We've lost the east wing, the closest part of the manor to where I lie.

The central hall follows, the wood whining before it snaps, caving my home inward.

Elves heal faster than humans. It's the only reason that my vision begins to clear. Ahead of me, Knight bucks and thrashes, kicking away the guards trying to capture him. He doubles back, trampling the fools who jump in his way.

My eyes close for a moment or maybe longer.

I awake to the crunch of breaking skulls.

Bodies land beside me. Some with arrows, others with indented faces. It's Father. He's helping me. He's here for me, as always.

Knight nudges me with his nose, urging me to my feet.

I try to move my hand. It's hard, but I'm able to push myself to sitting. There's so much of me to heal, even my elven body can't keep up.

Knight nudges me again when I make it to a knee. I lose my balance and fall right back to the ground.

Everything hurts.

I start to take deeper breaths, I start to hurt a little less, and I start to hate a lot more.

Good. Hate will fuel my vengeance.

And I have plenty to unleash.

CHAPTER
44

MAEVE

My feet sink into the soil as I push to a crouch, body shuddering with pain, and pull my sword from the dirt. Knight sidesteps closer, and I use his mane to pull myself up to stand, then finally walk. It's all I can do to remain steady, my normal gait impossible to maintain. But I am gaining some strength.

Knight lowers one of his front legs and bows his long neck, kneeling on a foreleg so I can mount. My motions aren't graceful or easy, but they're sufficient to permit me to ride.

Knight starts off slowly, trying to ease us into a canter. The guards hurt him when he fought back. No one would know it now. The way he chuffs demands war upon our enemies. We trot around the house. There's no more house to save. But there might be family, servants, and workers who survived. Who need me. I struggle to control Knight. He's desperate to attack despite the injuries he's sustained. A war horse, indeed.

I'm not as ready until Neela cries out in defiance. I urge Knight onto the sprawling front lawn. The guards kicking Neela are larger and stronger than she is. She's curled inward, using her body to shield a cluster of smaller estrellas.

I leap on top of one of them. One of the guards, an elf, catches me and tosses me away as if I'm nothing.

But I am something.

His dingy smile vanishes as he smacks at the back of his neck. He falls on his ass, struggling to remove my dagger from the base of his skull.

If he were human, he'd already be dead. And because the other guard is human, all it takes is one clean slice to the throat. They thought me weak and soft as a princess, and maybe I am, but not today.

As fast as I can, I hurry to where Knight sways in place. His head is down. He's nudging Bethina, my tiniest estrella, encouraging her to run. It's too late. Like the others, she's already dead.

My pace slows. At least a dozen guards are running toward us—some whose faces I recognize and have known since I was a child.

I learned to fight, to protect, to lead. That doesn't make me invincible. Nor does it grant me everything I need to bring down a gang of trained killers.

One lunges and knocks me off balance. My head strikes the ground first. There are voices. "Kill her or get out of my way."

Aisling.

There's a crackling sound that builds, and then I'm struck with jolts of magic, screaming as every nerve in my body convulses in pain.

"He needs her," a troll rumbles.

"And I need her dead!" Aisling shrieks in return.

"No, no!" someone else yells.

A shouting match ensues, and the atmosphere is drenched with Aisling's magic. I can't prepare for this death blow, and I don't. But it never hits me. Instead, she whips her power to the side at the last moment and destroys what remains of the library in one strike.

Aisling continues to demand my death. "Look at her! She isn't worthy. But I am."

"No!" the troll rumbles.

Aisling won't stop. "I'll give you gold. Is that what you want? All you must do is blame a dead guard."

"No," an old elven guard retorts. Isa is her name. "We'll say it was you. The princess shall live."

Princess. I laugh, sort of. It comes out as a pitiful, pained series of squeaks.

What kind of princess lies among the dead, too beaten to rise?

"Do it," Aisling orders, a sick sort of glee in her voice, "or I'll kill all of you instead."

Hands clutch my throat and squeeze.

I should fight back. Except I can't move.

It's too late to save most of me, anyway.

I want to hold little Bethina in the Afterlife and run through the lush green forests. I smile again, picturing the estrellas chasing one another through gardens packed with blooms. I want to sit on that bench. The one I had here, watching the sun set over and over as I wait for Father and Giselle to join me and Papa.

More than anything, I want to be with Leith.

Leith...

My vision clears.

My rage surges.

And my hands dart forward.

I dig my thumbs into the eyes of the dwarf choking me. He tightens his grip, and I sputter and wheeze and dig in harder. Our struggle ends with a squelching and splatter and two massive hooves to the head.

His body flies off me, and I lunge for the stunned elf who holds my sword. Air returns to fill my lungs from one gasp to the next. The fools who tried restraining Knight have been reduced to a bloody pulp in the grass.

Streaks of blood roll down my face as I stare in the direction where Father holds his bloody sword. He's covered in bruises and cuts, and blood gushes from his left shoulder. But he's still fighting.

"You will *not* hurt my daughter!" he yells.

I smile through my pain. I didn't have a good father. I had two amazing ones.

More guards arrive on horseback in green-and-blue armor. At least ten more soldiers. With only two of us left, we're ill-prepared for such numbers. Father and I exchange glances and run, sprinting across the lawn.

"Get to that wagon," he says. I follow his gaze to a covered wagon spilling with looted art and valuables. It's not far. Just across the lawn, abandoned near a copse of wizard's elm. "If we take out the guards, we can take Neela, the horses, and the surviving estrellas to safety."

"Yes, Father," I answer.

Despite his weakened state, he's faster than me, the way he powers over the grass appearing effortless.

No longer do I see the man with the broken heart. He's long gone. Nor is this the man who played with me as a child, who read to me every night, who held me when I hurt. This is the famed warrior he was before.

I push myself harder, trying to close the distance between us while every inch of my body screams in protest.

I want to share his strength, his wisdom, his kindness.

He is my father, the man who pledged to love me as his own.

And he is a wonder.

Father reaches the wagon.

I swing my sword, straining to help him. But the guards are many, and I don't see the one with the spear aimed at my back.

Father does.

He doubles back, leaping in front of me.

And spares my heart...

With his.

I drop my sword, trying to catch him in my arms. We fall together, the torment he feels reflecting in his dulling eyes.

No...

No...

No!

"Become the queen," he says. His words waver, each one barely above a whisper. "Arrow needs you."

"Father..."

I'm yanked away from him as a mountain troll breaks through the dense crowd of guards, rumbling obscenities through his jagged teeth. "Fools! You could have killed her," he says.

"If you kill the princess, Soro kills you, understood?" Another voice. Loud. Human.

I know that voice. Lord Ugeen. That sniveling opportunist.

The troll lifts Father by the spear and holds him up and away. Father straightens his feeble arms, his hands opening and closing as if trying to reach me across the several yards between us. His lips move, and his last words almost break me. *I love you.*

"Finish him," Ugeen spits.

An elf appears on horseback, coaxing his steed into a canter, his sword raised high.

It takes a moment.

Just a moment.

For him to swing, and for my father, my hero, to die.

Someone screams. And screams. And screams.

That someone is me.

I break loose from the arms holding me, slowing my pace to a jog as I near Father's unmoving form.

No. This can't be right.

Father isn't— I mean, he *can't be*. This is too impossible to be real.

Father—he isn't dead. Well, he's hurt, yes, but I can fix him. I fix people all the time. One of my potions should help. I must figure out which one. It shouldn't take long. We have time.

Yes, time.

A sob burns through my throat.

Please, let me have more time, *with* him, *for* him.

I stop short and look around, trying to make sense of how his head lies so far from his body. We almost made it. We almost won. The wagon isn't far away. I can still reach it. That's right, reach it. Escape is still possible. We earned it after how hard we fought.

"Father?" I plead as I hold back my tears.

Tears are useless.

"Father," I say again. "*Please*. We need you. Giselle and Papa and Neela and *me. We need you.*"

My eyes sting. No. No crying. Tears are *fucking* useless.

But they fall anyway.

No matter how hard I tell myself that Father isn't gone.

I leave his body just long enough to retrieve his head and position it with his torso, where it belongs. I stroke the side of his face. His skin is cool. "We're better together. All of us were always better together."

Thick fingers clutch my shoulders. Neela is here, her presence all the permission I need to scream.

And I do, until my vocal cords are raw with pain.

Neela kisses the top of my head. Like me, she's aware the guards have us surrounded. Like me, she doesn't care.

She lowers her bruised and bloody body beside my father, her arms wrapping around his torso. It's then I see the hilt of a dagger protruding from the center of her back. "I never had a friend before him," she says.

"Neela…"

"He chose me," she continues, her blood saturating the soil. "When no one else would have me."

I know what's happening. But she can't leave me. Not after everyone I lost today.

"He took me in and fed me my first real meal." Large tears zigzag down her face. "It was terrible. Burned fish and half-cooked potatoes." She sniffs. "I couldn't tell him, though. I couldn't offend him. I ate every last bite like it was the best. And because my friend made it for me, it was."

"Neela, *don't*," I beg.

Her tears run faster, coloring her face as her blood drains out of her. "My dear child. I must join him in death. Who else will take care of him if I don't? It was my time long ago. I only stayed for him. Now…now it's time for me to go."

And she does.

I'm numb, unable to feel anything.

Empty space is all that remains.

They're gone. They're *all* gone.

And they're never coming home.

My arms are brutally wrenched behind me and shackled, and then I'm thrown without care into a different wagon. It jerks forward, the squeak from the old wheels growing to a shriek as the guards force the horses to a gallop.

The last thing I see is Aisling unleashing her rage and her magic… and what's left of my home crumbling to dust.

CHAPTER

45

LEITH

The arena isn't that far. Today, though, the ride there seems to take hours.

Once we arrive, Gunther hurries forward to take the reins. I don't have to see him to know he's beaming. The boy is always happy to see me. I look regardless, wanting to assure myself that no fresh wounds mar him.

"Bloodguard. Bloodguard!"

I squeeze his shoulder and ask Caelen to buy him a good meal. I shouldn't invest so much in his well-being. There's nothing I can do about it, not right now. And yet, whether I mean to or not, I'm bonded to this kid in mutual torment. He may be young, but like me, he's known suffering. If I can help him, I have to. For both our sakes.

I'm going to talk to Maeve about approaching his family, if he really has one. There's nothing he deserves more than a home with us and my sisters and mother. Dahlia will insist they become best friends. I smile despite myself, hoping Gunther will agree. They can play in the woods and just be children for once.

My boots hit the muddy ground as I dismount, and the guards pull me away before I can bid Caelen a proper farewell.

I glance back, but he's already gone.

Instead of taking me around to the livestock entrance and leaving me in an iron cage under the audience seating like they have every day this week, they lead me toward the pens where the gladiators are held. It appears I will fight today.

I crack my neck from side to side. I stomp through the mud, kicking the muck back and onto the guards. "Beggin' your pardon, great sirs. I really should be more careful."

The guard in my line of fire curses and shoves me, then snarls when I keep my feet and shoves me again. We're almost to the pens where the other gladiators await. I steel myself, wondering after all this time—and all Giselle and Maeve's interventions—who's still alive.

The stench of unwashed bodies and swine hits me hard. I'm spoiled by the aroma of the forest and gardens that surround the cottage. And it's not only that. My belly is full, my wounds are healed, and I've had a full week of rest.

A large roach skitters along the boards between the pens. A gladiator snags it, shoving it into his mouth before another can insist he share it.

He's not alone. A cyclops, his knees crooked from malnourishment, sifts through the mud, plucking kernels from pieces of half-eaten corn flung from the swine pens.

Shame weighs me down. I've returned in optimal condition—more bulk to my frame from good meals, more strength from training, and more endurance from the distances I've travelled while hunting for herbs and mushrooms in the forest with Maeve.

Another whiff of this ripe aroma knocks me across the nose. I try not to grimace. I haven't wallowed in filth in a long time. I'm not judging them.

I still *am* them.

They will no doubt judge me. I'll spare them the good stuff—the wardrobe full of new clothes and my daily showers beneath the falls with my princess—and hope that the good we've done for them is returned with neutrality at least.

"By all the glory," Rye says. "It's Leith."

Murmurs erupt, spreading down to each pen. Gladiators I know pull against their restraints, trying to get a look at me as I pass. They're arranged in a new pattern. It's odd. There are too many unfamiliar faces intermixed with seasoned gladiators. The ones with the greatest number of wins are split far apart from one another.

"Oi," Ned calls. "Oi. 'Ere I thought you was dead."

The corners of my lips tug into a grin. It's a strange feeling to miss them. It's even stranger to hear warmth trickle through their surprise. My old barrack mates are happy to see me. Meatheads or not, we are one. It's something I learned from Maeve: you don't have to be blood to be family.

I pass Pega's pen. Rye's and Ioni's, too. They look good. So good they're almost unrecognizable. Their faces are clean and filled out, their stances solid. Before Maeve and her family, all we knew were injuries, illness, and pain.

After them, I don't recognize anyone. In my absence, more have died and even more have come to take their places.

Angry faces greet me as the gate of a particularly nasty pen is pulled open. I'm pushed inside and almost collide with an old human man who spits at my feet. The move reminds me of Sullivan. This man is not impressed by new clothes and sturdy boots. He sees me as weak and glares. I glare in return. He hasn't seen what I've seen despite his years. He has no idea the shit I'm capable of.

It becomes a mind game of sorts to see who looks away first. It's always someone else.

Today, it's me.

"*Leith.*"

I turn when a familiar voice calls my name from the back of the pen. Luther.

The giant recovered and beat the odds. He's shoved into a corner, waiting for his turn to go.

No one moves to allow me through.

Ah, yes, we're back to this.

I shove anyone in my path aside, using my shoulders to jab them.

There's no way I'm not talking to Luther.

I trudge over the muck, kicking aside rotting pieces of vegetables the newer gladiators lunge for.

Luther's giant bottom lip tilts up. I return his grin.

"Still alive," I say.

"Because you," he admits.

His foot is twisted, the leg thinner and plenty scarred, but it holds his weight. And like he said, he's still here.

Luther favors the damaged leg as he stands, but not so much that I'm not confident he'll keep fighting and keep winning. As long as he can move, Luther's better off than most.

"She good?" he asks.

"She's amazing," I admit.

I haven't told them who "she" really is. They presume it was Giselle, and none of us told them otherwise.

Pega surely suspects, but she's been loyal to her sponsor and to me.

"You good friend," he says. "Today win. Then next. Then Blood... guard."

"That's the plan," I say. I place my hand on his shoulder. With Sullivan gone, Luther and the others have become more than competition.

Luther keeps his voice low and his speech short, as always. "Saved me. Saved many." He jerks his large chin in the direction of the other pens. I catch sight of Ned and Ioni trying to draw closer. The others are too far.

I kneel or at least try to. The shackles and crowded conditions make it almost impossible.

"What happened to the others?" I ask. "Most here are new."

Luther shrugs. "Not have more...for all."

They ran out of medicine is what he means.

Luther keeps his voice low and scoops up a large handful of mud. He throws it at those surrounding us who are straining to hear. They were pretending to speak to each other. But you can't pretend around Luther. He's smarter than that.

Most shuffle away. But two—the closest man and the one who got smeared with the most muck—lunge for Luther. He swats the first away with barely a flick of his wrist. The other, I kick in the knee, knocking him face-first into the mud. He'll be all right if he's not thrown in the arena right away. But if they pull him now, he won't stand a chance.

I'm not trying to play the bastard, but if you come at me or mine, you need to come harder than that.

He's lucky I only hurt his knee.

"Guards not happy," Luther says. He mulls over how to form his words. "Plants...make us...better."

"I know," I agree. Maeve's work is genius. The remedies are designed to treat not only injuries but underlying infections and even shore up older wounds.

Luther eyes me, knowing I'm holding back information.

"I wasn't positive the remedies would save all of you," I say. "I'm glad they did, and that all of you shared them when you didn't have to."

"No," he says. "That you."

Luther is right, and I don't think I realized how right he is until now. Maeve's first treatments were meant for me—to heal my injuries and keep me going. I never intended to let anyone else have them. But when I saw Luther and what Soro's twisted games had done to him, I had to help. Just like Maeve helped me.

"Do the guards know what you did?" I ask.

Luther shakes his immense head. "No... Hid well," he says. "Small."

"They weren't easy to find," I interpret for him.

He nods, his small eyes moving left and right before he leans forward. "More?" he asks.

I lower myself as much as I can. To anyone who doesn't know us, they might mistake us for whispering or possibly kissing. Doesn't matter to me. Doesn't matter to Luther, especially when I reach into my waistband and slide the envelope of fresh healing herbs into his new shirt.

"Bad today," he says. "None come back yet."

"Do you know what we will face in there?"

"Fire," Luther replies. "Smell burning."

Fire is what Maeve learned, too. Hell, I hope that doesn't mean another fucking dragon.

My stomach sinks at the thought, but it's how much I hate these treacherous royals that returns it to its place. "Luther," I say. "What do you think about taking down Vitor and Soro?"

Maeve and I discussed this option should Vitor and the royal court try to deny her the throne. In truth, if we didn't have an entire royal army to deal with, me and the gladiators would have done this long ago. Maybe all we need is a princess on our side. Maeve wants her Papa Andres free— we all do, even if he *is* guilty.

I still think there's more to it.

If Vitor even tries to pull some shit like convincing the court to make him king, I will personally rip the crown from his cold, severed head. Enough is enough. Andres needs his freedom, and Maeve's people deserve more. I'm not naive—we're looking to take on a hostile and established regime. But seeing all the good that I can still have, I want others to have it, too.

Do we think we can manage on our own? Hell no. I'm not even sure we can escape these pens without a legion of guards raining down on us should word of an uprising get out too soon. But Luther is a fine place to start, and my fellow gladiators are a way to follow. We all fight. We're all ruthless. We are exactly what my Maeve needs.

If the damn lords didn't want an army of trained murderers after them, they shouldn't have conspired to break our spirits.

And they sure as fuck shouldn't have driven us to become Bloodguards.

Luther scrutinizes me. He seems on the verge of arguing. I have never argued with a giant. There's no point. I enjoy my limbs and prefer them attached to my body.

I half expect him to swat me away like he did the other man, but I hope Luther will consider my words.

"Yes," he says finally. "When?"

Fuck yeah. "I don't know. We need to organize."

He nods. "How many?"

"Two gladiators so far," I say.

He tilts his head. "Then…four?"

"No. You and me are the two."

Luther makes this odd choking sound. I think he's swallowed something the wrong way until I realize he's laughing. At me.

"Good start," he says.

He turns his head as my voice drops even further. "Get a feel for some of the others. Start with those you saved with the remedies."

"Yes," Luther says.

We talk at least an hour more, and I think it must be getting a bit easier for him. I'm glad. I always knew Luther had more to say than his anatomy allows. When this is all over, I will learn the language of giants. Maybe. The have a strong connection to nature, and I'm not completely sold I'll be able to speak "tree."

Gladiators are pulled left and right. Like my friend said, no one comes back. By the three-hour mark, there's enough room in each pen to easily move around.

The sun is high in the sky now, heating the stink around us. The body count weighs on me. Something truly wicked waits inside. Goody.

I stretch again. There's nothing better to do, besides panic, and that shit never helped anyone. Luther does the same, anxiety showing even on him. There's no guarantee he won't betray me. And I can't be certain someone won't betray him. But change starts somewhere. This somewhere is in a pen reserved for swine.

Luther makes a motion to signal that a guard is approaching. It's the only movement he makes.

The human guard strikes the metal gate with his sword, cutting three fingers off the fool dwarf who thought he could rest them there.

"Pretty boy," the guard calls.

I'm not trying to be cocky, but I don't think the guard is talking to the muddy bastard picking his nose.

The guard swings his sword from side to side, the possibility of my imminent death adding to his glee. "Let's go," he says to me. "Time to bleed."

CHAPTER
46

MAEVE

It feels like a fever dream. One I can't wake from.

One in which I can't see.

One in which I can't breathe.

Is this what it is to die?

Alone in a suffocating inferno, unable to move my limbs?

I turn my head, searching for my fathers in the darkness so they can tell me it's going to be okay. Or Neela so she may stroke my hair to soothe my fear. I keep turning my head or at least trying to. Where are the little estrellas? They need to sleep with Father so they may keep him warm and feel safe.

But *I* don't need warmth. I need water. My stars, why is it so hot?

"The princess is waking."

It's Tut, the ogren general in charge of surveillance. Vitor's loyal follower. I recognize his voice.

"Remove the covering," Vitor says. There's a long pause, and his voice tightens. "I said remove the covering."

Metal slides against thick leather as a sword is pulled from its sheath. "Now, gentlemen, there is no time for posturing," another voice says. Wonderful. It's Lord Ugeen. The kiss-ass worm sounds mere feet from me. "Let's just get on with it, shall we?" he says.

Something is yanked from my face, pulling strands of my hair. I'm upright, bound tightly to something hard and bumpy, but my vision is blurry and I cannot make out what it is. Immediately, I try to lash out, to kick and claw, but my arms, legs, and body are bound.

My face is swollen, my right eye reduced to a slit. That, combined with the dimness of my surroundings, makes it hard to see, but eventually my eyes adjust.

And when I finally make out where I am, I shudder.

Shit.

Though I've never seen them before, it's obvious where we are.

We're in the catacombs.

I had no idea a cavern so vast existed within them. Piles and piles of skulls and bones from past wars, including those who perished attempting to kill the phoenix, are neatly stacked like trophies between stalagmites of varying widths and lengths. Heat...so much heat...pulsates against me in waves.

The only thing remotely reassuring is the statue of my grandmother carved from the stalagmite across from the one I'm tied to. My head lifts upward as I take in the Great Avianna of Iamond. In her left hand, she holds her own blade against her side. In the other is King Masone's golden sword, raised in victory. *This* is where Vitor hid away the ancestral swords.

The statue mimics the painting in our former parlor, in which those who died following my grandmother lie dead around her. Except here, her likeness is depicted in greater detail.

The eyebrows are carefully chiseled, angled rather than curved, as they were in life when she was feeling exceptionally righteous. The dimple carved into her right cheek is set perfectly in line with her regal nose, which tips up slightly at the end. Her hair is cut short. She never liked it long—she was certain someone would use it to strangle her in her sleep.

The battle armor is perfection, the indentations of the mail curved and angled just right. But it's the weapons, not the statue, that are the true treasures.

Each is a masterpiece, a startling reflection of their personalities and indicating the stark contrast between them. Grandmother's sword is... *feral*, that's the word that comes to mind. The hilt is a large raw diamond snaked in silver-and-green ivy that matches the tones of the blade. Grandfather's sword is regal, the epitome of strength and endurance. The hilt is gold with a bloodred ruby fixed at the end. The blade is thin, long, lethal, and becoming of the king Leith deserves to be.

If he's still alive...

Good stars, he needs to be alive! Just like Giselle and Caelen. But if they were somehow captured while we fought in the raid...

The raid. Ah, yes, where I saw my entire world implode.

My head pounds. My body *burns*. Every injury I endured sings the melody of pain.

I loll my head to the side to see Vitor waiting several paces away to my left.

"You fucking traitor," I say, my voice raw and harsh.

The beating at the base of my skull makes it hard to think, hard to simply breathe. I try to focus, but incessant nausea surges, and my thoughts spin, leaving me faint. I'm dizzy from the blows to my head and weak from pushing my body to the extreme.

"Why didn't you just kill me?" I ask. "Why did you force me to watch my family die?"

Vitor does little more than press his lips together tight. But then he speaks, and I wish he'd kept his mouth shut. "It was never my intent to hurt you, Maeve. By the great phoenix, all I ever wanted was to keep you safe."

"You failed," I say, or I at least try to.

Vitor's hands are mildly crossed behind him, as always. Pua and Tut stand at attention on either side. Tut mutters something to Vitor, who responds with a few words I fail to catch. Pua lifts a piece of hair caught on the front of his tusks and lets it float away.

They stand in front of my grandfather's statue. Like my grandmother, it's also delicately carved into a stalagmite. "The Good King Masone of Iamond," I say, laughing without humor. "I suppose as regent, this is the closest to a king you'll ever be, isn't it?"

"Don't say that, Maeve," he says.

"Don't say what?" I respond, the effort causing pain like glass scraping over my vocal cords. "Don't speak the truth? Someone must. What a fool I was to think that maybe, just maybe, you were still the man I called my uncle."

Anger deepens his scowl, but then he looks to Soro—shouldn't he be at the arena?—and Ugeen, who are standing alongside a wall of stacked bleached femurs. They speak in low whispers, and Ugeen nods at everything Soro says.

I stare at Soro with fury flooding my veins. My lungs sting when my breathing picks up. I try to calm myself by making out the words chiseled into the rock formations.

The one closest to me tells a story in the language of my elven ancestors. It's of Skyla the Sun, who loved Milagro the Moon. They wanted to be together, but they always remained apart.

From the stone ceiling covered in wine-colored stalactites, moisture rains down along with the sounds of muffled but familiar cheers. We're below the arena, then, and a match is already in motion. Is it Leith's? My head sags forward, my body begging for sleep. Even if it is Leith, even if he is already fighting, he could never hear my screams. And if Grandmother was truthful with me, the catacombs are only accessible through the castle, where no one would let him in.

I fight the urge to fall asleep and force myself to focus on my surroundings.

We're on an incline of soil and rubble. Below, more bones and stones make up a maze that supposedly leads into and out of the catacombs, according to what little was shared with me in my childhood. But that's not enough information to help me now.

I shift my stiff shoulders, but the ties hold strong.

Vitor takes in how I absorb this unfamiliar place for any speck of *anything* that could help me escape. "By all of Old Erth," he says. "You really don't remember this place, do you?"

It's an odd thing to ask. Of course I don't remember this place. Grandmother was always so secretive, as if you had to possess a certain level of clearance and majesty to have the barest inkling the catacombs even existed. I reply with a scowl, hating the idea of speaking to him.

My ears twitch as the muffled sounds of screams and pounding hooves above us grow more pronounced. I think I hear a horn blast.

That can't be right. Didn't that match just start?

Perhaps not. All I'm certain of is that I'm badly hurt.

My body bellows from the magnitude of injuries I've sustained, punishing me with stabbing pains and dull throbbing aches.

It's hard to focus on anything. I try anyway. After all, I'm not dead yet.

A golden gate to my right separates us from the largest stalactites. They're immense, stretching from the cavernous ceiling to the hard gravel floor. Should any of these wine-colored monstrosities break, we'd all be crushed.

I peer closer, past the gate. There's a large mound of soil there but not much more. Could that be another way out? Maybe. The bars look spaced far enough apart for me to squeeze through. I must figure out how to break free.

"Maeve," Vitor says quietly.

I wish my voice didn't leak the misery I feel. It kills me just to look at him. "Don't," I say. "You've done enough."

"My darling daughter, forgive me for my part in this."

"I'm not your *fucking* daughter." The words tear through my throat. "And nothing you say or do will make me forgive the unforgivable."

I didn't think tears were possible in heat this wretched, but they are. I can't even swallow without coughing. Gone. My family is gone.

"Give her water, Soro," Vitor orders. "Now."

"*Shut up!*" I tell him. That's it. That's all that I have for a man I loved and learned from. From the man who threw me into the air as a child and who taught me to throw a spear not long after.

Vitor stares at me for a beat—long enough for me to ponder how to kill him, how to make Soro pay. How to gut Ugeen and the generals.

I jerk my head when the galloping above makes condensation drip onto my forehead. The screams from the arena grow in severity. Leith… Is he fighting for his life above while I'm trapped here, unable to help him? Has he even gone?

Is he dead already?

Soro raises his head from where he's speaking to Ugeen.

Another drop from above has me shuddering with disgust, which causes pains to shoot through my body. By all the stars, everything hurts like hell. I take slow breaths through my mouth. My nose is broken, and the tissue surrounding it is so swollen I can barely feel my face move even when speaking. I must have been close to joining Father and Neela if it's taking this long for just my face to heal. Toss in the awful heat, and every breath is grueling.

Father and Neela. I'm so sorry.

Soro looks up as more drips pelt my head. "You hear those screams?" he asks no one in particular. "No one's getting through today. This was my idea. *Mine.*"

Leith is still alive. He must be. He's the main event, and this monster wouldn't dream of missing his match.

Soro starts to say something but stops when he notices more drops falling on me. Slowly, he smiles, reminiscent of the smiles from his youth, before his bitterness turned him into who—or what—he is now.

"What a childish, hateful villain you are," I say.

He chuckles without humor. "I gave you a chance. I gave you a choice, Maeve. You could have had it all…" he replies.

"Soro," Vitor says. "Do *not* disrespect Maeve. She's exactly like her grandmother—a fierce warrior who took on everything thrown at her. You would do well to learn from her example."

From one short breath to the next, Soro shoves his face into Vitor's. He was always absurdly fast, his speed a marvel, even among elves.

"You believe her so special. Why? I've done *everything*, all my life, to please you. And it was never enough, was it?" He turns his head, glaring at me with unapologetic loathing. "No, your little Maeve *always* came first."

"Not little Maeve. *Queen*," I fire back. I spit out blood, straightening as much as I can while ignoring the pull of my strained muscles. My eyes, ablaze with fury, shift between Vitor and Soro. "That's why I'm here, isn't it? That's why you didn't kill me along with my family!"

Vitor maintains his composed demeanor, as he always has, hands behind his back and shoulders relaxed. I wait for him to degrade Soro for his insolence. But that well-earned knockdown doesn't come. He nods thoughtfully. "You're here to make my son a king, yes." Darkness overtakes the sharp planes of his face, and it scares me more than a strike ever could. "As a regent and his heir, we will never be kings unless we marry the heirs to the throne. With Andres out of the picture, you're the only one with the power to change our station and keep power consolidated in one house."

"Why even mention Andres?" Soro asks, scowling. "After what happened, he proved he'd never be strong enough to do what it takes to keep Arrow in power."

My throat is on fire. Everything I had is gone. And here these knobs stand, without care for anyone but themselves. "How dare you speak of Papa that way?" I demand, grunting when more of that damn condensation trickles onto my head. "He would have made my grandmother proud—"

"How?" Soro asks me. The faraway screaming switches to abject terror. But Soro stands before me unaffected. "Andres refused to do what needed to be done. And so did you."

What?

Vitor curses, then throws back his head and laughs. "What a fool I was," he says. "Why, *why* did I tell you?"

Soro spits on the ground. "Because like always, you underestimated me." Hurt punctuates each syllable, compounded by rage. He turns back to me. "You had everything, Maeve. Same as your father. Instead, you both fucked over our great leader."

I have no idea what he's talking about, but the darkness in his expression makes my heart hammer. "I know Papa didn't kill the queen. I know it!"

Soro saunters toward me, adjusting the dagger secured to the sheath at his hip. "Then who did, Maeve?" he asks, glancing over his shoulder at Vitor. "Tell everyone here who killed our queen."

"It was—"

I cut myself off, examining everyone in my cramped surroundings. Ugeen and the ogren generals wait for my response, curious as to who I might accuse.

Who will I accuse? It wasn't them—they're genuinely waiting for my answer.

Was it Vitor? No, not with how he loved the queen.

Soro raises an eyebrow. "It wasn't me. I was with these very men in the castle before the fire started and I was forced to intervene."

Vitor's forehead creases, creating four deep lines soaked in sweat.

It had to be someone who isn't here. Or dead, or...

I start breathing fast. Too fast. I start coughing, no, choking. I know Father was wrong about what happened. How could my sweet papa have left his beloved mother to die, let alone shoved her into the flames, as Soro accused?

The thundering hooves above force the stalactites to release their moisture like falling rain. Thick drops the size of pebbles fall from overhead

My body crumbles. No. Not my papa. They are all wrong.

Soro is mere feet from me. I should be thinking of ways I can secure his dagger—get him close enough to do something. But I can't.

"Tell her," Soro says quietly. "Tell her what you finally admitted to me."

Vitor's jaw clamps shut.

Soro removes his dagger from its sheath, tosses it into the air, and catches it. By my next pant of air, he's on me. He yanks my hair, pulling up my chin. As if he has all the time he needs, he skims the tip along my jugular.

"*Don't* hurt her," Vitor says.

Soro squares his shoulders, the tip pushing into my throat even as he replies in an eerily calm voice. "Then tell her, *Vitor*," he says.

Vitor doesn't move. And even in this heat, he fails to take a breath. Pain wells in his eyes along with tears. Pua shoves him forward. It's then I see the shackles binding Vitor's arms.

The ropes dig into my breasts when I startle. *Vitor* is Soro's prisoner... just like me?

Soro nicks my chin, making me jerk. I startle again when another drop of fluid falls from the ceiling and dribbles along my ear. "Tell her," he says. "If you really see her as a daughter..."

It takes a strange amount of effort for Vitor to speak. "You were right, Maeve. All these years, you were right to believe in Andres's innocence. Even when his own lover lamented over his sentence, you kept the faith."

Soro slowly releases his hold on my hair. "Then who killed my grandmother?" I ask.

Anguish destroys what remains of Vitor's resolve. "You did," he says.

CHAPTER
47

MAEVE

Soro takes point beside me. I sway in place, or at least that's how it feels.

"No," I say. "That isn't true."

Ugeen and the ogres lose their collective minds.

Ugeen rushes to Vitor and screams in his face. It's easy now that Vitor is shackled. "Andres was unjustly punished?" he demands. He regards me with disgust. "What kind of pathetic weakling stands idly by while her father pays for her sins?"

I try to deny it, but words fail me. Everything fails me.

Pua smacks his bardiche against the palm of his hands as he snarls. "The princess must die. We can't let her live if she killed the queen."

"And share the power with the other houses?" Soro snaps. "Are you truly this stupid?"

Tut fiddles with the hilt of his axe. He's grown out his tusks, and they're making it hard for him to speak. I understand enough. "You must pardon our Prince Andres," he says.

"And *she* will be sentenced to death," Ugeen growls. "And executed immediately."

Soro shoves Ugeen away when he tries to approach me. "Executing her won't make me king. I need the fucking title, and you shits need me to have it."

It feels as though I'm awake in a nightmare I can't escape. I don't speak. I whimper. "W-why?"

Vitor's shoulders slump, and his eyes focus on a point far away, his voice barely above a whisper. "We brought you down here that night. I didn't want to, but Avianna insisted that Andres was ready and that you needed to be, too." He shakes his head. "She believed an attack on Arrow was imminent, long before such chatter began. In the event Avianna or I were killed, two more needed to take our places. Andres, though, fought his duties, and you did, too."

My body sways with each intake of the hot air. A memory stirs within me — one I had convinced myself was no more than a recurring nightmare in response to my trauma all those years ago. I recall it differently now. My head aches, and my heart throbs. I envision myself in this very spot three years ago. I close my eyes and concentrate.

I hear my grandmother before I see her. "Take it," she says.

There, by the stalagmite that tells the story of the sun and moon, she stands in a silver gown. Vitor stands loyally at her side in a similar-colored robe. She offers the large dagger in her open palms to Papa.

"Andres," she says. "This must be done, my son."

Papa turns in the direction of the large gold gate, where I hover over a crying human girl from Amdar. In my black shirt and breeches, I'm almost invisible. She, in a gown of white, glows with ethereal light. Or maybe that's just my memory playing tricks. The tattoos on her cheeks are protection symbols her people have used for centuries. But nothing can protect her now.

I remember the symbols and thus remember her. She used to wash the windows in the castle solarium, buffing them to an impeccable shine. Lexanne. That was her name. She didn't have a family. She was an easy pick. No one would miss her.

That didn't make this right.

"Papa, no," I say. I twist from side to side, torn between keeping my sights on my grandmother, my father, and the poor girl wailing for mercy at my feet. In few words, I beg them not to hurt her.

Grandmother ignores me. "Understand this, Andres. When those we help across Old Erth turn on us, when those enemies on the brink of uprising come for us, the sacrifice of a few will keep the many of Arrow safe and in power."

"Hurting this child is inexcusable, Mother," Papa says. "There must be another way."

"This is the only way," Grandmother responds in that tone she used to dictate her word was law.

Papa is taller than Grandmother, yet she manages to look down at him. She adjusts her hold on the dagger, and in a few smooth strides she looms over me and the poor, frightened girl.

Vitor grips Papa's arm and yanks him back when he tries to intervene.

Papa responds with a hard blow to Vitor's face. Vitor doubles back and lifts Papa, slamming him to the hard ground by the collar of his bloodred robes. Papa snatches Vitor's hand and twists, spinning Vitor onto his side. They roll in a pile of swinging arms and legs, the echo of their pounding fists and pained grunts ricocheting along the walls of bone.

I position myself between my grandmother and Lexanne, attempting to block her.

"You can't do this, Grandmother," I say, taking several steps toward her. I hold my hands out, heart thumping, knowing I'm about to fight the notorious Queen of Arrow. "Please. This girl could be me."

Grandmother snatches me up by the throat and shoves her face in mine. "You could never be her," she says. "But for the sake of Arrow, *you must be me!*"

She flings me away like I'm nothing. I tumble backward, landing on the edge of the incline. I leap to my feet, intending to race back toward my grandmother, but the breath has been knocked out of me. Leaning over and clutching my knees, I shake my head to clear it and suck in a breath at last.

"Aurora!" Avianna screams as she strides away from me, toward the gates and the cowering girl frozen in terror before them. "Your queen calls you."

I rise and run toward them, but the ground shakes, causing me to stumble. I recover quickly and sprint full-out. I'm almost to them, almost in reach, but I'm too late. Grandmother slits the young girl's throat in one swift and merciless motion. Lexanne's blood splatters, spraying my face as I tackle my grandmother to the ground.

We slam against a stalagmite. I roll off her and shoot to my feet, my fists up.

But Grandmother doesn't rise. She lies motionless, bleeding from her temple. My hands fall to my sides. I'm reaching for her when something hard strikes the base of my skull, and the catacombs explode with light and fire.

"Someone had to take the fall, Maeve," Vitor says, bringing me back to the present. Numb and trembling, I stare at him wordlessly.

"But neither Andres nor I wanted it to be you." His voice breaks. "At eighteen, your life was just beginning. The insight you provided was well beyond your years. We knew you'd make a better queen than he would a king."

"Why did you tell Soro?" Ugeen asks him. "This was a secret you could have taken to your grave. Why tell him now?"

Those tears I hate soak my face. Soro watches them fall.

Drip. Drip. Drip.

More condensation dribbles onto my forehead, mixing with the tears soaking my cheeks.

More yelling from above.

More pounding of hooves.

More of me knowing I caused the injury that killed my grandmother, and that Papa paid the price.

"Soro?" Ugeen presses.

Soro sighs, perceiving my grief as weakness. "When I succeeded in ambushing him, he knew I'd take Maeve by force. But knowing he was fucked, there was little he could do." He motions at Vitor with a reckless swing of his dagger. "He didn't want anyone else hurt and thought in telling me this deeply guarded secret, he could strike a bargain." He cocks his head as he regards his father. "It didn't work that way. Did it, Vitor?"

"You swore as my son that you wouldn't hurt Maeve or House Iamond," Vitor says. "And yet, you ordered the slaughter of every member of her household, even if Maeve was all you needed."

"I did what a true king should do—sacrifice a small number for the greater good," Soro replies. There's no menace in his tone, simply unmitigated righteousness. "As for my word, that oath was never made in blood, and I stopped being your son a long time ago." His sharp features twist, his face plagued with the evil that met me in the cottage. "Call her," he says.

If possible, Vitor's mouth tightens further. He's had it with Soro. But Soro isn't done. "I said *call her*," he snaps.

Everyone present turns in the direction of the imposing golden gate, the ogres unsheathing their weapons and lifting their axes high. Unable to move my body, I turn my head as much as I'm able, struggling once more against my restraints.

"Aurora," Vitor chokes out.

Aurora...the same name Grandmother used?

"Louder," Soro orders, a growing sense of awe licking his words.

"Aurora, wake from sleep and accept your offering," Vitor says.

And nothing...

"Again," Soro insists, the sweat glossing his skin highlighting his menacing gaze.

Vitor's voice trembles, something I've never heard from him before. "Aurora, great savior of Arrow, rise from sleep and take your offering!"

The ground rumbles louder than the sounds of combat from the arena above. The mound of soil behind the gate stirs, releasing streams of blinding light and tendrils of smoke and clouds of...

Oh, no. Not...

That's not soil.

It's ash.

CHAPTER

48

MAEVE

Brilliant, flaming plumage of red, yellow, orange, and purple rises, shaking the remains of her nest free from her peacock-like tail and body. A neck stretches and lengthens until a majestic head looms about one hundred feet above us. She spreads her sail-wide wings, stretching them and cawing in a melodious song.

Wheel-sized fathomless black eyes blink back at me behind a hawkish beak, her head tilting from side to side with interest when she sees me.

"By all the glory," Ugeen says.

I didn't notice him backing away. He has the option. Still bound tight, I don't. Pua and Tut did, too, and they appear just as beholden as Ugeen.

For a moment, shock numbs my pain and all rational thought.

Soro flips the dagger over and over, repeatedly catching it by the hilt in his left hand as he closes the small space keeping us apart.

The point of his dagger nicks my chin again. I fight back the urge to cower, even as he glides the sharp tip down my throat. "Your sweet, gentle papa was too weak to do what must be done." He stops with the point between the swells of my breasts. "But I'm not."

In a flash, he's behind Vitor.

His speed too fast to track.

One moment.

And then it's over.

In horror, I watch helplessly as Soro slashes his father's throat and shoves Vitor's limp form toward the phoenix.

In her excitement, the phoenix explodes in light, flames sparking in all directions, burning the walls and ground and ceiling...exactly like she did three years ago.

The epiphany has just begun to bloom when a serpentine tongue shoots from Aurora's mouth, wrapping around Vitor and pulling him into her open beak.

Except for Soro, the others race away in the direction of the maze. Soro remains still, watching the man whom he'd loved and simultaneously hated slide down the phoenix's elongated throat.

"Eat, dear Aurora, eat," he says. "You belong to me now."

I take a shuddering breath and close my eyes, opening them again only to see Aurora regurgitate Vitor's bones. They land in a wet lump, and a sob escapes me.

But the horror show is not over yet. Aurora stretches her neck and frantically laps what I thought was condensation falling from the large "wine"-stained stalactites. As I tilt my head up, moisture splatters my face and shoulders. I stare down at the bloodstains on my chest in horror.

Another sob breaks through my throat for Vitor, for Papa, for Father and Neela and everyone I lost today. And another sob, and another for the knowledge I have gained. My grandmother didn't make sacrifices to make Arrow great. She *offered* sacrifices.

Soro saunters forward, wiping Vitor's blood against his robes, and stops right in front of me.

I look from the pile of Vitor's bones to the piles of bones that make up the catacombs, then back to the phoenix who quenches her thirst.

With the blood of gladiators.

Drip, drip, drip.

Every droplet hurts me now, knowing it has travelled from the veins of the innocent, through layers of sand and porous stone, and onto me.

Rage and horror join my sorrow, twisting my gut in a painful whirlpool. "Tell me what you want," I say.

Soro huffs. "Oh, Maeve. Always right to the point."

Now that Tut and Pua are no longer standing guard over Vitor, they've joined Ugeen at the entrance of the maze, where they deem Aurora can't suck them up and swallow them. This is the first time they've seen the phoenix. It's obvious by the fear and awe marching across their exaggerated features.

"You used the phoenix as a means to stage your coup?" It makes sense. Whoever commands the phoenix commands her power. If this motley crew turned on Vitor, it's because Soro revealed her existence and convinced them he could control her.

Soro sighs, as if he's the one who had a rough day. "Aurora is a gift — my gift, now," he says. "Why wouldn't I use my gifts to their fullest extent?"

Rage overshadows my grief, singeing my insides to liquid fire. "Well, now that show and tell is complete, I think you should know that I'd rather burn than marry you."

Soro pushes my soaking hair away from my face. Like a child outlining an image, his fingertip passes along the perimeter of the scars along my jaw. "I gave you every opportunity to help me and yourself. You could have made it easy," he whispers against my ear. His voice lowers. "You could have made it *good*. Now, it's too late." I curl inward when his lips trail over my skin. "Hear me well. You will do as you're told. Even if I must break you into a thousand pieces, you will bow to me." His tone is soft — regal, even — but so full of venom I could die from poisoning on the spot. "Or should I take your lack of respect out on your sister?" He smiles. "Or perhaps your gladiator?"

Despite my fear, I keep my voice even. "Do what you want," I say. "All he's good for is making me money."

Soro nods as he steps away. "I don't know about that, Maeve, especially not when my own father saw him as a potential king. When you saw him as someone to fuck." He squares his jaw. "Vitor alluded to what a wonderful couple you'd make. *To me*, knowing I sought you for my very own."

Only at his final words do I catch a glimpse of hurt overtaking his solid frame. But like before, that hurt dissipates, leaving only the rage it festered.

"Your gladiator — he won't win today. Even if he does, I'm certain he won't walk out of the last trial alive." He looks to the ogren generals. "In fact, why risk more of his brethren arriving to take his place? Find his family. Kill them. And bring back their heads."

"They died years ago," I snap and immediately regret it. Except, if Tut and Pua do send a squad to Siertos, innocent people could get hurt.

"That's unfortunate," Soro says, not bothering to pretend to mean it. "I have to admit, your plan to marry a Bloodguard was genius. Everyone else knows better than to screw with me. But...*but*..." His gaze dances to the arena above us. "He's up soon. And he's not a Bloodguard yet." His attention drops back down to me. "Should I punish him for interfering with what's mine?"

Soro's threats slow my beating heart. He will throw everything at Leith just because he *almost* had what Soro wanted. His attention flits to where Aurora preens herself, each feather she plucks igniting in yellow-and-green flames before dwindling to ash and adding another layer to her nest.

"Yes, I think I will," Soro says, his demeanor as inviting as a coffin full of vipers. "All of Arrow needs to learn not to touch what's mine."

"Free Leith from his obligation to the arena and allow him to live free in Arrow," I say quickly. "Do this and...and I'll swear a blood oath to marry you."

I may run my mouth, but I'm no fool. Soro and his murdering legion killed my family. They'll kill Leith, too, if he threatens Soro's title as king. At least this way, Leith will get to live.

Even if it's without me.

"That sounds reasonable," Soro agrees, smiling. "Consider it a wedding gift. Now, let's discuss my terms..."

Pua cuts me loose. I fall forward as the conditions of Leith's freedom flare against Soro's arm and form words. I swallow back the blood still pooling in my mouth and everything this day has cost me and take Soro's hand.

My teeth chatter from my body's uncontrolled trembling as Soro and I seal our oath. There is one brief moment of peace as the unbreakable bond is made. Leith will live. He'll never have to fight again.

But then I hear that rising chant above us.

"Bloodguard. *Bloodguard. BLOODGUARD!*"

Soro smiles. "Oh no. We're too late. Your champion is already in the arena..."

CHAPTER

49

LEITH

The guards manhandle me all the way to the arena entrance. It's bad enough that every gladiator before me damn well died, but everything in the arena today feels, well, *different*.

The horn blasts, and the chanting begins. "Bloodguard. *Bloodguard!*"

I'm thrown into the sand, tripping over the first of at least twenty dead gladiators.

The gates come crashing down. The severed hands of the body I tripped over are still gripping the bars.

Two possibilities occur to me as I rise. Neither of them is particularly cheery.

One: A large group of gladiators were all pitted against one another, as Sullivan and I were.

Or two: They were, indeed, thrown in one at a time, and whatever their opponent was killed them so fast they were replaced as quickly as they fell.

Deathly pale faces are all that greet me as I look to the stands. There are those whose partners are fanning them, trying to revive them, and more who are pouring goblets of water over their faces to wake them.

Even more are too frightened to move.

I step over the handless body and walk toward that of a young giant larger than Luther, but one who never learned to fight. He probably thought his strength would be enough.

It wasn't.

His open ribcage, absent a liver and one of the four kidneys giants have, tells me who was stronger.

Throughout the arena, the bodies lie almost in a row. They weren't arranged this way. The pattern isn't neat enough. There's also no clear cause of death.

The only thing they have in common is that they were all running toward the exit.

Nice.

Real. Damn. *Nice.*

They should have done me the favor of killing it, them, or whatever the hell I'm up against.

A dagger lies beside a dwarf whose smoking asshole was made larger than his head.

I pocket the dagger, not wanting to dwell too much on that. There are enough nightmares ahead to keep me awake for the next year.

There's another giant, this one smaller than Luther. Likely younger, given he's only as tall as me.

Oh, and look at this. He's holding part of his brain. He must have caught it as it launched from his eye sockets.

The eyeballs lie staring at the gladiator who has his foot rammed into his mouth. Another gladiator might have fed him the severed foot to silence his screaming. He must have choked on it. Considering how the others died, this was the best way to go.

There's a boomerang blade tossed beside him, and I know it's Maeve's doing. Though it's not my own blade, no guard in Arrow would think to include a Siertosian weapon like this. A piece of *my* culture in this twisted hellscape that poisons their own. I focus on the genius of its design. It's better than allowing my stomach to fall at my feet, like that poor bastard cyclops who was strangled with his own intestines. I'm trying not to be obvious as I search each row of the royal box. Maeve… She isn't here. I turn around, pretending to stretch, but there's no sign of her.

Look at the weapon. Look at the weapon. Damn it, look at the fucking *weapon.*

A week or so ago, when I was using the one she bought me to help her collect medicinal ingredients in the forest, I told Maeve how my mother taught me to use a boomerang blade. It was the same one her father used to bring down birds to eat. She spent weeks teaching me the right way to throw it. I'd toss it over and over, practicing with each hand until the muscles on my arms and shoulders threatened to tear.

Once I mastered the motion, it would smoothly return to land by my feet. Then the hard part began. I spent over a year learning not only how to strike my target but to catch it upon its return. It was tedious and frightening and so worth it. It was also a way to catch food, until the birds were smart enough to abandon Grey.

I toss the boomerang in the air with the confidence my mother insisted I demonstrate. It is larger than any I've used before but weighted perfectly, so I should have no problem adjusting to its size. When all my fingers remain attached, my confidence grows, as well as the enthusiasm of the crowd. Thank the moon that muscle memory is a real thing. And while I still can't find Maeve, I feel her with me in this weapon.

It should help me today.

Unless I end up like that troll over there.

And there.

And there.

I swallow hard.

He didn't need that spleen, anyway.

Panic should have set in. I'm halfway across the arena and armed to the teeth, having tucked three daggers into my waistband, two broken spears under my arm, a sword into one hand, and my trusty boomerang in the other. It's only because I'm allowed to take weapons from the fallen that I have this much.

A banging sound reverberates from the other end of the arena. The warning of impending danger causes several royals to faint and even more to clutch each other.

I stash the sword upright in the sand, remembering I was warned not to engage my opponent directly, and ready for one hell of a fight. A creak averts my gaze from the opposite end and to a concrete door I'd noticed but never seen used. It's part of the arena wall. It opens with a deep, thudded *crack* followed by a hideous snarl.

Within the darkness, white-hot flames ignite six hundred pounds of bovine muscle.

Oh fuck.

I run before the fire bull can charge. It's not to escape. There's no escaping these creatures who trample their food and then hold their shrieking bodies down so they can burn them alive and enjoy a homecooked meal. And let's not forget the ones they kill for pleasure.

The distance I create is long enough to pivot and toss my first spear. It nails the racing bovine in the chest.

Its hellish speed works against it. It trips over itself, driving the broken spear deep enough to puncture a lung. It rolls out of the way from another fire bull that appears, crashing against the wall and kicking up sand as it slowly dies.

The next fire bull is faster and smarter than I prefer my opponents. It closes in on me, weaving from side to side, easily avoiding the next broken spear I toss, plus another I come across.

When only yards remain between us, I lift my blade and run toward it, and, yes, another fire bull appears. I'd prefer to kill my enemies from afar, but they have other plans. My legs and arms pump as I accelerate. They mean to impale me as they did that poor sap who met them ass-first.

I slide between the legs of the one who reaches me first, its large body providing me the space I need to lift my spear and cut its underbelly. The flames encasing it flicker out as I roll away. That kill was surprisingly easy. Too easy for the chunks of gladiators who remain.

The final fire bull is smaller but more muscular and the fastest yet. I hop onto my feet, cursing when I realize that my haste to get out from under the other fire bull cost me a dagger that slipped from my waistband. But two still remain.

I barely have my balance when the fire bull slides to a stop and then doubles back. The quick turn slows it just enough for me to jerk to the side and bring my boomerang blade down on its snout.

The shock of pain impedes the fire bull's natural ability to maintain its flame. The dwindling heat is enough to singe my skin but not enough to burn me alive.

It jerks its head back and forth, shoving me to the side and trapping me against the wall as it tries to fling the blade imbedded into its face.

I feel every bit of its heavy, jerky movements. I dig my heels into the sand and push, scrambling free as I wrench my blade from its snout. With a tight grip on the handle—a short piece of leather connecting the two blades on either side—I bring it down hard into the fire bull's skull, shattering the dense bone and piercing its brain.

When it collapses, I raise my weak arms, expecting only thunderous applause.

A youngling dwarf who accompanies his parents yells, "Yay!" His parents don't notice him, continuing to clutch each other in fear.

Other than some less-than-heartfelt claps, there's nothing.

It's eerily quiet. And that was far too easy.

Until a metal-on-metal grinding sounds from across the arena.

The gate opens just enough for a humanoid head to peek through.

The creature's head is bald and its attention everywhere, glancing around and breathing through its mouth. A wave of visceral disgust washes over me. This creature is *wrong*.

Screeches and screams from the crowd immediately begin. I think I hear Maeve, but I don't dare look this time. No. This freak will require my undivided attention.

My shock is the only thing that silences the collective cursing my insides are doing as my opponent pushes its way into the arena.

Dark-green scales cover everything save its face. Four strong limbs armed with beast-like claws stained red with my predecessors' blood protrude one at a time. It stands, shaking out its body as its wobbly head bounces faster.

This...*thing* crouches and stretches, creepy gaze mesmerized by its surroundings, as if it wasn't responsible for the carnage in the first place. As absently as I would scrape mud from my boot, the creature lifts the head of a nearby human, cracks it open like an egg, and slurps down the brain.

It tosses the body aside when it finishes.

And reaches for a troll's...

Never mind.

I almost miss the parents of the youngling dwarf covering his eyes and hauling him away.

This…this *thing* thrown into the arena with me is unnatural and not a part of Old Erth. The others didn't stand a fucking chance. I'm not sure I do, either.

Whoever conjured this freak had a shit-ton of time and a twisted imagination.

Another gate creaks open, and a wizard with sparkling gold robes steps through. The aroma he carries is that of burning silkweed, the same malevolent magic said to emanate from hell itself.

Oh, shit.

The wizard's broad features are all business and his snow-white sclera absent of irises. "Au men. Au men," he says, lengthening each syllable.

"Aumen" snaps its neck in its master's direction.

Slowly, and as disturbingly as the rest of him, Aumen looks away from the wizard and sets its bobbing head and rolling eyes on me.

I'm used to these assholes scouring all of Old Erth to secure deadly opponents. I never imagined an opponent like this. This thing was born of evil. It's not just its freakish body—it's the awkward motions, as if it's only now learning to use its limbs.

Maybe it's partly human. But as it rushes toward me, its head bobbles back, its mouth splits open across the length of his face, and it exposes needle-thin fangs. Any sympathy I had vanishes like that last bit of brain stuck to its incisor.

The beast strikes in a cobra-like motion, spitting what appears to be shards or fangs. I use my boomerang to bat them away and charge, swiping my sword out of the sand as I pass.

Again, it spits. This time, I can't block them all. Like darts, some imbed in my stomach. I throw my sword out, hollering in anger and pain when the fangs twitch and burrow farther into my skin. Still, I run.

If it wasn't for my death grip on the hilt of the sword and the force of my weight lurching forward, Aumen would have gutted me with its claws.

Instead, it peers down, examining my sword protruding from its sternum. It lifts its bobbling head and hisses, spitting more needles. They pierce through my cheek and would have punctured my eye if I hadn't jerked my head to the side.

I push the sword deeper.

It doesn't respond in pain. Again, it bobbles, more fascinated with my weapon than it is with me. Did no one else get close enough to injure it?

As I use my weight to push, I realize its ghastly head was sewn on.

"Au-men," the wizard calls to it. "Au-men."

The word is foreign to me, more of a sound. Yet within it is power.

I drag my sword downward, gagging when Aumen's abdomen opens.

There are no visible organs. I wish there were and that I had somehow struck the creature down. Instead, a pouch like that of a marsupial flips inside out, revealing a mouth that punches forward and sinks its fangs into my abdomen.

I don't scream or cry out.

Some things are too painful for such marginal reactions.

My head falls back, my wide eyes burning beneath the merciless sun. Something else rakes at my skin. There's a tearing sound followed by the painful pricks of needles burying into my torso. Aumen screams like a tortured man, but so, so much worse. Even in my half-delirious state, every hair on my body stands on end.

There are shrieks. There are racing footsteps. There is violent retching and the crash of flopping bodies.

Spectators are yelling, fainting, fleeing, and hurling.

Spectators who are nowhere near this thing trying to kill me.

I sway in place, my grip falling from my sword and my spine bowing backward. The wizard deepens his chanting lustfully, certain another death is within his reach.

Somehow, the fear of death sharpens my senses.

Only years of practice help my aim. My boomerang blade strikes the wizard in the skull. He collapses.

No time to scream.

Less time to run.

The moment from when I'm bitten to when the wizard falls lasts mere seconds.

Seconds of agony I never want to feel again.

Aumen drops me. It scuttles away in awkward motions and…eats its master. Without its maker in control, I suppose it saw "daddy" as fresh meat.

If hysteria hadn't spread across the crowd before, it does now and then some.

My feet move slowly at first. Damn. The wizard thought he was in control, and he was, until his blood was too much for Aumen to resist.

My head reminds *me* we don't want to be the next thing it decides to eat.

Loud slurping sounds reverberate through the coliseum as Aumen devours its maker's corpse.

My goal is to strike when it's preoccupied. Except it hears me approach.

It spins and hisses, cutting my skin with more needle-fangs. I don't stop and drive a dagger into its throat. It barely notices.

The way my sword remains lodged, completely unmoving in its chest, explains why I couldn't kill it the first time. There aren't mere ribs protecting its heart. I should have guessed. Nothing of Aumen is like it should be.

A large, flat plate of bone protects Aumen's vulnerable organs like a shield. And my sword is stuck in it.

Once more, my rage becomes my ally, joining the strength I've built over my time with Maeve. With a roar, I use my sword to lift the monstrosity over my head, my arms shaking violently as I use Aumen's body weight against it. There's a crack as the hard plate shatters and my blade slides into its vital organs. Its limbs twitch in agony, but I can't bring myself to give a shit about its pain. Not with the corpses of my peers littered around us.

My back bows, and I lose my grip on the sword as the creature falls behind me. It lands hard, limbs scratching at the ground. I leap and ram my fist into the hilt of my sword.

The excited cries from the crowd are muffled. I take my remaining dagger and stab the mouth on its stomach when it tries to open again. With the last ounce of my strength, I wrench my sword free and slice open its jugular. I continue to saw into its throat until its head rolls clean off and I'm bathed in blood.

I don't stop, taking my blade and striking every part of Aumen's body I can reach.

I continue my strikes long after it's dead. The audience chants, celebrating not my victory but Aumen's defeat.

The monster they feared is dead.

My weapon slips from my slick hands, soaked with Aumen's insides and pungent with the reek of malevolent magic. And still I fight, punching and kicking its crumpled form.

From the exit, I hear Gunther's "Bloodguard. Bloodguard. Bloodguard!" chants.

I step away from the creature and almost trip on some random torso. I did it. I damn well did it. I lived. And I avenged. As I stumble forward, I begin yanking needles from my skin. Some don't give me much trouble. Others, Maeve's going to have to help me with later. I look around, trying to spot her or Jakeb, Giselle, and Caelen…where the hell are they?

Trumpets blare, and the audience—those who remain conscious—is on their feet.

But I don't care about them.

Where are my people? I heard Maeve, but I never saw her. She wouldn't just leave without acknowledging me somehow. Maybe she thinks I'm dying and ran off to prepare a medicinal bath.

Another round of trumpets sounds, proclaiming Vitor has something to say. That's glorious. Fine. Say it. The sooner he's done singing his own praises, the sooner Maeve and I can get back home.

But he doesn't stand. Ugeen, that bald dimwit, does instead, his robes of gold paling him further.

A young pageboy runs forward, hanging on to his floppy red hat with a wide brim. "All rise for Lord Ugeen," he says in a small voice.

It takes more than a moment for everyone to get to their feet. The royals clap within their ring. Others from the Commons and Middling follow but not many. Regardless, Ugeen smiles with his hands in the air as if *he* won the damn fight.

"My, what a feat. What a feat indeed, young gladiator!" He's clapping, but who the hell is he kidding? Asshole is probably clapping for himself.

His voice booms across the arena, his hands rising once more.

"It's time to celebrate, friends, not only in praise of our distinguished gladiator's monumental accomplishment but in celebration of a royal wedding."

Bloody hell. He's here to announce his engagement? Can't this prick see he lost half his audience by bringing that fucked-up crime against nature into the arena?

"Shall we meet her?" he asks no one in particular. Some clap lightly, still disturbed by Aumen and my fight. But everyone turns to see the lucky royal dumbass who will end up with another dumbass.

"See them, revere them, and praise them," Ugeen shouts, attempting to rile an audience he's losing. "Behold. Arrow's future king and queen!"

Ugeen lifts a crown from a velvet pillow.

My breath freezes in my lungs. I don't know what's real or not, unable to believe what my eyes are showing me.

No... Not... *No!*

Maeve, *my Maeve*, steps out wearing a bejeweled gold dress, her face hidden behind a veil. But it is her. I'd know her anywhere.

She's led to Soro's side.

He kisses her hand.

She curtsies to him.

Along the stands, some continue to clap. Others go still, the mix of confusion, resentment, and surprise keeping them silent.

Strong limbs band my arms to my side. The force required to keep me in place makes the soldiers grunt and tremble.

Ugeen lifts a rope of braided gold, blue, and green ribbon between Soro and Maeve.

"Soro of Revlis," he says, "beloved son of Vitor of Revlis, High Lord and General, Fist of the Law, Champion of Arrow, Ultimate Victor, and God of War, will marry Maeve of Iamond, Healer of Ails, Princess of Arrow and granddaughter of Avianna of Iamond, Finest Queen of Arrow, the Ultimate Sword of Justice, the Wisdom of One Thousand Truths, and Mother of Righteousness, on the day of her twenty-first year."

It feels as though Ugeen's animated words rip the flesh from my ears in bone-rattling pain with each syllable, singeing them into the remains so with every thrum of my pulse, the words reverberate and scald me.

Soro regards her with startling determination and unmitigated triumph.

Maeve turns to face me as Ugeen binds the end of the braided rope to Soro's wrist. I can't read her expression. That veil keeps it hidden.

It feels like daggers ablaze with fire puncture my organs and pin them to my bones. "No…" I say.

Ugeen rocks back and forth on his feet in delight. He lifts Maeve's hand, binding it to Soro.

"The promise is made!" Soro bellows, a sick grin spreading across his face. Though his words are addressed to the crowd, he stares directly at me. "And you're all invited to celebrate."

Maeve's free hand shakes—no, motions in a way that tells me not to do anything.

And she thinks I'll actually follow it!

"What's this shit?" I demand.

Ugeen regards me, stunned, if not offended. "What?" he asks.

"I asked you *what the hell this shit is*," I repeat a lot less nicely.

Ugeen fancies himself one of those proper lords. And proper lords don't appreciate being yelled at. "Settle down, gladiator," he says, more offended by my tone than my intent. "The woman is free to make her own choices, no? Unlike your family, Maeve of House Iamond is not dead."

The arena vanishes in an explosion of blurring sound. As it settles, there's only silence, even as pain shoots through me as if my muscles are tearing from my bones piece by torturous piece.

"You…you *murdered my family*?"

Ugeen is affronted. "Nonsense. They've been dead for years." He looks at Maeve. "He didn't know?" he asks her.

I break free of the arms holding me. Sand and chunks of flesh press beneath my feet. I'm running forward, I think.

Maeve just stands there, holding her hand out, trying to tell me to stop. As if I ever could.

Except right now it feels possible. Necessary, even.

I have to get away.

Her free arm clutches Soro's—her fiancé. Her future *fucking* king!

Someone jumps into the arena, running up on me. Caelen, urging me to leave the arena with him, telling me they'll kill me if I stay.

But I'm already dead. This nightmare—the reason I signed up for this shit in the first place—ends *with my family dead*. Giselle's next to me, her voice begging me to listen, saying we must leave, telling me something about Jakeb, Neela, and the manor.

The royal guards are approaching. That's what Caelen says.

I shove him aside like it's nothing.

I suppose it's not.

Compared to losing my entire *fucking* family!

"They're dead," I say.

Giselle's voice splinters. "I-I'm sorry."

And Maeve knew. She *knew* and she didn't tell me. How could she not tell me?

The arena suddenly clears, and noise destroys my ears. The guards charge. I do, too.

There's no reason left to live.

But there are plenty of reasons to die.

CHAPTER
50

LEITH

*S*lice.

That's seventeen.

Slice.

Eighteen.

Eighteen lashes. And six more to go.

I kept my feet for the first twelve. Managed to remain on my knees for the next five.

The eighteenth, though. That…that was a killer.

This might be a new record of overall shittiness for me.

And here I thought I won.

Won the perfect woman.

Won the right to fight in the finals.

Won another chance to bring my family here.

Lies.

They were all lies.

Slice.

My wrist cracks as my muscles fail and my weight pulls mercilessly against the rope that binds my hands above my head. Yeah. New record for sure. I think I could have gone without breaking it. In fact, I could have gone without a lot of things today.

The arena and all the hell I went through definitely lands on the list. Finding out my family is dead—yeah, right at the top.

And the woman who fooled me into falling in love with her despite caring so little about me as to keep secret the most important information in the fucking world...the one who neglected to tell me that tiny tidbit regarding my dead family...yeah, she ruined my day. No, *my life*.

Slice.

Dahlia... She was supposed to play all day in the woods with Gunther, chasing each other, getting dirty, climbing trees before we called them in for supper and filled their empty stomachs.

Mother...who gave me her food, going hungry so my sisters and I would get even a little bit more. She, for once in her life, would have had her fill, too.

And Rose, who held the one book she ever had like a treasure, even though she couldn't read all the words. I would have sent her to the best school in Arrow and built her a library if that was what she wanted.

Rose, Mother, Dahlia...I would have given them *everything*.

They're dead.

They're all dead.

And Maeve didn't tell me.

Slice.

I slump down, at an angle, I think. It's hard to tell where the worst pain is coming from. It's everywhere and in places I never knew could hurt this bad. Maeve, the cottage, and those hours beside our lake—was all of that just a dream? Was I just always here, in these filthy pens and cold barracks?

Shit, nothing makes sense in my head. All I know is pain and tragedy.

The ropes binding me to the post pull at my arms, my own weight working against me. It won't be long until I pull tendons, muscles, maybe both. Hell, I may even dislocate a shoulder all on my own.

Slice.

Nine...nineteen.

Was that nineteen?

"Oi!" Ned calls. "Is that a way to treat the next Bloodguard?"

The guards laugh. "If the future king willed it, he'd already be dead."

A few of the gladiators spit in their direction, muttering and demanding they release me. Some taunt the guards, itching for a fight.

"Arseholes!" Ned shouts. "That's all the lot of ya will eva be!"

He was already struck for cursing them. Pega, Rye, Ioni, and Luther, too. Some others I don't know joined in as well.

Rye whistles so he can drop his pants and slap his ass at them when they turn.

The gladiators are trying to distract the guards in hopes their strikes won't be as potent.

It's an interesting strategy. I wish I could lift my head and tell them it's absolutely not working. The guards keep switching off so everyone can take a turn at the gladiator with the broken heart.

Maeve… She was real. She *is* real.

But I can no longer stand the thought of her name.

She swore that she would do anything to become queen. Was I foolish enough to think she only meant it with me sitting on the throne beside her? All along, she meant to meet her own needs, and I damn well fell for it. It's why she motioned for me not to interfere. She didn't want me to ruin the big announcement.

About *her*.

And her maggot of a future husband.

Slice.

"Fuckin' animals!"

"Son of a whore!"

"Bastards!"

"Hang in there, boy," Ioni tells me. "They almost be done."

Slice.

Twenty, I think. Maybe more. The guards have never been good at counting. Or maybe they're just pretending they've lost count so I don't spoil their fun.

"He's had enough, ya filthy pigs!"

That might have been Pega. I don't know anymore.

My head drops farther than seems possible. The sound of shackles across the stony walk has me looking off to the side. It's nightfall. The gladiators should have been hauled back to the barracks long before this. But my punishment is an opportunity to show what happens when a dog threatens a king.

My back is on fire from the lashes and the injuries I received in the arena. Something bit me or stung my arms and belly. Or not. It's hard to tell.

Except nothing compares to the agony in the center of my chest. Where my heart is, or was, until Maeve destroyed it. I was an imbecile for trusting her.

Slice.

Sixteen? Are we back to sixteen?

"What are ya doing?" Ned demands. "He's had enough. Let 'im go."

I sustained more injuries than expected from my clash with the guards. I did quite a bit of damage before they were able to get me under control.

I laugh.

Control.

That's a funny word.

I thought I'd finally taken control of my life. I chose a cause. I chose my lover. I chose to keep going. And here I am, suffering despite all my supposed good choices.

Pink drool slides from my mouth. My hair is drenched in sweat and blood.

"Enough. His time is up. This man is free."

Caelen? *Is that you, friend?*

Nah. I watch the tip of the bloody whip withdraw as the guard readies for another strike.

Except then there's a loud crash, and a thump, and the guard's unblinking face staring at me in shock.

Well. Would you look at that? Caelen indeed has arrived.

A ruckus ensues. Someone demands for me to be freed. It's strange, but I don't hear the guards. There's only silence.

My body falls as I'm cut free, and Caelen catches me with my face only inches from the muddy ground.

"Leith. *Leith*," Giselle says. "I'm so, so sorry. We weren't allowed near you until now."

I start to fall asleep.

"Leith, can you hear us?" Caelen urges.

"Holy shitting dragon balls," Giselle says. "I can see his bones."

"I know," Caelen agrees. "He's in bad shape."

"Is that supposed to be there—"

I jerk when something pokes me, half conscious and hoping to be none.

"Giselle," Caelen says. "Ask him when conscious." And then, "*Giselle*, stop touching it…"

I fade into sweet oblivion.

Until I bolt up.

I'm drowning in ice.

Ice.

My body erupts in pain, then something else—something vaguely akin to relief.

My hands grip the edges of the tub. The room I'm in is small, dark, lit only by the moonlight trailing in through the high window.

I swipe at my face and hair, pausing when I see Caelen in a chair, watching me closely. Giselle is here, too, kneeling beside the tub. She tries to smile, but her face is swollen and bruised.

"He lives!" she says.

"Where am I?" I ask.

"New Arrow. That's what they call it," Caelen says, his features solemn. He looks down. "Jakeb put all his heart into it."

When he finishes, his lips press tightly together as if he's done speaking and won't ever do it again. If there's any doubt, he stands, turning in the direction of the door.

Giselle rises, moving quickly before Caelen can exit. She hugs him tightly, as if she's afraid she will lose him.

Caelen appears surprised by the contact. He curls into her small body, taking a moment all their own.

"Thank you," Giselle whispers. "For everything."

Caelen kisses the top of her head. "Always," he tells her.

Giselle watches him leave, wiping her face before turning around. She pulls out the chair Caelen was in and sits beside me.

"You need to get all the way back in," she says, motioning to the tub. "I can't see your bones anymore, but your back still looks like something the butcher would try to sell me, and I'd respond by slapping him hard enough to make his uncle twice removed bleed." She shrugs. "You've seen better days, Leith."

"How did you do it?" I ask. "Fix me, I mean."

"I didn't," she admits. "Your friend, the giant, motioned me over and passed me an envelope. It's one of Maeve's most potent remedies. I think it was meant for at least seven gladiators. Given how you're seven times worse than I've ever seen you, I dumped the whole thing in."

I nod.

"We thought you might need more. We left you with Uni and returned to the manor, but...there was nothing there."

Again, I nod. It's all I seem able to do.

"You won't heal completely, even with everything you're swimming in," Giselle says. "I don't possess healing knowledge, but it's already helped a lot, and it should keep you from infection." She sighs. "Whatever she made will serve you well, no matter what happens next."

Giselle knows Soro won't let me get off so easy. I settle back into the water, shuddering. It's almost as if Giselle laid a slab of ice in the tub and threw me on top to melt it.

I don't really care. My body—it's healing. It's getting better. As Giselle said, it won't be as good without...without someone else. But it may be enough. "It's cold," I say.

"It is," Giselle agrees. Her voice quiets. "Hot water is a luxury only whole, wealthy families have. We're neither anymore."

There's more wrong than I know. "Where is everyone?" I ask. "Where's Neela?"

Neela runs the house and takes care of everything and everyone. She should be here grouching over the mess we're making.

Giselle's face crumples with grief. This tough petite woman is seconds from falling apart. "Neela's dead," she says.

"*What?* Jakeb would never—"

"Allow anything to hurt her?" she offers.

I have trouble finding my voice. "Yes."

"No, he wouldn't. Except Father's dead, too," Giselle replies, and now she's weeping outright. "Pasha, Musy, Sonu...oh, and the estrellas. You know, those precious little fuzzballs of joy who bounced along all day just happy to be alive? They're all dead, too... Leith, *everyone* is gone."

I stare ahead, to the crooked fissure in the plaster. It's the only way I can ground myself, seeing as I'm about to explode.

Slowly, I turn my head in Giselle's direction. She's sobbing silently, if it's even possible, but holding nothing back.

"Tell me what happened," I growl.

"The royal guards invaded the manor and the grounds." She rubs her eyes with the sleeve of her cherry robe. "Caelen thinks they ambushed the guard station and went after my family as soon as you left. They must have already been in place, possibly on a neighboring farm. Father... I should have known something was wrong when I couldn't find him at the arena. Had I known, Caelen and I would have rushed to help. I don't know if it would have made a difference. Caelen is only one man, and I can't swing a sword worth a damn. But we all should have been there, standing as one like we have all our lives."

"You weren't there?" I ask.

"No," she admits.

"What..." I can't speak. My voice is becoming more primal. I don't want to ask it—don't want to even think her name—but I can't stop myself. "What happened to Maeve?"

Giselle takes a moment, trying to calm. "Oh, her? She's stuck with that murdering asshole Soro for eternity." She rubs more tears away. "But at least you're a free man."

My heart is trying to escape my ribcage. Hope rises like smoke in my chest, but I try to push it away.

"Because of Maeve?" I ask.

"Yes. It was part of the oath she made with Soro," she says. "The note from the courier said it was a wedding gift to his bride." She practically swallows the air with every breath, like she's desperately holding back screams. "You don't have to fight anymore. You're free, you're pardoned, whatever the hell you want to call it. She made sure of it."

The hope, the admiration, the love—they all come crashing back into my body in a massive tidal wave, knocking the air from my lungs. *She didn't just throw me away to be queen.* My fears, my doubts...they were all wrong. Maeve was and is the queen I know her to be.

She didn't tell me about my family, but I can't even touch that right now without fucking falling apart. I need Maeve to tell me why. And to do that, I need to find her. Now.

"What about Vitor? He had a role in all of this—"

"One would think," Giselle says. "Still… It might be trivial, but I can't imagine him letting Ugeen lay a hand on Maeve, let alone announce her engagement before the court."

"What happened to her?" I ask again.

"With Soro and Ugeen?" Giselle appears sick. "Nothing good."

I launch myself out of the tub, yanking my destroyed and bloody clothes from the floor. Giselle presses her back against the door when I barely have one foot in my pants.

"Giselle, move. No way in hell are they hurting Maeve."

She shakes her head. "No. We didn't come this far for you to screw it up, Leith."

"Get out of my way," I snarl.

Her eyes change from honey to a swirl of bright colors as magic she isn't supposed to possess seethes like the start of an inferno. "I said *no*."

There's silence.

Unexpectedly, it's exactly what we need.

We let it linger until I can't stand it any longer and I'm certain I'm tearing apart from the inside out.

The honey color returns to her eyes. She points to the bed. Aside from the chair and the tub, that's all that's here. I didn't notice the fresh set of clothes laid on it before. I didn't notice that I'm completely butt fucking naked in front of Maeve's sister, either. Not that either of us gives a rat's ass about something so trivial right now. Still, I turn around and dress myself promptly.

I sit, and it hurts. Despite the herbal remedies, everything fucking hurts.

Giselle sits beside me, smoothing her skirts with her leather-gloved palms. "The manor and stables were burned to the ground." I look at her, stunned, and she continues, "But not before they were looted. I guess you're not real scum unless you loot first and burn later."

I bury my face in my hands. "What of the cottage?"

"That was destroyed sometime after the manor. Hence why there weren't more potions to bring you." She shakes her head. "Maeve put up a fight no one expected. I always admired her, you know? When I was little, I was *real little*. The queen thought I was *too little*. So she gave me books because, and I quote, 'You're a little shit anyone could squash. Pick up a book. And then another. If you don't learn a thing, use them to throw at anyone trying to squash you.' Charming woman, the queen. But Maeve had it all—brains, brawn, kindness. It was a joy merely standing in her company. She was fearless and brave and everything I always wanted to be."

She's right. Maeve is all those things and much, much more.

"Giselle," I say. "How do you know what happened? The specifics about Maeve fighting."

"Let's just say riches buy a lot, Leith. And I've paid a great deal."

I curse, then curse again. "Who did you pay? Can you trust them?"

Giselle stares at the wall. "I have sources and favors owed. They're effective but limited. Most refuse to associate with me." She looks in my direction. "Father was the High Guard of Arrow—a royal guard, not a royal. I was born before Father and Papa met. Papa gave us our titles, and I was so proud, but I quickly learned that if you're not of royal lineage or married to said lineage with heirs to prove it, you don't count. It's why I was bullied a lot. I just never imagined my family would endure more than I did." Misery floods her features all over again. "They didn't deserve to hurt or suffer or die. And they did all of it."

"No. They didn't deserve that. Just as you didn't. Your only sin was not taking anyone's shit." I place a brotherly hand on her shoulder. This is Giselle. Someone snubbed all her life, like me, and someone who was fucking precious from the start. "Tell me what happened to you."

I think she'll cry again, but then, like Maeve, she just doesn't. "What do you think?" she responds. "I can't fight. My tongue is my only weapon."

"Is it?" I ask. "That's not what I saw in Tunder."

A long, heavy breath leaves her small body, and she holds up her gloved hands. "My tongue is the only weapon I can *control*," she says.

For the first time, I'm given a glimpse of Giselle's vulnerability. It saddens me. She deserves more than what she has. Especially now.

And Maeve deserves my loyalty.

In the minutes that follow, I'm certain I'll break down the castle doors. Soro could be hurting Maeve as we speak. I can't handle anything more happening to her.

"It's time to save Maeve," I say.

Giselle shakes her head. "No, Leith." She rights herself. "It's time to take back Arrow."

CHAPTER
51

MAEVE

I chose to save Leith's life.

So why do I feel dead on the inside?

I cradle my head, still sore from battle, and sit up. Be it from grief or my injuries, my stomach continues to roil, its contents swirling upward and burning my throat.

Those catacombs were horrors I won't ever forget. Piles upon piles of unidentified, desecrated remains, not just from war but from the limitless demands of Aurora the Phoenix.

The *fucking* phoenix.

The same one I killed my grandmother over. A cry breaks through me, and I curl inward.

I killed my grandmother.

Me.

But Papa paid the price.

It cost him his mind and his throne, and it may cost mine as well.

My knees knock together as I stand and stumble across the room. If memory serves, this apartment — one bedroom and a foyer in the royal wing — used to belong to Ugeen's wife. She hosted tea for me here once before she left him, mostly because he kept screwing her cousin.

I wish they were still married. Polasie was sweet and funny and would have loved to see me force-feed Ugeen his liver. That snively kiss-ass opportunist will pay for his role in the coup.

They dragged me here from the arena, knowing it was the only way to prevent me from ripping Soro's throat out and running to help Leith.

Oh, stars. Leith. He was so injured, and I wasn't there to heal him. Is he alive? He *has* to be alive.

Making me watch them destroy my family and home wasn't enough for these foul creatures. They forced me to watch Leith's match, which was horrendous. I broke free when he collapsed, begging him to fight when it looked like he'd never move again.

Except he wasn't done. My champion climbed out of the grave they dug for him and proved why he deserved to win.

And after he won, he lost.

I expected him to rage at the announcement, but it was worse. A frightening calm like the air before an ice storm ravaged, erasing the young man I've come to know and replacing him with the murderer the arena made him. When he saw me promise to wed Soro, I watched the rest of Leith be demolished.

I had no choice. Soro would have killed him if I hadn't agreed to his terms.

So, for now, I must act the part of the compliant bride to be, despite my desire to roast my betrothed's balls over a spit.

I force myself to rise and stumble to the basin in the corner. I pour cool water from the porcelain pitcher and splash it on my face with trembling hands. Uncle Vitor… He wasn't the bad guy after all—at least not completely. He made mistakes, *terrible* ones, but he didn't deserve to die as he did.

I wipe my face with a towel.

Or did he?

In the end, he became what he offered—a sacrifice to the phoenix.

What was it grandmother said? Something about one life to save thousands?

"No, Grandmother," I say aloud. "Papa was right. There *must* be another way."

I now know the point of all the death and suffering since that night three years ago. It's why Vitor and Soro were throwing everyone they could into the arena. They needed to feed the ever strengthening and growing Aurora.

I start to pace, choking back tears. The slate floor cools my battered feet, and while it offers some relief, the pain from my injuries keeps my mind focused.

By the stars, I will be queen. And I'll do it *my way*.

If it weren't for this pesky little life-and-death blood oath I have with that raging psychopath Soro, the crown I rightfully possess might be the shining light I need in all this darkness.

But the blood oath is there, and I must find a way out of it.

My feet sting, my head throbs, my throat aches, and every muscle and ligament in my body screams in vicious agony. Accelerated healing ability or not, I won't recover fully for many more days.

Furnishings of rich mahogany fill the room, including an oversize bed. While I don't find an axe in the wardrobe to murder Soro with, I do find plenty of overly accessorized silk dresses with matching hats, as well as—oh, goody—a wedding gown of white lace and stitched in diamonds I'm no doubt expected to wear at the blessed event. Next to it hangs a veil even longer than the one I was forced to wear to the arena to cover my face, which was still bloodstained and bruised.

If trees were middle fingers, I'd wave a forest at Soro.

Mercifully, I find a pair of men's breeches and a shirt. I peel out of the undergarments I'm wearing and change. My hand presses into the dressing table to keep my balance as I pull up the breeches. The table is stacked with sparkling jewelry—rubies, sapphires, and emeralds fastened to more flashy gold, silver, and diamond necklaces than anyone needs. And because my *precious* fiancé doesn't spoil me enough, look at this. A large bottle of belladom!

I loathe every bit of this space. This castle is nothing but a pretty prison.

Someone knocks on the door. It's a soft knock, so I don't immediately look for something sharp. "Come in," I say.

"Princess," stammers the servant. The door opens slowly, and a young human woman slips hesitantly through. Her skin is ebony, and her long hair is charcoal black.

"Ah, yes?" I say.

She walks slowly, shadowed by a young troll girl with short red hair. I saw her when I was dragged, or rather, "escorted" in.

"I am Lita. This be Brynne. We are here to serve you and have brought your supper," the young troll says. "Please eat. You mustn't displease Soro, our most distinguished and revered future king."

My mouth twists. "Is that what he told you to call him?"

Lita and Brynne exchange glances. "Yes?" Lita answers.

I curl my fingers into fists at my side. "Figures."

The young women watch me as I start to pace again. "Tell me, is anyone questioning what happened to the former lord regent?"

At Lita's nod, Brynne answers. "No."

"Why?" I ask, though I suspect the reason.

"Our beloved and most revered future king made a formal announcement that the former regent was a traitor. And that while he adored his father, Arrow will always come first."

Rage swells from deep within me and all but punctures through my skin. Of course Vitor will be painted as a traitor. This way, there will be no funeral and no period of mourning. I knew Soro resented Vitor. I just didn't realize how deep his hatred ran.

"Lord Ugeen and the generals produced evidence—"

"Sure they did," I grumble.

Brynne twists her hands in front of her. "Our future legendary and adored king also decreed that should anyone question him, they're questioning Arrow. And if they question Arrow, it will be considered treason, and they will be sentenced to death."

Just as I thought. *By the phoenix, Soro, you truly put the dick in dictator.*

Lita and Brynne bow and motion toward the meal they have delivered. I suppose they fear what will happen if they say too much. The food is served on a pewter tray. Lita lifts the lid and gracefully bows again.

My stomach is such a mess, I gag at the smell of broiled meat. She quickly covers it and offers me fresh rolls from an ornate wicker basket rimmed with wildflowers.

"He had you bring me bread," I say, gesturing to the basket.

They smile at having pleased me.

"Kindly tell our most revered and distinguished king to shove these rolls up his ass and not forget to butter."

They stop smiling.

Terror makes their round faces slack. They think I'll actually make them do it. I groan. "Hmm. I guess you're not up to poisoning him, either?"

Oh, and there's that terror again.

"Sorry. I'm joking." I'm not, but why upset them? Besides, if I intentionally kill Soro, directly *or* indirectly, I die with him. It's one of the many conditions he placed in our blood oath.

It's a last resort, and it's one I'll take if there's no other option.

But…there must be another option. My people need me as their queen.

"I'm not hungry," I say. "Please enjoy the meal yourselves."

They blink back at me, no doubt thinking I'm baiting them. They must be bound to the castle and know of me solely through court gossip. I can only imagine what the likes of Aisling have told them about me. Aisling—oh, yes, she's at the top of my kill list as well.

I ease toward the women, hating how they cower.

"I'm not going to hurt you," I promise. My words are cut short when I note exactly how thin they are. "Please. Eat."

"We can't," Brynne says. "It's not allowed."

"I'm allowing it," I say. "I'm also requesting extra portions so that everyone stuck serving these dipshits can eat." I don't mean to raise my voice and scare them, yet it's what I end up doing. "I'm sorry," I add quickly. "It's an…order?"

Lita looks hopefully at Brynne. "If it's an order, then we must obey."

"Yes," I say. "Yes, please obey."

They bow, leaving me standing here wishing I could do more.

As the doors close, my ears twitch at a chittering sound.

But when I turn, the sound stops. I make my way slowly back to the side of the bed, sinking to my knees. Tibeta, one of the tiniest estrellas, pokes her head around the leg of the bed. She's alive!

I sweep her up in my hands, covering her tiny, furry face with my kisses.

"Tibeta," I say. "My sweet little munchkin. My baby. I'm so happy to see you."

She presses her face against my nose, clutching me to her, tears running down her whiskers as she weeps.

Poor thing. She must have stowed away in the wagon and hidden until she could find me.

The outermost door to the apartment opens, and I hear the rumble of Soro's voice, along with Tut the ogre's.

Tibeta leaps onto my shoulder as I push a dresser against the double doors to my chamber. I open my palm, and once she's hopped onto it, I head to the one window in the apartment.

There's nothing but jagged rocks below it. I make a hooting sound, hoping she'll mimic me. Tibeta cocks her head and repeats the noise. Good. This is good. Estrellas have symbiotic relationships with avian creatures, and the nearest bird should answer her call.

I look around and focus on the large bottle of belladom. "Tibeta, nightshade," I say. When she lifts her large ears, I think she might understand me. "Nightshade," I say again, hoping she comprehends enough to return with it.

She chitters in panic, then quiets. She knows I'm sending her away, and I'm worried she's too scared to leave me.

A large black owl swoops in, landing on the sill. She looks at Tibeta once, then at me, as if curious why an estrella would summon her.

There's curt pounding at the bedroom door. I'm out of time. "Nightshade," I say one last time. I lift her and place her on the owl's back, where she happily begins rooting through its neck feathers for mites to snack on. "Be careful," I whisper.

And they're gone.

Soro tries to open the doors, meeting resistance from the dresser placed in front of it. He shoves it hard, forcing his way in.

He greets me with a scowl. "Did you seriously think you could keep me out?"

"No," I say. "I just seriously think you're an asshole."

He starts toward me, but it's the man behind him who holds my attention—Tut, with his long axe draped over his shoulder. I used to respect him. Now, I only see him as I do Ugeen. An opportunist who sold his soul to Soro.

His tusks are so long, they've begun to curl at the tips. And in the time since he shoved that stupid bag over my head and dragged me here, he's had time to file them to very sharp points.

"Tut will be your bodyguard," Soro says, not bothering to so much as smile.

"Bodyguard or prison guard?" I ask, glaring at both of them.

Soro ignores my question. "Call him what you wish. He'll see to it that you remain where I tell you to be." He places a proprietary hand on Tut's shoulder. Soro looks ridiculous, given how much taller and muscular Tut is.

I cross my arms. "Tut is here to enforce your orders?"

"Yes," Soro agrees like it's obvious.

I inch forward. "Then order him to kill me. I will obey you."

Soro is too damn fast.

He hits me so hard, my head slams into the floor with a thud. I fight to not lose consciousness, and with great effort, I pry my eyes open.

"You know I can't order him to kill you without losing my own life, Maeve. I'll find a way to get rid of you, rest assured, but first I need an heir to keep the throne." He shakes his head in disgust. "You could have made this easier. We could have worked as one." He huffs. "You never should have denied me."

My hands press into the cool stone as I push up, then stand. "I deny you now, like I denied you then. Not because of Leith but because of who you are." I circle him, spitting out my words and wiping away the blood pooling at the corner of my mouth. "You think yourself so grand, so deserving, but you'll always be second-best, and no crown or throne will ever change that."

I don't fall when Soro strikes me this time. Mostly because there's a stone wall nearby that I lean into for balance. I lock my knees to keep from sliding to the floor and wipe my mouth on the back of my hand.

"Do I get to die after the first heir?" I ask him, pushing away from the wall. "How many children would you like? Ten, twenty? Girls or boys?" I'm being sarcastic, of course. Elves as a species, like mages and shifters, have trouble conceiving. My guess is that it's a trade-off for a long lifespan.

I fluff my hair as if Soro's blows were nothing.

He studies me for a moment, eyes scanning me from head to toe, then approaches slowly, stopping to bend and whisper in my ear. "You know what?" Lust wets his words, making me sick. "Blood and bruises aside, you are exceptionally beautiful. If it weren't for your tongue and your bite, you could be more than a bitch to use as I please." He loses his small smile. "Clean yourself up. I won't be embarrassed by my future wife."

He leaves me with Tut, but not before slamming the door behind him.

Tut edges forward, and I back up, looking for something to use as a weapon

His thick eyebrows rise to his fuzzy hairline when I reach for the oil lamp.

"Touch me, and I'll set you on fire," I warn, holding the lamp out between us like a weapon. "I don't care if I burn along with you."

He pauses. I can't gauge if he'll attack or if I should attack him first. I steel myself, waiting for anything, prepared for everything.

Or so I thought.

Tut shakes his large, heavy head and walks to the window, the taut muscles on his leathery legs bulging as he sits on the wide sill and places the double-headed war axe down beside him. He's in his usual blue armor. The green leather belts across his broad chest stretch as he lifts his arm to fiddle with the end of the axe handle.

"It wasn't supposed to be like this," he says slowly.

"Which part? Killing my family? Torturing Leith of Grey? Or murdering Vitor?"

Tut used to nod at me respectfully. As a child, he'd greet me with a smile. But he's not smiling now. Tut is a few centuries old—still fairly young for an ogre. Too young for those wrinkles around the small eyes on his gristly face. "Vitor needed to die, Princess. Soro does, too, but for the time being…that's a harder sell."

CHAPTER
52

MAEVE

"You're a fucking liar," I tell Tut. "And a traitor, too."

Tut scowls, causing his tusks to rise.

I tilt my head. "Did I insult you?"

"Ya," Tut replies like it's obvious.

"Good," I say.

He lowers his head again, his skin bunching along his throat. When he finally lifts it, I can tell he has something to say. I'm just not sure I'm willing to listen. I already have a plan in mind—smash the oil lamp against his chest and watch him burn, just as he watched Vitor.

"I've been a servant of the court for a long time," he says. "Long before your father was born. I was there to watch him take his first steps. I watched him grow, Princess. I cared for him."

My mouth parts as my anger escalates to fury. As the general in charge of surveillance, Tut is tasked with executing "justice" at the ruler's will. I watched him escort my papa to the dungeons that day. I saw him— Vitor's freshly anointed right hand—lock my father up for a crime he did not commit. I was willing to believe he was just following orders, but *this*? To pretend he gave a damn about my papa while he did it...

He flexes his huge fist. He could kill me with just a squeeze. We can't go hand to hand…but we could go with my foot kicking him through the open window. I hadn't thought of that, actually. I could give the crows a bit of meat to munch on come morning.

"I did not want to hurt the good prince," he rumbles. "Andres…your papa… He was an honorable man."

"Don't," I say, rage simmering through my every word. "Don't you dare talk about him like he's not around. Like he's not suffering as we speak. Like he's not *fucking dying* in the cell you forced him into!"

Ogres don't cry, at least not in front of those outside their family, but tears glisten in his eyes for a moment before he blinks. "I believed he would not have hurt the queen. I even tried to speak on his behalf. Vitor would not hear me. It is only now that I see why."

"I suppose that makes you a hero," I taunt. "But it doesn't. In fact, it makes you worse. You were willing to let a man you believed *innocent* waste away to keep your own precious seat in power."

Tut takes a shaky breath, and I hope my words fucking hurt. "Believe me or not, Princess, I am here to tell you that he is safe." If untrue, I don't think a strike from his meaty fist could hurt me more.

I don't want to believe him. The love I have for my family is only a commodity to be used against me. "You're a liar."

Back and forth, side to side, Tut rakes his claws along the leather straps across his chest. "I'm not lying," he says, "Your papa is free."

Hope flickers in me like the wavering flame in the lamp, but I can't blindly trust his word, no matter how much I want to.

When I do not respond, he simply regards me and continues speaking. "I needed my position. I chose to bite my tongue to keep it. And because of that, I was able to get him out."

If I could lift the bed, I would throw it at him—for knowing that I can't trust his word and still giving me hope, which I absolutely can't handle being stolen away. "Where is he?" I manage, unable to settle my trembling voice.

He pauses for a moment as if deciding whether or not to tell me. If true, this information can be used as a weapon against me and any of my family who remains, so I'm surprised when he finally says, "Safe. With your friend Stasia."

"Stasia?" I almost stumble against the nightstand, hope rising.

"You helped her child, so she wants to help you. She doesn't know who he is. She thinks he's just a very sick man you're treating." He holds up a beefy hand and swears, "On the honor of my people, he'll be safe there until you choose to move him." It's a serious oath for an ogre and one not taken lightly. He would not lie on the honor of his people.

I blink back tears. My sweet papa is safe and free, but this is not the time to rejoice. There are still too many obstacles in my way—too many enemies, perhaps including this ogre who clearly wants something from me. I straighten my shoulders and lift my chin in challenge. "Regardless of any noble intent, you're helping an evil man."

"That was never my intent," Tut snarls, his tusks appearing to grow right in front of me.

I scoff. "And yet here we are."

Tut growls and snaps his fangs. I barely blink, my temper getting the best of me. "I fought an ogre earlier today. You probably heard, since you were a part of this whole, you know, obliteration-of-my-family debacle. It didn't end well for either of us, but I'm willing to have another go."

His top lip curls back from his gums. "I told you I freed Andres, and at great personal risk. Do you hear me? He is safe, and safe he shall remain, as he deserves."

"Why?" I ask, certain he is using my papa's life to barter for something.

He stills when bitter tears cloud my vision.

"I asked you why," I bite out once more.

"It was the right thing to do," he says. "He was innocent all along, and Vitor finally admitted it." The nails of his huge hand dig into the stone windowsill. "I would never hurt Andres. And as his child, Princess, I will not hurt you. It was not supposed to end this way."

My fingers tighten around the handle on top of the oil lamp. I know in my bones that there is more to his motivation than sheer goodwill. "Then tell me. How was it supposed to go?"

Tendrils of steam swirl from his nose as he eyes me closely. His emotions must be running especially high. "We were supposed to take out Vitor, and we did."

"You, Pua, Soro, and Ugeen?" I guess.

"Do not group me with them as an ally." He shakes his head, his frustration making it harder for him to form words. He slows his speech, enunciating each syllable carefully. "They are the means to an end. I, among others, have spent years infiltrating this establishment." His deep wrinkles expand across his leathery face, aging him further. "Some were caught early on." He pauses. "You can guess what happened to them."

"The arena," I offer. "Yes, a fabulous way to assure Aurora grows big and strong."

Tut shakes his head, and his shoulders slump as if he's exhausted. "None of this is her fault. She's a tool used by bad people to do inexcusable things."

I can't believe he'd defend that monstrous creature, but his words and expression seem sincere. "That's one way to look at matters." I ease away to sit on the bed, balancing the lamp on my knee just in case his mood, or my own, grows hostile.

"Your grandmother suspected traitors," he says. "And she was right to. So instead of revealing Aurora to us, she fed her in secret." He pulls down his cuirass when his plump belly pushes through. "We've spent decades trying to get close to the queen and Vitor. It took the queen dying for Vitor to seek a new ally. Yet as much as I did to earn his trust, he never trusted me enough to reveal where the phoenix was held."

"But now you know."

"Now I know."

The oil lamp balanced on my knee flickers, causing Tut's shadow to dance along the wall, highlighting how imposing Tut is compared to me. His shadow is three of mine across, and those three shadows could hold another three of me over their heads. But I'm not afraid. Not of him. I won't give him that power over me.

"So that I'm clear, you spent years waiting to meet Aurora so you could capture her to use as a weapon against Arrow?" I ask. "Was that your ultimate goal?" It's no wonder grandmother and Vitor were so damn paranoid.

"No," he grunts. "Not to capture as a weapon."

"What, then?"

Tut hangs his head low, clearly fighting for composure as he takes several deep breaths. When he looks up, he appears even more weathered. "Princess Maeve, please hear me. I need your help. We *must* work together."

"Work together why?" I ask. This isn't just about my Papa, and Tut proves me right.

He stretches out his arms, all but pleading. "My plight is much bigger than you or me or Arrow. Old Erth is dying, and she's taking us with her. Our only hope of salvation is to set the phoenix free."

CHAPTER

53

MAEVE

I stare at Tut, waiting for the punch line to this terrible joke, but he only stares back at me.

Free the phoenix? The same monster who swallows people whole and spits out their bones? No way will that ever happen. I push to my feet, ready to hurl my lamp and light this ogre aflame.

He points at himself, voice calm despite my clear hostility. "I'm the head of surveillance. I am sent to survey the outskirts of Arrow, where Erth-wide disasters have begun to encroach on Arrow's borders. I've seen the destruction with my own eyes." He blows out more steam. "Aurora was never your grandmother's to capture. She must be freed. Only then will Old Erth regain its peace."

He's serious. "Regain its peace or be massacred, Tut?"

As if he wasn't expecting this reaction, he does a double-take—an odd motion, considering ogres barely have a neck.

"The great phoenix was meant to roam the skies—"

"She's a harbinger of death!" I all but strangle him with my words.

"She's not," Tut insists. "That's only what she was purported to be. Untruths that your grandmother and Vitor spread and exploited for their own gain."

I narrow my eyes at him. "Tut, that makes absolutely no sense. You've *seen* her. She's a monster!"

"Ya. It does. Aurora balances nature. She keeps the winter in mountains where it belongs and drought in the desert where it should remain." He blows out more steam, but it's pathetic at best, mimicking his defeated state. "Your grandmother stole her from the skies to use as a weapon and to keep Arrow in power."

I set the lamp on the nightstand, still within reach, and sit again. "My grandmother didn't just take her from the sky. She killed her because Aurora was killing our people. There was no weapon to be had." As soon as the words are out of my mouth, I know I'm wrong. Tut, though, spells it out for me.

"Avianna killed her so she could rebirth the phoenix into something that she could control. She wanted Arrow to be great, and thus stole Aurora's greatness to make it so."

"You act as if Arrow is only what it is because of Aurora." I spread my arms wide as I motion with my hands. "Look around at all we've rebuilt that was once squalor. We did that, Tut. My grandmother and Papa did that. This has nothing to do with the phoenix."

Tut stands. I do, too, both of us squaring off. "You built those homes with wood from trees that grow tall and strong in the areas surrounding Arrow. You fed those workers *and* yourself with the bountiful harvests Arrow produces. You feasted on game that's hearty and plentiful from thriving off a land rich with nutrients while those around Arrow, those without the phoenix, starve and suffer and die."

I lower my hands. Okay. He has my attention now.

"You eat the best, you have the best, and you are the best. You know this to be true, Princess." Tut starts to pace. For someone tasked with subterfuge, he makes a lot of noise.

Slap, scratch.

Slap, scratch.

Slap, scratch.

Ogres' feet are so tough they don't need shoes. But this one damn well needs his toenails clipped.

"You hear the stories the immigrants share, Princess—about floods that ruin their crops, about freak ice storms in summer that freeze mothers holding their babies as they rush to shelter. Princess, you've cared for those who arrived sick with unheard-of infections that plague the young and strong."

Tut is right. I don't want him to be, but he is.

"Immigrants rush to this kingdom, wanting what they can't have in theirs because Aurora doesn't soar over their land to give it to them." He blows out more steam, this time in the shape of a circle that might as well be a broken heart. "My realm is dying, Princess. My people are so sick from decades of malnourishment, we haven't seen an ogren Liburi child born in more than seventy years."

I approach him slowly, and Tut eyes me warily. He should. But I don't mean him harm, at least for the moment. "If Aurora is set free, all the realms will benefit just as Arrow has?" He nods. "And if she is kept trapped, the rest of Old Erth will continue to suffer?"

Tut nods again, his lack of a neck causing him to tilt his entire upper half. "The great phoenix only exists to balance nature. It's the sole reason Nature created her."

I know the story of the phoenix. I learned it as a child and saw it play out within the stained glass windowpanes in Vitor's office.

Damn it. *Vitor*.

Still, there must be more to this. I find it hard to believe this ogre and others risked certain death to infiltrate Arrow royalty so they could release the phoenix on the unproven theory she will heal the world. It's more likely he wishes to take it for his own kingdom or sell it to the highest bidder. "What do you want from me, Tut?"

"I want you to help me release her."

I want to believe his theory. I do, but the risk is too great. "No."

"Princess," he snaps, affronted. "It's the right thing to do. Not just for your people but for all the world."

"What if you're wrong?" I ask, my voice harsh and louder than intended. So many people have died because of this creature. In the wrong hands...

He flaps his meaty hands downward, trying to silence me. "Hush. We mustn't be heard."

I pull my knotted hair forward and attempt to braid, trying to settle and not appear like a woman who's lost her damn mind. Even if she has.

"What's wrong, Tut? Are you worried you'll be discovered and, I don't know, fed to the phoenix?" I drop the strands of my hair.

He grinds his fangs, less than pleased by my reaction. "You don't understand," he growls.

I saunter closer. "Don't I? Aurora needs blood, needs *people* to survive. Say you do free her. If—*if*—I don't alert Soro to your plan, what's to stop her from eating every last person she can get her beak on?"

Tut's shoulders stiffen. "Aurora only eats dead things," he says as if I'm the one missing the point.

"What?"

Steam funnels from his nose. *Poof. Poof. Poof.* If he's laughing at me, I'm going to ram one of his tusks up his nose. "Soro killed Vitor, and Aurora feasted. Gladiators die in the arena, and Aurora nurses from their blood and bones."

"Do you really think this is motivating me to help you?"

There goes Tut, looking all offended again. Well, too damn bad.

"Aurora was never a threat, Princess," he says. "When she appeared at all those battles, it was only to feast on the dead. She's part of the ecosystem. But she was painted as a monster by the monsters who desired to keep her."

"How did she rise?" I take a moment to compose myself when his mouth shuts tight. I must demonstrate patience, even though I severely lack it. "General Tut, I know you don't want to tell me. But considering I haven't sung like a canary to Soro, the least you can do is tell me how."

"Two soldiers—Bloodguards, actually—bled upon her nest," he says. "Back before there was a coliseum, when it was just empty ground used for training and tournaments."

Horror replaces my anger, making my stomach turn.

"When Aurora was killed, Avianna and Vitor waited *for years* for her to be reborn from the ashes," Tut says. "But she didn't rise. They carved catacombs into the porous stone beneath your castle so no one could find her and left her ashes on an altar. When those men died, fighting each other for glory and coin, their blood soaked the sand where the arena now stands. Vitor—I think it was him—felt the ground quake. When he went down to the catacombs, he discovered a hatchling had stirred to life and was reaching up to catch the dripping blood of the fallen warriors."

I rub my face, wanting to scream at how truly sick and twisted this entire tale has been.

"Aurora was gentle," Tut says, eyeing me like I'm close to the brink of insanity. He's not wrong. "She let the queen and Vitor hold her. The queen sliced her own arm to nurse her, but Aurora wouldn't take her blood. They tried animals, with no luck. It wasn't until they offered her the corpse of a soldier that they figured out that Aurora only fed on the dead…"

"And that's when their murdering spree began?"

He sighs. "Yes. Servants first, because they were readily accessible and already within the castle… But her true purpose is out there." He inclines his arm toward the window. "It's why she soared around the realms. Eating dead things left behind — "

"And thus, creating new life with her spirit," I finish for him. "Balance." I curl into my stomach. "They didn't build the arena around the dead Bloodguards to honor them," I say. "They did it to feed Aurora."

"Ya," Tut says. "The bigger she got, the more she had to eat. And they killed and bled and fed her so that every ounce of magic she could muster would be trapped beneath that cursed arena. So Arrow would grow strong."

I understand all of it.

The games, the gladiators, the "criminals."

Every brutal action taken to ensure Arrow's dominance among the realms.

And look what it has done to the world. If freeing her will balance out the Erth so every realm can thrive, can I really fault Tut for his actions? Like Vitor said, a small sacrifice for the greater good. But what… what if Tut has no plans to free her at all and this is only a cover for something more sinister? Could I live with myself if I was fooled into Arrow's demise?

"I…I can't free Aurora," I say.

"I don't need you beside me, Your Highness. My people and I just need a distraction. Something that will occupy Soro and his cohorts long enough for us to get to Aurora and set her free."

His small black eyes blink back at me hopefully.

"I'm listening," I say, not because I'm going to help him but because

I need to figure out what is really going on here.

"All you have to do is keep Soro busy," he says, licking his fangs. "The only way to Aurora is through the dungeons. Keep Soro with you, distract him and anyone else close to him, *please*."

Something isn't adding up. I clutch my hands to keep them from shaking. This is the moment I've dreaded since Tut swore on the honor of his people and I knew he was telling me the truth about Papa. "What will happen to Papa if I say no?" I ask. Save one life for thousands? Grandmother and Vitor did all the wrong things, yet here I wait, tasked with the same choices.

Tut dips his head, and I steel myself for what is coming. Free the phoenix or lose my papa.

"A smart man would use him as leverage," he says. Slowly, he raises his head. "But Soro took everything from you, and Andres remains that little boy I saw grow into a good man. I've made terrible choices, Princess. But I won't be so terrible to you."

I don't fully trust him, even as I fear something worse will happen if I don't. "I'll think about it," I say.

He stands and bows. "That's all I ask," he says.

It's a hell of a thing to ask.

"You don't trust me, do you, Your Highness?"

I shake my head.

"Then let me prove it. I can kill Soro," he offers. "Break his neck in his sleep and stuff his skull with candy for you."

"As, um, sweet as that is, it won't work," I say. "You were there, Tut. I can't play any intentional role in his death, direct or indirect. It's one of the many provisions of our bond. And you killing him to prove your loyalty to me? Well, I'm not willing to bet my life on it."

"Then tell me what I can give to earn your trust," he says. "Whatever you want, you shall have it."

I glance past him and through the open window. I may not trust this man or his motives, but that doesn't mean an alliance with him couldn't be useful. "There is one thing…"

CHAPTER
54
LEITH

The following evening, I ride Star back to the manor alongside Caelen and Giselle. Pega wanted to join us, but the guards ordered her back to the barracks, where we're no longer permitted.

We cross the front lawn, my heartbeat pounding in dull, angry thuds when I catch my first sight of the manor's charred remains. Wretched anger bordering on rage awakens within me. I haven't slept, too focused on what could be happening to Maeve. Seeing what remains of her home doesn't damn well help.

Death came for Jakeb and almost every member of his family.

Maeve, though—that's a different story. She's going to live. I don't know how, but until my last breath I will fight for her freedom. This, I swear.

Jakeb's final resting place is the first we reach. He and Neela disappeared, as some ancient beings do. The impression of their bodies is pressed deep into the soil, including every wrinkle of Jakeb's long, elegant robe and the outline of Neela's small body tucked tightly against his side.

So help me, if any peace exists in the Afterlife, I pray these friends found it together. Their grave... It's quite a spectacle. Something I've never seen before and something I never want to see again.

I bow my head in gratitude. He gave me food, shelter, clothes, and kindness. It's through him that I connected with Maeve.

How do you thank someone like him? I suppose you can't, especially now.

Giselle, already weeping after finding her beloved father and governess, covers her mouth when she finds the first of the estrellas.

"Bethina," she breathes. I know this one. She was so small, harmless. She even liked me. These guards are nothing but cowards.

Giselle holds her in her palm as Caelen digs a small grave, his motions stiff and harsh. Then she carefully places her down, crossing her tiny hands over her heart.

"I was always too afraid to touch them," she says. "It's why they preferred everyone else to me." She sniffs. "That doesn't mean I didn't love them."

"I should have been here," is all I manage.

Giselle smooths soil over Bethina's grave. "We all should have."

Caelen is shaking hard with rage. I've never seen him quite so emotional. He looks at Giselle, then across the scorched lawn. "This shouldn't have happened," he says.

As twilight makes its first appearance, we take a moment to grieve.

"The numbers they sent were damn near an invading army," Caelen says. He motions to the multitude of bloody spots. "They never stood a chance."

Giselle can't seem to move. Caelen places an arm around her shoulders, but she flinches out of his reach.

"Come on," he sighs. "There are more graves to dig and more dead to mourn."

We don't find all the Iamonds' estrellas—hopefully that means some escaped—and almost miss Toso entirely. I kneel in front of him, remembering how he adored Maeve and how I couldn't blame him.

My shoulders hurt, the weight upon them unbearable. I place my hand over his soft, furry head. "Goodbye, my friend."

It's then that "my friend" stirs and tries to bite my finger off.

I leap backward. Caelen jolts. Giselle curses. Toso continues to move his head, hissing and snapping his small fangs.

"Toso," I say. "It's me, Leith."

He stops snapping, and his ears perk up. But then his head tips and falls back to the ground, his strength waning.

"I'm going to touch you," I tell him.

His head pops up, and he hisses, showing his fangs.

"Do *not* bite me," I warn.

Toso makes a pathetic sound. He's so close to death. I take my chances and stroke between his ears. He whimpers, his wide, blank eyes blinking several times.

There's no hint of the trademark yellow irises of a healthy estrella. His blinking increases. He's crying but too dehydrated to form tears.

"Do you think he's blind?" I ask.

"Partially but not yet completely," Caelen says. "If we restore his strength and tend to his wounds, maybe his vision will clear." If he lives, that is.

I change positions and lift him toward me. Stab marks cover his chest. Toso wasn't beaten. He was brutalized.

"Those damn monsters," I growl. "Look at what they did to him."

Caelen whips around. "Did you hear that?"

"What?" Giselle asks. He closes his eyes, his ears twitch, and he drops down, his hands clutching his knees as he breathes deep. Then he sighs as something in the brush catches his attention. "Leith, you better show the estrellas. They're worried sick for him."

I carry Toso to the edge of the lawn and hop down to the brush near the start of the path to the now obliterated stables.

Little feet bounce away like a herd of frantic newborn lemurs. "Don't go, little ones. It's Leith," I say. "Maeve's Leith."

The steps halt. I kneel and hold Toso out. "We're going to help him," I say. "And we've come to help you, too."

One by one, sets of glowing yellow eyes press through the darkness.

"That's right," I say. "I'll watch over you until Maeve returns."

It's Maeve's name that allows me to gain their trust, and probably my scent, too—that of her healing herbs. One of the smallest in the group, not much bigger than Bethina, ventures out first, a prominent limp slowing her pace. Her sad, frightened eyes remind me of Gunther. I wish they didn't. I'm no longer certain I can help him.

The little one inches closer. She holds up her tiny hands and presents a giant bejeweled ring.

Giselle gasps. "That belonged to the queen," she says. "It was her wedding ring. She gave it to Papa after the king died."

More estrellas follow the first, their hands carrying gold and jewels. Like many magical creatures, they're known to pilfer shiny things, which in this case is extremely useful.

They surround me now, some hopping onto my shoulders as though they can't wait to see the view from their new home. Even if that home is atop a dangerous gladiator like me.

Giselle gasps. "Caelen, look," she tells him.

We both turn to see where she's pointing. The little ones managed to save a pile of jewels and riches under the cover of the bushes.

Caelen nods, appearing relieved. We need gold and jewels with everything else destroyed. "It's plenty to hold us for a time."

A chuff comes from off to the left. *Knight.* My eyes widen. It's Maeve's horse and Hilltop, Jakeb's steed. They're both still saddled, their heads drooped as if injured and hungry. With only grass to eat, these massive horses are likely starving.

"Star!" I call.

My mare is their daughter. With a series of snorts, she races from the front lawn, bypassing me when she catches sight of her family.

If horses can cry, that's what Star and Hilltop do through their whinnies and bodily strokes.

I carefully hand Toso to Caelen. "Take Toso and the estrellas back to the city. Star can carry them. Leave Hilltop and Knight. Both need to eat before they go any farther."

Giselle claps as loudly as she can with those thick gloves. "All right. You heard him, little ones. You need to come with us."

"We'll place Toso and the other injured in the tub," Caelen says. "Giselle left it filled with healing herbs." The medicine that remains should help the estrellas. Star allows them on her back, on her head, and even permits them to cling to her tail and mane.

Hilltop stands before Knight, attempting to protect him from me. It takes me saying, "Maeve sent me," for her to hop aside. I edge closer and reach out to stroke Knight's head. I barely smooth the first few hairs between his eyes before it occurs to me why Hilltop is so worked up. A contusion the size of my fist protrudes from the side of his head. I've never heard of anyone knocking out a moon horse. Somehow these fuckers did, and poor Knight must have the mother of all headaches.

"It's okay, old boy," I say. "Maeve sent me here to take care of you." It's not explicitly true, but she would have if she could.

Knight flicks his ears. Maeve's name has power over everything and everyone, including me. Even in her absence, the love behind her name holds strong. And fuck me if Old Erth doesn't need more of that.

Slowly, I lead the horses past where the cottage used to stand, my heart feeling as scorched as the land. With Knight's injuries, it takes some time to reach the falls. I listen for any indication we're not alone as the horses follow me down the path and past the adoni wisteria, stopping before the small waves can wet their hooves. I remove their saddles, keeping only their bridles and reins to guide them.

In the moonlight, I get a clear view of what they endured. Soro's soldiers spared neither people nor animals. To them, it's hunting season all year round.

Hilltop bears gashes and scratches in need of attention, and Knight has been burned all along his hide. If the hair in those spots grows back, it will likely never have the same luxurious sheen.

Moonlight streams across the small waves batting at the shore where the horses wait. The smell of the minerals mixed in with the water bothers them. They snort and paw the ground, clearly uneasy. They may not be keen on drinking it, but giving them a drink isn't why I brought them here. I may not be able to fit them in a tub of Maeve's healing herbs, but I can do this.

I remove the boomerang blade from my belt and toss it up into the trees. It easily slices through the curtain of branches hanging above us, causing leafy limbs with large bundles of berry nuts to fall to the ground. Hilltop and Knight devour everything I offer. I forage through the perimeter of the trees, using everything Maeve taught me, and return with a stack of edible wildflowers. Knight munches steadily on the greens and Hilltop finishes off the nuts while I fill my empty flask with water from the falls.

Hilltop jerks as I pour water over her injuries, hitting me with what could only be described as a horse's dirty look. But her brown eyes soften as her pain eases.

"You want more?" I ask. Her chuffing is enough of a response. "Then get in the water, old girl."

She doesn't move, choosing to eye me while Knight chews on the last of the flowers. Again, I collect more water. She lifts her nose away from the scent, the mineral-heavy aroma making her suspicious. Yet the sense of relief she feels when I pour more from my flask is all the incentive she needs to step in.

She wades into the lake, creating ripples as she wanders deeper in to thoroughly soak her injuries. Knight lifts his head to watch Hilltop.

Trust is important. Tonight, it's everything.

As he chews on the last bits of wildflower, he eases his way into the water, pausing when he's about chest deep to flap his gums with relief. Yes, that's it. The cool and medicinal water soothes all those scrapes and superficial burns. It's the perfect cure for all those sore muscles. He has ways to go before that lump on his skull clears up, but he should be good enough to return to the city soon. Back in New Arrow, I'll get him everything he needs.

The water's reprieve tempts him deeper.

It doesn't take long for them to relish the waves. If anything, they can't get enough of the lake.

I stand with my arms crossed, alert to anything that may harm them. Regardless of my vigilance, they spot something I don't initially see.

A new wave of energy hits them, powering them across to the opposite side of the lake. And damn if I didn't realize moon horses could swim.

I don't really see the woman in gray. She's one with the moon, melding into her surroundings, her veil of silken mahogany hair blending into the darkness.

She wraps her arms around Knight's neck and turns in my direction as he stumbles to shore.

Maeve is here...*with me.*

CHAPTER
55
LEITH

Time stops, as does my heartbeat.

Maeve looks up from stroking Knight, and her gaze meets mine.

She may start running first. I don't know. I only feel the ground beneath me rip apart as I race around the lake toward her.

It's not a gentle reunion. We collide in desperation, kissing, touching, and afraid to let go.

Her hands sink into my hair, mine into hers, feeling the soft strands as the wind whips them around me.

Her familiar warmth takes me home. Every doubt, every fear, every bit of anger and rage melt away. There's only her touch, her taste, the feel of her skin.

"What are you doing here?" I ask.

Her hold on me tightens, her fathomless blue eyes filled with pain. "I came to honor my family."

I stroke away her tears with my thumbs and cover her mouth with mine.

We kiss for what could be seconds or hours, but time has no meaning. Maeve commands my everything.

"I thought I lost you." I breathe her in.

"Never," she whispers. "Not until the sun casts its last ray and the moon bids the sky farewell."

It seems the world has done everything in its power to tear us apart, but we refuse to let go. I kiss my way from her lips down her throat, pulling the neckline of her dress to lick and suck her breasts until I hear seams tear, granting me access to even more of her.

I lose myself in her taste, her scent, in the breathy little way she says my name over and over again.

She's real and alive and in my arms. Her skin is warm beneath my hands. I never thought I'd have the chance to touch her again.

"Leith, I..."

I know.

I think I've always known. With Maeve, there is a depth of emotion—of connection—that I feel down to my bones. I kiss her like these might be our last moments on Erth, and she echoes the motions, her mouth and body following mine like she's afraid to let go.

Desire, ache, and endless need take control.

The way her eager hands tear at my pants and stroke over the length of me makes me want to explode.

Her eyes widen to meet mine as she falls to her knees and takes me deep into her mouth. I curse, then curse some more, moving in and out as her nails dig into my hips, encouraging my rhythm and accelerating speed.

I tear my shirt off and toss it aside. As I fall back into a sitting position, she hefts her skirt and climbs my body.

Then there's bliss.

She sinks down on me, and we're one. It's only the two of us in this world and the pleasure we create. There is a second to savor the connection, and then our bodies are moving. Gripping, thrusting, barreling toward release.

It's hot and fast and hard. Mindless. An escape from the pain, because we've both lost...*everything*.

No. No, I won't let the pain intrude. Not in this moment.

She is alive and in my arms.

She moans against my mouth, her hips jerking as tiny tremors ripple through her body. I treasure every pulse, my own body flushing and growing harder still, the forerunners of ecstasy stirring at the base of my spine.

I fuck her through it, her cries of pleasure echoing across the lake.

When she comes, I follow her over the edge, cursing and claiming her as mine before we fall to our sides, living, feeling, breathing as one.

Tented by a willow, its thin branches laden with pink and white flowers, we make our bed entwined in each other's arms, resting softly upon her cape.

It's a while before our breathing slows. And even longer before we stop kissing. When we do, the lust that warmed her features has cooled, replaced by a sadness that makes my chest ache.

"I'm sorry I kept your family's passing from you," she says, running her fingers gently across the tattoo on my forearm that now includes a recently inked rose. "I never wanted you to discover what happened the way that you did. I planned to tell you after you won Bloodguard, once I knew you were safe and their death would not kill you in that wicked arena. But I was wrong, and I'm so sorry for that."

I pull her closer. Her eyes scrunch shut, and several tears slide along her bruised nose.

She tells me about the aviary and the shifter she cut to pieces. Ordering the place to be burned down? That's something I would do— except instead of an order, I would have lit the match and personally added more wood.

Across the lake, a moonlight dove sings her mournful tune. Another joins, and their brethren throughout the forest follow their lead. Tucked away beneath the canopy of sweet, fragrant flowers, the world feels perfect. Spread those branches, step out, and we'd quickly discover that it's not. There's so much wrong. And aside from the murder spree I'm planning to unleash, there aren't many ways to make it right.

"You *were* wrong for not telling me," I say. "I should have known. Their loss would have fueled my drive and made me stronger."

She stiffens in my hold. "Leith, I'm sorry—"

The slow shake of my head might as well be a soak in the cold lake with how much Maeve pales. I lift her chin with my thumb and kiss her. "That's what I *want* to believe, at least, Maeve," I say quietly against her mouth. "But I can't be sure. Not when I see this place—*feel* what it has done to me." I trail my gaze in the direction of where the manor once stood as tall and proud as the family who lived there. "You, like me, lost everything, and now we're here, damaged spirits that may never be whole."

Each tear that Maeve spills is a knife wound to my soul. "You'll find someone to fill that void," she says. "Someday."

I gently cup her face, growling my words. "You're the only one who can do that. Do you hear me?" Her breath hitches, and I continue. "I love you. I always have. There will *never* be another."

She sits up and hugs her knees, her voice cracking with each syllable. "I'm not worthy of love." She takes a shuddering breath. "I'm the one who killed my grandmother."

I push to a sitting position. "That's not true. You could never."

"And yet I did." She sniffs, the breeze fluttering over the lake blowing auburn strands across her face. "I used to think I was a good person. Not perfect, by any means, but kind and determined to heal, not harm. But I've hurt so many, and I continue to fail those who suffer."

I don't believe her. I can't. My jaw clamps, and I shake my head. "Maeve…"

"I caused Grandmother's death," she says, "and my papa's emotional collapse."

I put my arm around her and pull her close.

Maeve's shoulders rise and fall several times before she begins. "I didn't stop Grandmother from killing innocents, Leith. I didn't get Vitor to end the games. I didn't protect Papa, who lost his mind protecting *me*." She pauses and takes several breaths. "And despite being someone whose sole purpose is to be queen and protect all citizens of Arrow, I can't stop Soro from feeding Aurora my people's blood."

"Maeve…who is Aurora?"

And then she tells me the sordid tale of the phoenix.

Fuck the aviary.

I'm ready to burn the Erth down.

Sullivan, and everyone before and after him, died and bled for a fucking bird—a creature who never should have been caught in the first place? What kind of hell did we wake up in?

I stand abruptly and yank on my pants. Maeve slips back into her gown, her movements rote and gaze haunted. They broke her.

Those motherfuckers broke the most beautiful person I know.

"We're getting out of here. We'll regroup with Giselle and Caelen, find your papa, and get the hell out."

Maeve's head jerks up, confusion creating two delicate lines between her eyebrows. "I can't."

"Like hell."

She jerks her head to the side. I think she hears something. As she reaches for my hands and glances briefly behind her, I know we're no longer alone. But Maeve simply clutches my hands and brings them to her chest, the silk of her fine gray gown rising and falling along my knuckles with each breath.

Shit. She's a fucking mess. I'm no better.

"I need you to live," she says. Her voice quivers, but not with grief or fear—it's the steadfast determination this woman has demonstrated from the start, even as her blue eyes well and shimmer beneath the moonlight. "I need to know that I've done something right, that I've helped more than I've harmed. And I need that something to be you." She releases a breath. "I love you, Leith. If you hear nothing else tonight, know that my heart will only continue to beat because of you."

I haul her to me, my voice more beast than man despite the gentle way my forehead presses to hers. "I fucking love you, Maeve. Don't you dare leave me, too."

I shove Maeve behind me as someone approaches, causing Hilltop and Knight to whinny in challenge. They're gunning for a fight.

And so am I.

An ogre on massive horseback reaches for his axe when he sees my sword in my hand. "You said you'd only come to mourn your dead," the ogre says.

I don't take my eyes off him as Maeve speaks beside me.

"Leith...take care of Papa and Giselle, even though she won't let you. Find a wife, build a family... Most of all, be happy." There's a rustle of fabric as she draws closer, and misery drenches her voice. "That's no longer an option for me."

She strokes what feels to be a scrap of soft material behind my ear.

I turn at her touch—and the familiar aroma of belladom.

"No," I say, dread rising at the sickly sweet odor.

The way she looks at me parallels the agony I felt when I saw her promise to be Soro's bride.

Tears shimmer in her eyes as a small scrap of white fabric escapes her fingers and flutters to the ground. "I'm sorry," she says. "My stars, I'm so sorry."

It takes me falling to the ground to fully accept what has happened.

The steady stomp of heavy hooves expunges all surrounding noise. The moonlight doves no longer sing, the starlight sparrows no longer call, and the waterfall dissolves into silence.

I surrender to Maeve's potion. There's no fighting it. There's no escaping it. There never was.

"*Maeve.*"

It's the same name I call when I wake in the morning, alone at the shore of our hidden lake. It's the only name I need.

She thinks she should surrender to fate.

Fate can fuck off.

I'm not done fighting yet.

And if I know Maeve, neither is she.

CHAPTER

56

MAEVE

My hands glide over the smooth hair of a royal moon horse as I dismount and lead her into the castle stables. She's mostly chocolate brown with splashes of white along her nose and back, and her mane is white and braided. Bronwyn is her name. She's beautiful and, like the other horses in the royal stables, unaccustomed to kindness. To Soro, Tut, and the others, moon horses serve a purpose—to guard, to thunder into battle, to die for Arrow.

I press a kiss on top of her nose. To me, she's another I need to protect.

I release her and shut the stall door, not bothering to lift the skirt of my gray dress as I walk the length of the royal stables. Though my cape still lies beneath the willow, I am not cold. The air reminds me of home, where the grassy knoll ends and the forest begins. It's earthy, moist soil intermixed with the dry aroma of horse feed and grass.

Broken pieces of hay float through the air as I make my way down the aisle, the longer wisps swept up by my skirt to stick to the lacy hem. I take my time, petting each horse, cooing words of affection, but it's not just for them. It's for me, too.

When I asked Tut to take me to the manor, he readily complied, thinking it was one more way for me to owe him. One added step forward to freeing the phoenix. If so, he's wrong.

One of the many things Leith has taught me is that I owe my people but I also owe myself.

It's why I went to bid farewell to my family.

And why I gave myself so frantically to Leith.

He is my family, too. We needed a goodbye as much as he needed my truth.

I spread my pain and guilt at his feet like a puddle. Yet he stepped over it to comfort me and to forgive me. Even after everything I did, he forgave me so that maybe I can begin to forgive myself.

I choke back a sob. It's quiet, mercifully failing to echo and alert those just beyond the stables to how damaged I am. That doesn't mean I'll admit defeat.

My fingers ball into a fist. To hell with anyone who opposes me.

"Where have you been?" a gruff voice demands from the front of the stables.

Ugeen. Lovely.

He does his best to stomp forward. In fine leather slippers, it's hard for him to stomp anywhere, let alone on a soil-and-hay-covered surface. The moment he's to me, Ugeen snags my arm and pulls me to him.

My head whips to the side when he slaps me. I right myself, shock dulling the sting from that blow. "I asked you where you've been!"

He slaps me again.

This time, I slap him back.

I don't wait for him to gain his footing before I slap him again.

And again.

And again.

All the way the fuck down the hay-strewn length of the stables, I shove and slap him, until he trips over the hem of his robes and lands on his ass.

I turn and lift my chin, fluffing my hair and remembering whose daughter I am.

The guards race forward, including Tut. I keep walking. What are they going to do? Save Ugeen? Turn on their future queen?

No.

Not today.

Not ever.

I shake off the hem of my dress and smooth the skirt before climbing onto the stone steps of the castle. I didn't care about littering the stables or the walkway with hay. I do care about making a mess along the marble floor. Someone will have to clean it up, and I can't ask my dear subjects to do one more needless thing for me.

The guards cast their gazes down as I pass. My features no doubt reflect the downright rage Ugeen's presence stirred. Throw in how that ball-less ass sack *hit me* in an attempt to put me in my supposed place? I'm in no mood to play nice.

I'm almost to Polasie's old apartment when Soro's voice reverberates from the main hall up to the second level where I stand. "Where is she?"

Great. Ugeen ran to daddy to tell on me.

I hear that familiar swish of air of Soro moving at his top speed. My hand is on the knob. I twist it. I throw the door open, and suddenly he stands in front of me, the jewels sewn into his hair reflecting dull tones of yellow and red from the flickering torch set into the gray-and-black stone wall.

Brynne, one of the handmaidens assigned to me, stops polishing the silver tea set and runs. Simply runs. It's a good thing. I don't have to worry about Soro hurting her. "Did you strike Ugeen?"

"Yes," I say. "And I'll do worse if that knob ever touches me again."

He laughs when I walk past him. But it's the laughter filled with malice that I've grown to fear. "Should I strike you for him? You wouldn't hit me back so easily, would you?" I freeze when he pauses. He doesn't just want to hurt me.

Slow, steady footsteps approach, the volume increasing subtly as he closes in. He leans his left shoulder into the door leading to the bedroom. "I could," he says. "But hurting you won't be enough, will it? No, it will mean more if I hurt someone else."

His voice cuts off. When his leer drags down to my breasts and back to my face, I jerk away and ease my way into the parlor.

Soro's tone, which used to be playful as often as it was scary, is simply scary now. He pushes away from the door and stalks forward. "You fucked that gladiator tonight, didn't you?"

I continue to step backward, trying to play dumb, but the shock imbedded in my features—that he actually made the correct assumption—gives me away.

He marches toward me, his dark eyes flashing anger and betrayal. I edge away until my lower back brushes into the buffet and several goblets fall with a clatter to the floor. "You did. You fucked him even though you're engaged to me."

This isn't a good time to bring up the fact that he and Aisling screw any time they can.

"Are you trying to make me look like a fool? Or simply incompetent, like Vitor did?"

He shoves his face in mine, and I bow my spine backward, knocking over more goblets. I try to snag one to use as a weapon but come up empty-handed.

Can I kill him unarmed? I don't know, but if me dying means Leith and my remaining family stay safe, I'm ready to start swinging.

But just how did he know—

I instinctively clutch my neck, where Leith kissed his way down, tearing seams along my neckline to reach my breasts. Oh, stars.

Soro's glare heats my skin worse than Aurora's fire ever could. "Yes... the only way to hurt you is to hurt someone else more."

My eyes widen farther as I watch him walk away. The careful manner with which he shuts my door is more threatening than the loudest slam. I stumble into my bedchamber, beating back a whimper when Tibeta jumps on my shoulder, chirping her distress when she sees mine.

"It's all right, my little bean," I say. "It's all right."

But it's not.

The owl Tibeta befriended hoots as she swoops past my window. I throw open the glass pane and stretch out my hand, hooting so Tibeta repeats me.

The owl returns and lands on my arm. She permits me to stroke her. Perhaps I do have a bit of Grandmother's charms. Carefully, I pass my knuckles over the silky fullness of her feathers to give my racing heart a chance to slow. What is Soro going to do to Leith?

And what must I do to keep him safe?

Tibeta tugs at my hair, her chitters sad and afraid.

"You can't stay with me," I tell her, keeping my voice gentle. "As much as I want you to, it will only be a matter of time before Soro forces his way into my bed and you're caught."

It's why I mixed the nightshade with the belladom in the first place. If I can knock him out, I can possibly stay safe.

Tibeta chitters, not understanding everything but understanding my goodbye. "You must go. You must stay safe. Find Giselle. She and Leith will give you a good home, and you'll get to be with Papa."

Her little ears flop as she nods, recognizing the names of her family at least. In Tibeta's large eyes, I catch my reflection. I hate the woman I see. No matter what I must endure, I will become the queen Father asked of me, and I will fight to protect the ones I love.

The owl hops from my arm and onto the sill. I kiss Tibeta's fuzzy head one last time before lowering her onto the owl's back.

I jump at the harsh knock on the door. Tut barges in, larger than life, spurring the owl to fly. My vision blurs as I watch her carry away my last bit of home. Tibeta soars into the night, her paws clinging tight to the feathers along the owl's back.

"Were you petting a chicken?" Tut asks.

I frown. "No. It was an owl."

He shrugs. "They both taste the same."

"I'll take your word for it."

Steam billows through his nostrils. "Soro is ranting about you being with that gladiator tonight." Like Soro, he stares at the neckline of my dress, causing me to pull it upward. "You were foolish to leave your cape behind," he says.

I motion around. "Obviously I wouldn't have had I noticed the condition of my dress."

I slowly ease away from the window, fixating on Tut when I realize exactly what I can do to keep Leith safe. In a few quick steps, I'm in front of the vanity, pulling out the most expensive rings Soro gave me.

"What are you doing?" Tut asks me.

I turn, my voice flat but no less determined. "Getting ready. As soon as we can manage, I need you to take me to the phoenix."

CHAPTER
57

LEITH

Uni pours another round of ale for me and Caelen.

"Rough day, huh?" Giselle asks, voice raised to be heard over the laughter and stomping from the wooden dance floor and the energetic melody of the iplos on stage.

Caelen moves over so she can take the stool between us. She's wearing a brown smock similar to the one Maeve wears when working in her garden. She's trying to blend in, but with her mouth, it won't take long for everyone to notice Giselle.

Behind the bar, there's a clang of metal bowls and the aroma of venison stew wafting in from the kitchen. Another day, another time, it would make my stomach growl. But filling my belly is the last thing on my mind right now.

"Is he asleep?" I ask Giselle. *He* meaning Andres, who is now living with us in New Arrow.

"Yes, finally. Gabi made him a sedative tea with the hopes of calming him."

Caelen, still wearing his signature uniform, adjusts his scabbard on his hip. It's still within reach for a quick beheading, but he's more comfortable now. "Good. Stasia says he's been anxious since she first received him. It sounds like the tea was what he needed."

"No, he needed someplace small to feel secure, so we turned the linen closet into a bedchamber for him, and he seems much more comfortable. Thank you, Uni," Giselle says when he places a mug of ale in front of her. She takes several gulps before continuing. "By the time Gabi made it up the stairs, the tea was spilled and Papa was asleep."

She finishes off her ale, stealing a glance at Caelen before speaking again. "I miss Maeve. Everyone in the city today asked me if I plan to step into her role." She huffs. "Who could do that? She's a selfless leader who treats wounds, delivers babies, and last week repaired the broken wings of a pixie caught in a spiderwolf web."

Caelen strangles out a laugh, and Giselle rolls her eyes, then says, "I told you that pixie challenged *me* to go ale for ale. It's not my fault she was too drunk to fly."

"Don't talk about Maeve like she's dead," I say, my tone grim.

Giselle tries to smile when Uni refills her mug. "I don't mean to. It's just that I never counted on anyone presuming I could take her place." She opens her palms and stares at her gloved hands. "I'm the last person who should touch anyone, let alone try to heal them."

Caelen slips from his stool as the iplos end their fast-paced tune. He weaves his way through the crowded tavern and requests a melody. As the song begins to play, tears fill Giselle's soft honey eyes. She hops off her stool before Caelen reaches us and runs off.

Caelen watches her, then takes her seat beside me. "I requested that song to lift her mood." He sighs. "It didn't work as I intended."

Not long ago, I wouldn't ask about their business. But things are different now, and I could use a distraction from everything we've planned. "Why don't you go after her? Is it her magic?"

Caelen shakes his head, the quiet majesty he always carries crumbling as he looks to where Giselle stands across the room. "I can't," he says. "She won't let me. She's poison."

"What the fuck, man?"

Caelen throws back his ale, then slams the empty tankard down. And here I thought Giselle would be the loud one.

"Giselle has Areris," he says with a frown. "Maeve has tried curing her for years. Nothing she's ever made has worked."

There are battering rams that hit softer than Caelen's words.

Areris. Even I've heard of it. And Caelen wasn't joking—Giselle *is* poison to anyone else with magic in their blood. She can't have a child without killing it. She can't kiss another without sickening them. And when crying, she can't even lean her head on the person she adores without risking their safety.

"Is this why you're so willing to help me tomorrow?" I ask Caelen. "Because you think you have nothing to lose?"

Uni refills Caelen's mug, giving him ample berth when he starts to sprout fangs. But as quickly as they appear, they retract as Giselle returns to sit between us.

"I'm helping you because it's the right thing to do." His gaze flits to Giselle, who keeps her head down. "And because if we pull it off, it will benefit us all."

Giselle knocks back her ale as the tune Caelen requested comes to an end.

"So, we're in agreement?" Giselle asks.

I nod. "Yes. If I can't pull this shit off tomorrow, whoever's alive takes Andres and runs."

CHAPTER

58

MAEVE

"Out for a walk?"

I freeze when Soro calls out from the war room. That's what he's calling the study now that he thinks he's in charge. Tut is speaking quietly to the guards stationed at the door. Something about not allowing anyone who hasn't been cleared anywhere near our beloved future king.

The collar of my poofy black gown fastens high on my neck, making it hard to turn my head. Damn it. The only reason I'm wearing this monstrosity is because of the absurdly large skirt.

I turn and sweep into the room, pretending to fuss with the pins holding my hair coiled in a tight bun and very cognizant of not venturing too far in. "I am, actually."

Ugeen and a few soldiers huddle around a table where that familiar map of Arrow and the surrounding realms are spread out. Pua stands at the head. He straightens when he sees me, and the others abruptly quiet.

I wink at Ugeen when he scowls because I can and because I caused the bright-red raised marks covering his face.

Soro, our most revered jackass, sits on that ornately carved phoenix chair from Vitor's office. The back is low enough so as not to impede the sensual way Aisling massages said revered jackass's shoulders. Almost as sensual as how he strokes that fucking bird. She glares at me, and the movement of her fingers grows more aggressive as she stares me down.

I don't know what he means by bringing that stupid chair in here. My guess is that it's to remind Pua and Ugeen what he holds within his grip.

"A little late for a walk, my queen," Soro says. He steeples his fingers and smiles. "As tomorrow is our wedding, I've arranged quite a spectacle to celebrate and make it an event no one will soon forget." He licks his lips, all but drooling. "Return to your room and sleep, my beloved. You'll need your rest if you hope to take in the slaughter."

"I just need to stretch my legs," I say.

"I think you spread your legs enough last night," Soro says, causing everyone to erupt with laughter—everyone except for Aisling. I'm uncertain whether Soro disclosed I was with Leith or if they presume I was with him. Maybe they're simply trying to remain in good standing. My face heats as he bats his hand. "Forgive me, my beloved. I meant *stretched.*"

"Of course you did, precious," I reply. "If you'll excuse me."

"I said no."

He might as well have screamed the words, the way the silence drops like an anvil. "You're not to leave the castle." He smiles. "That's an order."

My, there's never a dagger around when you need one to launch yourself across the room and stab someone in the balls.

We glare at each other until Soro finally says, "Fine. Pua, go with her. Make sure she doesn't leave the castle grounds or your sight. If she breathes, you breathe with her."

Pua billows a ridiculous amount of steam, the funnels spiraling from his nostrils fogging the stained glass windows. His big foot slams onto the floor as he steps away from the table. "I'm not here to play nanny to some brat." He points with the broken nail of his middle finger back at the map. "I am trying to work out a plan. Don't you understand? The city-states of Nican and Recca have both assembled their armies. They're coming for us—"

Soro threads his fingers and places them behind his head. "Let them come," he says. "Arrow has all it needs to defeat anyone stupid enough to try."

Several guards gather around Soro when Pua takes a deliberate step forward, his round belly stretching his leather vest with each breath.

I've prepared myself for the worst-case scenario, and so has Tut. He stomps in and throws his hands in the air. "Enough. I'll watch the princess."

"She's not to step one toe outside the garden gates," Soro says. But he's no longer looking at me. He's smiling in Pua's direction. Tut huffs and yanks me by the arm into the hall, playing the role of an annoyed general tasked with babysitting a little too well.

I jerk free of his hold and start down the corridor in the direction of the kitchens, throwing a quick glance over my shoulder just in time to see Soro leap from that damn chair with unnatural speed and bring the tip of his sword down and through Pua's skull.

I walk hurriedly away, jolting when Pua's body slumps to the floor with a thud.

Tut quickens his pace and falls into step beside me, albeit a lot louder than me. Several more guards run past us to investigate the commotion. It's a distraction I'm grateful for when I realize the path to the dungeon is clear.

My words are released in time with my fast steps. "So that's it, isn't it? Don't question. Always obey, or else."

"Yes, but that's not why he killed Pua."

I must crane my neck to look all the way up at him. "Then why?"

Steam billows out through Tut's own nostrils now. "We're not supposed to tell you this, Princess, but *someone* broke your papa outta jail." He chuffs, clearly pleased with himself. "Soro suspects a traitor among his generals." He smiles, pushing out more steam. "He killed the wrong one."

And I'm headed to the catacombs with the right one.

Stars, I hope I don't regret this.

CHAPTER

59

MAEVE

We pass down the long hall of cells in the castle's dungeon where Papa was kept. There are only a few prisoners, and they appear to be asleep, huddled in corners with no covers or pillows. I sneak past them easily enough, more mouse than woman.

Tut, not so much. He's more scary swamp monster than man.

Slap, scratch.

Slap, scratch.

Slap, scratch…

"You really must trim those toenails," I mutter under my breath.

Tut growls, which makes even more noise. A bear shifter in the cell to our left rolls onto his side. Fortunately, he rolls toward the wall. "My brother told me long toenails attract ladies."

"Your brother was a liar," I snap. "Tut, you're being really loud. Keep it down."

Hopefully trusting this ogre will be worth the risk. He is the only person alive other than Soro and Ugeen who knows how to get back down to the phoenix. Not only do I need that information, I must retrieve my grandfather's sword before Soro discovers it.

My pace slows, eyes prickling with tears when I reach the stone cubby where Papa slept. I can't ever see him again, at least not while Soro is king. It's the only way to keep Papa safe. But maybe, if I play it right…

Tut points to a door farther down with a huff. Cobwebs encase it.

"That's the way down?" I ask. "It looks like it hasn't been opened." I take a closer look. "Ever."

Tut nods. "Some mage a while back placed a spell to make it look like no one's bothered to go through it in over a hundred years. People don't like creepy shit. And creepy shit involves doors that people have been too afraid to open."

I nod, then step aside for Tut to work the lock with two thin pieces of metal from his pocket.

He ordered the guard assigned to dungeon duty to fetch fresh meat stew for the prisoners' dinner tonight—in celebration of the future king and queen's impending nuptials, of course—but I'm beginning to wonder if we should have knocked him out instead. After what feels like an eternity, I hear a faint *click* and hurry us through.

Tut strikes a piece of flint across the wall and lights a torch, illuminating the ominous spiral staircase that descends before us. I don't remember these stairs at all, having been unconscious for part of my transport during my kidnapping and hooded for the rest. I never would have found this place alone.

I press my hand into the wall to keep my balance along the steep stairwell as it curves. As I spread my fingers, the row of rings I wear grows more uncomfortable, the prominent stones digging into my knuckles. I don't have access to gold, but Soro showered me with plenty of jewelry to use as currency.

"Can I ask you something?" Tut says, his gruff voice echoing to the abyss below.

"Only if you can be a little quieter."

Slap, scratch, slap, scratch.

Slap, scratch, slap, scratch…

Merciful moon, he must do something about those toenails. I'm uncertain how it's possible that he's causing such a commotion until I realize the big guy is walking sideways to accommodate his gigantic feet.

"The sword you're getting down here. Why is it so important?" Tut rubs his eyes to clear some dust particles floating upward. "I know you don't plan to give it to Soro."

I clear my throat. I need to be careful. I'm not certain where Tut's allegiances lie, and he's already in a mood. The last thing I want is to enrage an ogre who could snap my neck and bury me down here. "You are correct."

I have no intention of giving the sword to Soro, and frankly I'm relieved he hasn't thought to retrieve it already. Perhaps he didn't notice it, too distracted by murdering his father and all, or maybe he thought it was a replica created by the artist who carved the statues. But I knew better, recognizing it as genuine, even covered in dust in the near darkness.

"Tell me," he says, his annoyance releasing in bursts of steam that flutter strings from a pulled web into the air. "It's the sword that the queen used to bring down the phoenix. The one she took from her dead husband's hands." Oh, and Tut doesn't like that one bit. He grinds his fangs, his tusks appearing to lengthen in the dim enclosure.

Does he think I mean to use the weapon to kill his beloved phoenix? Well, that's not it. This isn't about war. It's about politics. If I am to take Soro as my king, my subjects must never view him as having more power or authority than me. He will only be king *because* of me. There is no symbol in Arrow more powerful than the Good King Masone's phoenix-killing blade, and he will never have it.

Not that I intend to reveal such machinations to Tut. Just because I'm using him to get to the catacombs does *not* mean we're allies, let alone confidants.

I pause to adjust my rings, attempting to act casual. The rings will go to Brynne and Lita in exchange for helping me smuggle the King Sword into my wing of the castle undetected. The coin from the jewelry will support their families for several years. I only hope that fear won't force them to report me. Soro *cannot* have that sword.

"You're dawdling," Tut says, obviously annoyed I didn't answer his question.

"Forgive me," I say in the same tone.

I hurry down three more steps and almost trip when, instead of another step, my feet strike flat ground. Tut lights the next torch and moves to where the maze of bones begins.

I cough when Tut kicks up enough dust to form a film along my tongue. It's sweltering down here. The close walls of the maze provide some relief, but it will only get hotter the closer we get to Aurora.

I cough so violently, I press my hand against the wall to keep my balance, only to jerk it back when my fingers slip into the eye sockets of a skull.

Disgust roils my insides when I think about just how many bones are in this place and how many lives were lost to make Aurora, and thus Arrow, stronger. It's wrong. All of it. But Arrow is strong with or without a phoenix. Somehow, we'll survive without Aurora. I just need to figure out how to release her myself without the risk of her falling into the wrong hands again. But not anytime soon. My first priority is retrieving the sword.

Tut coughs and spits on the ground when we take a wrong turn. "Ugh. I taste the dead."

I cover my mouth. *Me too, Tut. Me too.*

We pick our way through the veritable minefield of bones leading to Aurora's cage.

"I presume you plan to return here tomorrow?" I ask.

"Your birthday, wedding, and coronation are the distraction my people and I will need to free the phoenix." He narrows his tiny black eyes. "You have to do this, Princess. I brought you down here like you asked. You owe us this."

Something about Tut's tone feels off. I wipe the perspiration dripping from my chin with my sleeve. His quest *sounds* noble, but…as much as I need him, I definitely don't trust him.

I try to act casual. My sweaty hands grip my skirt to flap it.

"Why did you wear that down here?" Tut asks, sounding annoyed.

"It's how I'm sneaking the sword back to my people," I say. "The black will also hide the amount of sweat sticking to me."

"Ya," he says as he turns to face me, sizing me up like an opponent, not a coconspirator.

And that's when my suspicions are confirmed: Yep, I've walked right into a trap.

So be it.

CHAPTER
60

MAEVE

The sword hidden in my skirts—the one I'm planning to switch out for Grandfather's—isn't real. It's a mere replica that Lita located in Vitor's former apartment. It's slightly shorter and about as sharp as a spoon. It's made well enough that the real one won't be missed if someone journeys down after us, but the blade is definitively not enough to bring an ogre down.

I let out a breath when Tut turns to continue through the maze. Ordinarily, I would never go unarmed like this, but Soro stripped my room of anything I could use against him, going as far as removing anything glass, including the bottle of belladom. I can't imagine how he guessed my many fantasies about smashing it over his head and shoving the broken shards up his nose, but here we are.

I keep my eye on Tut's dominant hand as he lumbers ahead of me. If I don't reach Grandmother's statue in time, my speed and agility will be my only protection.

Tut's meaty shoulders droop with relief as we reach the end of the maze. The incline lies just ahead, ripples of heat pulsating from Aurora's nest and creating small waves in the soil.

He motions me forward. "After you," he says.

Ah, no. I don't think so. No way am I putting this ogre at my back.

I pretend to cough. With all this dust and surging heat, it's not that hard. I wave him ahead, my sweaty fingers so slippery, I fling off one of the emerald rings I'm wearing. It bounces off Tut's hard chest and to the ground. He doesn't pick it up.

"You first. You're the one who must figure out the dynamics of the gate to set the great phoenix free," I say, snatching the ring from the dirt.

He cocks his head, the muscles along his bulldog-like features tightening with distrust. Fine. I don't trust him, either.

"Tut, go on. My job is easy."

He grunts and stomps toward Aurora's cage, kicking up dirt and ash with every step, his fingers gripping the handle of his double-headed axe the size of my torso.

I untie the replacement sword and slip out of my skirt, revealing the breeches I wear underneath. Stars, it's wretched in here. I hoped losing a layer would help, but Aurora is far too powerful, her body generating heat like a burning star. At least if my fears are realized and Tut is not true, I won't be hindered by heavy fabric as I make my escape.

I strike out again when Tut is far enough ahead of me. Aurora isn't out, but her nest has grown in the days since I was down here last. I can already see it, and I'm not yet to the top of the incline.

Thankfully, the nest is still. Good. My biggest fear was that we'd find her preening herself and then she'd pelt us with fireballs and swallow us whole.

I'm not exaggerating, based on our last encounter.

Tut, being Tut, is making a lot of noise as he scurries from side to side, trying to locate an unlocking mechanism. I look up to the stalactites stained to a dark, dull purple. Mercifully, they're not currently dripping blood onto the composite of ashen soil and long-decaying bones upon which I stand.

But the same won't be said tomorrow.

"There's no lock," Tut grunts. He glares at me accusingly, as if I'm somehow responsible. "There's only one way to get her through."

I feel my body tense as Tut bellows a cloud of steam from his nose, speckling his face with condensation. He looks at the heap of ash covering Aurora, far out of his reach beyond the bars, and then back to me, eyes narrowing. Oh, and he looks *pissed* about it.

Chills race down my spine despite the heat. "You plan to kill her, don't you?"

Tut straightens, his full attention on me now—just how a murderer might look at his next victim. The moment he does, I leap onto Queen Avianna of Iamond, and I climb.

I pretend not to notice Tut pushing away from the gate, trying to keep my voice light so he does not suspect *me* of suspecting *him*. "It'd be easier to get her out, and yes, she'll be more portable, but that won't make you any better than my grandmother."

My full attention stays on Tut as I swap out the swords. But Tut is a general—stronger than me—without a speck of reason left behind those beady black eyes. I was right. He never planned to set her free.

He was a sniveling traitor all along.

"You're the one who's no better than your damn grandmother," he says.

Ah. It's going to be like that...

Tut marches toward me, raising his axe. "Like her, you ruin everything for everyone."

Fuck this.

I hold my grandfather's sword in my right hand, snatch my grandmother's in my left, and flip, landing in a crouch with both blades out.

Tut stops dead.

As he should.

Slowly, his leathery features tighten, and his eyes latch onto mine and stay there. "I'm getting her out tonight. Whatever it takes, I'm doing it."

"You said you were only coming down here to prepare for Aurora's release. You never said anything about taking her tonight," I say to keep him talking until I can come up with a way out of this.

"Killing her is the only way," he snarls, his thick tongue sliding over his tusks. "But I need fresh meat to call her forth."

Fresh meat meaning me. That's why he agreed to bring me here.

The damn nerve.

I twirl my swords to loosen my wrists. "Then I suggest you cut off a leg and toss it into her nest, because you will *not* be touching me."

The bottom lip of his protruding mouth slaps up and down like he's tasting me on Aurora's behalf. I don't know what it is about this bird, but it seems like everyone obsessed with her eventually goes mad.

"Say you succeed in killing me." I narrow my eyes. "Not that you will, as I will kindly feed you your right testicle the moment you think to try."

The space we occupy between rows of stalagmites and piles of bones isn't large, but it's enough for us to circle each other. One foot over the other—that's how we start. "You can't leave this castle without getting caught," I say.

I continue to sidestep, my blades at the ready.

"Watch me," Tut growls. He angles closer, his gnarly toenails digging into the dirt.

"No," I growl in return. "It's a mistake to free her now." Or kill and steal her, as he plans.

"Aurora needs to be freed. The Erth depends on it!" he screeches. "My people depend on it. On me. And I will have her!"

My back is to the golden gate. Not exactly the best place to be. But I have the swords now, and I can certainly run faster than an ogre. I just need to get past him.

"If I die, and I won't," I promise, "Soro will know it was you. He'll come after you and everyone you've ever spoken to, knowing you robbed him of the throne."

"No body, no blame," he snarls.

He charges.

And I meet him halfway.

He raises his weapon.

I raise both of mine.

Cling, clang, cling.

He swings one way, I the other, blocking him with Grandmother's sword, whirling and slicing open his gut with Grandfather's.

I spin away from his next blow and cut a new hole in his face.

Tut raises his axe in both hands and brings it down. I hop back and whirl out of reach, and he...explodes.

Chunky bits of Tut slide across the expanse, battle axe spinning through the air until it hits the golden bars of Aurora's cage with a massive *clang*.

That was unexpected.

As if summoned by the dinner bell, the ground trembles as the great phoenix wakes. And who should saunter toward me, sparks of the lavender magic she used to ignite Tut dancing across her skin, but Aisling.

She points accusingly at me. "You dare plot against Soro…"

A terrible heat builds at my back, crawling its way up my spine.

Aisling's jaw slackens as her gaze lifts and lifts and lifts. Her finger lowers, flames reflecting in her lavender irises.

Fire builds behind me as Aurora continues to rise, lengthening our shadows across the sweltering terrain.

My body overheats as I race past Aisling and dive over a high section of bones.

Flames of red and gold burst forth as Aurora spreads her wings and flaps, causing a wind so fierce that bones scatter like leaves, and I have to shield my face from the debris. Aisling screams when Aurora's serpentine tongue snakes out from behind the bars of her cage, lapping at the bloody chunks that once were Tut.

Another heat source builds, this time to my far right. I scramble up and over the next mess of bones as a sphere of lavender fire barrels down the row I just abandoned.

I don't have to wait for Aisling to build more magic. Her screams of terror and fury manifest more power in record time.

"You took him from me!" she says, somewhere to my left beyond a maze wall. "And now you seek to steal the phoenix from us, too!"

Yes, Aisling, that was my intent all along. All I was thinking about was you. I roll my eyes and hunker down, trying to pinpoint her location as her voice draws closer.

Aisling didn't know about the phoenix. Soro never shared that little secret. She knows it now, and she's taking it out on me.

"He's mine! Do you hear me, Maeve?" Aisling shrieks over the slurps and gulps of the phoenix. "All of this was always supposed to be mine!"

Shards of bones burst from the wall inches from me. I grip my swords and take off, leaping over pile after pile of dead gladiator as Aisling sends funnels of flame after me.

Her hands rise, fall, and turn as she manipulates her fire power to chase me down. Walls of bones explode into shards, imbedding in the dirt and walls.

A skull slams into my back. I lose Grandfather's sword when a piece of stalagmite strikes my wrist and knocks it free.

I double back to the opening of the maze as Aurora spits out Tut's moist bones. She watches Aisling manipulate a fireball of magic, her head tilting side to side with interest. She elongates her neck and tastes Aisling's flames.

Aisling's fire, powerful enough to burn down a manor, does nothing to Aurora, who simply shudders, unharmed and evidently unimpressed.

"Yes, great phoenix," Aisling says, her voice as disturbing as Tut's glistening remains. "Feed from me. You are my sister, as I am yours."

I fall to the ground, covering my head when another sphere of flame crashes into the maze. I crawl away, but not before finally catching sight of Aisling hidden behind a section of demolished bone.

She thinks that by ducking and shooting she's safe. Mages are like that. They tend to believe that nothing can touch them.

But I'm an elf and a warrior.

Fast.

Agile.

Strong.

I close in.

Aisling turns around, a sphere of white-hot lavender flame building in her palm as I cut her from her shoulder to her groin.

I use the momentum to roll behind my grandmother.

Aurora, still hungry and crazed for fresh death, ribbons her tongue around the two body parts that were once Aisling.

I turn and rest my back on the base of Avianna's statue.

Aisling was wrong. She and Aurora weren't sisters. Aisling was just a woman who bullied my Giselle to tears, cut me down every time we met, and destroyed my home. I do not even pity her.

My lungs draw air in painful spurts. I lean over, hands on my knees, catching my breath and waiting for my heart to slow. After a few moments, I poke my head around the statue in time to see Aurora spit out Aisling's bones.

"No body, no blame," I whisper.

CHAPTER

61

LEITH

The drumbeats started at sunrise and continue to bang away in that same steady, deliberate rhythm. They speak of war and death, which is…appropriate.

Caelen and I march our horses into the arena complex. "Is it odd being here when you're no longer required?" he asks.

"It is," I say. "But I wouldn't miss this for all of Old Erth." Not when it's my only chance to secure the title Maeve needs me to have.

Caelen grins. Not something he's known for. "Neither would I."

It's arena day. It's also Maeve's birthday, her coronation, and the day of her unholy union with Soro, who has surely planned a masterpiece of atrocity to celebrate.

Asshole.

Old and young, poor and rich, all have arrived today. Whether they are loyal attendees or first-timers just looking forward to watching the surprises in store for a final Bloodguard trial doesn't matter—the entire complex is packed. But I'm not here for them. I'm here for Maeve.

We slip from our horses, passing the reins to a stableboy who is notably not Gunther. My stomach twists at the thought that he may have been harmed for his show of loyalty toward me that night Vitor and

Soro dropped in at the manor. I will find him when this is over and make certain that he, at least, enjoys the life that my sisters could not.

"I wish you luck, Leith of Grey," Caelen says as we clasp arms. I nod, and he releases me. After a moment, he says, "You shared your plan for today with me in confidence, my friend, but sometimes confidences must be broken to protect those we love."

Prickly dread trickles through my bones. Has my friend betrayed me and alerted Soro? No. I know the man. His loyalty is to Giselle and her family. But before I can ask what the hell he's talking about, he strides away, calling over his shoulder with a wave, "I'll see you inside. We'll have the best seats in the house." And with that, he disappears into the crowd of people streaming through the arches.

By the time I enter, pandemonium has already been unleashed. Lines by the dozens form for keepsakes, food, ale, and more outside of the arena. Stasia waves from the cider stand she erected, pausing to sigh deeply when Gabi's backward-facing feet take her in the opposite direction to where Manu, a giantess, is selling sweet bread.

The dwarves who carried the cauldron of eels now stir a cauldron of boar hooves in lizard broth. The aroma of the broth and vegetables clashes in the most delicious way possible with the turkey legs Neh-Neh and Uni are coating with butter and herbs to sell to the masses. As much as it pains me to see them here, I know they've got three big mouths to feed, and I can't begrudge them the coin today's "festivities" will bring.

Spectators stop to watch me, point in my direction, wave, and, of course, heckle.

An elderly lord with gentle mannerisms and soft words lights up when he sees me. "Enjoy your freedom while it lasts, jackass!" he hollers.

I return his grin. "Not as much as I've enjoyed your wife," I reply.

Look at that. He's no longer smiling.

All the noise should overwhelm me. But my focus hasn't wavered since my mind was made up.

To the left, the line for the Commons has formed. At the center, the Middlings await. Those in the Noble Ring—closest to the arena floor— don't stand in line. The gentry cross the bridge that connects the castle to the coliseum. There's no wait, and there's no rubbing elbows with the riffraff or need to talk to anyone deemed beneath them. At the bridge, they're bowed to, given programs, and escorted into their designated boxes.

Through the archway of the gladiator entrance, I can see that the pens are nearly empty. The only evidence of the other gladiators is the imprints of bare feet through the mud toward the tunnel that leads into the arena. From here, I can see them stuffed in one narrow and cramped cell. They stand shoulder to shoulder behind bars that run along the tunnel wall. Their view is minimal. Those assholes have moved them closer to screw with their minds. They'll be able to hear all the torment and not benefit from it. Shit. I never thought anything would be worse than those damn pens. One more flex courtesy of Soro.

Well, by the great phoenix, it's time we change all that.

CHAPTER

62

MAEVE

There's so much bloodshed to be had today, and I want no part of it. At least Soro allowed Giselle to meet me at the entrance and escort me inside. It's the first time I've been allowed to see her since before my family and home were destroyed. I take a shuddering breath and square my shoulders, knowing all eyes will be on me today.

My white, diamond-stitched dress makes a swishing sound as we step from the bridge sectioned off for royalty to the slick stone floor of the arena complex. I tug at the uncomfortable sleeves as Giselle and I walk down the corridor in the direction of the royal box. I agreed to wear the gown, but I drew the line at the veil. I want Soro and everyone here to see my face when I'm forced to go through with this farce of a wedding.

I take my sister's gloved hand and pull her to a stop. "Any word of Leith?" I whisper.

An odd look crosses her face, like when she was caught in mischief as a child. "He's not happy about the situation, of course, but he is good otherwise. Caelen has spent time with him frequently."

Relief floods my chest, letting me breathe a bit more easily. He is well and will not be putting his life on the line in this horrible place ever again.

Beneath the first archway, a few ladies, their dresses in alternating pastels of silk and satin and their noses high in the air, whisper as a servant fills their bejeweled chalices with wine.

"She ran off, I tell you," Lady Zizi, a troll, insists. "She can't be queen here, but knowing Aisling, she'll be queen somewhere else."

Um. I don't think she will.

They fall silent when they see Giselle and me, and they huddle closer together. "Do you think Soro killed her?" Lady Urt, a cyclops with short green curls, whispers.

The ladies flap their hands and shush her, warning her to watch her tongue.

Too late. The servant pouring wine hurries away in Soro's direction, his thin legs moving fast and his feather cap bouncing in his haste.

The women gasp when Soro bends to hear what the young elf has to say. My, and doesn't that make them scatter? I don't feel sorry for Urt or Zizi for however Soro chooses to punish them. These "ladies" were Aisling's closest friends, following her lead in their relentless harassment of Giselle, who now shifts uncomfortably beside me.

I squeeze her hand, and we continue our slow progress through the crowd.

"I must tell you something," Giselle whispers when we reach the landing above the steps leading to the box reserved for top-ranking royalty.

I glance around to be certain we cannot be overheard. "About Leith?"

She shakes her head. "I just want you to know." She swallows. "I want you to know that I will always support you and protect you any way I can." She looks so serious I find myself holding my breath, but then something over my shoulder catches her eye, and her expression brightens. "Caelen has arrived. I must go."

The look on her face makes my heart ache. She loves him.

After giving my hand a squeeze, she practically skips away, but then she rushes back to me. "I, uh, borrowed a couple of things from your room last night. Hope you don't mind."

I know we are being watched by those around us, so I school my features to prevent my confusion from showing. Soro ordered that no one is allowed entrance to my wing except my maids. It would be impossible for her to borrow anything.

Before I can even take a breath to respond, she says, "Brynne and Lita are really nice. I met them in the city yesterday, and we had a long talk." And with that, she spins and pushes her way through the sea of jewels and silk and satin toward a box two down from mine, where her love awaits.

Chin high, expression neutral, I make my way across the landing to where Soro and Ugeen are deep in conversation by the arched corridor entrance. Ugeen is dressed all in pink, because he didn't look enough like a knob already. The color bleaches his already pasty skin, and since today is extra special, his head is polished to a high shine.

Ugeen steps away from Soro and the servant and shakes his head as I approach. "What a poor excuse for a queen," he says. He's speaking loudly, belittling me so others will, too—no doubt part of a plan to weaken me in the eyes of my people to allow Soro more power.

Soro sends two guards in the direction of where the ladies disappeared, their quick steps echoing along the high walls and ceilings of the immense corridor.

Ugeen leans into Soro and smiles. "You'll do better your next go around, my king."

He's still angry at me for slapping him.

I learned my lesson, though. No more slapping Ugeen.

"Pfft," he says, wrinkling his nose as if I smell bad. "Disgusting."

I respond with a regal wave to his face and a right hook to his jaw.

See? Lesson learned. I didn't slap him once.

Ugeen falls on his ass, as per usual, smacking the hands of the guards who try to help him up. He lunges at me but is cut short when the guards assigned to me swarm him with their swords out.

"Uh, uh, uh," I say. "Mustn't attack the queen. Her royal guards don't like it."

Ugeen no longer has anything to say.

But Soro will have plenty. I groan when he bypasses Ugeen and marches to my side.

Soro is all dolled up in dark-blue breeches and shirt with a matching robe for our special day. And don't get me started on the sheer volume of gems woven into his hair.

"Would it kill you to behave like a decent bride?" Soro asks.

"Hard to be decent when I'm engaged to an overly bedazzled prick." I don't finish speaking before Soro raises his hand to strike me, and I instinctively cover my face. I immediately regret it and lower my hands, not wanting to appear weak or cowed by this man. I'm the queen, dammit.

With a growl, Soro reins in his anger and drops his arm, hand clenched. "If I find out you had anything to do with Aisling's disappearance..." he warns, voice shaking in a way that suggests... My, does he actually have a heart in there?

Too damn bad.

I lift my chin and regard him as if his mere presence makes me ill. It's not hard. "You said it was Tut. That they fought when he tried to free the—"

His seething scowl cuts me off. "I don't think it was him. Tut was ruthless, but Aisling was, too." Coming from him, it almost sounds like a compliment.

I raise my eyebrows. "Aisling was an opportunist, just like Ugeen." I give the man a glare. "What makes you think she didn't side with Tut and make the catacombs appear as if they fought?" My, that doesn't sound so bad, so I keep going. I sidle closer, as if he didn't almost strike me—as if I want to help him rather than feed his paranoia. "What if Ugeen is in on it with her? Hasn't he already proven he's willing to lie about such things to suit his interests?"

Soro's features sharpen to obsidian blades. I tilt my head as if confused. It's better than appearing like I've knowingly gone too far, which I fear I have.

He stares at me for a beat, then hooks my arm and drags me forward. "Come on. You're late enough."

The bright sun stings my eyes as we step out into the stands. Soro releases me, not bothering to help me on the stone steps I want to push him down. So help me, if I ever get the chance, I'll fling him from the royal box.

The overhang, swathed in white, affords some relief from the sun's bright rays. White silk is draped over every seat, starting in the Middling section, and white petals are strewn along the rows where bet takers run up and down. Bouquets spilling with white-flowered vines are placed at each row. This is a spectacle indeed.

I slow my pace to take every bit of it in before focusing on the arena. An orchestra tunes its instruments just to our right on a newly constructed platform, also decorated in white.

On the arena floor, eight large crates are arranged in a circle. My attention shifts to the royals on my left. Everyone there is either casting their bets or trying to guess what fresh torment they're going to put the gladiators through today. Having been sequestered since Aisling's disappearance last night, I haven't learned a thing. But based on the size of those crates—my eyes widen when I glance down to see two of the boxes thrashing independently—these poor people are up for the torture session of their lives.

"Sit down," Soro hisses.

For a moment, I picture gouging his eyes out with my bare hands, but I resist the temptation.

I sit, horrified by a glimpse of caged gladiators through the arched opening at the other end of the arena. I desperately wish I could do something—anything—to help them.

Soro empties his goblet down his throat. A servant appears and sets the contents of a brass container on fire while another sets a quiver full of arrows beside it. A third offers Soro a bow. He examines it carefully and pulls on the string. My attention jerks back to the boxes in the arena. What are these gladiators in for? And how many of them are mere civilians who will die for the crime of seeking refuge in our land?

These "royals" have poisoned my kingdom, and I don't believe I can ever atone for my part in allowing it to happen.

The quieting of the crowd gives everyone around me pause. Their chanting begins low, building upon itself until it reaches a mighty crescendo, and everyone is on their feet.

"Bloodguard!"

"*Bloodguard!*"

Soro rises slowly beside me. I stand, too, when *Leith* enters the arena and marches across the sand.

I cannot breathe or even form coherent thought. Leith shouldn't be here. He *can't* be here. I agreed to marry this despicable man beside me today and live a life without him so he wouldn't ever have to enter this arena again.

So he wouldn't die.

It takes a while for Leith to reach the area closest to the royal boxes, given the massive diameter of the arena, and I swear to the moon and stars my heartbeat stalls with every step he takes. No guards escorted him into the arena. No one commanded him here.

He's here by choice.

His eyes meet mine, and I take my first full breath since he stepped onto the sand. My heart hammering so hard I fear it will break through my ribs, I place a hand over my chest. This warrior—the man I love—is here for a reason. He's here for *me*.

"You," Soro says.

"That's right. *Me*," Leith shouts back.

Soro's body stiffens, and he scowls, clearly unhappy that the crowd is losing their collective selves at Leith's presence. But then, Soro smiles.

Oh, mercy. I glance between them. All Soro has to do is find an excuse not to put Leith in the arena, but he's too cocky for that.

"You vowed he would not be called into the arena to battle," I say, panic causing my voice to come out thin and raspy.

Soro's smile remains in place. "He was not called here."

No, but he intends for Leith to die today regardless.

And Leith couldn't give a damn.

"You think you call the shots? You think we fight for *you*?" Leith says, his ire elevating each word to a credible threat. "Today, *I'm* the one in charge." His voice reverberates through the massive amphitheater as his gaze sears to mine. "Today, I fight for Maeve of Iamond, my queen."

CHAPTER
63

LEITH

My gloves and boots are leather, my pants and shirt black, as I prefer. I'm here to fight on my terms. I'm here for the title, because so help me, I owe Maeve as much.

As the crowd settles, Soro raises his arms, his voice booming for what I intend to be the last time.

"Gladiator," he calls.

I raise my arms, too. "What?"

That earns a few bouts of laughter he doesn't appreciate. Maeve takes turns looking from him to me. She's scared for me, but I'm more scared for her. That asshole still has her for now. Fortunately, I will kill him, no matter the cost.

Soro tries again. "It's time for the *real* games to begin."

"Do your worst, you sadistic *fuck* of a wannabe king."

The crowd goes wild at my proclamation. Bet takers are flipping through their notes and looking around helplessly as they're overrun with orders.

Like it or not, Soro has no choice but to let me fight. The masses assembled would tolerate nothing less.

He acknowledges me with a regal wave of his hand, and the red-and-purple banners designated to me are hoisted.

I watch them rise, and in moments, odds are posted.

It is very, very clear that Soro does not expect me to win.

Maeve wrings her hands. She did everything in her power to keep me out of this very arena. And yet, here I am.

With a motion of Soro's chin, a full woodwind orchestra takes over. Its music drenches the arena, the notes of a melody I know from my youth vibrating against the stone walls.

"My people!" Soro projects his voice with that magic the royal box permits, and the arena goes quiet. "Today will be a fine event—one worthy of celebrating your future king and queen!"

Cheers rise again, albeit less enthusiastically.

Soro has inflicted so much fear of retaliation among his people that no one is certain how to respond to him.

"Place your bets here," a young dwarf calls out.

A band of sprites zips up and down the rows. "Ale? Some ale to quench your thirst," they call out in unison.

It's some time before the arena is prepared. The betting takes place as musicians play and performers dance around the periphery of the stands.

And then, the drums toll the onset of my match.

Boom, boom, boom...

I take everything in as I stride toward the center in time with the drums. There's something different about the arena today, something less obvious than the circle of crates fanning out from its middle. I can't put my finger on it, but the dynamics are off somehow.

Everyone is on their feet as the music switches to a faster tempo. The closer I am to reaching the center, the more the already hyped-up audience loses their collective shit. Some grab at one another and point in my direction. Even more shove each other aside for a better look. Royals dripping with jewels motion hurriedly to place more coin.

"Bloodguard! *Bloodguard!*" they chant.

A red-painted circle takes up a large part of the arena's center. Eight large wooden boxes have been placed at equal intervals within it. The crates are all closed, solid, and large enough to fit four Luthers comfortably. Three large padlocks line one side of each to secure the contents. Some boxes rattle and shake. Others with more vocal occupants hiss or snarl or claw at the wood. One is shredded from the inside on multiple sides. Whatever is in there wants out. And soon.

I stride confidently into the red circle, knowing this match won't begin until I stand where the sicko gamemaster intended. The nearest crate teeters back and forth with growing vigor, each tip preceded by a harsh strike. From within, a crazed laugh bursts forth, making every hair on the back of my neck stand on end.

My eyes widen. No. Not *that*.

The disturbing, high-pitched laugh echoes again as the walls are struck from within. With the next blow, the crate almost topples over.

Only one animal makes that sound, and it's one animal I never wanted to see again.

Inside that box is a vampire colt. Sickly gray and somehow beautiful, their white manes hang over fire-red eyes. Their thin, sharp tails can kill with one deliberate whip. If you're unlucky enough to encounter one, you're lucky as hell if it's the tail that kills you.

Bony protrusions poke out from either side of their necks. Designed to protect the colt's jugular vein and carotid artery, they are two features among many that make them hard to kill.

Immense despite their name, carnivorous unlike their cousin the moon horse, and armed with short spikes that project and retract from each hoof at will, these are among Old Erth's greatest nightmares.

These creatures don't eat their prey. They mutilate it. They hunt larger animals, and they win. And instead of killing what they catch, they use the spikes on their hooves to shred the body alive.

As their prey squirts hot blood, they slurp with their long tongues until the body is dried.

Their victims die crying, begging, or screaming—usually a combination of all three—maniacal laughter the last sound they hear. Well, maybe it's wrong to say that. In all fairness, they're not really laughing. That's just their deeply disturbing whinny.

Most are female. Males only appear to mate and are devoured by the females the moment they dismount.

Damn it, why can't I face cave boas or wraithions? Even giant leeches would be preferable to *this*.

It's best not to focus on that, so I don't, my attention falling to the ground. That's when it hits me. It's the arena floor that's different.

That sickly brown color from years of blood soaking through the sand is gone. But more than that, the sand lies and feels different, too. It's groomed flat with a pattern to it, starting from the crates and radiating inward toward the center of the circle.

The ground feels deeper than before, my feet sinking slightly with every step. What else? My attention drops to the grooves in the sand, searching for anything I can use to my advantage. The harsh sunlight makes it difficult to see, but what I do make out is significant.

Between the crates, thick lines stretch to the perimeter of the circle. They're hiding something down there to use against me. It's why they needed more sand.

I look up to Maeve in the stands and flash her a wink. I don't want her scared, even though I can see the fear in her taught features from here.

But fear aside, if I win, I'm going to bring this whole establishment down.

I came here of my own free will. There will be no help today. No collusion with Maeve ahead of time to assist me. No hints or warnings. Today, I'll rise or fall by my own merit, and the thought strengthens me.

I cannot fail. I must win.

For myself.

For Maeve.

For Arrow.

I think of the gladiators in the barracks, the poor people in parts of this city who suffer because of Soro and the abusive royals who serve him.

It's time for change.

And that change begins with me.

A smile as slick as poison cuts across Soro's face as the music changes tempo. The lord behind him — Ugeen, I think — is dressed head-to-toe in pink, his bald head providing the finishing touch on his dick costume. He clears his throat and takes over speech duty. Soro leans forward in his seat as if he can't wait to see what happens next.

The underling begins, his voice as loud as Soro's, puffed-up chest suggesting a twisted sense of pride in his role in today's proceedings. "The Bloodguard match today is unlike anything Old Erth has ever seen.

Created specifically for this ultimate battle and engineered by the *best* in the land, this is a test of power, agility, and wit." He smiles and puffs himself up even further, feigning importance beyond his station. "In each crate, a different opponent awaits. Will the gladiator win or fall?"

"Fall!" the crowd in the Noble Ring shouts. They cheer as if I'm not standing right here. To them, I'm merely an insect to dispose of, incapable of escaping a spider's web. But the spider is just another pest—like Soro—that I'm more than capable of squashing.

The lord shifts his weight. The crowd ceases their chatter, permitting him to speak. "The entirety of this match will take place within the red ring at the center of our arena. Once the match begins, the gladiator will not survive any attempts to leave it. He will circle the inner perimeter, moving to the speed of the music."

This really is a sick fucking game to them.

The sunbeams stretching across the light-blue sky have intensified, heating the sand at my feet. Sweat dribbles down Ugeen's forehead. "When the music stops, the gladiator must also stop. Whichever crate he stands before is the one he's to open and face the contents of. The gladiator may not stop in front of a previously opened crate or an empty space. It's only during combat that the gladiator has free rein in the circle and the musical requirement does not apply. Some will be easy kills..." He clears his throat. "Others will not. The decision falls to the gladiator. Choose life as a victor or death in disgrace."

Stop in front of crate, open crate, kill contents of crate. Not too complicated.

Soro grins like a spoiled child, as if the contents of these crates were a gift to him personally.

"Should the music stop while the gladiator remains between crates, he'll die a miserable death and maggots will feast on his flesh."

What the hell is this shit?

"You may fell your enemies in whichever order you desire"—Ugeen glares down at me now—"and as befits the generosity of our revered kingdom, the gladiator may choose whether or not to engage the opponent or opponents within his final crate."

So, if I play this right, I won't have to fight the vampire colt. I don't know what else is in each of those crates, though. There could be something more dangerous—unlikely but possible.

This small mercy is far too suspicious for comfort, but I'll have to take that chance. Gladiator or not, I can't kill a vampire colt alone.

Ugeen lowers the scroll, his dick tip of a head now drenched with sweat. He wipes his brow with his sleeve and continues. "To exemplify the genius of our cherished engineers and to test the gladiator's endurance, spinning saws will break through the sand at random." He sniffs. "As always, best of luck to our gladiator."

Spinning saws will break through at random?

Anger burns a hole through my chest. This isn't a match.

It's a death sentence.

CHAPTER

64

LEITH

I'm not given a moment to breathe before the arena erupts, demanding carnage.

I don't know what I'm facing except the vampire colt. I can't even be sure I'll survive long enough to worry about it. If that stupid music stops and I don't land in front of a crate, it's over.

My mind wanders to Maeve. In the time we've spent alone, I've memorized her face, the way her eyes sparkle when she's up to no good and her sweet smile when she is.

I can avenge my family today, but that is not my primary focus.

Today, I fight for Maeve. For us. For the future she gave me faith to believe in.

I crack my neck from side to side and walk to the perimeter of the circle to examine the weapons scattered in the sand. They weren't here when I studied the arena earlier, no doubt placed—perhaps by the use of magic—during the reading of the rules.

A close-range weapon is the smartest choice. I find a dagger and slip it into my belt. No matter the situation, I can always use a dagger. I bypass a rusted helmet and a breastplate that would almost certainly take the rest of my prep time to put on. I almost walk past a partially buried sword, not wanting to waste the precious seconds it would take to dig up, but something stops me. The bit of crossguard sticking out from the sand appears old and dusty, but when I eventually wrench it free of the ground, I discover a pristine weapon, shining like a star beneath the sun.

A gasp spreads through the crowd as I raise it. Sunlight glints off the massive ruby secured to the hilt, and the crowd goes *fucking wild*. I can barely hear my own thoughts over the cacophony of screams let loose by the good people of Arrow.

I recognize the ostentatious weapon from a portrait back at the manor. This is Maeve's grandfather's sword—that of the original king—but how? She had no idea I would battle today.

I glance up to find her standing, eyes wide, hands over her mouth, looking as surprised as I am.

Sometimes confidences must be broken to protect those we love.

Two boxes over, Caelen, grinning, salutes me as Giselle bounces up and down waving vigorously at her sister. That answers that.

I have friends who care about me. My eyes sting when I look to where Maeve continues to stand—to where Soro glances from her to me. She's smiling, but I think she's crying, too. And if I didn't know I fucking loved her before, I sure as hell would know now.

She wants me to live. And dammit, for her, I will.

I find the sheath that goes with the sword and secure both to my waist. I take another look at the scattered weapons and the crates. This sword is magnificent. But no way am I going to use it to cut through the crates or those damn locks.

I hurry around the ring, well aware I'm running out of time.

It's not until I come across a familiar battle axe that I'm sure it was smart to wait. I lift it, wondering how I know this weapon. When I glance back at Maeve and see Soro gesturing wildly as he screams at her, his ever-present ogren generals conspicuously absent, I realize who this axe belongs to. My gaze flitters to Caelen and Giselle, who are looking damn well smug.

The horn blasts. I'm out of time.

The orchestra begins to play.

At first, the melody follows a standard rhythm that I can steadily jog to without much effort. Without warning, the tempo picks up. I'm not quite to the next crate when the music abruptly stops.

The audience screams.

The only thing that saves me is the force of my jump. I leap as rows of iron spears shoot upward from the space between the crates. The eruption is fierce, and I'm plowed with a blinding spray of sand.

As my vision clears, the spears retract, vanishing as if they'd never existed.

The degree of danger hits me hard.

Impaled. I was almost *impaled*.

I rise carefully and lift my discarded axe from the ground. I've reached the first crate. I press my ear against the door.

Nothing. Only silence. As I strategize, what sounds like an angry swarm of hornets buzzes from the ground.

Having been stunned into immobility by the spears, I expect actual hornets. I forgot about the creative efforts the engineers undertook developing this torture chamber, and it almost costs me.

More out of instinct than skill, I skid out of the way of a spinning saw. The blade doubles back. It doesn't traverse back and forth, side to side, or even zigzag. It doesn't follow any pattern I can memorize. Instead, it travels as unpredictably as a fish in a large lake.

The diameter of the blade is about the same as a supper plate and the thickness comparable to a thin sheet of ice. It can tear up my feet and calves with ease. And if I fall, it will finish me off.

A second saw blade appears as the first continues on. I avoid it and the other when it returns. And as quickly as they appeared, they disappear beneath the sand.

The audience cheers, either for me, the saws, or the contents of the crate. It doesn't matter. They all suck.

My need to survive heightens my reflexes. Fueled by rage, I lift the axe and bring its butt down in a straight line.

One.

Two.

Three locks break open from my single strike.

I kick open the door and sidestep left to avoid anything that might charge.

The time it takes me to break the locks and move aside is a matter of seconds. So is what happens next.

With the taste for war burning deep within me and my weapon in the air, I release a battle cry and prepare to attack, but I never get the chance to swing. The moment I see my opponent, I know I'm done for.

Wrapped in chains and wearing nothing but a burlap sack is Pega. Blood oozes from two large gashes on her head, staining her wild yellow hair orange.

Those bastards.

Those *ruthless*, conniving bastards.

To become Bloodguard, they expect me to kill another gladiator.

A new kind of wrath envelops me, tightening my throat.

I don't think things through. In fact, I do everything a gladiator who wants to be Bloodguard shouldn't do.

Instead of taking my opponent's life, I offer it back. I tug at her chains—they're knotted. Pega should have been able to get free, but her eyes open and close when they see me. "What did they do to you?" I ask.

"Drug," she slurs. The injured side of her face is droopier, and she's drooling. "Druuuug," she says again, dragging out the word.

I undo the chains and slap her. When she doesn't wake up, I slap her again. She startles this time and slaps the ever-loving shit out of me.

I fall backward and laugh. "Good girl," I tell her. "Now, time to go."

I glance behind me when that buzzing sound returns. The saws are back. "I'll keep you safe," I say. "You just need to keep moving. Understand?"

Pega nods slowly. I help her to stand, and that's when I realize she's holding on to her broken arm. "Shit," I say.

"They wanted to get back at me for having nice things." She mumbles something else, but I don't catch it.

"It's all right," I say. "Let's get out of here so you can have all the nice things you deserve."

The buzzing vanishes. That doesn't mean we're safe. The rattles increase in the next crate, and the one I already passed rumbles with an escalating chorus of growls.

"Now or never," I say.

She nods but is having a hard time staying focused. I all but drag her with me. The moment we step out of the crate, the music resumes. "If the music stops, you stop. Understand?"

Outcries from the crowd erupt all around us.

Pega's eyes dart back and forth, and she sways. "Yeah," she mumbles.

The music slows, and I have to hold her back when she starts to move faster. "Follow the rhythm, Pega," I tell her. "If it's fast, you go fast. If it slows, you do as well. Whatever you do, don't leave the circle."

I haul her out of the way when the saws puncture through the sand and charge. A third emerges, chasing the others.

How many of these things are there?

I check behind us. For now, it's only these three.

Only? What am I thinking?

With Pega, it's a fight to avoid the saws. Throw in that wretched music, and it's all I can do to keep a level head.

Pega, as doped up as she is, does her best and permits me to lead. As the saws disappear, the music picks up. We bolt, her hand clutched tightly in mine.

If I can save her, I will. But to do so, I first need to save myself.

We race at high speed to match the orchestra as the crowd screams and cheers.

When the music slows, so do we, and Pega gasps for air. Whatever they gave her makes her barely fit to walk, much less run—yet she does her damnedest.

I speak as quickly as I can. "There's something waiting in each crate. If you're not with me, I can't be sure it won't go after you." Still walking with Pega in time to the music, I glance up. "Can you climb the crates?" I ask.

She doesn't hesitate. "Yeah."

The tempo picks up again. We're short on time.

"Can you leap from one to the other?" I ask.

She looks up at a crate as we pass, checking out the distance. "Yeah."

I'm not so sure, but I keep that tidbit to myself.

"All right, Pega, listen," I say. "The moment we stop in front of the next crate, climb it. Don't wait for me to open it. When whatever resides emerges, leap to the next one."

"There could be anything in there," she mumbles.

"I know," I agree.

Her words are getting easier to understand. After years as a seasoned gladiator, her metabolism seems to be burning through whatever they drugged her with fairly quickly. At least that's my hope.

The music slows, taking up the familiar, slow melody that began my match. "The only way to win is to kill everything that attacks me until only one crate remains."

I steal a glance in time to see her pupils dilate in and out. "I'll make it if I'm on that last crate?" she asks.

"I don't know, Pega," I admit, trying to go over Ugeen's rules in my head. I'm not confident in my assessment. "But that's all we've got, and we have to try."

Something that resembles hope fills her expression. "I trust you, Leith," she says clearly.

I nod. Yeah. It's all come down to trust.

"Ignore the music once you're up there and stay low," I instruct. "Only move if there's no other choice."

The music stops. Again, I narrowly miss being impaled, taking Pega with me. I pull her to her feet in less time than it takes the spears to withdraw.

"Climb, now," I order.

I take in our surroundings. We passed Pega's crate at least three times—no doubt an effort to tire us out. We are immediately to the right of it now, the vampire colt on its other side.

My plan isn't perfect. I'm not sure we'll make it. Still, Pega has hope, I have hope, and sometimes, that's enough.

Pega reaches the top of the crate, and I'm readying myself to break the next set of locks when a streak of fire blazes in my peripheral vision and the crate Pega was in explodes.

We're thrown so roughly and unexpectedly that my ogren axe flies from my hand. I land in a roll to protect my body, the hilt of the king's sword striking me in the ribs. When I realize how far I rolled toward the edge of the red circle, I scramble away. The sand I kick in my haste strikes the red line, and a wall of fire erupts, the heat as unbearable as if I were tossed into the inferno myself. Well, that answers what happens if someone steps out of the circle.

The blast angers the beasts inside the crates. They roar, howl, and claw, except for the colt. She slams her hooves against the wood, neighing in that freakish way.

The noise rattles my senses. Has the melody resumed, or is the orchestra waiting to start? I stumble to where Pega lies on the sand just in front of the crate she was blown off of. Her face is deathly pale and her broken arm twisted in the wrong direction.

I press my back against the unopened crate and look toward where Soro waits. He leans one foot along the stone edge, and the other is planted on the floor of the royal box. His hands carry a bow, the servant beside him ready to light another flaming arrow at his command. His face is lit up in sheer childlike delight. He set fire to Pega's crate.

Two guards are holding Maeve by the arms as Ugeen watches her. She curses and kicks and fights her way to Soro only to be hauled back to her seat. As it is, the flames are eating away at the crate and its surrounding space.

I ball my hands into fists so hard my knuckles crack. I glare at the door to my next adventure.

Slowly and deliberately, I turn my head in Pega's direction. "Climb," I say. "Now."

My voice is no longer patient. It's cold, it's lethal, and it belongs to a man who needs to get shit done.

Pega attempts to scramble up with one arm, but she doesn't get far.

I boost her up by her heel. I'm so frantic, I practically throw her to the top, muscular dwarf or not.

The colt shrieks out another whinny while long claws protrude through a damaged crate across the circle from me. At this pace, they won't need me to break them free.

I need to keep going.

I don't know what's going to emerge from this crate in front of me. Whatever it is, it's hissing. It will either crawl or slither out, then immediately target my throat.

Let it. I didn't come this far to cower.

CHAPTER
65

LEITH

I jump up and latch onto the top of the crate. Using the heel of my boot, I kick down and strike one of the locks.

Again and again I come down on it hard until my ankle threatens to break.

I'm almost forced to use the sword. Almost.

But my next attempt does it. I bust the latch free and break open the corner of the door.

That's all it takes for a sea serpent to shoot through the opening and attack. It's young, probably four feet long and a quarter as wide. I doubt it's ever fought a human before.

I punch the thing so hard in the head, its fangs clatter.

The skull is rock hard, and my fist throbs. In the time since Maeve began treating me, my left hand has recovered enough to mostly make a fist, so I punch it with that one, too.

My knuckles on both hands hurt now, and my sore heel throbs under my weight. Guess what? I'm not the only one hurting. The serpent bobs its head from side to side, the rest of its long, yellow body motionless. It's stunned and partially blinded by my first blow. It won't take long to recover, so I don't waste any time.

I dive toward the axe and fall into a roll, clutching the handle to my body. The momentum gives me extra speed, and I come up swinging, slicing off the head of the next serpent that escapes the crate.

The familiar buzz of saws tugs my lips into a smile. I edge backward and toward the sound, allowing my ears to guide me. The buzzing escalates, as does the shrieking crowd. Maeve screams, trying to warn me. But she more than anyone knows how well I move my body.

Another serpent slides out, its long, heavy body creating deep grooves in the sand. This one is older and smarter, maybe six feet in length. It avoids every swing I take.

Except it's new to the arena.

I'm not.

As it rushes me, I slide to the side and toward the crate. It doubles back, hissing, enraged, and unaware of what's coming.

The first saw slices off the serpent's tail. It wails and slithers diagonally, trying to avoid the two that follow. And failing miserably. The saws crisscross, chopping through its slick, leathery skin. As it lunges in a last effort to survive, I swing the butt of my axe up and into its jaw. It falls into what are now four spinning blades.

Blood sprays my face.

And I like it.

I wipe it away and crouch lower to the ground. The first, smaller serpent comes to its senses. Still partially blind, it strikes and misses, slamming into the battered door. One swing is all it takes to send its head flying.

A fourth serpent glides out between splintered planks, its mass and weight shattering what's left of the door. This one is an experienced hunter, huge and fast. It easily avoids my blade and coils around me, causing me to drop the axe.

I expand my limbs, trying to create space for myself as it constricts, but my strength is no match for it. I use my weight to pitch left and right, but it's useless. I can't break free.

The serpent squeezes harder and buckles my frame hard enough to break one of my ribs.

I suck in shallow breaths and force myself to keep fighting. The saws that finished off the other serpent are headed my way.

This one must have missed the show. It whips me back and around, squeezing tighter.

My eyes fly open as the serpent drops closer to the charging blades. With all my strength, I arch my back, attempting to throw us the other way.

Except the serpent won't surrender its hold.

It fights against my weight, rolling us back and onto the spinning blades. We fall sideways onto all four saws as they cross. One of them slices through the creature and into my left arm. It stings like hell, but I can still flex the muscle, so hopefully the damage isn't too bad.

The serpent worked against itself. As the blades sliced through its flesh, its dense muscles and bones shielded me.

Its hold loosens, and I push through the corpse, shoving the heavy coils away.

Still acutely focused on the location of the buzzing sound, I avoid the blades multiple times.

I skid along, grabbing my axe the moment I spot it.

I'm out of breath and holding my side to quell the shooting pain in my ribs. When the fifth and final serpent attacks, my sliced arm is practically useless. I swing the blade, and it cuts into the beast's throat but doesn't clear it.

No matter. It's enough to weaken it. I hold out my arms and snag it, my left arm around its neck and the other grasping its thick body, preventing the serpent from coiling around me. As the next set of blades arrives, I pitch it right on top of them.

I fix my glare on the royal box, axe draped over my shoulder as I stalk to the beat of the music. Maeve is no longer trying to lunge at Soro. She's pacing.

Pega leaps onto the next crate with more difficulty than I wish. The way she cradles her broken arm against her chest throws off her balance. I nod my encouragement. Right now, she's on her own.

The melody ends at the next crate. I almost forget to stop. This was easy. Too easy. I don't waste time worrying about it. As with the first crate, I break down the locks with one strike of the axe.

I whirl to the side when I kick the door open. Nothing happens. Like with Pega's crate, all is quiet. I sneak a glimpse, and that's all I need.

Luther... Fuck me. Whatever mental game they're playing, it isn't going to work.

Like Pega, he was drugged. But unlike Pega, he's already halfway through unwrapping his chains. I enter slowly as he makes it to a standing position. He hobbles forward, leaning heavily on his diminished left leg.

I'm covered in a mix of blood and sand. All in all, I resemble a swamp creature parents warn their children against feeding. "Hey, Luther," I say.

He smiles. "What the plan?"

"You're going to the top of the crate. Pega will explain the rest."

"Pega?" At my nod, he narrows his brown eyes. "Bastards."

"Yeah," I agree. "Ready?" I ask, not really asking. Ugeen called them a test of endurance, so I'll wonder if the longer I spend in one place, the more likely those blades are to "randomly" appear underfoot. I'm not eager to test it.

He shuffles forward. It takes Luther stepping on my shrieking back and Pega pulling him up, but he makes it to the top, half drugged and glistening in the sun. That's my buddy, Luther. The crate creaks, and I'm not sure it'll support his weight.

But then the music resumes and it's not my problem anymore. It's fast this time, forcing me to take off in a sprint.

"Tell him, show him," I shout over my shoulder.

I can't be sure they'll stay safe, but I can't help them if they're not.

I run at full speed to match the tempo, and as I pass the crate where I found Luther, it explodes. The blast propels me at an angle, and I land in a roll, hanging tight to my axe and sword.

The music keeps going, and so do I.

I circle the perimeter twice more before the music abruptly ends. I slide, digging my battered heel and my axe into the sand to stop. The front of my boot barely grazes the space between the crates.

The spears shoot up as if on springs, and I'm showered with sand.

"*Damn!*" Luther shouts a few crates behind me. That's the quickest that giant has *ever* spoken.

If not for that shrill laugh of the vampire colt, I wouldn't move right away.

Aside from the anxious whispering, the arena is quiet as I prowl forward.

Luther and Pega peer over from a crate three down from mine. They know what it is. It's why they're hiding.

Pega curses.

Luther does little more than shake his head.

Just another few feet and I'm at the crate door.

Again, the colt laughs. Again, she kicks. She's ready to eat.

I'm ready to feed her—just not what she expects.

I charge, the last few yards between us vanishing beneath my feet. With a roar, I bring down my axe.

On the last two locks.

The colt rams the door. Bitch doesn't realize she has to kick herself free the rest of the way.

I edge away from the door in the direction I came from.

I watch.

I wait.

I buy some time.

It's not much.

It's just enough.

The rules state I'm supposed to open the crate. Nothing says I have to open it all the way.

The colt uses her back legs to kick, exactly as I thought.

She breaks through, stumbling backward and facing away from me. I don't wait for her to gather her wits. She's out. That means I can run anywhere within the circle.

I crash my axe down on the locks of the next crate, which is home to some bellowing, snuffling beast, and circle behind it. Ugeen said I had to open the crate in front of me but never that I couldn't open others. That eerie laugh grows shriller and closer. She's tickled pink and coming for me.

But the troll bear I just released is coming for *her*.

He's a big boy. A strong boy. The kind of boy that's more than capable of breaking the rest of the crate door. The door slams into the colt just as she spots me. She may be a killer, but so is the troll bear. He shuts her down, jumping on the remains of the door and pinning her to the sand.

The colt hisses. Yes, *hisses*. Her long tongue shoots out to ensnare the bear's throat. The bear must have had a relative killed by a vampire colt, because he reacts instantly, slicing her tongue with sharp claws.

She doesn't appreciate that, and for all his brawn, the bear lacks serious brains. He smacks at her, disregarding the deadly points protruding from her neck.

My rescue bear ends up stabbing himself through the paw. Twice.

That familiar buzzing sound zings through the sand. It's time to move.

I don't wait to see what happens next.

I take off with my buddy the axe and my best friend the sword. I don't care who wins between the monsters behind me. Either way, the victor will be famished once their fight is done. It's up to me to provide the meal. I bypass the clawed and splintered crate. I won't waste my time breaking something open that can break free on its own.

It's my mistake.

And I pay for it.

I pick the next crate, busting down the hinges secured by the padlocks. Then I press my back against the side wall, waiting for something with fangs to skitter out.

My shoulders droop. It's quiet. Just as it was when I found Pega and Luther. The door creaks open when I push it with my axe. I don't have to see the face of the person cowering in the corner to know who it is.

The scars covering his head are telling enough.

CHAPTER

66

MAEVE

"Ugeen. Take the queen back to the castle," Soro says.

Soro doesn't like me cheering for Leith, but I can't help it. Just as I can't help my response. "Fuck off, Soro," I snap. No way am I leaving Leith.

I cry out in pain when Soro snatches my wrist. "I wasn't asking."

"Did you not hear me? I won't go anywhere—"

His next squeeze breaks the bones in my wrist and brings me to my knees.

"Take her," Soro orders.

I go back on my promise not to slap the unholy hell out of Ugeen. He falls on his ass, since that's all this knob knows how to do. I reel on Soro, knowing everyone in the royal boxes is watching and can hear me. I straighten my shoulders and speak clearly for our audience. "You are unworthy to lead Arrow, just like your father before you. You threw in those gladiators—those friends of Leith, who have stood by him—on purpose. You must have known he would fight today."

"I knew he would hear about the fate of his...*friends* at the hand of another gladiator during today's battle," he says under his breath with a sneer. "But I never imagined he would enter the arena of his own free will."

I point an accusing finger at him. "What kind of man—no, what kind of *king* relies on devious mental games and trickery mere hours before he's to sit on the throne?" I inch closer and drop my hands to my sides like a disappointed mother whose brat son went too far. "How can I ever trust you? How can our entire *kingdom* trust you?"

Around us, murmurs rise, and I'm emboldened. "What did you hope to accomplish with your cruelty? Did you want to win the pot? Was this all about money, just as it was when Vitor called the shots?"

The grumbles in the royal stands grow, the discord loud enough that I will have to shout to be heard. The arena isn't about making money for Soro, but money is what this group of dunces cares most about, so I continue with the lie, hoping to rile them further. "You always wanted all the gold in all of Arrow."

Soro may have doubted my involvement before, but he recognizes the game I'm playing now. And boy oh boy am I playing it well.

His gaze slams into mine as he stares me down. "You killed Aisling," he says. More gasping from onlookers, this time directed at me. "You killed General Tut," he adds.

I frown. It's easy—I'm enraged. "Oh?" I say.

His hot, ragged breaths strike my face.

I smile sweetly. "Prove it."

He points toward Leith. "That axe. That sword!"

Soro edges back as I straighten to full height. "What about them?" I ask. "I can see that it resembles Tut's axe. But he's an ogren general." I purposely use the present tense to imply that murderous oaf may still be alive. "Are you saying your queen is stronger than your generals?" And by implication, stronger than him? Soro blinks several times. "Are you claiming I can bring down such a warrior single-handedly?" It's hard not to smile as the royals in the box with us react in agreement. "And what of the Good King Masone's sword? How would I possess such a weapon? Where would I find it, when it's been hidden for years?"

What's Soro going to say? I'm stronger than he wants anyone to know and I found the sword hidden in the secret catacombs where he keeps the damn phoenix?

As if I'm not daring him to kill me, I tug on the sleeves of my gown and settle back into my seat, eyeing him as my heart continues to pound at record speed. I insolently cross my arms as I take in Soro's scathing expression.

Stars above, please let Leith survive this, even if I don't.

CHAPTER
67

LEITH

Gunther peeks over his shoulder, his eyes red and swollen from crying. He breaks down when I step inside the crate. He hobbles forward, dragging his injured foot, and I catch him in a one-armed embrace.

His frail body is mere bones around a broken soul. He hugs me harder. "Bluh guar. Bluh guar, blood guar," he says, crying so hard he can barely speak the words.

"Not yet," I say.

I ignore the pain his tight hold inflicts on my broken rib and pass a hand over the ridges of the scars on his scalp, flattening the few spiky hairs that survived the years of cruelty dealt upon him.

My eyes squeeze shut. This could have been Dahlia or Rose had I tried to bring them with me. Being girls wouldn't have spared them from the abuse immigrants to Arrow are subjected to. Far from it. Not that living in Grey spared them, either.

Fuck, this world is heartless.

My family didn't make it.

Gunther *must*.

Another crate explodes—*fucking Soro*—and the monsters are on the move.

Sand shoots past us as the ferocious colt races by. The explosion adds to the crowd's unrelenting excitement. I can't hear much inside this crate, and the noise outside makes it impossible to figure out exactly what's happening.

Thunderous gallops have me whirling with my axe and sword out. Gunther yelps, clinging to my thigh and almost making me lose my balance. I shove him away, ready to fight.

The colt doubles back and storms by, her gray body and white mane bloody from the deep claw and fang marks the bear made.

Not that he won. Not that I expected him to.

The bear hangs from the colt's left pointed horn. He isn't moving, and his entrails drag along in the sand. Behind them, the saws follow. But that colt is too smart and clears them with ease.

It won't take her long to finish her victory lap and suck down her meal.

Unless she's still in the mood for a hunt. We must get out of this crate before we're shredded by saws or, worse, trapped in here with her.

I grab the boy by the shoulders. "Listen to me, Gunther. You can't hang on to me, understand? I can't protect us if you throw me off balance."

His eyes well with apologetic tears, and I'm reminded that he's just a scared little boy.

He opens his hands and shows me the bent nail he's carrying. "I h-h-help. I-I-I fight."

I soften my tone. "Yes. You fight and you protect the others."

"Others?" he asks.

"Yes," I say. "Exactly."

I yank us back when the colt reverses and trots in the direction of her burning crate. It doesn't surprise me—they're curious creatures, taking in everything that might help or hinder them.

My back is pressed against the wall, and my free arm keeps Gunther beside me. The partially closed door is barely enough to conceal us. I hold my breath as the colt stops in the space between the crate we hide in and the next, allowing me a glimpse of her head and neck.

We remain quiet as she grabs the troll bear's corpse in her sharp teeth and trots away from the flames to eat, giggling loud enough to be heard above the bone-rattling cheers from the audience and the whirling saws in search of flesh to maim. The cut along her long, thick tongue doesn't appear to impede her appetite. The gross thing burrows into the bear's gut and fervently sucks.

With a sigh that does nothing to relieve the stress weighing me down, I return my attention to Gunther. "I want you to follow me, stay quiet, and do *exactly* what I say."

Gunther nods and holds out his small hand to offer me his nail.

"Keep it," I say, maintaining a calm tone, heart aching at the valor of this child who has suffered such cruelty. "You'll need it to help the others, remember, Gunther? They need you to protect them." Again, he nods in that way of his. "You're going to get on top of the crate where our friends are."

"Friends?"

He asks in a way that makes me think he's never had one.

"Yes, friends," I repeat. "Get up on the crate and listen to whatever they say. Fight to stay alive."

"A-a-nd potect dem," he says.

"Yes, Gunther. You protect them."

I hold out a hand to keep him still and edge toward the opening. Using tremendous care, I poke my head out. The colt is a few crates away now with her back to us. From here, I can't judge where Pega and Luther might be. With the crackling of the burning crates, the smoke, and that frenzied crowd demanding I appear, I can't get a fix on anything.

If I go right, I'll interrupt the colt's meal, and she's almost done. The bear's body has shrunk inward and is collapsing into its skeleton.

There's no time to waste. We must move now.

I sheath my sword and motion to Gunther, cringing at the slapping sound he makes as he hobbles across the wooden floor. As he reaches me, I slip onto the sand.

The colt raises her head, her ears twitching. My knuckles ache from my grip on the axe. I don't move. I don't breathe.

The crowd's gasps and eager murmurs work to my advantage. The colt fixates on them, slurping her tongue inward to whinny in that blood curdling way of hers. The crowd eats it up. She's enjoying the attention. As tall as she is, she can see over the wall of fire that continues to burn around us, trapping all of *us* in here with *her*.

Her tail flicks. She's not scared of anything and is probably thinking about how to jump the fire wall and pick her way through the royals.

Okay. Maybe she's not all bad.

I ease away from the crate, motioning Gunther out. My nerves, already on edge, actually sting when Gunther steps onto the sand.

We start backward, and I swallow a curse. Gunther's pace is slow and conspicuous. He's trying to be careful, except the way he bears his weight creates a scratching sound in the sand.

Every drag of his foot kicks up dust and adds to the cacophony of sound.

I'm doubting whether I can get us through this.

That doubt triples when the buzzing sound resumes behind us. I throw Gunther over my shoulder and run in the direction of the saws. There are now six saws—two crisscrossing in the front, three spinning side by side, and one more taking up the rear.

Plus a raging vampire colt in full gallop behind us.

Without much thought, I leap over the zigzagging saws. I time it just right.

If I wasn't carrying Gunther, my balance wouldn't be off. And I could have cleared the next few blades.

But I *do* have Gunther.

My balance *is* compromised.

And I don't clear those last few saws.

I throw Gunther to my right and stumble to the left.

He's safe and rolls away.

The first saw cuts through my boot and slices my instep.

The second scrapes the skin off most of my upper arm.

The third cuts into my shoulder blade when I roll.

Agony blinds me with white-hot pain as my screams are swallowed whole by the crowd.

Gunther cries out, pleading with me to get up.

I murmur in response, telling him to run.

If I can't save him, he must save himself.

At first, he doesn't listen. But then he hobbles away as another terrified voice calls my name.

Maeve.

Maeve remains with me. She tells me to stand, pleads with me to fight, and her sweet voice echoes softly in my head like it did the night she told me she loved me.

But then the saws burst through the sand, and she screams.

Her terror is enough to jolt me to action. I scramble to my feet as the latest of the buzzing sounds pass by me and rebound toward the colt, who kicks and leaps and races to safety.

Of course she doesn't get cut.

Of fucking course.

I fumble ahead, the first few steps I take further punishing my mangled foot. I almost fall when I reach for my discarded axe.

The energy I had when this match first started is long gone. My left shoulder is too weak to help me power through all the locks at once.

Two crates left.

Which can I open to cause the most havoc?

Hell if I know.

If my friends can make it and I can make it along with them, we stand a shot.

I curse myself for not opening that mangled crate earlier. I would have had a better chance of helping Gunther.

Would have. Could have. Should have. These words have plagued me in every arena game. They won't plague me now.

Squaring my shoulders, I position myself in front of the mangled door. "Get to the last crate!" I yell.

I don't know where the others are or if they can even hear me amidst the chaos. More and more crates are up in flames and splintering into shards. Chunks of burning wood litter the sand, shrinking the open space inside the circle.

Last one, I tell myself. This last crate and then that damned colt.

"Leith, she's coming," Pega calls out, coughing from all the smoke. "She knows where you are. *Run*."

CHAPTER

68

LEITH

I run *and* leap, ignoring the agony of my mounting injuries. I break open
the first lock on the splintering crate. The force I must use to break the
next causes me to lose my balance, and I land flat on my face. I spit out
sand, looking up as three sets of long claws drag down the mostly broken
door. They hover over my ass just as the colt rounds the curve.

Really?

The saws shoot up in front of my face. The only thing that saves me
is that they don't immediately rotate. Without meaning to, the engineer's
design affords me time to roll out of range before they engage. The colt
races away, as freaked out by those things as I am.

I scramble upward, taking aim at the bottom lock.

My remaining strength only enables me to bend the lock. I assume
a better position, but before I can act, I'm thrown out of the way when a
giant lizard with three sets of legs slams its heavy body against the door.

I'm tossed toward the fire wall, because why not? I throw out a
hand, catching the corner of the lizard's crate and slowing just enough
to prevent my impending death by fire. As I struggle to rise, the lizard
drags herself out, tasting the air with a black forked tongue, watching the
spinning saws appear and roll past.

What the hell? Am I the only thing left these discs of death want to shred? *Random, my ass.*

I push up on the axe and take in the scene. Talk about the Erth in flames. Fire surrounds the ring, and smoke billows upward, discoloring the clouds. Blades—*sharp* blades—appear from nowhere and come at me from all directions. And bonus, two deadly monsters are eyeing me as their next meal.

The colt races toward me but stops when she notices the lizard. I don't know if she's trying to be cute, but she scratches lightly at the sand with her hoof. And then she charges, laughing maniacally. There's that monstrous, unhinged child I know.

The lizard tilts her head from side to side with curiosity. I'm certain she's done for until, at the very last moment, she shoots forward and takes a chunk out of the colt's side.

Yes!

The shrill whinny makes my ears ring. She whips her head left and right, barely grazing the lizard, whose only concern is taking another bite. And she does, throwing the colt into survival mode.

I leave them to it and search for the others.

"Gunther. Pega. Luther!" I call out. There's one remaining crate. I can only hope they made it there.

My legs barely work, and my vision is blurry, eyes stinging from the terrible flames. Something pokes out of the sand between the first crate that exploded and the other still burning beside it. When it doesn't come at me, I keep moving.

Until I reach the space between where the next pair of crates once stood and realize what it was.

I race back to it, unable to believe my luck.

Between the explosion and the gust of air created by the fires, there's no more camouflaging this large device. I step carefully around the spears. It's easy. They're visible now. As are the springs used to launch them.

I call out again to the others.

No one answers. The only sounds that cut through the roaring fire and the next explosion are pained and hissing moans.

Fuck my life. I've never heard a lizard make any noise. I didn't really think they could. But if I had to imagine what one would sound like dying, it would sound exactly like this.

I turn around. I don't curse this time. To be honest, I think I'm all out. The colt trots toward me with half the lizard's body dangling from one horn and the other half on the other.

That buzzing resumes just ahead.

Well, I've had enough.

The fires continue to burn around me. I'm hot. I'm tired. My body is destroyed, and I'm mad as shit.

This ends now.

Calling up all my remaining adrenaline, I rush in the direction of the final crate, doing my best to avoid the piles of smoldering debris. I can't outrun the colt, and I'm in no condition to leap over the saws.

I take my chances with the blades, swerving left until I'm racing dangerously close to the fire wall. The saws don't reach me, and they sink back into the sand. They have a limit to how far they can travel. Something helpful at last.

They can't get too close to the fire wall.

I can't get close enough.

Sweat sizzles against my skin, and the smoke and fire threaten to cook me alive.

I keep going, screaming through my teeth.

The colt isn't willing to risk her hide. She's plenty willing to risk mine.

She charges me as I run away from the fire wall and head to the spot beside the last crate, jumping over the row of spears and the spring mechanism that launches them.

I leap one last time. The colt gives chase, the weight of the lizard slowing her just enough.

As I come down, I bring my axe down with me, right onto the spring.

Too many things happen at once. The spears shoot from the ground, their recoil stronger with less sand to push through. It's perfect, a sudden shock of noise joining the clamor of slowly grinding metal and the screams of the people who watch us.

An arm's length away, saws bounce against each other, dinging like raindrops on a tin bucket, except much louder. A few blades snap off, spinning through the air. At least two almost cut my head off, but damn if it isn't all worth it.

Look at that.

I guess the saws connect to the same device that controls the spears. It wasn't my intention to destroy the machine. The crowd thinks otherwise. Fine by me. Let them think I'm just that good.

I only meant to skewer the vampire colt.

And I did.

She whinnies that piercing, evil laugh even as spears puncture her immense body. No matter—she rips them out of the ground as she flees. The laugh grows louder and more shrill as she gallops toward me, steps faltering but not fast enough. Her tongue, more leech than anything, slithers out to grab me.

This is a good time to reach for my sword. In one fluid motion, I throw my arm out, slicing off the vampire colt's disturbing tongue. I bend my screaming knees and lurch upward, plunging the tip of King Masone's blade into her skull and out the other side.

I've heard cheers when I've done well in the arena and cheers when I didn't think I'd leave here alive, but I've never heard anything like this.

A new Bloodguard has risen against all odds, and the audience responds in turn.

"Bloodguard!" they chant over and over.

I'm supposed to bow, I guess. I don't. I was never here for them. I was here for my mother, who gave what little she had to her children, even at the expense of her life.

I was here for Rose, who placed her heart into each word she wrote.

And for Dahlia, who told me I was a hero long before I became one.

They're not here. So now *I* must be. For *me*.

And for the one I will love for eternity.

Me and Maeve, we're going to be together, build a family, and take back Arrow.

Pega stumbles to stand atop the crate. "You did it," she slurs.

Hell, yeah, I did.

Pega, Luther, *and* Gunther made it. The two gladiators gape at me, dumbstruck.

Not Gunther. He always believed in me.

"Bloodguard! Bloodguard!" he chants along with the crowd and leaps off the crate, expecting me to catch him. Which, of course, I do.

My friends jump down beside us, Luther lowering Pega to the ground. She holds out her arms, and Gunther wriggles free to throw himself into them. Luther claps me on the back, and I hug him in retaliation.

"It over!" he bellows. "Blood guard! BLOOD! GUARD!"

"BLOODGUARD!" Gunther joins in, jumping and shouting beside a misty-eyed Pega. "BLOOD! GUARD! BLOOD! GUARD! BLOOD! GUARD!"

Holy fucking shit.

It's really over. All the mind games, the pain, the injuries, the starving—the not fucking knowing if when that horn blasted, it would be the last time I'd hear it.

Five horns blast in a row now. Five horns to announce the new Bloodguard. I raise my arms and roar. I did it. I *fucking* did it.

Three swishing sounds in quick succession have me whirling. I move on instinct, adrenaline still coursing through my veins. I knock away one arrow and catch another.

A wave of gasps and screams comes from all sides of the arena. I toss the arrow at my feet and look up to where horror blanches Maeve's face, her hands lifting to cover her mouth and hold back a scream.

Next to them, Soro stands, bow in hand. "You think you won, gladiator?" he says. "You are *dead wrong*."

Dread fills my chest to the point I can't breathe.

Soro shot three arrows.

I only defended against two.

Time is a horrible thing, slowing down so I don't miss a damn detail, like Pega's bright, bloodstained hair fluttering in the wind, and Luther's stricken face...and Gunther's unmoving body.

The arrow I failed to catch punctured straight through his heart.

He was an easy kill. Mostly starved, there was no muscle to shield him—just small, frail bones that never had the opportunity to grow.

He lies quietly, his head against Pega's lap as he stares up at the sky.

She smooths her hand across Gunther's brow, showing him kindness he was for *so long* denied.

I collapse on my knees beside him.

He smiles when he sees me, opening his palm to show me the bent nail, his sole weapon against the monsters.

I cover his hand with mine, willing my strength, *my life* into him.

But I don't have that kind of magic. I'm only human, after all.

Pega openly sobs. "Soro aimed that arrow at me, Leith." She points accusingly at herself. "It was meant for *me*. Gunther stepped in the way."

"I f-f-f-ight," Gunther says. It's then he weeps. "I po-tect."

They are his last words.

Rage fills me and boils over. "Go," I tell them.

Luther starts to speak, but I don't give him the chance. "Go," I growl.

I rise and face Soro, the aspiring king who is so noble and brave that he murdered a child—already battered, already suffering.

I'm mildly aware of the shock making its way around the arena.

Luther carefully cradles Gunther's body in his arms and walks away. Pega follows, weeping. They're quick. Almost as quick as Gunther's slaughter.

I bend, pick up Gunther's nail, and pocket it for safe keeping, like I did with Sullivan's hair. Maybe they can be buried together.

And then I straighten. I wrench my sword from the vampire colt's skull... The sword of the original king. And I set my sights on Soro.

I stalk forward, kicking through the sand. I couldn't save Gunther, I failed Sullivan, and I was far from my sisters as they died scared and alone. But I *will* save my queen.

Soro smiles. "Come now, gladiator. It was only a game."

"I'm a *fucking* Bloodguard!" I fire back. "And you, you *cocksucking coward*, just murdered a child!"

There's a collective murmur in the crowd. Some boo him—even the surrounding royals. I don't care about them. Soro has my full attention.

"He was small and defenseless," I bite out through my teeth. "His name was Gunther, and he was my friend!"

Soro tosses his bow and arrow aside. "And what if he was?" he hisses, knowing he's losing part of his loyal audience. "I will be your king!"

"No, you won't," I growl. "I challenge you, Soro, for Maeve of Iamond's hand."

The audience isn't murmuring anymore. They're screaming.

I pay them no mind. "I challenge you for that little boy's senseless death, for Sullivan, and for every gladiator you've forced to fight in this wretched arena. I. Challenge. *You*, Soro, to a fight to the death."

CHAPTER

69

LEITH

Soro and his cohorts exchange a round of stunned glances.

"What's wrong?" I call out. "If you're not brave enough to accept a challenge, you'll never be brave enough to be king."

The murmurs of the audience questioning Soro's leadership are nothing compared to the excitement that builds.

"Bloodguard! *Bloodguard!*"

Soro raises his chin, takes in every section of the arena cheering for me, not him, and curses through his clenched teeth.

If I win, it's over for him, and he knows it. But if Soro wins, it's over for everything good in Arrow.

"Very well," Soro says, his tone flirting with boredom. "If this is what you want." He holds out his hand, where a servant is quick to place his sword.

As if he has all day, Soro makes his way down the arena level, but he doesn't climb the retaining wall to enter.

I wait, eager to unleash the ass-beating that's long overdue.

Soro takes the stance of a soldier prepared to fight. The wind is strong enough to flutter his ridiculous sparkly braid, and that evil grin gleams against his skin.

I relax my stance. My sword out.

He shouts to that snake Ugeen, who scrambles to his side. Soro mutters something. Ugeen nods in my direction, not that dick-suit bothers to engage me directly.

From one hell-bent breath to the next, Soro leaps into the arena, rage reddening his face. Resolute to prove he's the better man.

I think I'm ready for his speed, but I'm wrong.

I don't think I'm that hurt, but I am.

Something swipes me across the face and knocks me to the ground. I roll to the side, barely avoiding Soro's sword as it comes down.

As I start to rise, I'm kicked in the head.

Another kick belts me in the gut, spinning me away from the royal box.

I land with a grunt, the side of my face scraping against the sand.

My body demands I don't move, begs me to rest.

It's my own stubborn will that allows me to force myself to my feet.

The blur coming at me is impossible to track. I pivot and slice my sword up and down in quick motions that do absolutely nothing but cut through empty air and make Soro laugh.

He's no wimp. He is a fighter like me, but he's healthy and using his elven speed to his advantage.

Something hard nails me in the gut and sends me whirling and crashing to the ground once more. I try to spit out sand, but I can barely do more than keep breathing.

Except then Maeve cries out in pain, and everything that hurts me turns to nothing.

This is the woman I love.

My pain will *never* best hers.

I lie still, pretending to be more injured than I already am. It's not hard. I've had a hell of a day.

Soro kicks my leg.

My stomach.

My chest.

And a second rib snaps.

The pain in my ribs is overpowered by the stinging cuts that crisscross my palms when I push my hand into the sand intermixed with salt.

Soro is still here. He's not far. He's behind me somewhere, gearing up for that next blow.

I rise slowly, purposely leaving my back vulnerable. Surrendering myself completely to instinct and intuition, I react to something I sense rather than something I see or hear.

I spin on my heel, the butt of my sword coming down in an arc and slamming into Soro's sternum. His spine bows, and he falls. I flip my sword, hovering over him as the point of my blade pierces the flesh above his heart.

My breaths come in quick bursts full of pain and rage.

"Go ahead," he dares me. "Do it. But if I go, she goes with me. No way in fuck will I ever allow someone like you to take my crown."

My eyes dart to the royal box. Ugeen has my Maeve by the hair, her neck exposed and a dagger pressed to her throat.

I fall to my bloodied knees.

No.

Not her.

Every ache in my body, all the pain from my injuries—they don't hold a candle to the deep chasm breaking open inside my chest. There is no choice here. I told myself I'd die for her, and I will, without hesitation.

She shakes her head to stop me, her eyes ramming closed when the tip of the dagger cuts a shallow line along her throat. Drops of blood well, staining her snow-white dress.

Soro is already on his feet, sword raised. I toss the king's sword to the side. "Do it," I say. "Just spare the woman I love."

Maeve locks eyes with me. "Leith," she says.

"No," I say. "No life is worth living without you."

There are calls for action from the spectators, some demanding I fight, some begging for Maeve's release. But then the air shifts between me and Maeve, and suddenly we're back behind the cottage on that day we first sparred. "I'm sorry, Leith," she says, just like she did that day. "I'm not like you. I can't make them bleed. I can't make them pay."

Yes. She can. And with those words, I know she will.

Soro brings down his sword, aiming for my throat—knowing I'll kill him if he doesn't finish me first—as Maeve slams her head back to break Ugeen's nose.

I throw myself backward and roll away.

Soro misses me by inches.

I leap, tossing my sword into my left hand and taking one long swing.

There are images that are etched in our brains forever—my mother's somber features when she told me goodbye, Rose's silent tears as she held tight to Dahlia, who begged me not to leave her behind, Sullivan's face when he knew his time had come, and Gunther as he clutched that bent nail in his small hand.

This is one of those moments and the first for which I am grateful.

Maeve launches herself into the arena as a swarm of guards tackles Ugeen.

Her feet stomp into the sand, releasing puffs of dust into the air as Soro's decapitated head rolls past her.

Soro's problem is that he learned to torment and humiliate in a fight.

Three years in the arena taught me to dominate, to anticipate everything and to respond to the impossible.

It's what secures me my final win.

The thunderous applause and cheers I received in the past pale compared to the cacophony now threatening to tear the arena apart.

"Bloodguard. *BLOODGUARD!*"

I pay them no mind. They're not important. All that matters is the woman throwing herself into my arms, begging me to never leave her and vowing to love me forever.

My vision blurs, and tears, those *fucking* tears I was never supposed to shed, fall for my Maeve.

Those who are scared always cry.

I'm no exception.

EPILOGUE

MAEVE

"It's hotter than a fire bull's ball sack down here," Leith mutters as we make our way down the cramped winding staircase leading to the catacombs.

"Aurora has a way of doing that," I agree.

Leith lights another torch protruding from the wall and glances over his shoulder at me, dark hair sliding along his charcoal tunic, and winks.

I smile. It's our wedding day, and I should be happy. Hours ago, standing before my people and introducing Leith of Grey as their new king, I was. But down here, it's difficult not to think of how far Arrow fell under my grandmother's rule. How far I will have to go to make up for her transgressions.

I brush the dust from his shoulders, encouraging him to keep moving forward.

It's a tradition for grooms to wear their house colors on their wedding days. I offered him the navy and green of my own, but he chose to dress in shades of gray, because "Get it?" Arrow's new king or not, Leith remains humble, true to himself, and every bit the man I love.

Leith pauses when the faint sound of music drifts down from the castle above. Specks of dust spin in time with the crescendo of a delicate melody. Less delicate is the percussion of massive feet upon the ballroom floor.

"Luther and his wife must be dancing," he says, smiling despite our circumstance.

"And his son and all their cousins, from the sounds of it," I respond, feigning levity of my own. "You did a good thing, you know. Making him castle librarian. He seems so happy now."

"He's suited to it," Leith says, resuming our descent. "He's clever and organized."

"And the only one who can reach all the books," I add, laughing.

It's a forced laugh, and he knows it. We spent the last week in meetings with our new high general, Caelen, and his handpicked officers, discussing the state of Arrow and the changes we plan to institute. Discontent is brewing in every realm. Disasters, natural and political, are on the rise. In Aurora's absence, all of Old Erth has begun to die.

"This is the right decision," I say, and Leith nods solemnly.

His eyes, full of love and trust, meet mine, and for a fleeting moment, I wish we were not king and queen—that we were everyday people in a healthy world where we could just be together, the two of us, at leisure to remain in each other's arms as long as we wish.

The torch closest to us flickers as a wave of heat wafts up the stairs, and we continue because we are not everyday people in a healthy world. We are the King and Queen of Arrow.

We round a curve where darkness awaits to swallow us whole. Without releasing my hand, Leith lights the next torch and five more after that.

It seems to take forever to reach the maze of bones, but when Leith pauses, his shoulders square, and the heat climbs from suffocating to torturous, I know we've reached Aurora's realm.

"Shit," he says. "Just…*shit*." He looks across the vast cemetery of bones. When formulating our plans, we discussed the layout and particulars of the catacombs, but hearing about it and experiencing it firsthand are entirely different.

In silence, we walk through the stifling heat for what feels like an eternity until we finally reach the area beneath the arena.

It's lighter down here, though not a single torch has been lit. Instead, a soft glow emanates from behind a pair of massive, golden gates. Dust rises as Leith steps onto the cavern floor, and the hem of my green-and-navy gown scatters even more.

I allow Leith to lead. I can tell he's feeling protective, now more than ever. Perhaps it's because, like me, he senses the souls that will forever haunt this place where their bones lie carelessly discarded. A cruelty even we cannot undo.

We begin to ascend the small hill. The very one I sprinted so long ago to stop Grandmother from killing that poor girl. Only for me to...

"Are you sure you want to do this?" he asks just before we reach the top.

I stop a little too abruptly, then gather my wits and motion to his arm, where the full Bloodguard insignia glows. It's not as bright as when the mage first finished the last stroke of the crown, but just enough to remind him what it means, what extra bit of magic was infused in the ink to link our lives. "Are you sure you want to do *this*?" I ask, tapping his forearm.

He pulls me to him, the love behind each brush of his lips against mine lifting the dread we've shared since deciding to leave our marriage celebration and descend to this morbid place. At the time, it felt like this couldn't wait a moment longer. Now that I'm here... I'm pretty sure it could've waited till tomorrow.

He pulls away, his soft smile the sunshine I need in this darkness. "You're stuck with me, my qu—" His smile widens to show me his teeth. "No, *my wife*. As long as you live, so shall I."

I choke out a laugh and don't even fight the prickling in my eyes. It's the good kind of tears this time, ones overflowing from a heart that knows Leith will always be mine.

Human lives are so painfully short, whereas we elves are functionally immortal, unless mortally wounded. It's something I chose not to dwell on before, back when I was more concerned about Leith living through the week than the ages. After all, I would rather spend the rest of *my* existence missing him than fail to love Leith for even a moment of his own. It is a pain I was willing to accept for the privilege of having him now.

But the mage who placed his tattoo told me that the Bloodguard insignia could be imbued with something else. A stronger kind of magic.

One borne of love and sacrifice. One that would tie his life to mine. By agreeing to this, illness and the years alone would not kill him, but should he fall, my own existence would end.

I worried he wouldn't agree, that I'd have to fight for the right to be vulnerable for him. But there was no hesitation. Despite his instinct to protect the ones he loves to the point of self-destruction...Leith looked into my eyes and chose *us*. And in that moment, I fell for him all over again. Not only as the gladiator he was but the man, the king, the *husband* he promised to be.

We reach the top of the incline, the gold metal bars of Aurora's cage shimmering from base to tip.

Leith stares hard at Aurora's cage, then nods. "All right. Okay. Let's do this."

We ease our way forward. The mound of ash that makes up Aurora's nest is now unnervingly enormous. As I approach the bars, Leith hooks my arm through his. I think he's worried about me being so close to the cage, though I've seen that she can do plenty of damage—whether by tongue or flame—from inside of it. Eventually he motions for me to go to the left of the golden bars while he moves toward the right. I gasp, choking on the sweltering heat as I shuffle the sand at the base of the gate with my feet. There, just like Papa said, partially buried, is a locking system similar to the one Leith has just uncovered on the opposite side.

Leith and I look at each other. Papa's ability to speak has been improving, but he is still hard to understand sometimes. What we could make out is where the mechanism was, that he'd overheard Grandmother and Vitor talking about it, and that it took two to open it. He didn't know the particulars of how it operates because it has never been opened since Aurora's capture and imprisonment. My attention bounces between both devices. Again, equal in appearance, save that the one on the left is affixed to the bars, and the one on the right to the base.

"It makes sense that it would require two people to open it," Leith says as we meet in the middle so we can keep our voices low and not disturb Aurora. He swipes the sweat beading along his brow with the back of his hand and briefly glances at the bloodied, ashen floor. "It wouldn't be right for one person to hold her captive or free her. The responsibility is too great."

"It is." I squeeze his hand. "Our people have benefitted from holding her at the expense of our neighbors."

"The people of Arrow are strong," he says, brushing my hair over my shoulder. "Resourceful and resilient. We have stores of food to last for a while if things get tough."

I nod. "Even though it might bring temporary hardship to Arrow, freeing the phoenix will restore equilibrium to Old Erth. It is the right choice for my people. Arrow is a just and honorable kingdom. We will get through whatever comes."

His expression is solemn. "I agree. It's the right thing to do."

I don't think my hands have ever felt this heavy letting go of his, nor have my footsteps felt this slow. Still, we make it, each taking position over our designated mechanisms.

The gold wheel is too warm for my liking. I jerk my hands away several times until they grow more accustomed to the uncomfortable heat.

"Let's turn to the right first," Leith suggests. We both turn our wheels to the right two clicks only for the bars to close in tighter. His eyebrow lifts in a true *what the hell* motion.

"Left?" I offer.

We each try four clicks to the left. The first two return the bars back to their place, but the next two tighten the gate further with an awful *clang, clang*.

The mound of ash stirs, and a thin ray of excruciatingly bright light pushes through, spotlighting the bloodstained stalactites above it. Leith reaches for Grandfather's sword, which is strapped to his waist from now through eternity, and he watches the trembling beam closely.

When the yellow circle of light doesn't grow in size and its jittery movements cease, Leith returns to the wheel and my heart to a much steadier beat.

I tap my fingers along my side, carefully eyeing the mechanism. But it's not until I turn back around, my gaze catching on the story of the sun and moon etched into the stalagmite, that a thought occurs to me.

"It takes two," I repeat. At his stiff nod, I say, "Two either belong together or stay far apart."

Leith follows my gaze, appearing to understand. "Go back to where we started."

I glance back to the mound of ash as it stirs, and another beam of light—this one red and angled to the left—pushes through. I bite my bottom lip and grip the wheel.

Two clicks to the right. *Clang, clang.*

One...two...three more streams of light push through the now-quivering mound of ash. Two green. One blue. All shifting left and right, puncturing the hot, wretched dimness of the catacombs.

Leith mutters several curses. I do as well, although I'm not as creative. This time, I think I return to my wheel first. "Again," I mouth.

The wheel squeals as I click one time to the right and Leith clicks once to the left. My rubbery legs almost give out completely when the cage opens wide enough to allow me through. More green streams of light emerge.

Another *click*.

Another *clang*.

Another stir from the mound.

Green, blue, orange, yellow, and red streaks burst forth and widen. All that's missing is purple.

Never mind—there it is. A circle of bright purple illuminates a fissure forming along the ceiling at the center of the catacombs, just beyond the cage.

The influx of heat burns my eyes, eliciting tears. But it's fear that chills me to the bone. My hands tremble as I reach for the scalding wheel, knowing the next click or clang may be the one to fully awaken the phoenix.

Vitor had it all wrong with the calling-Aurora nonsense. All he ever needed to do was throw rocks against the cage from a safe distance.

"Now or never," Leith says, whisper-yelling as only he can. "All the way until this thing opens or she breaks out."

"For Arrow," I say.

"And for our future family," Leith replies, the sincerity and promise lighting his sea-glass eyes even from this distance. "No matter what, I will get us out. You and me will fucking live, Maeve. I swear it."

Yes, we will.

After everything we've endured, we *must* survive.

I tighten my grip on the wheel, and so does Leith.

"Now!" he yells.

We spin the wheels toward each other as fast as we can. I keep my head low as dirt, stone, and ash pepper my scalp and crumble against my arms.

The first stalactite falls beside me, shaking the ground and making me jump. Then another behind me, and another, and another, and still I don't stop spinning the wheel.

Blue, green, yellow, orange, red, and purple bathe the catacombs in blinding light.

My body screams in agony as blow after blow from the avalanche of broken stone crashes into me.

And still I spin, even as waves of heat slam into me and I fall to my knees at the searing pain of it all.

A sudden blast of roasting air knocks me away from the wheel as if I weigh no more than Tibeta. I curl inward, slapping my hands over my ears when Aurora screams, the sound reverberating through the catacombs and causing more of the ceiling to come down.

Leith is suddenly here. He yanks me up, pulling us not in the direction from which we'd come but away. I'm retching and coughing, but Leith doesn't stop. He pulls us up and up and up. I see enough to notice what he already did—a series of steps have appeared, carved into the stone walls of Aurora's cage. Not that they'll last.

Our means of escape crumbles behind us as we race upward. Sand pours over us as if streaming from a broken hourglass. For a moment we're buried, just buried. It's only the feel of the sand sweeping down and away from us that keeps me from completely panicking. I brace myself against the onslaught, determined to keep my feet.

From one long moment to the next, I catch enough breath to keep me alive. Leith continues to pull me higher and higher, despite the torrent he must fight for each inch we gain. With every ounce of my strength, I follow him.

After what feels like an eternity of punishment, we reach the top, Leith grunting as he slams Grandfather's sword against something hard.

More sand rains down upon us, striking and destroying the last of the stone steps.

The floor bottoms out beneath me. I start to fall. It's over. And I cry out, hoping that at least my beloved Leith has made it.

But then there's moonlight, and air, and Leith wrenching me upward. He pulls me from the brink of death and into the royal box as what remains of the arena floor collapses, and a beautiful, powerful, *free* phoenix takes flight…

ACKNOWLEDGMENTS

Once upon a time, I was a poor immigrant who couldn't speak English and who found herself in a new world, far away from anything remotely familiar. One day, a man knocked on my family's door. He had his teenage daughter with them and was canvasing my neighborhood to bring food to those in need on behalf of his church. My father opened the door and welcomed him in, and he and his family welcomed us into their hearts. So, this is to Mr. Harte, who was more father than friend, and Mrs. Harte, who was gentle and kind, when the world seemed empty of both. This is to their son Jimmy, who made my smiles wider and my enthusiastic laughter that much louder, and to their other son, Johnny, a tender spirit whose compassion shone even in the darkness. This is to their daughter, Kathy, who, along with her husband Jim (Gilsenan), offered guidance, love, protection, and helped me to navigate into adulthood and independence. This is to their children, Kelly, Conor, and Brendan, who I spent a summer raising and who I will spend my entire life loving.

To my husband, Jamie, the most patient, supportive, and generous man I know. You are my best friend. You kept the faith even when mine crumbled. You wiped my tears when I was too devastated to move. You believed in me. You are my world. You promised me that everything would be better than okay, and look, it is!

To my vivacious, strong, and fierce Lily. You taught me to believe in love at first sight. Whenever you fall, rise with your head up, fluff your hair, and remember whose daughter you are.

To Logan, *my* Wolverine, your strength and intelligence surpassed mine from the start. And you're almost as funny as me. Almost. Never cower in the face of the storm. My beloved son, that storm is your bitch and a dwindling cloud in your presence.

To my Maggie, my very own unicorn. You are magic. Life is better because you sprinkle it everywhere. Don't ever stop dreaming, believing, or sharing your stories. They are worth exploring just as much as the world before us.

To my wonderful brother, Douglas. I love you. I'm convinced there were seven of us but only you and I survived. No seatbelts, no supervision, driving when we sure as hell shouldn't have been driving, lighting fireworks we had no business owning, and running into bushes we shouldn't have hit. But, hey, memories, am I right?

To Alyssa, my other child who grew in my heart. I'm so proud of you. Your life is an adventurous mountain. Keep climbing to the top.

To Nicole Resciniti, my agent, my friend, my sister, you believed in me. When no one would sign me, you offered me the pen and paved my way to success. I remember you telling me I was going to be a *New York Times* bestseller one day. I think I finally believe you.

To Liz Pelletier. You took a chance on me and Leith. You loved him from the start and helped turn a fighter into a hero. Thank you for welcoming me into your home and for all your hard work. This novel would not be what it is without your grace and brilliance.

To Rimmer, Mair, and Steve, who left us too soon, their babies, and to the rest of my DeSales University crew. Our college experiences were the best of times, they were (sometimes) the suckiest of times, but they were packed with memories, laughter, and love that continues to bond us. Hey, look, the degree paid off after all.

And to my readers, past, present, and future. Thank you for coming along. Strap yourselves in—it's one hell of a ride.

WANT MORE?

If you enjoyed this and would like to find out about similar books we publish, we'd love you to join our online Sci-Fi, Fantasy and Horror community, Hodderscape.

Visit hodderscape.co.uk for exclusive content from our authors, news, competitions and general musings, and feel free to comment, contribute or just keep an eye on what we are up to.

See you there!

HODDERSCAPE

NEVER AFRAID TO BE OUT OF THIS WORLD